The Girl with the Turtle Tattoo

Daniel Basil Lyle

LylePublishing

Sulphur, Oklahoma

The Girl with the Turtle Tattoo

ISBN 978-0-9794101-4-7

Published by LylePublishing
505 W. 12th Street, Sulphur, OK 73086
(www.LylePublishing.com)

Printed by CreateSpace, an Amazon.com company. Available from Amazon.com and other retail outlets. Also available as an ebook on Kindle and other devices.

LCED10132018

DISCLAIMER and FORWARD

Although this book draws heavily from some of the author's own experiences, all characters are fictitious. Any resemblance to real persons, living or dead, is purely coincidental. Also, turtle tattoos are no more dangerous than any other tattoo. And, although loosely patterned after the author, the religious views of the character David Richard King are his own.

Chapter 1

CHANCE ENCOUNTER

Should you wait or go

when the light turns Green

but Red lingers stubbornly...

—trusting your cautious eyes

or honoring your eager heart?

It's an issue of both sight and mind.

Beware the random toss of the dice.

The Luminary Chronicles, 1:18-19

"Is that a turtle?" he asked, peering down at the checkout lady's exposed wrist.

Dave was bored and in a rush, just making polite conversation. He had no idea that the next few moments would change his life entirely, plus alter the fate of humanity.

To him it was just a chance encounter at a grocery store.

She glanced up at him from the items she was expertly sliding through the scanner.

"Yes, it's a baby turtle."

He marveled at it for a few seconds as he leaned there against the check-writing platform—steadying himself as he recovered from a bought of abrupt dizziness he'd experienced just a few minutes ago. Must be low blood sugar... *Maybe I better munch up one of those store-baked cupcakes once I get into the car with my purchases,* he thought to himself.

"It's so bright. I've never seen a tattoo so bright," he marveled as he poised, ready to hand her another of his carrying-bags to put more of his purchases into when she finished filling the present one.

Indeed, the little tattoo gleamed with vivid greens, rich browns, and deep blacks.

1

And it had a wry smile on its little green face.

It almost looked alive.

"Thanks," she said as she expertly slipped his items past the scanner and then into his waiting bags. "I just treated myself to it the other day."

"I thought it might be one of those stick-on ones," he continued, fascinated. "I've never seen a real tattoo as bright as that one."

She flicked a quick, shy smile at him. "It's brand new, that's why. That's when the colors are brightest. It will fade with time."

She paused in her work behind the counter to slide upward the sleeve of the ocean-blue, light sweater on her left arm. Other wonderful creatures were briefly revealed: a creepy black spider with white specks, a flapping red and yellow parrot, and a coiled orange snake with blue highlights.

"Wow! Those are beautiful. Thanks for showing them to me."

She slid her sleeve back down as she placed the last of his items into the opened bag.

"Happy to do so."

Well, back to business...

She surely knew that she was attractive. He was certain that at five foot four inches, lean and trim, in her early twenties, fitting well into her slim white jeans, she often got admiring looks. But she didn't seem the flirtatious type, rather a girl who'd just let compliments slide past. But Dave had a fleeting hope that she might recognize this middle-aged, longish-haired, bearded guy standing at the counter, as something...well...*different*.

He wasn't just coming on to her. He had a genuine interest in her body art.

"Your total is nineteen, even."

He reached into his back pocket, pulled out his billfold, and handed her a folded twenty.

"Where do you get your artwork inked?" he asked, absently accepting his one dollar change along with the receipt, placing both of them securely with the items in one of his bags that was sitting there in his cart.

She glanced up the line, seeing no one was waiting on her, and relaxed a bit.

"I go to Ada to get them done," she grinned. "There's a parlor there that does real good body artwork. Actually, I got this one as a gift to my mother, to cheer her up. She's having an operation soon."

"Oh, sorry to hear that," he stated sincerely. "But you're right, that little turtle is very cheery. I bet your Mom got a kick out of it."

"Yep," she smiled back, nodding regretfully, "more so than my other ones, that's for sure."

"You've got others?"

She ruefully shrugged. "Well, they're not so cheerful. On other places on my body I've got a lady's face melting into a skull, plus zombies fighting, bloody knives—that sort of thing. My mother doesn't fancy those as much. She thinks I'm a weird kid."

She shrugged, handing him the last filled bag of groceries.

He noted that her arm with the tattoo was firm and tanned. Indeed, she was quite fit—with no fat on her thin, short frame. Her longish brownish red hair well-framed her pixy-like face. But there was nothing much out of the ordinary to her except for her eyes, which were a startling *deep green!* They harmonized well with the color of the little turtle's shell painted into the flesh on the inside of her left wrist.

Her long brown-red hair on her lean, small frame made a nice match with her blue shirt and white jeans. She was an attractive, pretty young lady.

But Dave didn't want to offend her by treating her just as a sexy lady, rather to see her as a talented fellow artist.

"It's true that art often does originate from horrendous situations," he nodded as he slid the bag into the grocery cart next to his other filled bags. "Some of the greatest paintings are of things we'd normally hate. But beauty is beauty, no matter where it comes from. And your body-art is spectacular."

He liked all things of beauty. Indeed, he had a "catholic" appreciation—seeing art where others often saw only junk.

And though he'd never tattooed his own body—too skittish of needles and unwilling to have permanent art on his body—he still carefully maintained his own appearance. In a similar fashion to those who tattooed their skin, he wanted his body to reflect his inner preferences. He had straight long brown hair held back in a ponytail with a gold clip. Also, he sported a neatly-trimmed mustache and beard—quite the "professor" look. But he definitely drew the line at needles repeatedly puncturing his skin. It was fine for others to make their bodies into works of art, but not for him.

The only tattoos he'd ever allow on himself might be the stick-on types. If you didn't like them you could always just peal them off. And if you got tired of them you could change them. But since he preferred long-sleeved shirts, vests, and suits—they'd never be visible anyway. But other people could have the permanent kind if that's what they wanted. He tried hard to be respectful of the decisions of others.

"Have a good day," the nice clerk smiled at him.

He waved in a friendly manner as he pushed away from the checkout stand.

He was vaguely aware of other customers arriving at the lady's checkout stand as he pushed his cart through the crowded exit. From there it was just a few hundred feet out into the parking lot.

"Ohhhh!" he grunted in surprise as he exited the grocery store's main doorway, rocked by another wave of vertigo. For a moment it seemed that the whole world was *spinning* around him and the ground *dropped away* beneath him!

"What the hell?" he gasped, squeezing his eyes shut in pain.

He almost fell onto the pavement, but clutched the cart's handle tightly. Then, just as fast as it had struck him, it was over.

He blinked rapidly to clear his vision, seeing a parking lot filled with cars. Other shoppers pushed past him, with empty or filled carts. The sun shined down bright and warm out of a cloudless blue sky.

"Huh, maybe I'm coming down with something," he muttered to himself, pushing his cart onward.

But that was an amazing Turtle Tattoo, he vaguely thought to himself. Such a perky little turtle with a smile on its little bald head! Indeed, he was a great fan of reptiles. Being single, he had the freedom to pursue his own deepest interests. His house was a virtual zoo, each room featuring well-designed, attractive habitats he'd built himself. His tame, nonpoisonous, harmless "house-mates" were various small and large lizards, tortoises, and even snakes.

Keeps those pesky females at a distance, he thought to himself, picturing his gorgeous reptiles waiting at his house. From his observations, the first thing a girlfriend or wife insisted on was "it's that snake or me!" Indeed, he'd gotten several excellent snakes from young husbands ruefully making the sad choice between their beloved pet and their intolerant wife.

Actually—come to think of it—that young girl at the checkout stand was definitely intriguing. She obviously liked reptiles enough to put one permanently into the flesh of her arm. Maybe he should go back and ask her for a date? But, no...a girl as attractive as she, certainly had a boyfriend, or even a series of them. Probably her latest lover was some biker-type who appreciated her "tats" and would just punch the face of anyone who dared to smile at her, let alone ask for a date. Hah! No need for that sort of trouble.

And, besides, he was much too old for a young-looking kid like that. He must be twice her age. But she was definitely cute.

He grinned appreciatively as he loaded his carry-bags into the back seat of his bright yellow Chevy Cavalier, pausing at the last bag to take out the receipt that was sitting on top of the groceries. He folded the receipt twice and carefully slid it into his top shirt pocket, for putting with his other receipts once he got home.

Then he picked up the dollar bill to put it into his wallet...

—and *froze!*

The denomination jumped-out at him. There in his hand wasn't just a single dollar bill—it was a *one-hundred* dollar bill!

"Oh, my God!" he gasped out-loud, blinking in surprise at the denomination of the note. "That nice young lady gave me the wrong change. She'll probably get docked in her pay for this mistake. And I'm sure grocery clerks don't make that much money to start with, so..."

He closed and locked his car before turning back to the grocery store.

I'll give it right back to her—he thought. *That way she won't get into any trouble. I'll give her the one-hundred dollar bill and she'll give me a one dollar bill in exchange out of her register. Simple! I can fix this problem if I act fast enough.*

Back in the store, he trotted into the exit door, sliding past the out-going carts, and walked up to the backside of the checkout stand he'd just used.

He saw a gray-haired, chubby lady cheerfully scanning a customer's items. The customer was a tall, thin lady holding a gurgling baby in her arms.

"Oh, excuse me," he said from the departing side of the station to the clerk. "Where's the lady that was just running this stand?"

The chubby lady looked over to him, raising her eyebrows questioningly.

"She gave me something by mistake when she checked me out that I need to return to her," he quickly explained.

"Sir, I don't know what you're talking about," the clerk shrugged. "What?"

"I've been running this stand all morning," she smiled at him in a friendly way as she continued to work. "You must have checked out at one of the other stations, not this one."

"I...b-but...w-what?" he stammered.

"Are you sure it was this one?"

"Uh...well...now...come to think of it..."

"I can call over the floor manager if you'd like?"

He nodded, confused, as she paused to speak into a mike. He was sure that this was the stand. Yes, it was the "20-or-under" isle he'd used because he didn't have too many items. There was no doubt of it. There was only one "20-or-under" stand. This was it. What the heck was going on here? Was this new lady joking around with him or something?

Another lady was walking briskly up to him. She was short-haired, squat, with a "manager" badge on her shirt, and had an authoritative air.

"Is there a problem?" she asked.

He turned away from the busy lady at the checkout stand and tried to quickly explain the situation: "Uhm, no—no trouble. It's just that by mistake I got too much change when I checked out my groceries a few minutes ago. I didn't notice until I got out to my car. But I wanted to return it so the lady who gave it to me won't get into any trouble."

"Oh, that's real good of you sir. Was it at this stand?"

"Yes, but it wasn't this lady. It was another lady. She was a young-looking girl with straight reddish hair past her shoulders, bright green eyes—oh, and on her wrist she had a brand-new turtle tattoo."

The floor manager frowned.

"Well, first of all, Sir—Mary's been working the 20-or-less stand here all morning. There hasn't been anyone else on her stand. In fact, she's just now coming up to her first break, so no one's taken over for her. You sure it wasn't her?"

"No! It wasn't her. But...I *was* here! It was the speedy checkout stand, *this* one. I even talked briefly with the girl. I complimented her on her *turtle tattoo* and..."

"Sir," the manager stated firmly, "we have a strict work code here. Visible body art is strictly forbidden."

"Forbidden?"

"We don't hire anyone with visible tattoos. You never know what will be offensive to a customer, you see."

"Well...maybe that was it, then. She had on a long-sleeved shirt. Until she was scanning my purchases the tattoo wasn't showing. And...maybe...I guess I might have been at another stand. But I was so sure it was this one...?"

"Look, Sir," the manager patiently explained, "we can just take back the excess money and use it to pay-down any discrepancies registered this morning. You don't have to identify the particular clerk. With the volume we have here, mistakes happen fairly often. Do you have your ticket?"

"Oh, yes I do," he said, reaching up into his top shirt pocket to pull out the folded receipt. "And I've the change she gave me. I'm sure it was just an honest mistake. Instead of giving me back one dollar, she gave me a hundred-dollar bill instead. I suppose it was in the wrong slot in the register and she just grabbed it without looking too close. We chatted briefly. I probably distracted her without meaning to do so. I'm sure it wasn't her fault."

He handed her the bill.

Both her eyebrows shot upwards as she studied the note.

"May I see your receipt, please?" she coldly stated, holding out her other hand.

"Oh, certainly, here it is," he handed that to her as well.

She carefully studied both of them, her eyes going from one to the other.

"Is something wrong?" he asked, confused. "I'm just trying to be honest and keep that nice clerk who waited on me from getting into any trouble and..."

She firmly handed both pieces of paper back to him.

"Sir, I don't know what's going on here—but since you're trying to give *us* money, not the other way around, I assume it's just some mistake that *you've* made. So please leave and there's no harm done, ok?"

She started to turn away from him.

"But...what are you talking about?" he blurted-out. "You don't want your money back?"

Her eyes narrowed as she turned back to him, speaking distinctly, sounding as if she was carefully keeping her true emotions in check.

"Sir, that receipt is not from our store—in fact, I've never heard of its name. Plus the address printed on it says it's here in Sulphur, but it's on a street that doesn't exist."

Dumbfounded, he focused on the receipt. She was right!

"And that supposed one-hundred dollar bill..." she just shrugged, grinning lopsidedly as if in response to a silly joke.

"The money?" he gaped stupidly, looking at the green bill sitting in his hand.

"It's some sort of play money," she stated, turning away to deal with another customer.

He forced himself to focus on the details of the green bill.

Instead of the face of Benjamin Franklin on its front, there was a picture of the Queen of England. On its back, instead of an image of Independence Hall there was the wide expanse of the English Parliament.

What the bloody hell?—he gasped again to himself. He shook his head in bewilderment as he turned and slowly walked out of the store.

Chapter 2

MEDICAL COINCIDENCE

Pain is more than discomfort

Illness is more than dysfunction

Injury is more than breakage

Crippling is more than slowing

Death is more than ending

And Life is more than living...

Don't think of it as a choice,

It's a willful distraction.

The Luminary Chronicles, 2:1-2

"So how you feeling, Mom?" he greeted her.

"Oh, I'm ok," she wanly smiled. "I'd be better, though, if you'd shave that shaggy beard off. Won't you do that for your poor, old, sick Mother?"

She didn't look ok, sitting there in her wheelchair, listlessly watching T.V. in her small living room. The little remaining hair on her head was in tattered scraps, sticking out in random directions. She was thin, almost skeletal. Her thick red robe was rumpled, smelly. Her hand trembled as she restlessly punched the remote, trying to find a soothing station to watch.

"Now, you know this is who I am, Mom," he gently chided her. "I was clean-shaven while living as a kid in your house. I was trim and proper while in the military, always within regulations. But now I'm my own man I get to look like *I* want to look—which is *not* with my face sliced up each morning cutting off hair that just grows back. I'm sorry if that offends you, but I'm not changing."

She snorted.

"Some son—who won't even cut off his hair just to please his Mom...*then* we could be twins, hah!"

She started to laugh at her own joke, but ended up coughing uncontrollably.

"Maybe we better cancel church today," he suggested, sitting on the sofa to the side of her wheelchair. "Maybe you should go back to bed, get more rest? If you felt up to it, we could go to the evening service or just..."

She cleared her throat, finally getting the coughing under control.

"No!" she loudly protested, her wavering voice now brought into stern control. "This stupid cancer's taken most everything away from me—but I'll *not* let it take away the Lord! You just go into the kitchen and fix yourself breakfast, dear—I'll go get myself dressed."

"Are you sure that...?"

"I know what I'm doing. I'm weak, sure. But all I have to do at church is just sit on a pew. That's not hard. Well the pew's kind of hard. But there are cushions. What I mean to say is that sitting there is no chore. And I feel like singing those beautiful old songs. My voice isn't what it used to be before the chemo and radiation therapies, but I can still hit a few notes, maybe..." her voice trailed off.

He sighed, knowing not to argue with her, and headed on out to the kitchen.

"I got your Ensure at the grocery store," he called out in a loud voice so she could hear him clearly. "It's strawberry, just as you asked. Plus I got eggs and chicken strips and lettuce and tomatoes. I thought I might make you a tasty omelet this morning and..."

"Strawberry?" he heard her weak voice sputtering back. "Oh, honey, you know I prefer the Butter Pecan ones. *You're* the one that likes strawberry. And don't even bother trying to cook something. You know you can't cook. You'd burn up my pans. It's nice of you to want to try, dear, but the Ensure is all I can keep down nowadays."

"Ok, Mom," he sighed, picking up one of the Strawberry Ensures and cranking the top open. He looked at its list of ingredients for a minute as he held it in his hand. It was just a high-calorie milkshake with added-in vitamins. But that didn't sound so bad. He swigged it down in one long gulp. Yep, it wasn't bad. He opened another.

"Is Cat coming by tomorrow to take you to your doctor's appointment?" he called out.

"Yes!" she called back. "Catherine's a sweetie, for sure. You should be more like her. Maybe you'd get married one of these days and have a happy family like hers—*if* you had her sweet disposition instead of being such a workaholic *grouch!*"

He sighed again, careful to keep the noise to himself.

"Yes, you're right," he loudly replied. "I'm just a grouch. I admit it. And I do work hard. But it's *important* work. No one else is doing it."

"At least you're being honest," she smiled as she rolled back into the kitchen in her wheelchair. "You're just a grouchy workaholic. But I still love you."

It was a remarkable transformation from the sad condition she'd been in just a few minutes ago. Instead of her shapeless red robe she now had on a neatly-pressed, blue, long-skirted dress. Instead of her nearly-bald skull she now sported a nicely-coifed blueish wig. Her pale skin was livened up with carefully-applied makeup. Sitting on her lap was a matching grey purse. Next to the purse was her large black Bible.

"I'm ready to go," she grinned. "How's my wig look?"

"Nobody would know it's not your real hair," he politely lied, ignoring the scraps of white hair sticking out from beneath the forehead edges.

"I didn't bring you up to tell fibs," she scolded him. "But thanks for the compliment. At least it looks better than the scarecrow I've become. Ah well, going to church is better than shriveling away in bed. I do appreciate you coming on Sundays to take me to church. So let's go," she resolutely stated.

He held out an Ensure to her.

"Strawberry, really?" she grimaced, wrinkling up her nose in disgust.

He continued to hold it in the air in front of her face.

"Oh, ok," she relented, taking it and sipping at it delicately. "I'll drink it on the way."

"Now who's lying?" he sighed.

Getting her into the car was the usual chore. They needed to take the wheelchair with them. That meant it had to be folded up and levered into the backseat, since the trunk wasn't big enough for it. With parts sticking through the middle divider, that left just barely enough room for Mom to be sandwiched into the passenger seat in the front.

"...and if you had a normal-sized car this would be so much easier, Dear," she rambled on, cheerfully popping from one subject to another without the benefit of intermediate steps. Earlier in his life this had annoyed him terribly. But in the last few years he'd come to realize that his mother was a strong "extravert" who did her thinking out loud, instead of silently inside her head as did strong introverts such as he.

He knew just to nod politely and now and then mutter agreeable grunts in response to her incessant jabbering.

Yep, if he ever did get married-off, he'd be well prepared for the "listening" chores.

The sermon at church was as boring as ever. He'd stopped going years back, but he grudgingly took his Mother on Sunday mornings as a gift to her. What was the point of it? These people—no matter how nice they were—were just lost in their traditions, trying to reassure themselves that death wasn't the end of everything. But dead is dead. No credible evidence existed that anything existed beyond the grave. Soon, very soon, his Mother would pass over that divide—into nothingness. She'd just slip into a coma, her mind would dissolve, and that'd be the end of her.

Looking over at her doing her own dutiful nodding to ponderous pontifications by the droning-on preacher made him both sad and glad. He was sad for her delusions, causing her to waste so much of her time, money, and energy just sitting through mindlessly plodding, repetitive rituals. But on the other hand he was glad she was still here, now weakly singing "Trust and obey" as they both rose from their pews for the invitation song.

It's good to have a mother even if she irritates you in many ways, Dave mused. *There's a connection that goes beyond the physical.*

Sure, it's just genetically-programmed familial connections, nothing more. But maybe that's where the "spiritual" truly matters: connections that cause you to rise above your own momentary selfish desires. In that sense, maybe religion had a purpose, no matter how feeble—to reinforce a tenuous "community."

After services, holding her thin arm firmly, supporting her as she weakly shuffled out of the church's front door, the minister caught his eye: "David, it's so good to see you!"

"Uh, sure...hi Cliff. Uhm, good talk today...gotta get Mom back home and..."

But the white-haired, paunchy preacher didn't take the hint, instead choosing to step in front of him and his Mom. He jovially reached out and shook her thin hand: "So nice to see you with us, Jean—and good of you to bring David."

She smiled back at him, suddenly gripping the Preacher's hand so tightly that he visibly winced.

"You've got to preach harder to reach him, Brother Davis," she insisted. "He's a tough nut to crack. You know that, hah!"

David sighed, just wanting to escape, but forcing a wan smile. "Thanks for coming and checking on Mom during the week, Cliff. I know she appreciates it."

"So what was it you thought was so good in my sermon today?" Cliff grinned back, pointedly "putting the screws" to his "lost sheep."

"Uhm...well," David struggled, trying to remember even the subject of the preacher's long, scrambled, confused talk. "I thought the image of the clasped hands you had as a background on your Power-Point slides—well, it summed your talk up nicely and, uh..."

"Actually, I was talking about the crucifixion, but that's close enough," Cliff good-naturedly laughed. "It *is* all about connections, isn't it?"

For a moment David was startled, thinking that the minister had read his prior thoughts about the true nature of "spirituality." But, no, now that he was prompted, David did recall some of the disjointed subjects having to do with Jesus reaching down to mankind to pull us up to God.

Too bad Jesus had failed so miserably.

"Right," David politely nodded. "God is great," he weakly finished, attempting to step around Cliff.

But Cliff reached out and grabbed his arm, stopping him in his tracks.

"I know you didn't hear a word I was saying from the podium," he whispered into David's ear. "But I've known you since you were a little boy, my friend. I know you have a good heart. And I know you're hurting right now. If there's anything I can do to help, just let me know. And please don't cut God out of the picture. God *is* great, greater than we can ever imagine."

"Ok, sure," Dave said, trying to wriggle past.

"And when things look the darkest and bleakest," Cliff continued whispering into Dave's ear while still firmly grasping his arm, "— when you are confused and scared, why don't you just say a little prayer? You don't have to jump up and down and get some 'revelation'—just accept your own weakness with a tiny dose of humility. David, do it for me. Won't you?"

Suddenly angry beyond his self-control's ability to moderated, David jerked his arm away and continued on.

The presumptions of that chubby preacher! The arrogance of that man! How dare he think that he could just reach out and drag him back into that religious nonsense? Just "say a little prayer"—sure, *that* would instantly cure the cancer that was eating up his Mother's body from the inside, right? Or, it'd instantly straighten out his obvious hallucination at the grocery store, right? And his wooziness would just vanish, right?

Wrong! The "God" that they prayed to so fervently was just a figment of their own imaginations, put there to make death seem more palatable.

But—he sighed to himself, *then again, "humility." Maybe I do need a dose of it.*

After all, he wasn't doing that great by himself, was he? It seemed that the world was spinning out of control, conspiring against him.

Then why not give it try?

What did he have to lose?

Silently he worded a short prayer: *God, help me. If you're really up there, then please do something. I don't expect it. I know I don't deserve it. But I sure could use some of that "divine intervention." Whatever bone you'd like to throw my way, I could use it. Thanks...and Amen.*

Embarrassed by his mental lapse to pray even half in jest to a Deity he didn't believe in, he shoved his key into the lock in the car door and angrily yanked it open.

"Trying to hurt your poor, innocent car?" Jean laughed.

David jerked like he'd been slapped by the "snicker" from his Mother. It almost seemed like she'd heard his silent prayer for help. Nonsense! She was just laughing at the preacher cleverly buttonholing him after the services.

"The door sticks sometimes," he peevishly lied.

He knew that leaving the church once he'd grown up and was out of her house had hurt her greatly. She seemed to have some secret insight that he'd eventually see "the error of his ways" and return to become the biggest "Believer" of them all. Dream on, Lady, dream on.

God had no power except to comfort weak minds.

At the restaurant where David took his mother for lunch, she seemed to grow stronger—nibbling on a salad while pattering on interminably about the people she'd talked with on the phone in the prior week, things she'd read, shows on T.V. she'd watched, the present news crises erupting around the world, her annoyance with her doctors—jumping from one subject to another, or from one outrageous unjustified conclusion to another, with nary a pause.

"Uh huh...how about that...is that so?" he muttered, only half-listening to her. It was sad that she could barely make it from the car into the restaurant in her wheelchair—church having exhausted her—and then once inside was eating almost nothing. But at least she wasn't totally bedridden. However, it was something of a spectacle to the other patrons when she loudly ordered the waitress to get the table's chairs out of the way for her to roll up close to the table.

"—and then the nurse told us to put on those ugly blue gowns with nothing in the back. I told them I wanted a full gown to hide my naked rear end, but they said it was the only thing they had. Oh, they were nice enough but..."

David chewed resolutely at the dry hamburger he'd ordered for himself, nodding politely while keeping his mouth visibly filled with food or grimly clamped shut.

He just tuned her out—as he'd taught himself to do while growing up trapped in her household. He concentrated his thoughts instead on his present experiment running in his garage at his own house. While he wasted time here in Sulphur the instruments were waiting for him in Edmond. He had to get back so he could eagerly study the readouts. Maybe this time he'd get some positive results!

Yes, I'm due a break—he dreamily thought to himself.

Who knew if maybe Mother Nature would finally cut him some slack? Sure, "cold fusion" was a colossal flop in the past. Yes, no one except himself had any interest pursuing failed research. But he was convinced there *was* something to it—he just knew it! One more test, one more step down a supposed "blind alley" and maybe...just maybe...

—when something his Mother said suddenly caught his attention.

"Uh, say—Mom, what was that again?" he asked.

She snorted. "Not listening to me again, huh? I know I ramble on, dear—but I'm not a stupid person. I don't get out much, but I do listen to the news and watch everything around me. If just once you'd listen to me and respond, talk with me, interact with me, I know that we could..."

"*Mom!*" he cut off her oft-repeated complaint. "My mind just wanders sometimes. I'm sorry! Now what was it you said to me just before this present topic?"

She had a fit of coughing before replying, catching phlegm in her napkin before setting it aside with a disgusted wince. "I...oh, Lord...I'm ok now, Davey. I was *telling* you about my last radiation treatment in Ada, last week—where the Doctors were *so* disrespectful even though the nurses tried to be nice. Those radiologists treated me like a slab of meat on that cold table when they..."

"No, no Mom," he interrupted her, "it was something else. Was there perhaps another patient there that you were visiting with? Did she say something to you that you thought was really cute? Did that happen?"

"Oh! Yes! There was another old woman like me, waiting to get her head zapped. They were trying to shrink a tumor in her brain enough to let her go into surgery in the near future because the metastases were..."

"That doesn't sound 'cute', Mom."

"I'm getting to it! Don't rush me."

"I'm sorry. No rush. It just caught my attention, is all."

"Alright, then," she gulped, stopped talking, and had another coughing fit. People at a table nearby looked over, clearly annoyed though trying to look sympathetic.

He apologetically nodded back to them, motioning with spread hands that it was ok—that she would stop soon, that the embarrassment of having a dying person near them would soon cease.

"Oh...goodness," she gasped, recovering.

"Maybe we should go ahead and leave, if you're not up to continuing?" he gently suggested, starting to rise from his seat.

"No, no! I'm fine now," she grimly stated, motioning with a thin hand for him to sit back down. She took a ragged sip at her water glass. "Well anyway, there was this lady. She was an old person like me. We visited as we waited our turns to get fried in the x-ray machine. She was telling me about her daughter, a sweet little girl. I was telling her about *you* and she got to laughing, saying maybe it wasn't so bad she had a hippy-freak for a daughter after all. At least her daughter didn't have any live snakes crawling about her bedroom, hah! And she'd actually *talk* with her at the end of each workday. Hah! Not at all like you when you..."

"Something else," he motioned with one hand in a circular "let's speed it up" type of movement, trying to encourage her to remember. "Was there something else about the lady that you were telling me that...?"

"Oh, the 'cute' thing?"

"Yes, I think that was what particularly caught my attention: the cute thing."

"Well, her daughter did something really strange—but also nice—that got a chuckle out of her Mother, don't you know?"

"What was it?"

"Well, she got this 'tat'—that's short for 'tattoo' because..."

"Yes, I know that, Mom. What sort of tattoo?"

"It was a cute little *green, smiling turtle*—right on her wrist, can you imagine that? Right on her *wrist!* Don't you think that would *hurt?* And wouldn't it get *infected?* I mean, there's so many big fat veins right under the skin on your..."

"Mom."

"Yes, Son?"

"Did you get the lady's name?"

"What...why? We were just sitting there in the waiting room about to go in for our treatments. It wasn't like we were having lunch together or something, or had a lot of time. And it was cold, you know. They didn't even give us blankets to..."

"Did you get the *lady's name?*" he loudly asked her.

The people at the other table looked over again, this time frowning at his outburst, not just embarrassed at his Mother's coughing.

He ignored them.

"Please, Mom," he said more quietly, getting his emotions back under tight control. "This lady at the clinic in Ada, did you get her name?"

"I...well...we did exchange names, I think. Maybe it was Cloe, or Zoe. No it *was* Cloe! Now I remember. It was Cloe Kleever—I remember because it sounds so beautifully. It was like 'Edger Allan Poe,' remember him? That name just sort of flows. You should use your full name on your little research reports that you write, 'David Richard King.' Isn't that beautiful? Your father wanted to name you 'Spike,' because your hair stuck right up when you came sliding out of me. Wasn't that silly? That's a dog's name. And Edgar Allan Poe wrote all those spooky stories. In fact, I saw 'The Pit and the Pendulum' the other day on the classics channel. It was *so* funny. The special effects were so clunky. It wasn't scary at all. Now what's scary is the medical channel. Oh my God, the program I saw the other day about..."

David hurriedly pulled a small notebook from his top shirt pocket, writing down the name his Mother had remembered, as she proceeded on with her fragmented radiation-muddled thoughts.

Sure, it was only a phonetic spelling. Who knew how it was actually spelled? But there couldn't be that many alliterations for "k-k" sounds in the Ada phone book, right? At least he had something that made sense to pursue concerning that strange girl at the checkout stand—not just a crazy hundred-dollar "play" bill and a totally-impossible grocery receipt.

But wasn't this amazing? His Mother just this last week sat right next to and visited with the mother of *the girl with the turtle tattoo!*

That's assuming it was the girl's mother. Maybe she wasn't? But how many girls got a Turtle Tattoo on their wrist recently in that immediate area? And didn't that checkout lady mention she'd gotten it inked in Ada?

Maybe there *was* something to that prayer stuff?

Ridiculous!

It was just a coincidence. Amazingly improbable and possibly helpful, but just random chance...

—in a cold and uncaring Universe!

Involuntarily he shuddered as he motioned for the waitress to come over and give them the check. There were too many mysteries and not enough answers. Humanity's sad complacency hid a frightening abyss. He should know.

Mother Nature hated him.

She was the true "bitch." She was *laughing* at his pitiful research failures!

Now that's a "god" you can believe in.

Chapter 3

FUNNY MONEY

Give me all you have

And I will give you nothing back

Give me only your very least

And I will give you everything.

Don't laugh—it's not a transaction.

The Luminary Chronicles, 3:89

Dave arrived back at his house in Edmond, Oklahoma totally exhausted.

"Whew," he gasped, leaning his head down upon the steering wheel before opening the door and staggering out.

It was a two hour drive on the crowded freeway, I-35, between Edmond located in central Oklahoma and the small town of Sulphur situated in the south part of Oklahoma. A large section of the ride was through the thick traffic of Oklahoma City. He knew he should stop and take a break about halfway through, but each time he chose to grimly continue. It was better to get it over with than stop for a milkshake.

As it was—after getting up early in the morning for the two hour trip to Sulphur, going to the grocery store, taking his Mom to church, then taking her to lunch, and then wheeling her to do the personal shopping that she insisted upon rather than just have him pick up stuff for her...and *then* finally making the long drive back—it'd been a long and tiring day for him, even though it was only 7:00 in the evening.

"Some day today, huh?" he waved in a friendly way as he entered his house to a big green iguana. The lizard sat behind a pane of glass sunning itself on a thick branch beneath a heat lamp. Its habitat extended from the floor of the small living room to the ceiling, totally covering one of the walls.

The lizard did not reply. That was ok. It'd be nice if he could, but reptiles were simple animals with small brains. But still Dave treated them as if they were people, perhaps hoping in the back of his brain that one day his critters would perk up and chat with him.

"So how'd *your* day go, Topper?" he said as he opened up the glass door and stroked the lizard on its back. The five foot-long lizard arched its back, lifted high its head, and closed its eyes in pleasure at Dave's hand ran along the sides of its sticking-up spines.

"I'll be back in a while to give you a nice fresh salad to munch on," Dave told the lizard, closing and locking the glass door. "I gotta check on the experiment before I totally crash."

Walking into his bedroom he opened the locked door leading directly into his garage. Walking through it was like entering another world. The small space was packed with large instruments sporting myriad knobs and dials. A low "*hmmmmmmmm*" permeated the air, just at the lower threshold of Dave's hearing.

He wormed his way through a tight corridor between the machines to stop before an ancient paper-spool printer. He lifted up the folded papers sitting in the out-tray, quickly scanning the intersecting lines on the continuous graph. Nothing...no excess of neutrons, rats! Well what did he expect, magic? Instead, it was just Mother Nature screwing him as usual, laughing at his silly little human presumptions.

"Ok, then," he sighed. "Increasing the copper interfaces in the matrix does nothing. Changing the slope velocities of the permeating electrons does nothing. Enhancing the hydrogen drift does nothing. Oscillating the core temperature does nothing. *Nothing* does nothing—*damn* it all!"

In frustration he crumpled the printout, dropping it on the concrete floor. It joined a number of other similarly smashed paper wads.

"Jesus Christ...I'm a total failure."

He'd really thought he was onto something this time by tweaking the copper content of the matrix. But...maybe the fusion of the hydrogen ions was happening just beneath his level of detection. After all, at best he'd be only fusing a few hydrogen atoms at a time—*damn surplus junk he had to work with!*

"Ah, to hell with it," he shook his head in disgust as he started to flip down various switches and levers, to shut down the running experiment. But then he paused.

"It won't hurt to let it run a bit more," he shrugged. "Maybe it just needs a few more hours," he muttered as he turned away and threaded his way carefully back down the tight corridor between the ancient, bulky equipment.

Stepping back into his bedroom he kicked off his shoes, took the car keys out of his pants pocket, stuck his billfold up on his dresser, and collapsed fully dressed onto his bed.

"I can feed the critters in the morning," he mumbled, face down on the bed.

Instantly he fell into an exhausted slumber.

It was only the *incessant ringing* of his cellphone that woke him up from his dreamless stupor...

—to jerk awake, suddenly scared breathless!

He never gave out his cellphone number except to a few close friends, with strict instructions for them to only use it for real emergencies. He preferred his landline phone for routine calls, tied to a screening messaging service and caller i.d. so that he could stop all those irritating robot and spam calls.

Did something happen to his Mom? Was there a crisis at the school?

"Oh, man, what's going on?" he muttered to himself, seeing from his illuminated wall clock that it was only 7:45 in the evening. He'd been conked out for only less than an hour!

He fumbled for the ringing cellphone on his nightstand in the darkened room, pressing it up to his ear: "Uh...h-hello?" he groggily stammered.

"Is this Dr. King?"

"Uhm...yes it is, who...?"

"Your life is in danger. Get out of the house. *Do it now!*"

"What?" he gasped, trying to wrap his head around the strange command, "Who are you and what...?" he asked.

But the phone was dead.

Blearily, he blinked his eyes as he pulled himself onto the side of the bed and up to his feet, fumbling to put on his shoes. Then he started out of the door of the bedroom. He only paused to grab his wallet and keys from off the top of his chest of drawers, just in case.

"Was that a crank call?" he shrugged as he walked past Topper's cage, confused, but determined to at least look out the front door of his house, check if anything suspicious was out there.

Stepping out onto his front porch Dave saw that there was nothing even vaguely wrong or unusual. The street in front of his old, small house looked the same as always—just boring row houses in an older section of Edmond. There was nothing exciting. The sun had just gone down across the horizon, so even though the light was fading there was still enough to see any suspicious cars or strangers on the street. Nothing!

Turning back to re-enter his house the *explosion* knocked him off his feet!

"You were lucky, sir," the fireman said to him. "If you'd been in your bedroom on the other side of that garage, you'd be dead for sure."

Dave looked in bewilderment at the remains of his garage. It was a smoking, burned-down mess. He was still in shock, dabbing with a handful of tissues at throbbing bruises on one side of his head where he'd hit the pavement when he fell.

Off to the side, a number of his neighbors were standing around, gazing with curiosity at the sad results of the fire. Dave didn't even know their names. He barely said "hello" when he departed for or return from work and happened to see one of them out on the street.

"I guess so," he mumbled. "Thanks for getting here so fast. Otherwise I guess my whole house would be gone. As it is, only my garage and bedroom are gone. I guess I should count my lucky stars, huh? I've still got my wallet, lost my cellphone—but didn't use that much anyway. Even my critters made it through ok."

"You some sort of a biologist? Those are nice reptiles you got in there. My son has a pet red-tailed boa constrictor just like yours."

"Yes, boas do make nice pets," Dave groggily replied. "But I'm not really a biologist. I'm a physicist. Reptiles are just a hobby of mine. I teach at the local junior college."

"Well, glad we could help, Mr. King. Sorry about the destruction," he said as he began to move away back to the fire engine.

"Right," Dave sighed—then quickly asked the retreating man: "Hey, any idea what could have caused it...maybe a gas leak or something? I think that my kitchen gas line ran through there. Could you tell?"

"There will have to be an investigation," the man called back, marshaling the rest of the crew as they coiled their fire hoses and stowed their other equipment. "It could have been from various causes. You had a lot of old equipment in that garage. Were you storing anything dangerous?"

"Dangerous?" Dave laughed, looking down at the tissues that were lightly stained pink from a small amount of blood from his cuts and bruises. "The only equipment I had in my garage that was active was operating at a total of about 100 watts. Otherwise everything was at room temperature. In fact, that was the point of what I was trying to do in there. The surplus research equipment I had in the garage couldn't even heat up a cup of coffee. Anyone's microwave in their kitchen was more dangerous than the equipment I had running."

"Well, sir, the fire is completely out," the fire chief nodded to him. "So we'll be on our way. We've got another call to get to. We're short on resources these days so we probably won't be able to do any extensive investigation. I'll just put it down as a gas leak. You'll get the official paperwork in the mail in about a week. Meanwhile just tell your insurance provider that the probable cause was a gas leak. They'll advise you on getting the debris cleared out and rebuilding the structure if you wish."

"Ok, then...thanks again."

"Right."

"Oh, wait!" Dave called out, running over to the fire truck as it started to move away.

The truck stopped. The fire chief poked his head out of the side window, sitting at the wheel.

"Yes, Sir?"

"You didn't say how you got here so fast. Who do I have to thank for that? Was it one of my neighbors?"

"Could be, Sir," the man called from the high cab. "We got a call at 7:30 concerning a fire on this street. Fortunately our firehouse isn't too far away and the traffic wasn't bad. The caller hung up before we got his name."

Dave frowned, puzzled. "Was it exactly 7:30? Are you sure?"

"We log in each of our calls. It was 7:30 on the dot. Is there something wrong with that?"

"Uh...no...I was asleep then. I had a long day...got up early this morning. Good thing someone noticed something."

"Alright then," the Chief called down from the cab. "If there's anything else, just give us a call."

Dave turned away from the retreating fire engine back to the still-smoking ruins of his garage, puzzled. He was sure his wall clock had said 7:45 when he woke up in the bedroom. That meant that the call to the firemen at their station had come *before* the explosion took place. How could one of his neighbors know about the explosion before it even happened? But then again, a low-level, simmering fire might have triggered the explosion. Did someone see some smoke?

"But then again..." he whispered to himself.

—unless it *wasn't* one of his neighbors?

Just who was it that called him as he slept on his bed, *saving his life?*

He'd be dead right now if that caller hadn't gotten him up! And his house and creatures would all be ashes if the fire truck hadn't gotten a head start through the ever-present thick traffic of Edmond.

"Or," he forced himself to look at it logically. "Maybe the anonymous neighbor seeing some smoke after reporting it to the fire station then called me up on the phone and saved my life—but how'd they get my cellphone number?"

Well, whatever, it certainly made more sense, didn't it?

For a moment he'd almost been considering some sort of a *conspiracy!*

Hah! Who'd want to conspire against *him?* He was the *least* important person in the whole wide world. He was without doubt the most worthless, miserable, total failure of them all.

The next morning at college he sat in his small office organizing his lecture notes and PowerPoint slides for a long day addressing bored, crowded classes. He was numb, just going through the motions.

Yes he was back at work doing his job, but still confused, almost in shock.

"Hey, I heard you had a fire?" Professor George S. Johnson asked, sticking his smiling, bald head through the opened doorway of Dave's office.

George was a tenured professor of Economics who had an office right next to Dave's. Being tenured, the short, chubby instructor had a much easier workload than Dave, plus relative job-security. If he were to show up late to one of his lectures, George wouldn't be fired on the spot—as Dave might be after repeated prior offences!

Dave sighed, stroking his beard absently. He didn't have time to idly chat with George.

George, though, was the closest thing Dave had to a friend at the college. Like Dave, he had a "thing" for reptiles. But George hadn't had a snake as a pet since his single graduate student days. That was a long time ago. Getting married put an end to him having pet snakes in his house.

So whenever Dave had to go for an extended trip of more than just a day or two, George was happy to "snake sit"—knowing how to take care of Dave's lizards, tortoises, and snakes.

Normally Dave would love to sit and visit with George for a few minutes. But Dave's first class was in twenty minutes. George had the freedom to "shoot the bull" about nothing in particular while untenured, lowly associate professors like Dave did all the work!

"Yes, my dear Professor Johnson, I had a fire last night," Dave shrugged, "but fortunately my house didn't all burn down. It was just my garage plus my bedroom that got toasted. The firemen got there almost instantly. I was lucky, I guess. Even my critters are ok."

"But your garage? All your research equipment! You don't mean the whole...?"

"Yep, I'm afraid so," Dave concluded the thought, a catch in his voice. But then he continued firmly: "But that's finished now. I can't continue without my equipment. It's for the best, though, George. You know I wasn't making much progress. I've cried on your shoulder enough times about it. Now it's finished."

"Oh, man, that's so sad," George commiserated. "You put so much work into it. But don't you need to take care of insurance and things like that? You should take the day off."

"No time, George," Dave said as he gathered his lecture materials together. "And there's no one to teach my courses if I did take sick leave or whatever. I've been warned about unscheduled leaves of absence—threatened with being fired if I'm late for another class even if it's due to my 'super-important' experiments making me stay up late. I phoned my insurance company. They're sending an inspector out this evening to appraise the damage. So it's a regular workday for me. But thanks for your concern, my friend."

George nodded sympathetically as he simultaneously slid fully into the opened doorway of the cramped office and settled his chunky body into the only guest-chair.

"Well, if I can help let me know," George sincerely stated. "Tell you what, though, this teaching-college job saves you from the research-blues, that's for sure. It's not so bad to have to give up active lab research, Dave. Most of the time it's just frustration chasing down blind leads. Why back at the University when I was doing my post-doc research, I got so mad at..."

"George, I'm sorry," Dave cut him off. "I've got a lecture in fifteen minutes. I'd love to talk more but I've got to get going."

"Oh—sorry, Dave, I'll get out of your way," he said as he pushed himself back up out of the chair and started to leave the office.

Dave nodded politely, turning back to hurriedly cram the proper lecture notes plus the relevant textbook into the outside flaps of his laptop case—then thought better of it.

"George, wait a minute, would you?"

"Yes?" George answered, turning back.

"I know you mainly teach general economic theory. But if I remember correctly, you also know about currency manufacture and distribution?"

"Of course, Dave," he grinned, his double-chin flapping with enthusiasm. "I probably mentioned to you at that my doctoral dissertation was about the manufacturing requirements of treasury notes responding to cultural imperatives. That's probably what you are remembering. It's quite fascinating. In fact, I found that..."

With a wave Dave cut him off.

"I'd love to hear more, George," he sincerely stated. "But I've really got to run. However, I was given a peculiar bill by mistake from a grocery store checkout clerk yesterday. I've never seen anything like it. Of course it's obviously just some sort of play money. But you'd swear it was real. It feels just like a real treasury note. I wonder if you could take a look at it and maybe tell me where it came from?"

"Sure! I'd be glad to look it over. Do you have it with you?"

Momentarily, Dave was perplexed. What had he done with the note? The receipt from the store was still tucked into his top shirt pocket, he knew—he hadn't changed his shirt from yesterday. But what did he do with that funny-money?

Oh, now he remembered.

It was in his wallet with his regular money. He stuck it in there without thinking once he left the grocery store after being laughed at by the floor manager.

In his wallet!

He frowned as the thought flashed through his mind—*If I'd not grabbed my wallet yesterday evening, that bill would be ashes right now!*

Could there have been more to the fire than just an accidental gas leak?

Shaking his head to push out those vaguely-troubling thoughts, he reached into his back pocket and took out his wallet.

Yep, there it was—right at the front of the rest of his bills.

"Here, George," he handed over the weathered, green note.

George took it, curious, holding it up to the light.

"Amazing," he chortled, pleased at the novelty. "This is a great party-prank, for sure. Hah! The Queen of England! That's rich. It'd be a great conversation starter during cocktail hour at a bar. But it *is* superb workmanship. Where'd you say you got this?"

"Change at a grocery store. Can you find out where it came from?"

"I don't know. Maybe. I can go over to the University and use their microscopes to track the origin of the paper fibers used in its manufacture."

"Well, I don't mean to cause you any trouble. I'm sure it isn't important. I'm just curious."

"Oh, it's no trouble, Dave. I don't have anything on my schedule today, anyway. I'll let you know what I discover."

Dave felt a strong sting of resentment. *Right! Nothing on his schedule while I'm run ragged, hardly able to keep up with just grading the ocean of test papers I'm drowning beneath. But, it is nice of him to look into it. No need getting mad at him. He is a good friend.*

"Thanks, George. I appreciate it," he said as he dashed out of the door and ran for the "physics 101" classroom located across campus.

It's been a crappy couple of days, he thought to himself. *But as the old saying goes: "there's a silver lining behind the darkest cloud." Without my surplus equipment my "illustrious" research career has finally come crashing to a sad end. Now I can just relax—stop trying to write, submit, and publish my few pitiful findings in my "free" time—and set my sights on becoming nothing more than...George.*

Yep, everybody can't be a "Nobel Prize"-winning scientist.

Teaching introductory science courses to students that don't give a damn about the subject, at a mediocre small college, was still good honest work. It was the same as working as a clerk in a grocery store. It may not be a world-changing quest, but it was performing an important service for real customers. After all, his student needed their passing grades to get their "Associate of Art" A.A. degrees to be able to go and do other stuff.

All he had to do to achieve that serenity of achievement was to abandon any pretense of greatness.

I'm a failure, he dutifully instructed himself. *All the big things I've tried to do in my life have ended in failure. Sure I accomplished some big things getting to where I am, but none of my highest goals. And in my stupidity I sacrificed way too much in my pitiful attempts: family, a wife, kids, my church, and even my mother's respect. My whole life is a fiasco.*

But so what?

So he wasn't a genius. So he wasn't some great scientist. So he wasn't going to make a world-shaking discovery. So he was never going to win a Nobel Prize.

So what?—he stubbornly repeated to himself.

Why couldn't he be happy just doing an honest day's work?

That supposed "tragic" fire had finally thrust him into the honorable ranks of the workaday "everyman"—and maybe that wasn't so terrible.

If he ever found that mysterious girl with the Turtle Tattoo, he might even ask her out for a date. After all, they were now both exactly the same—everyday working stiffs. And, for the first time in his whole life, his evenings were free.

He should feel happy.

But instead, he felt a profound emptiness...as if he'd given up his birthright.

He *knew* deep in his heart he could figure out how to make his experiments work. He *knew* it! But Mother Nature begged to differ.

"Cold fusion" was just that: cold and *dead*.

Chapter 4

COLD FAILURE

Misery has its rewards

The mundane garnishing glory

While heroic efforts go unnoticed

Even the lowest enjoying their day

If only to gloat about it bitterly

How the mighty have fallen

Yes, I talk about you.

The Luminary Chronicles, 4:16-17

"Alright, folks—here we are again!" he cheerfully greeted the students assembled in the large auditorium.

There were several hundred students present. So much for the "advantages" of their attending a small junior college! To make it affordable for the students—most of who were from the local area—it wasn't unusual to have large classes, even introductory physics. Normally few students were interested in physics, but the junior college pretended to be an inexpensive "pre-science-major" school. Physics 101 was a requirement for everyone.

More work for him, more pain for the students.

"I'm sure everyone's read the assignment for today," he said, ignoring the scattered groans coming up to him on the podium, "so I won't just go through slides of what you've *already* looked at on your own laptops or tablets. Instead we'll start with any questions you may have. You can put *me* to the test. So please remember to walk over to the microphone in the center isle and speak directly into it so everyone can hear. Ok, then—who's first?"

He was one of the few instructors that allowed questions from the floor. Most of the rest in the faculty just dully recited their lecture notes, not even bothering with projected slides.

He looked hopefully across the sea of seated students. No one moved. No one seemed at all interested in the subject. They were quietly chatting with their neighbors, tapping on keyboards, or swiping at cellphones. Clearly Physics 101 wasn't the most popular lecture course around.

And he didn't blame them.

Science only comes alive when it is hands-on. Their small two-year college didn't even have labs for "canned" experiments, let alone attempting any true research.

Coincidentally, the topic of the lecture from the textbook was his main research interest. Dave felt this to be timely and appropriate. Here in public he could summarize his obsession—then dismiss his part in it, once and for all! It would be cathartic.

It would be his "last hurrah."

It would be his formal, public, "goodbye" to his ambitions.

"I remind you, my friends, of the topic of today's chapter: '*Bringing the Sun's Fusion Power to Earth*'—a remarkable goal, for sure. This has many implications, both economical and societal. Technologically it would be a feat akin to putting a colony of humans on Mars. It would be a great leap forward in power generation, potentially replacing the carbon-polluting fossil fuels. It might be the one thing to stop and reverse catastrophic global warming, saving our planet. Does anyone have a question on general implications before I move on into the physical aspects of the current government-funded large projects?"

No one stirred from their seats.

He sighed to himself at the total lack of interest by his students. The standing mike in the central isle of the large auditorium stood alone, abandoned.

"Ok, then," he continued, trying to maintain his externally-cheerful dynamism, "I'll explain to you how 'ITER' is doing: the '*International Thermonuclear Experimental Reactor*'. It uses gigantic magnetic fields to contain burning plasma. And, if we have time today, I'll get into how 'NIF' is doing: the '*National Ignition Facility*" which uses powerful lasers to heat and compress hydrogen fuel. What I'm going to show you in my slides isn't in the textbook. I'm giving you the latest up-to-date results that..."

"Professor!" he heard a voice call-out from the audience.

He paused, seeing a young, brown-skinned man wearing a black sweater get up from his seat and make his way to the central microphone.

"Yes?" Dave happily called down from the podium to him. "Do you have a question?"

The tall young man stood straight and serious at the microphone, leaning forward to speak directly into it.

"Is it really worth the price?" he spoke, the sound of his voice booming from the auditorium speakers.

"What do you mean?" Dave asked. He leaned his head also a bit forward so that the lapel mike attached to his upper shirt would produce a bigger sound, matching the kid's antagonistic tone.

"Well, sir, isn't the present world-wide effort costing billions of dollars? What if that money was spent instead on alternative energy research? Isn't successful economic power generation from fusion power is at least decades off? And the problems are so huge, commercial production might never be achieved at all. In the meantime, we've wasted all that money which might have brought green power up to a level to finally and completely replace the carbon-polluting fossil fuels."

"Well said, my friend," Dave nodded politely. "But what if there were a way to achieve fusion energy *not* requiring a massive, multi-billion-dollar, radiation-spewing power plant? Wouldn't that be worth the small price to pursue its investigation?"

Behind the tall fellow with the black sweater another student lined up, a pale-skinned lady with long blond hair. And behind her, a short, white-haired Asian-looking man was getting up from his isle seat to join them.

Good!—he thought to himself as he waited on the black-sweater's response. *We're getting discussion. They can always get the physics formulae and atomic pathways out of the textbooks. It's the implications for humanity that will stick in their brains, plus make for a damn interesting class.*

And it would let him speak his heart without acknowledging that he was now a broken man.

"Are you speaking of *cold* fusion?" the black sweater person hesitantly replied.

"I am, indeed," Dave smugly answered. "There's more than one way to 'skin a cat'—or, in this instance, to get hydrogen atoms to come close enough to fuse together: releasing massive amounts of energy normally only generated at millions or billions of degrees in the heart of a star! This so-called 'cold' fusion at room temperatures, if it could be achieved, would put the Sun into a small device operating on a benchtop...or beside your microwave, in your kitchen, inside your own house."

"Well, Professor," the black sweater kid nodded, "I guess that would be amazing, indeed. But if that's really possible then why are the governments of the world only funding hundreds-of-billions-of-dollars giant 'hot'-fusion projects?"

"I can tell you why," the blond-haired lady interjected, rudely pushing the first student aside to take his place at the central microphone.

"Please, tell us," Dave encouraged her, enjoying the uncommon enthusiasm taking place.

"Because cold fusion was a *failure*," she flatly stated. "There was some excitement over it back in the 1990's—but it turned out to be just sloppy experiments, or bad measurements, or outright fraud. You just can't expect for the Sun to come down and sit inside a microwave."

Most of the class broke out in laughter.

"I did exaggerate a bit, didn't I?" Dave good-naturedly joined in the snickering, feeling giddy at this public-though-private humiliation. Like Catholic radicals of centuries past, he was torturing himself for his sins. In his case, it was the sin of Pride. "But there was a time when the idea of cooking a turkey without a fire would have been unimaginable, wasn't there?"

She nodded, but persisted...

"But it's not just a matter of discovering new principles," she insisted. "It's a matter of physics and mathematics—exactly what we're supposed to be studying in this class. It's the Law of Nature. To get a significant amount of hydrogen atoms to fuse and release energy they've first got to be put under immense pressure and heat!"

A few "boo's" sounded in the auditorium.

"Ah, but there *is* a theoretical underpinning, my dear," Dave patiently continued from the podium, glad to finally be laying it all out in the open. "Palladium electrodes that suck up large amounts of hydrogen allow the nuclei to get close together—without the need for monstrous temperatures or pressures. This is precisely the basis of the 'failed' experiments by Fleischmann and Pons to which you refer. It's true that neither they nor other scientists could get their apparatus to work reliably. But the electrolysis of heavy water within suitable catalytic matrices is still—even today—a hope for cheap and abundant room-temperature fusion energy. Or so think a few maverick researchers who..."

"—that no one funds," she bluntly interrupted.

He sighed, looking down at the podium.

"True, very sadly true," he gulped, remembering the surplus equipment he scrounged on what he could set aside from his meager salary, now mere burnt junk in his destroyed garage. "But a few diehards still exist out there trying to make cold fusion work. And besides them there exist alternative projects to the billion-dollar high-energy plants, which cost 'only' millions or just tens of thousands of dollars per year. Those 'mainline' renegade projects are exploring alternative ways to get tiny amounts of fuel to ignite in a controlled fashion. I assure you—and I'm happy to expand my overview of them for your amazement and edification—that there's a whole array of ongoing research projects for bringing reliable fusion power to earth. Some are crackpot, but others are based on reasonable suppositions."

"But it's wrong!"

It was the Asian man. He'd just joined the other two students at the mike. His hair was trimmed short, a fuzz of pure white. He had a prominent, jagged scar on his left cheek. In fact, Dave now saw by the heavy lines in his face that he was elderly. He hadn't noticed the man's age before because the man was remarkably fit. His bare arms were well-muscled. He had a thick neck. He was barreled-chested.

"Wrong?" Dave calmly replied. "How so?"

"*God* will not permit us to make a mockery of His nature! We are too stupid to have the power of the sun in our hands. Even if we could figure out a way to do it, we are unworthy."

"Tell that to your kind at Hiroshima and Nagasaki!" someone shouted from the audience. "God let them get incinerated, didn't He?"

"Yes, as a lesson to us," the man shouted back. "That's what happens when you spit in the face of God. The world gets destroyed!"

"Hey, hey, hey!" Dave interjected from the podium up on the stage. "Folks, I enjoy a good debate as much as the next person—but we are a *science* class, *not* a religious class. I'm quite happy to leave the moral implications to the philosophy and religious professors, and so should you. We need to stick to the physics of..."

"And that is just the trouble!" the Asian man shouted again, not even needing the microphone to be heard all over the crowded auditorium. "You arrogant scientists think that if something can be done then it should be done. You have no limits. You have no humility!"

Dave was at a loss for words. Who was this old Asian guy? He was aiming his words right at Dave's guts!

"But God gave us brains," the blond girl insisted, grabbing back the microphone in one hand while shoving the elderly Asian man back a step with the other. "I'm a religious person too, but I'm also majoring in Physics. We've got moral choices, of course. And scientists *do* struggle with those issues. We *don't* just charge blindly ahead!"

"That's what *I* was talking about!" the tall, black-sweater, brown-skinned guy excitedly interjected, pushing the blond girl backward to grab the microphone himself. "Green energy is *moral!* It uses just what God gave to us: gravity, sunlight, and heat from the depths of the earth. It's not contaminating our environment with radiation or carbon. It's not making only the big companies rich. It's something we can be proud to leave to our children and..."

"—you mean your billions of kids swamping the earth with their excess population!" another person yelled from the audience. "If *your* kind didn't breed like rabbits then there'd be no problem with having enough energy for the entire world!"

The bored, dispirited, class suddenly erupted into *shouting* and *shoving* as many rose in protest while others cheered the incendiary words!

At the mike, the brown-skinned boy shoved away the pale-skinned girl who was nodding in agreement to what the person in the audience had just shouted.

In response, she balled her fist and swung at the black-sweater kid who ducked out of the way, her fist smashing into the side of the elderly Asian's head—who staggered back, then launched a karate kick at her torso.

"No, no, no!" Dave shouted, pulling off his lapel mike. He jumped down from the podium and raced over to the standing mike to try and pull apart the clutch of now-wrestling students.

"So you caused a riot, did you David?" Dean Kelly intoned sadly.

She was a trim lady with thick blue plastic glasses dominating her stern face. Her short-cropped hair was dyed a bluish blond to match. She wore a pink-spotted blue dress. She liked blue.

And she did *not* like what she saw sitting across from her.

She'd been around a long time. She'd slowly risen within the small college's management to become the Dean of Science. She liked everything neat and predictable. This wasn't the first time that Dr. King had sat across her desk for her chastisement.

But it was sure as hell going to be the *last* time!

"I'm...I'm terribly sorry," he shrugged, looking dead-tired.

"The campus police had to break up the riot," she stated matter-of-factly.

"It was totally spontaneous, unexpected. You see I was just trying to provoke student participation, get a good discussion going and..."

"—in an introductory *physics* class?" she marveled, shaking her head from side-to-side in disbelief.

"Dr. Kelly, physics is the basis of everything!" he vehemently argued. "All of our screwed-up, competitive, arrogant human biology is based on physics."

She laughed.

The man was simply too arrogant to fit in at a small two-year, junior college.

"No, you're wrong, Dave," she coldly shot-back at him. "*Mathematics* is the basis of everything. You are correct that physics is the basis of biology. But mathematics is the basis of physics. This is un-deniable."

"Ok," he sighed. "I understand that you're a professor of mathe-matics. Everyone sees things from where they stand. It's just a mat-ter of perspective that..."

"It's a matter of *fact*, Dr. King!" she interrupted him, *glowering* at him. "And the fact of the matter is that your class broke down into a riot because of the situation you created! What were you thinking? Physics isn't a matter of philosophy and religion. It's about energy, space, and equations. How could you be so stupid?"

He looked to her like he was struggling with what to say next. Well, he'd best struggle hard. He'd already insulted her in the worst way possible, insinuating that her science discipline was merely a matter of perspective.

"It...it won't happen again," he replied apologetically and softly.

"That's certainly true," she agreed, "—because you are *fired!*"

She had a deep feeling of satisfaction at uttering those clear, mathematically precise words.

His expression was one of *devastation*.

"B-but, I-I..." he stammered, "I didn't start it! It was a religious kid that got excited about some religious position. Then it just snow-balled from there. It wasn't my fault!"

Ah...he looked like a little kid on a playground, caught in having started a fight.

She was enjoying this. He'd been a thorn in her side for much too long.

"It is never 'your fault', David," she glared at him. "The many times you were late to faculty meetings, forgot to go to your lectures, didn't turn in your committee assignments on time, then showed up at work disheveled and smelling of sweat, didn't have time to even bathe—none of that was your fault."

"Please, Dean Kelly," he pleaded. "I was trying to keep up a re-search effort at home. It was very difficult. I was doing the best I could under the..."

"We are not a research college!" she yelled at him, half-rising from her desk. "How many times have I told you this before? I know you regarded us as just a temporary stop-gap position before getting a

University position—even though you've been with us for ten years. But that's not how we work. We hire people who want to teach, *not* do research. And we want people who give us a commitment. You *don't* have tenure and never will. You're *not* what we need here. I've given you every chance to get your act together and you've blown off me and the college every single time. Well, that's not going to happen anymore. You're gone! Pack up your office and *leave*. If you are not gone by the end of the day I'll have the campus police bodily throw you out."

"But who's going to teach my classes?" he protested. "It's the middle of the semester!"

"We'll call the University and tomorrow have ten graduate students applying to teach each of your introductory classes," she smugly stated, "—at *half* the wages we paid you! And you damn well can bet that they will appreciate their part-time work here enough to be on time to their lectures and not cause riots."

She was enjoying this. He looked like he was on the verge of crying. Making out like he was some great "researcher", looking down on the rest of them as mere "lecturers"—he was finished!

"Dean Kelly—*Georgia!*" he gasped. "My house almost burned down yesterday. My research equipment was destroyed. I'm totally out of the research business. I'm willing to give everything to this job. I realize now my extracurricular research efforts were just a colossal waste of time. Please, can't you give me another chance—just one more chance? *Please?*"

She grimly shook her head in the negative. She was getting rid of this arrogant fool. Let him go get a job cooking hamburgers at a fast-food joint. That would teach *him* a powerful lesson.

"I've already talked to the College President. He agrees with me. There could be lawsuits stemming from the disaster in your physics class today. Students were injured, fortunately none seriously—but enough to cause lawyers to come running out of the woodwork! President Sawyer agrees that our best legal strategy is to let you go...immediately."

Then, seeing the devastated look on Dave's face, she continued more gently.

She could be magnanimous now that she was finally getting rid of his useless butt.

"Go on over to Personnel," she ordered him. She stood up and came around her desk to lay a comforting hand on his shoulder. "Even under these circumstances the Union requires a reasonable severance package. You'll be ok. And who knows, maybe this is the best thing for you. I'm sorry about the fire at your house. I heard about it this morning. We were going to offer you time off anyway, before you went and caused a race-and-religious-riot in your class-room! Take some time to get your head on straight. Figure out what you really want. Maybe you can still find a post-doc position doing the research you are interested in, if you gave the search a full-time effort, unencumbered by a 'day-job'. We're rid of you. But you're also rid of us. Take some time to get your head on straight."

He unsteadily rose to his feet.

"Ok, Dean," he whispered. "I'm sorry about everything. I tried my best. Thanks for the chances you gave me over the last few years. I guess I'm just a failure at everything that I..."

She sharply *slapped* him on his cheek.

He looked shocked, holding a hand to his reddened cheek, staring at her in surprise.

"Get over it, David," she glared at him. "I'm a woman in admin-istration when I'd much prefer to be a full-time teacher. I'm a single mother with three kids. I bounced from position to position before I finally wound up here. I'm not working the ideal job I'd prefer either. Everybody's got it tough nowadays. You've just got to roll with the punches. Get it?"

For a moment she feared she'd gone too far, perhaps provoking that hated "wrongful dismissal" lawsuit.

He held a palm to the side of his face where she'd slapped him. Then he lopsidedly grinned.

"Ok, Dean Kelly. I get it. All the best to you, then," he mumbled, turning away. "And that's a mean fist you've got there..."

"And all the best to you, Dave," she primly answered. "And as to my punch, in my younger years I was a mixed martial-artist. I had ten professional fights, won half of them."

She shouldn't have slapped him. That wasn't professional. But it sure had felt good.

He was a real jerk. He richly deserved the slap—and being fired!

Dave was dejectedly clearing out the contents of his desk into a large paper box when Professor Johnson came barging in.

"It's authentic!" he exclaimed without preamble, waving the wrinkled green bill high up in the air above his head.

"Uh...say what?" Dave blinked, dazed.

"Your 'funny-money'," George repeated. "Everything checks out. It is authentic!"

Remembering the assignment he'd tasked George with, Dave stopped his packing. It was just that morning. But the morning seemed like a year ago. Getting everything straightened out with Personnel had taken the entire afternoon. Now it was early evening.

Things weren't quite as gloomy for him as when he'd left Dean Kelly's office, though. Due to the ten years he had worked at the junior college, he was getting half a year's lump-sum as severance pay— as long as he signed a "no-contest" agreement. He'd done that readily. A half year's pay would give him time to sort things out, figure out what he really wanted. They cut him a check there on the spot. Actually, Dean Kelly's advice was right on point.

"What do you mean, George?" he asked the short, chubby man who was practically jumping up and down with excitement there in front of Dave's soon-to-be ex-desk.

"It has all the proper seals. It has the proper borders. It has a real serial number. And the paper has the proper embedded color fibers! Everything's perfect—except of course for the images and a few other details."

"But how is that possible?"

"I don't know. Neither did the techs at the lab where I examined the bill. It's a total mystery. They wanted to keep it and examine it further."

"Well—how about that?" Dave gasped, shaking his head in amazement. What a day this was turning out to be. Now he discovers that the girl at the grocery Megastore gave him a completely genuine *fake* hundred dollar bill!

It was just too weird.

He reached over and deftly nabbed the note out of George's waving hand, placing it securely back into his wallet.

"But that's not all," George said, coming around the desk to speak in a quiet voice so that no one happening to be walking past in the hallway might hear.

"There's more?" Dave marveled.

"I did some tests with an electronic detector. You know, for fraud detection. They're just coming out—you slide the bill through and it tells you whether the bill is counterfeit or not."

"And?"

"It read legit—even with the false images."

"But how could that happen?"

"It has embedded microcircuits," he softly stated. He paused before repeating himself more forcefully: "Dave, *it has embedded microcircuits!* Even our legitimate bills aren't that sophisticated. It over-rode the programmed algorithms in the detector's program and declared itself to be legitimate. It's the ultimate fake currency except for a few details plus those damn pictures that contrawise are flagrantly proclaiming it to be *counterfeit*. It just doesn't make any sense. Actually it's impossible. It can't happen. And yet there it is!"

"Wow..."

"Oh, yes 'wow', my friend—and that's not the worst."

"There's more?"

"I also did a swipe on it to test for cocaine residue."

"Cocaine?"

"All one hundred dollar bills have trace cocaine worked down into their fibers—because they've all at some point or other passed through drug-dealer's hands. It's the preferred medium of exchange for drug deals, not too bulky like small denominations and not too large a denomination to attract undue attention."

"What did you find?"

"Not a trace, Dave."

"But it looks beat up, wrinkled, worn, and used. It's probably passed through thousands and thousands of people's hands."

"That's also what I thought and..."

"Then how's it clean?"

George paused, shaking his bald head in bewilderment.

"It's like it came from a world where cocaine never existed," George marveled.

George was definitely getting Dave excited. The shock of the fire and explosion, the loss of all his research, the horror at being fired from his job, were all replaced by a *nagging curiosity*.

Where the hell was that *Girl with the Turtle Tattoo* from?

He shook his head, trying to clear it. Maybe it was just Mother Nature kicking him again in the pants one last time.

"Or, like we figured before," Dave puzzled, frowning in concentration, "maybe it's just some elaborate joke. Could someone take a brand-new hundred dollar bill and replace the images—then deliberately weather it so it appeared to be a used bill...and then embed microcircuits into its fibers?"

George shrugged his rounded shoulders.

"I never heard of such a thing," he finally replied. "I guess it is theoretically possible. But it would take a master craftsman using the best equipment. But why would anyone do something so crazy?"

Then George seemed to notice what Dave was in the process of doing.

"Cleaning out your desk?"

"I'm fired," Dave grunted, closing the top of the box and hefting it up under his arm.

He stuck out his other hand to George.

"Thanks for checking out the bill. I don't know what it means. But now I've the time to try to figure it out on my own."

"Fired?" George repeated, gaping foolishly.

"Maybe it's the best thing that ever happened to me, I'm thinking," Dave sighed, his voice trailing off. Then, with more regret at not being able to see his only real friend daily, "I'll be in touch, George. But I'm sure I'll need your 'snake-sitting' skills in the near future. I'll be job-hunting and traveling once I get my head on straight."

"What are you going to do now?" George asked, his rounded face twisted in concern. "You're probably not thinking too straight at the moment. Why don't you come over for dinner tonight with me and Alice? It's our night for family bridge and we'd love to have a third player. It might be good for you to have human companionship instead of just sequestering yourself in your house with your reptiles. Do you even have electricity?"

"Hmmmm..." Dave thought, pausing. "That's not a bad idea, George. And thanks for the invitation, but no. There's an even more urgent priority I think I need to pursue now that I've got the time to do so. And yes, I think they've got juice back. I'll need it to power up my computer at home for the search."

"What search?"

"I'm going to find that *damn girl* with the *turtle tattoo!*"

Dave squeezed past the dumbfounded George, leaving behind the cramped, little office. Then he resolutely marched down the corridor past curious stares from other late-working faculty.

He didn't look back. He'd burnt his bridges, in more ways than one.

These disasters weren't random.

There was a *pattern*, no matter how obscure.

And he was determined to tease it out.

Chapter 5

PATTERNS

Have you ever appreciated sand
Flowing like water over your hand?
A marvelous liquid made out of rocks
Ground-down by Mother Nature
Smooth, rippling, and soft...
Yes, it was made out of you.

The Luminary Chronicles, 5:32

As he drove his yellow Cavalier up to his house he saw two cars already parked there on the street. One of them had a sign on its side advertising his insurance company. The other was a black sedan with darkened windows.

It was an older subdivision. Big trees lined the sidewalks. The families were mostly retired, their children gone. Nothing much happened on that street, at least until recently.

Oh Christ—Dave groaned to himself. *This is such a pain!*

A man wearing a hard hat stood astride the blackened beams of the garage which lay on top of the crushed remains of his destroyed research equipment. He must be the insurance inspector.

More sinister, a burly man in a dark suit was talking animatedly with the inspector. The second man was big, wore dark glasses, had crewcut short blond hair, and wore a black suit. An even heftier black-suited fellow hovered off to the side. Likewise, he also had on dark eyeglasses.

They were either government or mobsters.

Either way, Dave felt a chill go down his spine.

A heavy wind was blowing, stirring up black soot. The evening air was thick and heavy. It was an ominous setting.

"Uh, hi there," Dave said as he walked up the garage driveway. "I'm the owner of this house."

47

"Dr. David King?" the dark-suited man interjected

"Yes?"

"FBI—Agent Anderson," he said, holding out a badge and federal I.D. to Dave. "And that's agent Cooper over there."

"FBI?" Dave dumbly repeated, closely examining the I.D. badge, which seemed authentic, before handing it back.

"Could we have a few words with you?" the Agent asked. "Perhaps we could sit for a couple minutes inside your house?"

"Uh, well, can I speak to my insurance representative here first?"

The two agents exchanged glances. Cooper nodded. Anderson stepped carefully over the burnt debris to join him over at the side, all the time keeping a careful eye on Dave. It was unnerving that the two FBI agents stayed close enough to hear everything.

Dave had never been in trouble with the law. He didn't want any trouble now. But why was the FBI interested in his burned-down garage?

Anderson took a small pocket mirror from his pants pocket and held it up as he stood off to the side, looking in it as with the other hand he carefully combed his short blond hair into place.

What a vain jerk—Dave thought to himself. *He's almost as much a jerk as me. But am I really that bad? Did I just lose myself in my failed experiments and reptiles?*

Dave mentally shook himself, forcing himself to focus on the immediate situation.

What the hell was happening? Was he about to be arrested? But for what? He hadn't done anything wrong! Although...he wondered if George talked to the wrong people about that funny-money? Did these agents think he was a counterfeiter?

"Mr. King?" the insurance inspector said, reaching out a beefy hand. He had the look of an experienced contractor who knew his business. He was bald with a wide face, bushy black eyebrows, and world-weary eyes.

"Yes, thanks for coming out so quickly," Dave gushed, trying to get his head together about the FBI being there, deliberately speaking-up so that the agents could easily hear him.

"The fire only happened yesterday evening, as you know," Dave continued. "In fact, I was almost killed! Lucky some neighbor saw something and gave me a call to run out of my house. There was an explosion. The Fire Chief thought it was probably a gas explosion. Once they had the fire under control they switched off my gas at the main line. What have you found?"

"Well, that's what I wanted to point out to you, Mr. King. There's a lot of mangled metal and cables in here. A spark from a bad connection could certainly have set off any accumulated gas, if you had a leak. I traced the line along the wall but it was too badly damaged to know if the connections were leaking. Did you smell any gas earlier in the evening?"

"No, can't say that I did," Dave replied. "I was in here to check on readouts of an electrolysis experiment that I had running just about an hour before the explosion happened. I didn't smell anything unusual."

"You had some sort of experiment in progress?"

"Yes, I'm a physics instructor at the local junior college—well, I was until...no matter. I do high-school level physics experiments as a hobby."

"Do you have a permit to use that sort of equipment in a residential area?"

Irritated, Dave replied a bit forcefully: "None needed, my friend. Like I said, I wasn't doing anything dangerous. It only took a few watts to run the equipment."

"Well, I'm not here to deal with any legal issues. And don't worry about your compensation," the inspector assured him. "Your policy covers accidental fires. Clearly this was an accident. A rapid gas leak could have accounted for the explosion. You certainly had enough electrical equipment in here to provide a spark. However, the pattern of the explosion and subsequent fire doesn't jive with a gas leak."

"Say what?" Dave dumbly replied.

"Come on over here," the inspector invited him, stepping through the crumbled wood and mashed equipment.

Dave carefully followed in his footsteps.

"Look there—and there," the man pointed out various clumps of smashed and burnt metal.

"What am I looking at?" Dave replied.

"The pattern of the explosion," he explained. "You can clearly see how the force of the explosion blew outward from a central point. Also, the plastic and metal are melted towards the center of the pattern. That's clearly where the explosion originated. And it wasn't over by the wall, where the gas line runs."

Intrigued, Dave saw what the inspector was pointing out. Yes, at the center of the roughly circular pattern was a blob of fused metal, hardly recognizable as a piece of equipment.

"Do you remember what you had at that spot?" the inspector asked.

"Uh...it's difficult to get oriented with the garage blown apart and burned down...but...I think," he paused a moment, sighed, then decided that truth was the best defense, "—that was where the central combination chamber was for my electrolysis experiment," he admitted, his mind racing.

How was this possible? Even if somehow he'd achieved maximum possible fusion of the hydrogen ions—an unthinkable achievement—it could only cause an increase of a few degrees in the reaction chamber. He just wasn't working with enough atoms in his jerry-rigged setup to produce anything close to the explosion that almost killed him!

"Not to worry, sir," the inspector said. "Even if something in your gear exploded, my report will confirm it wasn't deliberate. You are still fully covered."

"Ok," Dave tentatively answered, unsure of what was happening.

"The first thing you need to do is hire workers to clean up this mess," the insurance inspector continued. "Get three estimates and we'll pay for the lowest one. After that, we'll cut you a check for the standard compensation, which the adjustors will determine from my report and your policy. You can use that to repair the damage to your structure. I see in your policy, here on my tablet, that the contents to your house weren't covered, so we won't pay for any of your equipment that was destroyed in the garage. Any questions?"

"Uh no, I guess not. That sounds reasonable," Dave nodded, threading his way back out of the charred remains following the inspector. "Thanks for your help."

"Oh, no problem," the bushy-eyed man responded, waving a hand as he strode back to his car, "just doing my job."

"And we're doing ours too," Agent Anderson reminded him, stepping up beside him. "Can we sit and talk in your house—or do we need to go back to the station?"

"Say what?" Dave said, alarmed. "Am I being arrested for something?"

"No, no," the man replied in a deep, gravelly voice. "We're just doing *our* job checking things out. We're with Homeland Security. Explosions in garages catch our attention."

"Oh, you mean like terrorists building a bomb or something?"

"That's right," the man nodded as they entered his house. The other agent stayed outside on the porch. "Nice snake you have there. Do you live by yourself?"

Dave laughed. He opened up the top of the floor cage to lift out his pet king snake and hand it to the inspector. The snake was four feet long, a couple inches wide at his fattest point, black with white specks.

"Do you think a wife would put up with snakes and lizards filling up the living room?"

The agent let the king snake crawl up his arm before gently handing it back.

"Any poisonous ones?" he asked.

"No, Sir," Dave stated firmly. "I'm a strictly amateur herpetologist. I leave dangerous reptiles to the real experts. My harmless creatures were purchased in local pet stores. I just like them. I've always liked reptiles. When I was a kid I was fascinated by dinosaurs."

"I know what you mean," the agent laughed. "I was the same. When I was a kid I couldn't get enough of T-rex stuff. My dad bought me a one-twentieth scale T-rex plastic replica skeleton and it was like he gave me a treasure. Of course what I didn't fully realize is that they were true monsters. A grown T-rex could swallow me as a kid in one gulp."

"Or even you as an adult," Dave added.

"Wouldn't that be something," the Agent grinned, with a fingertip moving his dark eyeglasses up a notch on his nose from where they'd slid down. "What an ending that would be—a snack in the belly of a dinosaur. Hah!"

Despite his suspicions, Dave was starting to like Agent Anderson.

"It'd still be fun to see a live one—from a safe distance," Dave laughed, knowing the agent was playing "good cop" with him but not caring. It never hurt to have sympathetic connections.

"Well, back to this business of your garage," the Agent stated, sitting on a chair at a table that served as Dave's eating and reading place.

"Right," Dave said, sitting across from him.

"It seems that something unexpected happened with your experiment."

"Well," Dave swallowed, thinking furiously. Was he getting into deep trouble here? "Yes, clearly something happened at that spot. But I don't think it was from my experiment. It was probably just an equipment malfunction. I have—well, I *had*, before the fire—surplus World War II-era neutron and heat detectors trained on an electrolysis matrix. They were really old. Anything could have gone wrong with them."

"You're kidding, right?" Anderson grinned. "WWII surplus equipment? Where'd you get them?"

"You'd be surprised what's still in dusty heaps in government surplus centers. I couldn't afford anything up-to-date. That sort of research costs millions of dollars. All I've got is just my small paycheck."

Anderson shrugged.

"But you don't think it was the experiment itself?"

"I don't see how. In the combination chamber I was only working with a few atoms of deuterium. I was trying to initiate what's known as a sustained 'cold fusion'—but even if I'd totally succeeded it would have only warmed up the chamber by a maximum of a few degrees. That's what my calorimeters were set up to detect, to document any excess heat above the input energy."

"Fusion? Isn't that what powers a nuclear bomb?" Anderson mildly stated.

"The least powerful atomic bombs are from *fission*—where atoms are *split* apart and release excess nuclear energy catastrophically. But yes, a step up from the fission bomb is the so-called 'hydrogen' bomb: where the power of the sun is released in a few nanoseconds. But for that to happen it has to be triggered by incredibly high temperatures and pressures from a fission bomb going off first. I assure you, Agent Anderson, I wasn't playing with anything like that!"

"But you had an explosion."

"Probably just an equipment malfunction," Dave stubbornly repeated. "It was likely a spark that ignited a gas leak. Ask the inspector. That's what he said."

Anderson shrugged.

"And this 'deuterium'—what's that? Is that an explosive fuel?"

"It's one of the two stable isotopes of hydrogen. It occurs naturally in water at low concentrations. If you increase the concentration enough, it's what's called 'heavy water.' It's not explosive. It's part of the water. You could drink it if you wanted."

"So why are you using it in your experiments if it's so inert?"

"Well, if you can get the deuterium ions to fuse, it releases nuclear energy—plus neutrons. That's what I was looking for in my experiments, excess heat plus excess neutrons—beyond background levels."

"It still sounds dangerous to me."

"Well, on a commercial scale it might be—though nowhere near as dangerous as the fission reactions currently used in atomic power plants. As I said, what I'm doing—or was doing—is on the level of high school science-fair stuff, though with more sophisticated equipment. Even high school kids have gotten a few atoms to fuse. Me, I was trying for a more sustained reaction by tweaking the conditions around a sophisticated palladium matrix that I developed when I did my doctoral research."

"So you're experienced in this methodology?"

"Yes, I studied at Yale with Professor Victor Volodymyr—one of the pioneers of electrochemically-assisted nuclear reactions. He wasn't doing cold fusion research, though. That was discredited way back in the late twentieth century."

"So why are you doing it? And why in your garage? Why not at a local university?"

"Just stupid, I suppose—answering your first question," Dave grimaced. "I've got a fascination with it. I thought that if you laced the palladium electrode with the proper mix of other metal ions you could vastly increase its catalytic potential for hydrogen fusion, enough maybe to provoke a sustained hydrogen fusion reaction. But science is littered with the corpses of 'great ideas' that Mother Nature happily shot down. And mine, sadly, is no different."

"So no one will support this research because it's been so thoroughly discredited?"

Dave sighed.

"You hit the nail on the head, Agent Anderson," he grimaced. "Even funded out of my own pocket—what little I could scrape together—it would have been far better to do it in a real physics lab. But my job situation doesn't...or, I guess, didn't...allow for such. So..."

"So you're piddling around in your garage."

"That's about it."

"What about this 'palladium' electrode of yours? Could that be what caused your explosion?"

"Well, it might, yes—in sufficient purity and quantity," Dave admitted. "But since I funded the research out of my own pocket, I had only a tiny amount. Plus it was bound up in an inert crystalline matrix that I perfected in my doctoral research. It enhances the normal body-centered cubic form of a palladium crystal structure."

"I don't need all the details, Dr. King, just the 'take-home message.'"

"Oh, sure," Dave shrugged. *He* didn't need this interrogation. He just needed to answer the questions as briefly as possible and get rid of this annoyance. "Actually, my thesis professor allowed me to take a small quantity of it to a postdoc—otherwise I'd have none of it today. But it was destroyed in the fire, both the working sample and my stock," he glumly finished.

"Isn't metallurgy dangerous and complex? How could you do that in a garage?"

"Like I said, Agent Anderson, I did most of the metallurgy during my doctoral work, at Yale University in a fully stocked and certified research laboratory. After that, making minor additions to the matrix was relatively easy."

"You say you did a post-doc?"

"Yes, for a year. Then my Mom got sick. I had to move back here to Oklahoma to help take care of her. That's when I took a job teaching at the local junior college—which turned into a career. I've been there for ten years now...until today, that is."

"And just where was this 'post doc' of yours?"

"It was in France at the *Cadarache Research Center*," Dave grinned, his mood picking up a bit recalling the excitement of being part of a serious "big-physics" research team. "I had a small job in the development team for the 'big-science' fusion experiment going on there. It uses gigantic magnets to trap burning plasma of deuterium and tritium—another isotope of hydrogen—at a temperature of around 150 million degrees."

"Now that's a hot fire, for sure," the Agent nodded agreeably.

"Very hot indeed," Dave grinned. "And that's the place to finally achieve sustained, controlled 'ignition': where the energy output is greater than the energy needed to get the thing started. So if you're looking for explosions, Sir, you better go there rather than sniff around my pitiful, ancient, destroyed apparatus."

"Must have been disappointing for you to have to quit working in France?"

Dave felt his throat choking up. He fought back the glimmer of tears starting to brighten his eyes.

"Well, family comes first," he shrugged. "It's just me and my sister left to care for my mother. And my sister's got a big family, a full-time career—three kids plus a dope of a useless, ne'er-do-well husband. So I came back. And here I am."

"Do you blame the establishment?"

Dave slowly arose, an expression of indignation spreading over his face. "Certainly not, Agent Anderson. What are you implying?"

"Home-grown terrorists typically have irrational bones to pick with their government, official agencies, companies, or society in general. Are you angry at someone, Dr. King?" he mildly stated, his eyes hidden behind his large dark glasses.

"Maybe...*God*, perhaps...Mother Nature *certainly*," Dave barked. But then he sighed, relaxing. "But stuff happens, I know that. Sometimes you get the breaks and sometimes you get broken. But it turned out that my job at ITER wasn't some 'dream' job. I was just a small cog in a gigantic research enterprise, working on narrowly assigned problems. I didn't have any future there. Hardly anyone even knew my name. And I certainly wasn't able to pursue my own research initiatives. In fact, I was relieved to have a reason to cut it short."

He stood up and moved over into the adjoining small kitchen.

"Would you like something to drink?" he said, opening his refrigerator door. Inside was an old pitcher of lemonade, a single can of Pepsi, and a carton of milk that smelled well past its due date.

"No thanks," the agent said, getting up from his chair. "I've got enough information...for now. We might have more questions for you in the near future. If you go out of town please let my office know. Here's my card."

"Ok, I can do that—but why? Do you think I'm a terrorist?"

"No, Dr. King," he matter-of-factly stated as he stopped by the iguana cage and tapped on the glass. "I think you're probably just a nice guy who, like you say, had some bad breaks. But we may need your expertise, if you don't mind. Something's going on out there...and we don't know what. Strange things are happening. Your little explosion is just one of a series of curious events. By themselves, in isolation, they are easily explained. But put together, it may be part of a *pattern*."

There it was again. The agent was also seeing things in terms of some obscure "pattern." The mystery was deepening.

"What sort of a 'pattern'?" Dave asked, simultaneously concerned and intrigued.

"Can't say for sure," the Agent softly replied. "But that's my job. I look for disturbing trends. I tie together things which by themselves, superficially, seem to be merely curious. Maybe you're not part of it. But just maybe there's more here than meets the eye. You see, I have a special perspective on how things fit together."

He calmly removed his sunglasses, allowing Dave to see *empty sockets* where his eyes should have been!

And glinting in those shadowy pits Dave could have sworn he saw *swirling diamonds*—yet another hidden pattern?

"You're...blind?" Dave gasped, stunned.

Agent Anderson snapped the "glasses" back into place on his head. Dave heard a solid "click" as unseen interfaces locked back together. The "diamonds" must just been a trick of the light in the room...

The man slipped the small mirror from his pocket, again using it to comb his disturbed short blond hair meticulously back into place.

"The end-pieces of my glasses connect with neural implants in my head," the man grinned. "It's the latest medical gadgetry. I can't see as well as Geordi did in the Star Trek series, what with his fabulous visor three hundred years in the future. But I can see shapes well enough, and something more—something beyond just the visible outward contours of physical objects: how things unexpectedly connect."

"Really?" Dave gasped. "That's amazing! Uh, 'patterns', you say?"

"Oh, yes," the agent nodded. "Of course patterns are just lines drawn between otherwise disconnected events. For instance, I 'see' that you, Sir, are more than you claim to be. One of the 'shapes' I see concerning yourself is you being fired this very morning from your teaching job. It wasn't for incompetence, no far from it. The official reason they got rid of you was you supposedly starting a small riot amongst your students. But that was only an excuse. The truth was that they couldn't trust you. You were driven by something that scared them. Isn't *that* true?"

Dave remembered the fearful expression of the Dean, her violent reaction against him.

It made sense what the Agent was saying. He was speechless, his mouth hanging open.

"And certainly despite our 'freedom of speech' constraints," Agent Anderson continued, "volatile public discourse is of deep concern to Homeland Security. Zealotry is dangerous whether it's direct or facilitated. Even scientific compulsions can be perilous to society— especially when individuals feel they must continue on so-called 'impossible' quests, if you know what I mean?"

Dave frowned, trying to comprehend what the FBI Agent was implying.

"But...?" Dave started to protest.

"—and a good day to you," the Agent abruptly concluded the interrogation, stepping out the front door onto the porch and closing the door solidly behind him, joining the other agent.

Dave heard their heavy feet "clomp" down the sidewalk back to their black sedan.

Things were getting more and more confusing. How could he possibly "scare" anyone? He wasn't hiding anything!

But *was* there really some "pattern" to all this? Or was it just a congruence of random events?

Dave only knew that he must keep at trying to figure it out. The agent was correct—Dave was possessed by an obsession beyond his own control.

And despite whether it scared other people, it scared *him*.

"*Damn* it!" he yelled at Topper sitting placidly on his branch under his heat lamp. "It's got to be in here. Why can't I find it?"

The big green lizard just sat there, not helping at all. For the umpteenth time, Dave wished reptiles could speak.

It was the next afternoon.

After a fitful night spent trying to sleep on the small couch in his living room—trying to breathe past the smoky musk that still permeated the house—he got up tired and congested.

He had a fit of coughing before clearing out the accumulated mucous in his nose and throat.

"Oh, man," he groaned. "Maybe I've caught my Mom's cancer."

Bad joke. Don't say things like that!

Choking down some old cereal moistened by the going-bad milk didn't help either.

"Well, at least I don't have to go into work today," he snickered to himself, a bit hysterically. "Might as well make some calls."

He set up appointments with local construction companies to come give him bids on clearing out the debris and rebuilding his garage and bedroom. Most of them were happy to send someone out that very evening.

Setting up the appointments and then calling his insurance agency and then going and getting the proper forms had taken most of his morning.

Finally he was able to do his daily chores with his animals, going through the cages in the small rooms of his house: the living room containing Topper and Speckles; the storage room containing habitats for his large red-tailed boa and ball pythons, and the weight-room where he kept his assorted smaller lizards and tortoises.

He refreshed their water bowls and replaced the "salads" of his lizards and tortoises.

"You guys eat better than I do," he said as he placed the fresh confections for them in their cages: bowls containing lettuce, diced potatoes, corn, fruit, flecks of dog food pellets, and vitamin & mineral supplements.

Then he was finally able to start to work on his laptop, connecting to the Internet: searching online phone books of the city of Ada, Oklahoma.

"I need some combination of z's or c's or k's for first name and last name," he muttered to himself, grimly intent, sitting at his kitchen table.

There were many suitable combinations.

However, there wasn't anything that resembled the "Cloe Kleever" that his Mother had remembered.   All he was collecting was a huge long list of numbers. There's no way he could call them one by one asking if they had a daughter with tattoos—they'd think he was crazy.

Where was the damn "pattern" when you needed one?

"So what do you think, Topper?" he said to the big green iguana sitting lazily on its branch. "Do I have it wrong? Did my Mom get it wrong? Instead of landlines, is the lady's phone a cellphone number I can't access? Does she actually live somewhere outside of Ada? I'm not a private detective who knows how to do searches like these!" he yelled in frustration.

Just then his own landline rang.

Angrily, he snatched up the receiver and jammed it against his ear.

"*Yes*?" he snapped.

"Is that any way to talk to your Mother? Are you home already from teaching? Did you have a bad day? You know that I..."

"Oh, hi Mom," he sighed. "Sorry to answer like that. I should have looked at the caller I.D.—I've had a rough day and..."

"Oh, that's too bad," she cooed. "You should take a nice hot bath. That really helps me when I've had a bad day. And then you should go out for a nice meal. Get out of that stuffy house with those smelly animals, don't you know? Maybe you'll meet a nice girl. In fact, that's why I'm..."

"Mom, I'm busy," he cut her off. If he didn't keep her on subject she'd jabber happily on for hours at a time. "Can I help you with something?"

"Oh, no dear—I'm just fine, as always," she cheerfully answered, ignoring his interruption. He knew she was lying, but didn't want to interrogate her on her declining health. It was just too depressing. "In fact," she continued, "I was calling to help you."

"Me?"

"Yes, dear," she continued. "I just got back from my appointment at that torture chamber in Ada. Catherine just dropped me off at home."

Ah, an opportunity for a specific update. That was good. He needed to know her true state of health in order to do his duty toward her. If he had a job, no matter how odious or painful, he always did his best.

"So how are you? Are you feeling ok?"

"Oh, don't worry about me," she insisted. "I take things one day at a time. Anyway, I saw that lady again, the one you asked me for her name? She was just leaving when I was arriving. She recognized me from the week before and sat with me for a few minutes there in the waiting room."

"The lady you told me about?" his interest perked up. "You talked to her again?"

"Yes, that's what I just told you," she laughed over the phone. "Are you having hearing problems, Davey? You said you had a rough day. Now what's been going on with you? You know that I'm always here for you. I'm your Mother. You can always call me up and talk whenever you..."

"Mom!" he got her back on track. "You saw Cloe Kleever again? Did you happen to find out if she lived in Ada or..."

"Who?"

"Cloe Kleever."

"Who's that?"

"That's what you told me her name was!" he yelled into the phone.

"Oh, right," she laughed. "No, that's not her name."

"What?"

"Oh, as usual I got it all wrong," she laughed. "She remembered *my* name. But when I called her 'Cloe' she corrected me. I was so embarrassed. But she's a real nice lady and wasn't mad. In fact, we struck up a nice conversation about our beautiful children. I told her about your..."

"What was her real name?" he interrupted her. "Did you get her real name?"

"Oh, sure, Davey," she paused a second. "Her name was Samantha Smith. Very easy to remember—it rhymes! Of course I guess that's why I thought it was that other name because it rhymes also and I was thinking about getting new kitchen knives like a new cleaver for hacking apart steaks to cook in the oven that..."

"'Samantha Smith,' you're sure about it?" he probed, choosing to ignore her confusing rhyming with alliteration.

"Of course I am, dear," she chuckled. "When I *want* to remember something I can do it perfectly well."

"That's helpful, Mom," he congratulated her. "Did it happen to come up what town she lived in?"

"Are you looking to find her daughter?"

He paused, not wanting to acknowledge an interest in a girl to his mother, knowing that he'd never hear the end of it, but...

"I actually think I saw the daughter Sunday morning working as a clerk in the grocery store in Sulphur," he grudgingly admitted. "She gave me too much change by accident and I was worried it'd be taken out of her pay. I didn't know who she was. I didn't discover it until afterwards. I wanted to return it quietly if I could, without getting her into any more trouble with her management."

"Well, that was nice of you," she cheerfully replied. "Maybe all that church attendance as a child actually helped you some?—no, I'm just joking, dear. Don't take it personal. You've always been a moral person. I admire your dedication to your work, to your research, and to me. And I'm glad you always want to do the right thing. I'm proud of you."

He felt a few tears of gratitude choking him up. Should he tell her about his present problems?

"Was she pretty?" she slyly asked.

Oh, right—he sighed to himself. *That's what I get for opening up a crack. It's back to her wanting a second batch of grandchildren.*

"I don't know, Mom," he lied. "All I noticed about her was that she had a tattoo on her wrist. You know that I like reptiles. That's what caught my attention and..."

"Oh, you and those stupid snakes of yours..."

"They're wonderful animals," he insisted, getting exasperated again. "You insist that God made everything five thousand years ago. Snakes were an important part of that Creation, we're they?"

"Sure, that got Adam and Eve thrown out of the Garden of Eden!"

"That was the Devil pretending that he was a nice, friendly, tame snake," Dave tried to debate. "It doesn't mean that snakes are devils."

"Pish-pash," she snorted. "It certainly does. That's why God made women to be instinctively afraid of snakes. In order to get yourself a beautiful wife you must get rid of those nasty snakes in your house. Now a lizard or two, that's not so bad. You can keep those in cages out in your garage. But snakes that are ten feet long? Oh, my word! That's just too big for..."

"Mom!"

"Yes?"

"Please focus," he sighed, "—the lady! Did you happen to find out the town where she lives? If I knew that, I could maybe find her telephone number and..."

"Oh, I did better than that," she happily asserted.

"Really?"

"I told her that you had an interest in her daughter," she gurgled with excitement. "And she was so pleased! She always wanted her girl to meet a nice, educated man. She was so impressed that you are a Scientist when I told her about you. My son, the Ph.D. 'Doctor'! Well, not a *real* Doctor, but..."

"What did you find out?" he eagerly cut her off again, this time not bothering to be polite.

"Well, I'm getting to that, Dear," she laughed. "It turns out that her daughter is just as stubborn and headstrong as you. Getting tattoos all over her body—isn't that peculiar? But it's just what young people do when they're growing up nowadays. They rebel. They want to show they are their own person. Just like you and that shabby beard of yours. You'd look so much nicer if you'd just shave it off and..."

"Mom, please—about that girl?"

"Oh, right," she remembered, cheerfully turning the conversation back to the girl. "Her mother said if you or I tried to introduce you to her she'd reject you just because we were the ones that did it. So what Samantha suggested is that you just show up at her place of work, strike up a conversation—since you both seem to like reptiles so much—and things can go from there. What do you think?"

Finally some good news! Perhaps the girl would know about that impossible currency note. But, then again, maybe she'd just picked it out of the drawer by mistake with no idea at all that it was different from the pile of one dollar bills in the register and...

No! She had to know something about it. Besides, she *was* kind of pretty for a young kid...

"I'm not interested in romancing her," he insisted. "But I do want to return the money I owe her. I have an obligation that..."

"Oh, right," she giggled. "You have an 'obligation'—alright, then. I've got her present work address right here. I wrote it down and stuck it in my purse so I'd remember."

"Well..." he said, pausing. He was impressed. "Good work, Mom! What is it?"

"It's *'Georgia's Happy Home Kitchen'* on 14th street, downtown Ada. Samantha says it's just half a block off Main Street on the same corner as the closed movie theater. She says you can't miss it. Her daughter just started working the morning shift, from six in the morning till two in the afternoon. She's a real hard-working girl. She supports both herself and her poor, cancer-ridden mother. Remind you of someone?"

Hmmmm—she just started, he thought to himself. *She must have changed jobs, maybe to be closer to her mother in Ada.*

If he turned in early, he could be there when they opened up in the morning.

"That's great, Mom," he thanked her. "Good work! Oh, someone's knocking at the door," he said. He wasn't just making an excuse to stop the conversation. There actually were loud knocks on his front door. They were probably from the contractors come to give him bids on rebuilding the garage. "I've got to go. Thanks again, Mom. I'll call you back soon as I can..."

"Wait!"

"Yes?"

"You said you had a hard day. Tell me what happened or I'll worry myself sick."

"Nothing much, Mom," he said as he got up from his seat. "Don't be concerned. My garage burned down, my research is destroyed, I almost got killed, I started a race-riot at work, I got fired from my teaching job, and the FBI almost arrested me—but that's it. Everything's fine now. Love you! 'Bye!"

"But...?"

He hung up and went out to deal with the contractors.

He was now determined to take charge, to get things done. No taking forever to leisurely rebuild his house. He wanted the garage and bedroom back functioning in days, not months. If they wanted his money then they'd have to sign an iron-clad contract that included penalties for delays. Hah!

To be a researcher one had to be stubborn to the point of stupidity. Maybe that's why he felt such an affinity with that checker-slash-waitress?

According to Jean the girl was stubborn, headstrong, and rebellious—yet was still faithfully helping her own sick mother. In addition she was hard-working and liked reptiles!

No "pattern" needed there.

They were like two adjacent pieces in the grand Puzzle of Life.

He was suddenly certain they'd get along just *famously.*

Or, at least, she might at least give him a clue about that strange money?

Finally he was going to confront the *Girl with the Turtle Tattoo!*

Everything started going bad the moment he met her at the grocery store in Sulphur. And somehow, confronting her once again was going to set things right.

At least, he *hoped* there'd be a happy ending.

If not, he was going to be *very* disappointed.

Chapter 6

SAD ENDINGS

Things are often not as they seem

Made up instead of obscene things

Nailed together in sad disarray

They conspire to spin your head

Thinking that you've triumphed

They trample you into the dirt

And you don't even know

How much it will hurt.

The Luminary Chronicles, 6:87-89

The trip from Edmond to Ada should have taken only an hour and a half. Instead, it took two hours. He hit a construction delay on I-40, where the early commuting traffic was required to narrow down to just one lane.

Stopped dead in the crush of traffic, inching forward now and then in first or second gear, was a pain. But it gave him time to think.

He knew he had unrealistic expectations.

"She's probably just an ordinary high school graduate," he sighed to himself. "She works at low-level jobs to get a few bucks, helping out her Mom. She's probably not at all interested in any 'science' things, hates real snakes, and has zero interest in dating a man who's maybe twice her age. She's certainly not a wonderful, open-minded, curious, 'soul-mate' of mine. Hah! And to top it off she probably doesn't know a thing about the origin of that funny-money. She's just a cute clerk, you dope—to whom you happen to be mildly attracted. So don't get your hopes, up, 'Romeo'."

But his "positive self-talk" didn't do any good. He was already stressed-out and devastated from the events of the last couple days. Despite his intellectual warnings, his heart wanted the cute checkout girl to fix all his problems romantically and actually.

But things weren't starting out good at all.

To arrive there right at 6:00 in the morning he'd had to get up at 4:00 in the morning. He wasn't used to getting up that early. He liked to stay up late doing research, writing, or just watching recordings of a few of his favorite T.V. shows. Then he liked to sleep as late as possible, making a mad dash for work—often arriving late.

Perhaps being a "night person" was part of his problem at the college? You think?

"Well, that's all behind me now," he sighed as he finally steered his car into a parking space on Main Street in Ada. "I'm on a forced 'vacation' going on a wild-goose chase looking for some dopey girl with a turtle tattoo."

He was parked on Main street right in front of a boarded-up, long-defunct, unoccupied movie theatre. A tattered billboard read: *"The Phantom of the Opera."* That movie was about a disfigured genius who had an obsession with a gorgeous but horrified girl. He loved her obsessively, but hid in the shadows. She feared him as much as he loved her. But perversely she was drawn to his magnificent voice. The Music brought them together.

Was the poster a warning to him?

"Nope!" he laughed out loud. "I don't sing that well. Hah!"

But inside he was deeply disturbed. He had no wish to be some sort of lurking monster, to do harm to anyone. Perhaps he should just give up on the mystery of that weird money and go directly back home?

But, no, that would be just as wrong as letting his inner male instincts run wild.

So he locked his car and marched around the corner seeking the restaurant.

Sure enough, there it was: *"Georgia's Happy Home Kitchen"*!

It had a big bright sign high up proudly proclaiming its name. Large picture windows adorned the front. Dave could see a wall-sized blackboard inside spelling out the day's specials.

He'd expected it to be empty so early in the morning.

He was wrong.

Even though it was only 6:30 in the morning, Jeeps, trucks, and cars were crammed into an empty lot a block down from the restaurant. All sorts of people were walking in—the elderly, truck drivers, families with kids—of every skin-color and shape.

It was a popular place.

He paused in the doorway, surveying the interior. The walls were lined with shelves sporting antique pots, knick-knacks, and pictures of dogs and cats. The lighting was a soft yellowish glow. And smacking Dave in his face like a load of bricks was the enticing smells of cholesterol-laden, high fat breakfast: *fresh oven bread, sizzling pork-products,* and *cooling pies.*

Absolutely scrumptious!

Maybe he *would* have a bite to eat.

"Hey, honey," a middle-aged waitress casually called out to him as he entered. "Sit wherever you want. We'll be by with a menu in a jiff."

"Thanks," he called back.

The place was at least two-thirds full. There was an array of tables, booths, and a high-stool bar. People were quietly visiting with each other, happily shoveling in eggs, bacon, and sausage—and laughing.

Several waiters and waitresses bustled about...

There she was!

Yes!

It was the same long-haired, green-eyed girl from the grocery store! There was no mistaking her. And even though she again wore a long-sleeved shirt, he caught glimpses of a green tattoo on the inside of her left wrist.

She was servicing the back end of the restaurant. He spied an empty booth along that wall.

As he slid into it, she came up to him.

"Morning," she politely greeted him, handing him a menu. "What would you like to drink?"

He took the menu, laid it flat onto the table, and looked directly into her deep green eyes.

"Do you recognize me?"

She briefly frowned, focusing in on him.

"Uhm, I'm afraid I don't. Should I?"

"You took care of me this last Sunday morning at your work. I think by accident you gave me too much change. I didn't notice it until afterwards. I heard you were now working at this restaurant and wanted to return it to you."

He took out his billfold and lifted out the 100 dollar bill.

She squinted at him in apparent puzzlement.

"But...we aren't open on Sundays," she said.

"Oh, not here—at your *other* job."

"My other job?"

"Sure, at the grocery store in Sulphur?" he earnestly stated. "I was there early last Sunday, got some stuff, and you checked me out through the 'twenty or less' line."

She shrugged. "Sorry, sir, you must be confusing me with some-one else."

"No, it was you!" Dave insisted. "You gave me this hundred dollar bill instead of the one dollar change I was expecting. You don't re-member? Here, take a look at it!"

She backed up a step.

"Uh, sir," she squinted, frowning. "I don't know what you're try-ing to do, but I haven't been to Sulphur in years. I have a second cousin that lives there. Maybe you're confusing me with her? We do sort of look alike. But I never go up there. And I've worked this job here for several years. In fact, I've never worked in a grocery store at all."

"I asked you about your turtle tattoo!" he protested, profoundly confused.

"Lots of people get tattoos," she said, hitching down the sleeve on her left arm to cover the little reptile grinning out of her flesh.

"Are you *really* telling you've never seen me before?" Dave insist-ed, still holding out the hundred-dollar bill. "Please, take a look at this. Maybe it'll jog your memory. *Please!*"

Reluctantly, she took hold of the bill, held it up to the ceiling light, and then abruptly dropped it back onto the tabletop.

"Look, mister," she coldly stated. "We're a family restaurant here. I don't know what type of scam you're trying to pull, but maybe you'd best just leave if you're..."

"You told me about your *other tattoos!*" he desperately asserted, reaching out and impulsively grabbing her arm. Momentarily he felt a bit dizzy as if the world were whirling around him. Then he relentlessly continued, thinking maybe he should have eaten some of their delicious food before confronting her.

"You showed me the other ones on your arm—a black spider, a red and yellow parrot, and an orange snake, right? Pull up your sleeve! They're there, *right?*"

She firmly jerked her arm away from him.

"Sometimes I wear short sleeves," she frowned, pulling her arm tight to her body. "Anyone could have seen those."

"And what about your *others*—the ones that scare your mother? Are those where anyone could see them?"

"What are you talking about?" she sharply replied.

"The..." he desperately tried to remember what she'd mentioned in passing to him, "A woman's face melting into a skull. The...bloody knives! And—zombies that are fighting with each other!"

She gasped.

"How the hell do you know about those?" she now whispered softly, leaning forward to not be heard by patrons at nearby tables. "I'd have to be *naked* for you to see those tattoos. Have you been spying on me? Are you a *stalker?*"

"No, no!" he hurriedly stated, holding his hands palms-up, fingers spread wide, in an attitude of innocence. "Like I said, you *told* me! At the grocery store! Sunday morning! In Sulphur!"

She abruptly turned away, calling out in a loud voice.

"Bill, come quick! We've got trouble out here!"

The other patrons stopped talking and were now looking around curiously towards the back of the restaurant...

—as a big, fat, bald man in a cook's apron came running out of a back doorway, waving a bloody butcher's knife!

"What is going on, Sally?"

"That man there's been harassing me."

"Is that true?" the man bellowed at Dave, who eyes were now stretched wide in confusion and fear.

"No, not at all," Dave quickly jabbered. "I was just asking the waitress some questions. I thought she was a girl who checked me out of a grocery store a couple days ago and gave me too much change. I was just trying to do the right thing by returning the money. See, here it is!" he pointed shakily at the crumpled bill on the booth's tabletop.

The beefy fellow laid down his knife, took the note, and held it up to the light.

"Is someone messin' with my girl?" another, slender man broke in—his voice slurred as if he'd been drinking.

He was also wearing an apron, a hairnet on his head holding his long black hair into a tight bun. A cigarette dangled from his thin lips. He sported a scraggly goatee. On his bare arms there were numerous tattoos of every color and shape. On the left side of his face a black tattoo of a cobra was etched from his forehead down to his throat. In his hand he held a wet dinner plate he'd obviously just been in the act of washing.

"Your *boyfriend?*" Dave laughed, impulsively adding, "Not much to look at is he?"

Dave immediately regretted his words as the lean but strong young man dropped the plate and grabbed him by his collar. With a jerk he dragged the struggling Dave out of the booth, spilling him onto the wooden floor.

The thin young man stood over Dave threateningly, slowly balling up his free hand in a fist. The cobra on his face seemed to coil in anticipation of a lethal strike.

"Snake!" the girl barked at him. "Don't hurt the customer! He *wasn't* coming onto me. He was just pestering me with some stupid questions."

"*Snake?*" Dave gagged, the twisted collar on his neck making it hard to breathe. "Really?"

"Yep, I'm a 'snake' and I'll bite yore head offa yore body if yore upsettin' my sweet little Sally!"

"It was just a mistake," Dave managed to croak...

—as the glass picture windows at the front of the restaurant *exploded inward* as a pickup truck *smashed* through the front wall into the restaurant!

Patrons screamed as they were tossed to the side or crushed beneath its wheels.

"What the hell?" the beefy man screamed, stumbling backwards, dropping the hundred-dollar bill...

—as a black-clad, black ski-masked man with a pointed pistol emerged from the pickup and started *firing* into the dazed crowd!

Bill dived behind the bar, emerging with a shotgun in his hands.

BLAM!—the sound of the shotgun being fired briefly deafened Dave as he lay on the floor, broken glass and plaster showering down upon his body.

—as he saw the window of the pickup truck *shatter* from the blast...

Bang! Bang!—the masked man's pistol barked, catching Bill on his shoulder and spinning him around...

Dave felt a heavy weight pressing down on his chest.

It was the prone body of the girl, who appeared to be stunned. She'd been struck by hurtling debris.

Snake grabbed a stool and hurled it at the approaching gunman, who disdainfully knocked it to the side with a karate kick.

"You god-damned...*window-smasher!*" Snake shouted as he jumped at the shooter, his thin arms flailing around in the air like a three-dimensional living tattooed painting.

But just as fast he was dropped by a brutal punch to his throat.

Snake fell off to the side, clutching his throat, gagging...

—as the shooter stepped up to Dave who was still lying prone with the girl sprawled on top of him. Dave saw the man's hand reaching down to grab the girl's hair.

Dave jabbed the man through webbed eyeholes in the black ski mask, using two stiffened fingers.

The gun dropped and Dave struggled to roll over to grab it as the shooter immediately recovered, *stomping hard* on Dave's outstretched hand!

"Jesus Christ!" Dave moaned, jerking his hand away from the crushing pain, while with his other hand he grabbed the fallen dinner plate and *hurtled* it at the man's concealed head.

"CLUNK!" went the plate as it smashed into a thousand pieces on the shooter's head...

—who momentarily staggered backward...

—as Dave finally got out from under the girl's body and launched himself at the shooter, kicking the man's feet out from beneath him, spinning him around while simultaneously slapping on a *rear naked chokehold!*

Thank God for the many cage-fighting T.V. shows he'd watched over the years. He'd never actually been in a fight before. But adrenalin and countless cage fights can fuel desperate efforts.

"Call the police!" Dave yelled out to the rest of the people strewn across the smashed restaurant's cluttered floor. "Call 911!"

—when the shooter deftly jerked out of Dave's grasp, leaving behind the black ski mask dangling in Dave's hands.

In one smooth swoop the intruder snatched up the gun from the floor.

"You!" Dave gasped, falling backward, recognizing the man.

It was the elderly oriental "student" from the riot in his introductory physics course! He had that same jagged scar on the left cheek of his face. There was no mistaking the man.

"Why are you out to get me?" Dave angrily shouted, trying futilely to shield himself from the menacing gun with just his hands, stumbling backward.

"Not you," the white-haired man snarled, "*her!*"

"What?" Dave gasped, now fallen again upon the floor, lying on his back, his head raised up to see...

—the shooter calmly pointing his gun straight at the girl's head...

"No!" Dave shouted...

—as the shooter *fired* one bullet through her skull!

Blood spurted from her forehead, then rapidly pooled on the floor beneath her shattered head.

—as the black-clad man calmly reached down to the floor and *plucked-up* the fallen hundred-dollar bill!

"I don't think you'll need this anymore," he stated, sliding it into his pocket.

Then he turned, calmly walked around the crashed pickup, paused to snatch-up the fallen half-opened cash register, and vanished into the street.

"I thought I told you to inform my office if you went out of town," Agent Anderson matter-of-factly stated.

He was casually leaning against one of the black-on-white local police cars, combing his blond hair, peering into his pocket mirror.

Dave sat on a mobile stretcher as a paramedic bandaged his throbbing hand.

"What, to go and do local chores?" Dave dazedly retorted. It'd been a long couple of hours since the brutal attack on the restaurant. And he still hadn't eaten any food.

He was shocked, confused, angry, and hungry.

"And just what 'chore' brought you to yet another site of *mayhem*, Dr. King?" the FBI Agent pressured him, slipping the mirror back into his pocket.

"I came here to talk with my mother's oncologist," Dave angrily claimed, speaking loudly to be heard above the babble of the many converged police, emergency workers, ambulances, and fire trucks.

"At a restaurant?" the man retorted, his dark glasses peering at Dave inscrutably.

"I was getting breakfast," Dave weakly protested. "Is that a crime?"

"Not if it's just bacon and eggs instead of mayhem and *murder!*"

"I don't have any idea what happened," Dave protested again, shaking his head in genuine bewilderment. "I was just ordering breakfast when everything went to hell. One moment I was talking with the waitress and the next a black-garbed *ninja* was shooting her *dead!* Why aren't you out catching that murderer instead of harassing me?"

The Agent grinned, pushing his wide dark glasses up on his nose.

"You give an interesting version of what happened in there," Agent Anderson calmly stated. "The other witnesses tell a different story. They say you were arguing with the waitress. They say a couple of the employees came out and had to restrain you. They say that this 'ninja' went straight for you. You seem to be a 'nexus' Dr. King—at the center of riots, explosions, and *murder!*"

The FBI agent's words stung Dave deeply. He had to deny them but in his heart knew they were true. He was even less than just a miserable failure of a man—he was a walking disaster!

Dave grimaced as the paramedic dabbed alcohol on the cuts and abrasions on his face and arms—acquired from the flying debris and glass when the pickup smashed through the front plate glass windows.

"I've already answered the questions from the police," Dave angrily snorted. "Go get their report if you want to know anything else."

"They were focused on the *supposed* killer," the FBI Agent grimly stated. "But they don't know you like I do. In fact, I know you a lot better than you know yourself."

Dave shook his head in stubborn denial.

"I didn't cause any of that," Dave again protested. "I *don't* know what's going on. It's awful, just awful!"

Indeed, it was a horrific panorama stretched out around him. Ambulances were loading in moaning people laid out upon stretchers. The pickup's rear end stuck obscenely out of the smashed-in store's front. Firemen were still hosing down the exposed kitchen where a dislodged oven had caught a wall on fire.

"So just why are *you* here, Agent Anderson?" Dave demanded, standing up from the stretcher to confront the Agent directly. "Why is the FBI interested in a small-town robbery and shoot-up?"

"We've evidence that your 'ninja' wasn't just some random thief whose robbery went wrong," he said. "In fact, we have solid confirmation that he is a domestic *terrorist*, pure and simple. Oh, we'll get him soon enough now that his little organization has stuck its head up. But *you* are not an innocent bystander, 'professor' King. In fact, you are quite involved. Am I not correct?"

"I'm not a terrorist!"

"Sure you are," the agent quietly stated. "You'll stop at nothing to get what you want. You have impossible objectives. You make outrageous demands. Society is just a backdrop to your arrogance. It doesn't matter how many people get hurt to achieve your goals. You may be within the technical limits of the law at the moment, Dr. King—but you're just as much a criminal as that murderer."

Dave was struck speechless. How dare this man accuse him of such terrible things?

But...what if it was all true?

"That's outrageous!" he gasped, taking a step backward.

"Hey, man," sobbed a skinny young man who came staggering up to Dave.

Dave recognized his long black hair, scraggly goatee, and garish face tattoo.

"Snake?" Dave said, pulling back from the approaching figure...

—who grabbed Dave around the shoulders, hugging him close with his tattooed arms, and burying his greasy head into Dave's chest.

"They say you tried to save her!" the man cried, trembling in Dave's automatically-cradling arms. "You tried to fight that monster off and I..."

"Uhm...I'm so sorry, Snake. I couldn't stop him."

"But you *tried*," he sobbed even louder. "You tried to save Sally, and I was so *mean* to you."

"Hey, we'll get through this. Just hang in there," Dave tried to console the grief-stricken young man, simultaneously attempting to disentangle himself from the man's clinging arms...

—turning to see that Agent Anderson was gone.

What did that FBI Agent mean accusing *him* of being a terrorist?

He could definitely believe that the old oriental was a religious nut. He'd encountered their ilk from time-to-time in his scientific career: those that believed all animal research—even on lowly rats and mice—was a crime against nature; those that were committed stop at any cost "modernity" in every form; those who felt global warming and any other costly ecological disaster was a vast conspiracy to force people to pay slightly-higher energy bills; those who felt that tiny collections of developing cells were fully-developed humans; those who gave the same value to monkeys as to human babies; and those who insisted that literal understandings of ancient religious writings trumped scientific fact.

Dave considered most of those "religious nuts" to be nice people blindly clinging to doctrinally constricted worldviews. Others were just ignorant. But a few of them were dedicated militants, determined to force everyone else to accept their views. Theirs was a brutal evangelism done "by the sword"—convert or die! Do what we say or you get a *bullet* in your head.

Dave shuddered, recalling the blood spurting from Sally's shattered skull.

"They'll catch that murderer," he comforted the still-sobbing Snake, gingerly patting him on his thin shoulder. "He'll pay for what he did to your girlfriend."

"I'll never forget her," Snake quietly sobbed, turning away.

And neither will I—Dave sighed to himself, *neither will I.*

Whatever the Girl with the Turtle Tattoo might have eventually remembered and told Dave about the mysterious hundred-dollar bill was gone: taken with her to the grave.

"Either I'm crazy or she was lying," he bitterly whispered to himself as he staggered back down the crowded street to his car. He was relieved to see that his faithful, yellow Chevy Cavalier was still parked outside the closed movie theatre.

But he was convinced that it was *her!* She must have been lying. It was a good act. It certainly looked convincing. But she was without any doubt the exact same person that checked his groceries through the checkout stand in Sulphur. It was her, not some similar cousin. So, somehow, she must have been in on this conspiracy—to make him think he was losing his mind!

That vile black-robed ninja succeeded.

He murdered the truth.

But could *resurrection* still be a possibility?

The funeral was both striking and pathetic.

Cliff, from his Mother's church in Sulphur, conducted the service. It turned out that Sally and her mother didn't attend any church. But when Dave's mom found out about the tragedy, she insisted on stepping in and helping. So, whether Sally would have wanted it or not, she was given a nice Christian funeral service.

It was held outdoors, with the few attendees sitting on folding chairs around the open grave. A *graveside* service...

—the closed casket sitting forlornly on a lifting mechanism, poised to be lowered into the ground.

It wasn't much to look at, just varnished, plain wood. Sally's Mom didn't have any money. The only reason they were having a funeral rather than a cheap cremation was that Georgia, the owner of the restaurant, kindly contributed part of the restaurant's insurance payment.

"Ashes to ashes, dust to dust," Cliff was solemnly intoning. "Looking to that last great *resurrection* where all in their graves will be raised to the final, glorious judgment and..."

Dave sincerely wished for the resurrection, not religious fantasy but him getting to the truth.

Still, the solemn ceremony was soothing, peaceful, an oasis of cam in a raging sea of uncertainty.

The graveyard was outside the city limits, set within low rolling hills, richly-green with springtime fresh-mowed grass, wide tall trees sheltering the visitors, with live flowers interspersed among the gravestones cheerfully waving in a gentle breeze.

"—so we commend the spirit of our dear, departed Sally Jessica Smith to the Lord," the minister concluded. "Shall we pray?"

Dave respectfully bowed his head—though he kept his eyes defiantly wide open.

He knew all the theological arguments as to why a supposed loving God allowed bad things to happen to good people. He'd heard those sermons many times growing up as a kid dragged against his will to church. But they'd never rung true to him. And now he recognized them for what they were: apologies for *unrealistic expectations*.

"Stuff happens," he whispered to himself. "There's no rhyme or reason, it just *is!*"

That would have been *his* "funeral speech" if he'd been somehow tasked to do the service. Short and *sour*. You've got to make the most of the moment right now because the next moment you might be gone—by no fault of yours. One moment you're eating a tasty breakfast in a safe, comfortable restaurant and the next you're crushed by a car smashing through the wall, or shot through the head by a madman.

Fortunately, Sally was the only fatality from the vicious attack. But others were seriously injured. Some of them were still in the hospital, recovering from snapped bones, crushed sternums, and lacerated arteries.

A few of them were hit by the initial barrage of bullets. But, thankfully, those wounds were mostly superficial. It seemed that the seemingly-expert ninja couldn't shoot straight, except up close.

"—asking for your Divine Love and Limitless Compassion upon the heads of these relatives and friends of our dear departed Sally..."

Hah! "Love and compassion"—sure...what a lie! If by some freak circumstance there really was a "supreme intelligence" behind it all, he was a sadistic monster. He deliberately allowed the most vicious and hideous things to happen to his "beloved" children.

"—comforted in the knowledge that they will indeed see their beloved Sally again..."

Dave wanted to either vomit or fall asleep from boredom, he couldn't decide which.

It'd been a week now since the terrorist attack. The FBI Agent was right. The terrorists' Manifesto was released to the media that very evening. Those insane criminals got what they wanted most: a national audience.

Still listening to the interminable prayer, Dave played the video "manifesto" yet again, for the hundredth time, inside his head....

—seeing a man in a black ski mask against a featureless white background...substituted in Dave's mind for the present, praying preacher: but similarly pontificating.

The snide terrorist was railing against the supposed "evil" of modern-day scientists presuming to usurp "God's nature." The speaker in the video claimed to be one of a group of thousands calling themselves *"The Revelation-Revolution"*, or "RR", dedicated to exposing so-called "godless-heathen-secularist-heretic-scientists." And the speaker calmly named "David Richard King" as one of the worst offenders!

In previous times Dave would have basked in the attention, using it to leverage grants for his research. Now he just wanted to slink into the shadows, singing his sad songs in the background of the opera of life.

"...giving solace and knowledge of the eternal Glory awaiting the Faithful..." Cliff droned on, delivering his concluding sermon as a thinly-disguised, boring prayer.

Him! On national T.V., *Dr. David King* was named as one of the worst "secularist scientists" who was supposedly "playing God"!

This whole mystery was just getting crazier and crazier.

Oh, sure, the deranged killer also named the prime players in both the ITER and NIF high-temperature fusion-power projects. So Dave wasn't left hanging out there by himself. But the terrorist singled-out electrochemically-assisted nuclear reactions for special denunciation. Before concluding, the video even named Dave's doctoral advisor at Yale, Professor Victor Volodymyr—promising further retaliations against everyone!

"At least some things are starting to make sense," Dave whispered to himself.

Yes, the terrorist claimed credit not only for the restaurant attack, but also for the fire at Dave's house and the riot in his class. Supposedly the terrorists had managed to sneak into Dave's house and put an explosive device at the center of his experimental matrix—even though the FBI admitted they couldn't identify any known explosive volatiles in the wreckage that they'd appropriated without Dave's knowledge from the contractors.

It seemed that the "Revelation-Revolution" wanted to shut down fusion research not just by directly attacking its main advocates—who, after all, were mostly high-level scientists that no one knew or cared about—but indirectly by disrupting their everyday associations: classes, homes, and even the restaurants which they happened to frequent.

It really didn't make any sense.

"None of you are safe!" the black-masked man in the video ominously threatened in a booming voice inside Dave's bowed head. *"Unless this obscenity against God's Nature is shut down in all its many aspects, you will all pay a terrible price!"*

"...amen," Cliff solemnly finished, jerking Dave's attention back from his inward musings.

The chubby minister stepped around the front of the casket. In a professionally-sad "funeral director" way he shook the hand of the grieving mother. She sat there crying silently with a scarf covering her bald head. Then he shook the hand of Dave's Mom, who sat in her wheelchair beside Samantha, sporting her blueish wig hiding her own bald head. Next was Snake, who swayed from side-to-side, tears dribbling down his sallow cheeks. Even the cobra tattoo on his face seemed to be crying. Finally, there was Dave sitting beside his Mom.

Behind the front row of seats sat a scattering of other friends, relatives, and acquaintances. Big Bill, dressed in coveralls, sat dejectedly with his arm in a sling.

"So sad for your loss," Cliff was saying to Snake, patting him gently on his thin shoulder.

Dave wasn't waiting around to be "comforted" by Cliff. He slid from his seat to dart around the back of Snake and whisper in his Mother's ear.

"I'm going," he said, before quickly retreating.

He was breathing heavily, trembling—funerals always affected him this way. If he could believe in a loving God, it might make things easier: that this was just a harsh "boot camp" for heaven. As it was, Dave saw *no* redeeming hope, just a bottomless black pit symbolized by the empty hole in the ground awaiting Sally's corpse. It all seemed so futile.

"Can we talk?" Agent Anderson coolly greeted him at the back of the funeral chairs, stopping him in his tracks.

"Why are you here?" Dave groaned, continuing walking on past the man toward the parking lot.

"I wanted to pay my respects," the man mildly replied, falling into step beside him.

"Like hell," Dave snorted. "You just wanted to gloat!"

"Gloat?"

"You got me. I'm—what did you say to me a week ago—a 'nexus'! You said that I *attract* disaster. Well, maybe I do. *But it's not my fault!*" he yelled at him, then, more quietly..."How am I responsible for a stupid religious radical who just happens to have a thing against trying to get commercially-viable energy from nuclear fusion reactions? What the hell *is* that anyway? Is there a contest out there to find the stupidest radical-cause possible? If controlled fusion happens it will probably solve the earth's energy crisis. How the hell is that going against any religion?"

Back at the funeral gathering, behind them, a network T.V. crew was leaving—now moving toward Dave, having spotted him arguing with the FBI Agent.

For a couple days, they'd pestered Dave mercilessly, even camping out on his lawn as the construction crews started rebuilding his garage.

He refused to speak to them.

What could he say to them—admit he was just a "nobody" with no funding who got fired from his job for trying to be a philosopher when he wasn't?

And, yes, the junior college administers were publicly sympathetic to him—even admitting that the supposed "riot" in his class was catalyzed by the terrorist who'd slipped into the building posing as a student—but still adamant in their dismissal of him. They claimed he'd been let go not just for the unrest in his classroom but for "administrative" issues. Right... They wanted him gone and found an excuse to make it stick. That was their "issue."

But plenty of government, academic, and industrial spokespersons and big-wigs were eager to jump to Dave's defense. They strongly defended both the "individual researchers" doing unconventional research along with the cross-national large and small hot fusion-power efforts. The scientific community as a whole rallied around all the fusion researchers, even Dave. As one, they condemned the RR members, no matter if the group was composed of just one deranged madman or his claimed thousands of adherents.

But their "support" of Dave was always given with a "wink and a nod." He knew in their eyes he was still a bumbling incompetent, a dabbler with no real scientific talent.

"If you want to arrest me than just do it!" Dave taunted the FBI Agent as he continued his rapid walk to his car. If he had to be an abysmal failure, he might as well be notorious!

Fortunately, the media quickly lost interest in the unknown Dr. King to focus on broader issues.

Now, however—with a media-friendly visible funeral of an innocent young woman to cover—Dave risked being drawn ever deeper into unwanted questions.

"We have the receipt, you know," the agent walking beside Dave quietly announced.

The receipt!

It was Dave's last bit of tangible evidence that this convenient "terrorist" explanation of his recent troubles *didn't* answer all the questions.

Dave had looked for it, couldn't find it, and figured he'd lost it in the struggle and turmoil of the restaurant attack. Yes, he had still been wearing that same shirt.

"What receipt?" he peevishly denied, yanking open the door of his yellow Cavalier.

His mom was going home with Samantha to help her with the wake. Snake and Big Jim were bringing over donated food from Georgia's Happy Home Kitchen, which had not yet reopened to the public. Sally's few acquaintances and relatives were gathering at Samantha's house to eat together as a final memorial to their slaughtered friend.

—and though Dave would not admit it to that annoying FBI Agent, it *was* all because of *him.*

He was a jinx, a curse, a *bad* person to be around.

That innocent girl with the turtle tattoo would still be alive if I hadn't pursued her—he groaned to himself.

No one publically blamed Dave. But he knew with certainty that it *was* his fault. And he knew they were all out there behind his back agreeing with the Agent, labeling *him* as the real murderer.

"We'll be watching you," Anderson coldly informed him, rapping on his side window.

Dave hit the gas and shot away, leaving the FBI Agent cringing from a spatter of thrown-up gravel.

This couldn't be the end of it. Dave knew he had to take things to a new level.

Sure he was a jinx—but fundamentally he wasn't all that different from anyone else. Something else was going on to make him into such a *nexus of disaster.*

He had to find out what was *really* happening.

—and to do that he had to return to his *alma mater.*

He had to retrace his footsteps, back to the very first.

Chapter 7

<u>YALE UNIVERSITY</u>

Oh brother, my brother

Why must you go away?

With only a broom

To make your living

As you clean your room

And fly to the moon?

Was it something I did

Or, perhaps, left undone?

Or was it my gift

Disguised as a gun?

I so wish you could stay...

The Luminary Chronicles, 7:16-20

Dave stood in the middle of the old campus courtyard of Yale University, his traveling bag slung across one shoulder.

He was traveling light and fast. In his bag he had only an extra set of clothes, his toiletry kit, and laptop. As outerwear he just wore a light brown sweater.

"I've missed this so much," he whispered to himself choking up.

The stately old brown brick buildings were spread out around him across neatly-cut green lawns. Looming above everything in the center of the stately buildings was Harkness Tower. The bell tower invoked not so much scholarly excellence as an actual spiritual experience.

It was like coming home to a Cathedral of Knowledge.

"Welcome, my boy, welcome!" a distinguished, white-haired man heartily called-out as he approached on one of the wide, intersecting concrete-blocked sidewalks.

Dave smiled broadly, breaking into a run towards the spritely gentleman.

"Professor Volodymyr!" Dave happily exclaimed as they met in a warm embrace. "I'm sorry you had to walk all this way from your building to meet me. But with my notoriety I'm afraid that security would never let me get near the physics labs unaccompanied so..."

"It is not a problem, my boy," the man cheerfully interrupted. "I still walk two miles a day, keeps me young. And the old courtyard here is a favorite destination of mine. It is steeped with so much history. It connects me to the intellectual giants of the past—not that I'm one myself," he modestly concluded.

Victor Volodymyr was a tall man wearing a casual blue cardigan sweater. He was fully a head higher than Dave. A mass of white fuzzy hair drifted around the top of his head. His thin, smooth-shaven face was lined and spotted, betraying advanced age. But his blue eyes sparkled with the excitement of a newborn baby.

"Professor Volodymyr, you're truly a lifesaver. I know I didn't tell you much over the phone. I couldn't. I'm sure my communications are being monitored. And yet you invited me here with no reservations to..."

"Oh, please call me Victor," the professor broke in, chuckling, stepping an arm's length back from Dave to look him over with a critical eye. "We are long past a student-teacher formal relation, are we not? I have considered you, my boy, as my valued colleague for what...fifteen years now? And what do I care about FBI Agents? What can they do to me? Put me in jail for talking to one of my many former students? Hah!"

Dave laughed also, relieved.

"I guess it *has* been a while since I had the great privilege of being one of your many graduate students. I'm so grateful to you for seeing me that..."

"Nonsense, my boy," the old man chortled while grabbing Dave around his shoulders with a thin yet strong arm. "You are quite famous now, are you not? I saw you on all the newscasts. I'm fading away now, just happy to bask for a moment in *your* glory."

Dave snorted in denial although he was surprised to find himself disproportionately pleased at the man's generous affirmation. After more than a decade of obscure failures—relegated to puttering around in his garage while classmates published important papers on their way to prestigious academic appointments—a compliment from his major professor meant a great deal.

"All for the wrong reasons," Dave grated, now dead-serious as he walked along beside Professor Volodymyr. "I never imagined I'd be the target of a crazy terrorist."

"Yes, such a sad business," Victor "cluck-clucked" in disgust, "when people try to stop the progress of science by killing innocent people! But I suppose the ignorant, fearful, and insane have always done this. Was that young girl who was so hideously executed a friend of yours?"

"Actually, Victor, I barely knew her," he choked out, his throat now constricted with anger. "But the shooter deliberately killed her when he could have just as easily have shot me. I feel responsible for her death. But I'm determined to not have my research stopped because of a criminal's actions. If the girl's death is to have any meaning, I've got to persist, to finally find something of value to..."

Dave's voice choked up completely. He stopped speaking, suddenly overwhelmed with emotion.

"I'm such a fool," he whispered. "I'm so sorry I've not lived up to the effort you put into me here at Yale. I should have gone on to honor your legacy with my work. Instead I..."

His voice trailed off as he felt warm tears trickling down his cheeks.

"It's ok, my boy," Victor quietly comforted him. "It's true you pursued a path I cautioned you against. But many of the greatest discoveries in the history of science came from stubborn 'fools' just like you. They looked into obscure corners where none of their peers saw any utility. They pigheadedly tried to do the 'impossible.' Most of them were squashed by Mather Nature. But a few did succeed, more by luck than anything else. It's been said that Nobel Prize winners are scientists whose grand ideas actually worked. But it's not the Nobel Prize that's so noble. It's the indomitable persistence of scientists curious to the point of stupidity. I greatly admired your persistence, my boy. I was—and still am—proud to count you as one of my best students."

With fierce determination Dave resisted the impulse to wipe his embarrassing tears away. Victor's words were indeed comforting, but not motivating. What Dave needed to retain was his grief and anger!

He had one last thing to try, regardless of the results.

They walked on in silence. Dave further appreciated Victor not embellishing on his supportive speech. Dave knew the Professor was kindly allowing his returned "prodigal student" to regain his emotional balance.

The leafy trees of the large courtyard sheltered them from the rising sun's rays. It was springtime in Connecticut, warming yet cool enough to stroll along without sweating in pervasive humidity.

Dave had to remind himself that they were on the East Coast of the United States, where the vast Atlantic's store of atmospheric moisture was just an "arm's length" away.

Oklahoma tended to be on the dry side. Indeed, the pervasive worldwide global warming was accentuating a long drought. While other parts of the United States were experiencing record deluges and flooding, Oklahoma was presently parched. Grass that here in New Haven was leaping up out of the ground in Oklahoma was unseasonably brown and dead.

"I was so glad to get your phone call, David," Volodymyr now continued. "I'm not sure what I can do to help, but whatever you need—I'm at your disposal."

"That's so kind of you, Victor," Dave smiled back, ducking his head in embarrassment. "Hopefully I'll not pester you for long."

Indeed, Dave had to get back to his pets. George had kindly agreed to look after them for a few days while Dave caught a quick flight from Oklahoma City to the East Coast. But reptiles were a specialized challenge. Keeping them healthy and happy in captivity required a particular expertise.

George could certainly change the water bowls and prepare the daily salads for the omnivores in Dave's small collection. But things like the weekly feeding of the snakes were beyond him. Even just the process of properly thawing and warming frozen mice, chicks, and rats had to be done properly or the food would be ruined or rejected by the fickle snakes. And that wasn't even mentioning the live cricket colony or the...

"Nonsense!" Victor firmly insisted, interrupting Dave's meandering thoughts. "Stay as long as you need. Indeed, you are to reside with me and Ivanna at our country retreat. It's been a while since we've had a live-in guest, what with our kids having their own lives. And that's not to mention my kids being occupied with *their* kids and even grandkids. The house is empty with just me and the wife puttering about. We're delighted to have you."

"You have great-grandchildren?" Dave asked, genuinely surprised. Victor had always been so energetic he seemed eternally young. Somehow he happily balanced a full teaching load plus graduate students plus a world-class research program plus administrative duties plus consultation requests. His graduate students in the lab never viewed him as aging.

"Hah..." Victor grinned, his eyes twinkling. "I just had my first *great*-great-grandchild! She's a beautiful little girl. They named her 'Anna Marie,' after my own mother. How about that, my boy? There are indeed advantages to living long enough. You get to see the generations thriving behind you. And shouldn't *you* be thinking of settling down, finding a cute young woman, and making your own chubby little babies? Hmmm?"

Dave politely ignored the marital advice. He got plenty of that from his mother.

"Just how old are you now, Victor?" Dave marveled, shaking his head in disbelief at his vigor.

"I am a proud ninety-two years old, this very next month. It does sound rather old, doesn't it? But I don't feel old—at least where it matters most, in my heart. But my body *is* letting me down, that's true. Do you know that I've had all my major joints replaced? It's true. I am a 'bionic' man. Hah! I'm literally a walking robot. But the marvels of modern medicine can only keep you going full-speed for so long. That's why I'm finally giving up my laboratory, as I told you over the phone."

"I was so sorry to hear that," Dave sighed. "Your departure will be a great loss to both the University and to Science."

"Oh, pish posh," Victor casually brushed-off the compliment. "It's well past the time for me to go out and concentrate on enjoying nature at my country house with Ivanna. To tell you the truth, I'm getting tired of these burdensome responsibilities. I even renounced my emeritus status as a past President of the American Physical Society. I told them I want to watch birds landing in my yard. Do you know that I made a bird feeder, with my own hands? Yes, David—I started out as a young boy wanting to be a carpenter. And I'm still good at making things. My dear wife is not as old as me, of course. But she is in her eighties now, old enough. It's definitely time for me to finally step away from the many irksome duties of academia and research. I'm finally kicking my 'addiction' that which all my life has monopolized my time."

"Few others have equaled your amazing career here at Yale," Dave sincerely stated.

"Well, my superiors have been kind to me these last few years in my 'Professor Emeritus' status, as I've wound-down my active research program," Victor casually deflected the praise. "But I see the envious looks directed at my 'palatial' laboratory space. It is definitely time for an eager young man to step into my shoes—someone like *you*, my boy."

Dave appreciated the compliment but knew it was merely cosmetic. They both knew that his track record wasn't anywhere near good enough even to warrant even a submission to a major appointment at such a prestigious institution. Sure, he'd managed to publish a couple of trivial research papers during the last decade. But the person hired to replace Professor Volodymyr at Yale would sport a list of publications as long as your arm, plus already-established, dedicated funding sources, plus a world-class reputation of acclaimed research results in a narrowly-targeted expertise.

All Dave had to show was a burnt-out garage of ancient, ruined equipment and a handful of minor published papers.

"Well, that's not in the cards," Dave sighed as they walked beneath the trees out onto the sidewalk of College Street, heading north. "But I've been thinking that once I sort out my present mess I might pursue a low-level teaching position at a dynamic campus like this. After all, I've lots of experience teaching introductory physics classes these last few years—that is if you don't count supposedly causing philosophical and religious riots?"

"I never believed for a moment what I heard on the TV," Victor huffed, strongly striding-along beside Dave. "Your students here always loved your lab classes when you were my teaching assistant. And, of course, I'd be glad to give you a glowing recommendation—plus under-the-table arm-twisting, calling in my many decades of accumulated favors—for you to start teaching here *tomorrow* as an adjunct professor, if that's what you want. God knows what with twelve thousand students at Yale we always need excellent beginning instructors."

"Actually," Dave sheepishly admitted, "I just finished submitting a general teaching application at Admissions, since I was here to meet with you, Victor," he nodded. "And indeed I did list you as a reference. Thank you very much."

"My pleasure, David—it is invigorating to deal with the young people. They are what give me limitless energy. Hah! I hope I don't just turn to dust and blow away when I am finally completely retired and no longer have daily contact with them. That is my greatest fear."

Walking past Dave and Victor on the street was a stream of single and grouped students: fine young men intent on their destinations sporting thick dark hair, some with neatly-trimmed beards, and all with fresh, unlined faces—plus spritely young girls in unseasonably short dresses, slacks, and revealing blouses.

"They get younger every year," Dave mused affectionately.

"—and even more *sexy!*" Victor exclaimed, eying a particularly well-endowed young lady in a tight T-shirt hurrying past them, doubtless late for a class.

"Victor!" Dave chided him. "You're in your nineties!"

"I may be old," Victor agreed, pausing in a mock-serious fashion, pretending to totter on a non-existent cane, "but I'm not yet dead."

"Of course, admiring beauty *is* a Godly pursuit," Dave paused as well. He cast a covert, appreciative eye towards an approaching pair of young women—a long-legged, full-figured blond and a pert redhead.

The two men broke out in laughter, prompting curious glances from the passing lovely ladies.

Professor Volodymyr's laboratory was located in the *Department of Applied Physics*, in the *Becton Center* just a few blocks away from the Old Campus Courtyard.

In stark contrast to the venerable, stately buildings of the Old Campus, Applied Physics was housed in a minimalistic, plain-rectangular, formidable, *concrete fortress*.

Yep, he'd have gotten nowhere trying to gain entrance on his own.

But they did have a lot to protect.

In addition to working on the physics of novel materials—the research area in which Victor was one of the world's leading experts—they also conducted cutting-edge research into understanding and controlling the physics of optical processes: particularly novel and complex laser systems. And all that research was converging on trying to build the world's first truly "quantum" computer—moving beyond the binary "yes/no" operational system of present computers into the bizarre behavior of fundamental particles undergoing "superposition" and "entanglement".

Exciting stuff...

Dave felt his pulse race faster just by being back in his graduate environment.

Just giving lectures to huge classes of introductory students would be well worth the sacrifice to be back here.

The Professor's lab was on the top floor, luxuriously occupying a full corner of the building. They'd had to go through several layers of strict security to reach it. The department was taking no chances after the infamous "Revelation-Revolution" Manifesto's recent video-publication.

"Whew, I thought there at one point I was going to have to strip naked," Dave ruefully laughed, fingering the large "VISITOR" badge hanging prominently from a thin chain around his neck—as Victor unlocked a *large* chain physically preventing opening the one main entrance to his lab-complex.

"We're lucky they even allow *me* to come in here," the old man chortled. "Even before you started your little war with those terrorists, administration required me to chain up the door. Without all my post-docs and technicians occupying my space, it was open-season for vultures and other scavengers. I can't tell you how many of my instruments and supplies mysteriously vanished to surrounding labs before my Department Head clamped down. She wants a functional materials laboratory sitting here to help attract a world-class replacement—not a hollowed-out, embarrassing shell of a lab. Hah! Good thing she did that, or I'd have nothing to offer you, David. But regrets aside, here we are."

Dave stepped inside, overcome with nostalgia.

"It's...it's wonderful," he said as he happily peered around the lab.

Large and small machines occupied the space, plus numerous wide lab-benches. Unlike when he'd worked there last, everything was in reasonable, though dusty, order. In his frenetic graduate research days fifteen years earlier, he'd had to fight for every inch of coveted bench space. Professor Volodymyr's lab was at that time a hotbed of cutting-edge research. It was crammed to the hilt with competing post-docs, grad students, technicians, and support staff nudging each other out for a bit more working space.

Now it was "mothballed", waiting on a new owner.

It saddened Dave to see it silent, still, and unproductive. But, on the other hand, it was better this way. There'd be no curious eyes spying or interfering with what he wanted to do.

"I admit it's a great idea, David," Victor said, carefully locking the main entrance tight behind. Then he proceeded to shut the blinds to each of the windows that opened out on the public corridor.

"Well, I was only going to ask you for some of my doctoral compound, if you still had it," Dave hesitantly replied.

"Nonsense," Victor huffed. "I've all the latest equipment and components you'll need here to duplicate your garage device—but much smaller and more powerful. I'm just leaving all that behind. I'd much rather give you my resources than meekly hand them over to a snotty successor."

"You're very kind," Dave quietly replied as they walked deeper into the lab.

"But are you sure we can pull this off in a couple days, my boy?" Victor eagerly stated, rubbing his long-fingered hands together. "Any longer than that and my Department Head may get suspicious about 'unapproved' projects. Oh, she is a stickler for the rules. Of course I don't blame her for her caution in today's fearful climate, but it's *my* lab and *my* projects."

"Yes, I myself suffered from an over-anxious Department Head, Victor. I understand perfectly. But if you've still got my doctoral thesis matrix samples, I don't see why we can't complete the job fairly quickly," Dave firmly responded. "That's the basis of everything I've done subsequently. The crystal matrix configuration was published, of course, but extremely difficult to reproduce. I don't think anyone else has even bothered to try to duplicate it. After all, it took me three years of full-time work to make it here in your lab. And that was just the starting point from which I progressed on my own: tweaking it considerably subsequently, infusing various exotic metallic ion additions in various combinations."

Victor nodded thoughtfully.

"Oh, a considerable amount of your matrix is indeed safely locked inside my vault...I *think*," Victor uncertainly replied. "I may be carefree with my published results, but the actual key materials are precious to me. I guard them with my life. I did send out a few milligrams to others who requested it after your thesis was published in various journals. But I've also not seen any further work in that particular research area, so they probably didn't find it too useful. Of course there were many more projects in my lab since then, so I can't guarantee it's there, or if it's there that I can locate it. But I'll give it the old 'college try'."

"I do appreciate your trying, Victor. I was going to just give up and quit once my garage went up in smoke. But I feel that I've got to make just one more attempt before..."

"If the rest of our community had seen the genius of your work, we wouldn't be in this mess of scratching through vials of ancient chemicals," Victor angrily interrupted. "They were blinded by past failures of many others trying to achieve cold fusion. Your work on the matrix characteristics was brilliant."

"Doubtless the others working in my constricted area had higher-priority areas to pursue," Dave charitably replied. "This was always a long shot. In fact, I remember you tried to discourage me when I initially proposed it. You explicitly advised me it was way too close to the discredited experiments of Fleishmann and Pons to warrant pursuing."

"Yes, but then you properly focused on describing the physical properties, not trying to do the impossible," Victor replied, his soft voice echoing-about in the tomb-like laboratory. "Your departure from the accepted science road occurred afterward."

They were almost to the back of the crowded laboratory.

"Regardless, you did right by me, Victor. Without your guidance focusing my work onto acceptable data sets, I would never have graduated with my Ph.D. degree. But you knew from the start I was dreaming far beyond the constraints of acceptable results. So you're not totally innocent in my failures."

Oh, had he gone too far? Here the Professor was being so kind and Dave had to insult him...

"Of course not, my boy," Victor laughed good-naturedly. "How could you be an innovator if you were merely a good technician? I expected *vision* in all my graduate students. And you had that by the truckload. Come on, dear boy—one last try?"

"Ok, then," Dave grinned. "Let's just see if my crazy 'vision' has any legs. Did my latest experiment actually result in sustained room-temperature fusion—or am I, like so many others times in the past, just sadly deluded?"

They stopped in front of what appeared to be a closed closet door.

Victor unlocked it with a key, opening it to reveal a large safe that was set-into the masonry wall. He busily started dialing in a combination.

"But even if that wonderful result had happened to you," Victor frowned, "that could not have resulted in any explosion. From what you told me over the phone, there just wasn't enough reactant-mass present. Such an explosion as you describe was clearly impossible."

Dave sighed, shrugging in agreement.

"The terrorist video claimed they set off an explosive device they'd secreted at the heart of my apparatus," Dave snorted, eagerly awaiting the opening of the safe. "Not likely. I may have been working in my garage, but I was never careless on security. I had alarms rigged up to let me know if anyone tried to break in. None of them were triggered. Also, none of my security cameras showed any suspicious activity in the immediate vicinity of my house. The first thing I knew of any strange going-on was when the whole damn place exploded around me!"

Victor grunted, focused on putting in the proper combination.

"I of course know some of the details of your subsequent work, my boy, after you graduated from here," Victor said as he swung open the heavy door of the wall safe. "The couple of theoretical papers you published on frequency oscillation and wave dynamics within the matrix were well written. I read them with great interest," he stated, now carefully pulling out containers and examining their labels before placing them back in their exact positions. "But those published manipulations could not trigger fusion within your palladium adsorbent. Was something else at play, do you think?"

"Damn right there was—and it wasn't a phantom sabotage. I'd gone far beyond the results of those two papers I published, Victor. Now I was using an *array of micro-lasers* embedded within the matrix directed and recombined with nano-lenses. I adapted the latest video-player technology. I pulled-apart a 3d projector and cannibalized its operating chip."

"So you are saying?" Victor gasped, pausing in his search.

"Yes, my dear Professor Volodymyr, I was trying to use micro-laser technology to control individual deuterium ions. My final experiment was methodically stepping through a number of sequential, layered conditions trying to discover optimal combinations."

"Oh," Victor froze, lost in contemplation of what he'd just heard. "But the computational power to control all of those many variables would be..." he visibly gulped. "You were not dealing with single, isolated pellets of fuel like at NIF, or simply using the lasers to generate heat, or attempting to contain a single isolated plasma-cloud like at ITER."

Dave enjoyed a rare moment of pride.

"Oh, my dear God," Victor continued, "—*you*, dear boy, were trying to use nano-lasers to direct the actual atomic reactions! But, how could you do it? Even if our esteemed colleagues here in the Applied Physics Department were to perfect their rudimentary operating quantum computer, still I don't think even that could handle the incredibly-complex control functions. How did you do it?"

"Yes, Victor, I completely agree," Dave shrugged. "But I wasn't stopped by what is obviously impossible. One of the great virtues of being forced to play scientist in a basement was my not having to document failures."

"I...don't understand," Victor responded, seemingly baffled. He returned to his search of the many cartons and containers packed within the safe.

"When I failed I just moved on, jumping to the next possibility," Dave grimly explained. "I wasn't stuck with trying to justify or live up to a grant plan that was written months or years before. Since I had no grant money, I had no constraints. I didn't have to understand my failures. I had, in essence, the freedom to *ignore* failures and pursue *hints*."

"So you...?"

"I moved on from one thing to the next with nary a pause. I jumped at and followed any lead I wished. It was exhilarating! Versus the present scientific state of the art that requires a multi-disciplinary team paid for by multi-million dollar grants, it was like being *Edison* again."

"You don't say," Victor grinned as he kept searching deeper into the safe.

"Yes, Victor! Thomas Edison fiddled with a thousand different materials and conditions before he finally chanced upon how to light up a carbon filament. It changed the world, resulting in the first practical incandescent lamp powered by clean electricity instead of primitive fire. And he did it all by 'fiddling' mostly by himself in his lab. Well, he did have assistants, but not like today where..."

"You are right about one thing, my boy," Victor broke in. "The age of the individual researcher or inventor is surely over. The big 'easy' things have all been discovered. Now to make real progress you need ten million, a hundred million, even a billion dollars for a comprehensive attack. It's quite presumptuous to even dream of being another Edison who..."

"And I completely agreed," Dave stated flatly, slamming his hand upon a black benchtop in frustration. "But I didn't have any choice, Victor. It was either give up or *try*. So I chose to try."

"Very commendable, though completely stupid," Victor laughed. "I am thinking that maybe I would have gone bird-watching instead."

"But then, at the last, I thought—like Edison—that I was onto something," Dave continued. "And then that damned *explosion* stopped me in my tracks! In an instant, everything I'd worked for years to construct was gone—up in smoke. Even my stock of basic matrix was destroyed. Without that, any hope of proceeding onward was gone."

"That *impossible* explosion..." Victor mused.

"—that *we* are going to at least replicate its *absence*," Dave fervently concluded.

"Hmmmmm..." Victor replied absently, his blue eyes glittering with reflected light from the safe's lamps—now poking his entire head into the half-emptied space as he reached far to the back.

"Ok, then—which we're going to *try* to replicate," Dave amended himself. "Aren't we?" he weakly concluded.

For a moment Victor was silent. Dave was afraid he'd reconsidered his "romp" with his former graduate student as was about to slam the safe shut.

"It's like being a kid in a candy store!" Victor *whooped* as he pulled his head out of the safe and pranced around in a circle, his white hair bouncing up and down, his thin arms thrust high up into the air. "And here is your *magic matrix!*" he exclaimed in triumph, lifting high a nondescript large jar containing a white powder.

"Wahoo!" David exclaimed, dancing around arm-in-arm with the Professor in the empty lab. "Magic matrix! Magic matrix! Magic matrix!" they both chanted together.

"And I get to play in the lab!" Victor happily shouted-out to no one in particular. "It's been years since I got to do research with my own two hands. Now at the very last I get to do it one more time. Oh, I'm so *glad* you showed up, David."

They stopped their impromptu jig and began excitedly looking about to assemble the proper equipment and components.

For two whole days they didn't leave the laboratory.

They hardly slept or ate. They took quick catnaps on a pulled-out cot. For food they consumed power-bars from a cache in the enclosed, small coffee/rest area.

Fortunately there was a small bathroom in the large laboratory complex, so they didn't even have to exit into the outside corridor.

It was exhilarating, grueling work.

But the *apparatus* quickly took shape.

What would have taken Dave months or even years to achieve in his garage if starting again from scratch was accomplished in mere hours. Miniaturized neutron and gamma ray detectors were slapped into place—not the ancient vacuum-tube powered, refrigerator-sized, surplus equipment Dave had scrounged for his garage, but small, sleek, state-of-the-art hand-held units. Instead of intrusive thermometers, tiny microchips were liberally sprinkled throughout an expanding reactor core.

Even the carefully-positioned micro-laser array was better.

Dave had ripped out the heart of a thousand-dollar 3D home-movie projector as the starting point for his innovative previous setup. Victor, though, had in his possession the latest, tiniest optical arrays loaned to him by one of his colleagues, so sophisticated that a computer interface controlled millions of tiny lasers at once. Of course they were not intended to do what Dave and Victor were trying to achieve. And the computer program was only capable of the crudest targeting within the actual matrix of Dave's reactor core. But it was far better than Dave had been able to achieve in his destroyed reaction chamber in his garage in Edmond.

Enhancing and loading in the crystalline latticework was the most exacting step. Here it was that David had to duplicate the accumulated iterations he'd achieved over the last decade in his garage. Fortunately, Victor's stock of exotic chemicals and application methods was up to the task.

The last thing to install was a compact lithium battery capable of independently powering the entire apparatus for several days if needed.

"It's done," Dave blearily concluded as he slumped onto the floor of the lab, spreading his arms and legs wide. He looked up in exhaustion at the white ceiling above him.

"*They* are...*both* done," Victor marveled, sitting on the floor beside Dave, leaning back against a cabinet, breathing heavily.

"Great idea you had, Victor," Dave complimented him, "—of building *two* of them at once. It was only a little more work, but now we've got a backup if anything happens to the original."

Sitting before the two bedraggled men on an open space of the lab's floor were two gleaming, rectangular, metal construction-frameworks. The grid-works were packed with snaking tubes, electrical cables, and myriad equipment.

The two loaded frameworks were identical.

They were each the size of a small bathtub, roughly four feet by two feet by two feet. Each looked like nothing more than sophisticated satellites waiting to be boosted into orbit. And at their hearts were the closed reaction chambers where Dave and Victor hoped to bring the *sun* down to earth!

"We do good work," Dave wearily smiled.

"*Damn* good work, my boy!" Victor grinned.

"But how will we ever get these out of the building?" Dave abruptly gasped, suddenly realizing that security wasn't going to let conspicuously-dangerous devices depart the campus let alone the building.

And to make things worse, it was now evening. The light, as seen through the windows on the outside walls, was rapidly fading. Surely scrutiny would be even more intense now due to their late departure.

"Oh, not to worry, my boy," Victor brightly replied. "I've got a *plan*."

"Mike, my good friend," Victor called-out jovially to the uniformed, dark-skinned guard sitting reading a book at his isolated guard-station.

They were in the locked, heavily-secured loading dock located at the back of the building. Victor had already gone out the main exit of the building, brought around his van from the parking structure nearby, and positioned it by the loading dock before returning again through the front-entrance security.

Inside the loading dock at the back of the building the receiving area was cavernous. A few empty, smaller pallets sat over against one wall.

—and rolling along behind Dave and Victor was what looked like a small train car.

They had, with difficulty, gotten the two large devices up onto an especially-long, self-powered, motorized delivery pallet. Then they'd concealed the devices behind taped-on squares of cut paper boxes. On top, they'd piled other paper boxes filled with conspicuously-protruding laboratory journals.

"Hey, Professor," the heavy-set, dark-skinned man cheerfully replied, setting his book to the side. "Doing some more moving out?"

"Yes I am," Victor laughed cheerfully, walking up to the desk. "It's amazing how many personal files you accumulate over a career, isn't it? Fortunately I've got my colleague Dave here to help me move them out. It's a lot for an old man like me to try to pack into my van."

"Oh, I'm happy to help you load them, Professor," Mike grinned. "But it looks like you do have an awful lot there. Before, you just had a couple boxes now and then to take out...but that's a *mountain*. You must be retiring for sure this time, eh?"

Victor positioned himself between the guard and the long pallet that Dave was slowly wheeling past.

"I'm afraid so, my friend," Victor sighed ruefully. "They're finally kicking me out for good. But I'm going to miss your cheerful face. You've always been here whenever there's been the slightest need or trouble. I always knew I could depend on my good friend, Mike."

The guard waved a big hand in denial though he was obviously pleased with the acknowledgment of his work.

"Just doing my job, Professor," he replied in a deep, booming voice. "Always glad to help out."

"Here's my authorization to take this load of old junk home," the Professor stated, placing an official-looking form on the desk in front of the guard. It appeared to be properly signed by the Chair of the Department. "I suppose I should just throw away my many accumulated journals from the electrochemical society, of applied electrochemistry, of plasma physics, and IAEA nuclear fusion," he pretended to muse, "—but I just can't. They're my *babies*," he pretended to pout. "And I've got a whole wall of bookshelves cleared out at home in my library just waiting for them."

"It sure is a load that you've got there," the guard agreed, pushing a button for the loading-dock's reinforced freight door to start sliding upward, revealing a long ramp outside. The ramp was lit by external lights against the now-thick darkness of the night. Mike was starting to get up from his desk to go inspect the piled-high pallet.

"Say," Dave called-out, neatly slipping the control unit of the motorized pallet to Victor while smoothly taking the Professors place at the desk. "Is that '*The Girl with the Dragon Tattoo*' you're reading?"

"Yes, it is," the guard grinned, lifting it up and handing it to Dave, now settling back into his seat. "It's a great book. I've read about a third of it and..."

"You know what made this book so terrific?" Dave eagerly interrupted, thumbing through its pages. "It was the author, who really knew what he was talking about. The great tension in the book about secret organizations, subversion, and evil Nazi monsters—he knew about them firsthand. He lived those things himself."

"You don't say?" Mike marveled as the pallet, guided by Victor, slowly trundled on past them.

"Yes!" Dave hurriedly continued. "Stieg Larsson, who lived in Sweden, was himself a journalist at a major left-wing magazine, just like the hero in the book. Did you know that he personally trained female resistance fighters during WWII? He knew from his own experience what he was writing about in his book—opposing *extreme white-power cultures* in Sweden."

"Now ain't that's amazing," the African-American gentleman nodded, clearly resonating with this new information. "No wonder the book seems so real."

"Yes, it's what makes for a great read, for sure—when the author writes about what he's actually lived," Dave grinned, slapping the paperback book firmly back onto the desktop.

"Damn!" the deep-voiced man shook his head in wonderment. "Now I'm really stoked to finish reading it."

"And did you know that there are *two more* of them after you finish that one?"

"Really?"

"Yes, Sir," Dave stated firmly, *whomping* his hand down on top of the book to detract from the big load still moving past the guard station. "The next one is *'The Girl Who Played with Fire'* and the last one is *'The Girl Who Kicked the Hornets' Nest'*. They've sold tens of millions of copies each."

"Just incredible..." the man marveled, shaking his head from side-to-side in appreciation. He started to stand up again from his desk.

"But do you know the saddest part of it?" Dave interjected, leaning forward over the desk, peering straight into the man's eyes, encouraging the guard to yet again settle back into his chair.

"What's that?"

"Stieg Larsson, who wrote those three books, never lived to enjoy their incredible success," Dave quietly stated.

"Say what?"

"It's true," Dave shook his own head sadly from side-to-side. "That man," he pointed to the picture of Larsson on the back binder of the book, drawing the guard's gaze to it, "he *died* shortly after he turned in the completed manuscripts for those three blockbuster books."

"What happened to him?" the guard said, fascinated.

"The elevator in his office building wasn't working. So he climbed up seven flights of stairs—then dropped dead from a heart attack."

"No!"

"Yes, Sir—it's true," Dave sadly intoned, again directing the guard's gaze to the picture of the bushy-haired, glasses-wearing, youthful-looking author.

"Good thing we've got great service elevators and powered carts in our building," the guard sighed appreciatively. "You need help unloading all that stuff? We sure don't want the Professor to keel over from a heart attack."

"No need, I've got it," Dave cheerfully called-back as he quickly walked through the now fully-opened fright door, down the sloping ramp, and up to where the powered pallet sat parked behind the opened back of Victor's black van.

"Let's get this stuff in as fast as possible," Dave whispered to Victor. They began lifting the true journal boxes quickly over to the side as, with great difficulty, they managed to push in the large, concealed devices.

Then they hurriedly started piling the journal boxes back on top of the devices, burying them as best they could.

"Wow," Victor gasped, sweat beaded up on his high forehead. "I wasn't sure we could get it all inside or..."

"Lucky you have such a large van," Dave huffed, also getting his breath back.

"I had the back seats taken out of it some time ago," Victor grinned. "I really did intend to take home all these journals someday," Victor weakly laughed. "Plus the open back is great for deer hunting—hauling back your catch. That is, if I don't shoot them too far from a main road. Otherwise, I'd take my faithful Ranger."

"You hunt?"

"We've deer on and near our property in Vermont. I kill at least one buck each year to load up the freezer with venison steaks."

"Sounds tasty."

"You want me to have maintenance return the pallet to your lab?" the burly guard stated, now standing right behind them.

"What?" Dave said, startled—jerking upright from where he was bending over to pick up one of the last boxes of journals. "Uh...right!"

"And if you folks aren't coming back in, you'll also have to sign out," the man insisted. He was now firmly back into his official capacity.

Victor hurriedly slammed the backdoor of the van closed after Dave just managed to jam in the last box. The back of the van was filled to bursting. But if you looked just right through the back window you could see the *gleam of exposed metal* where concealing cardboard was pushed aside.

"Right! Thank you so much, Mike," Victor quickly replied, moving spritely around to take the sign-out sheet on its clipboard. He deftly maneuvered his body so that the guard was turned-away from the van.

The Professor signed the sheet with a flourish, glancing at his watch to mark down the exact departure time.

"You too," the guard gestured to Dave who was now perspiring from his efforts and breathing heavily. "And I'll have to take back your temporary badge."

"Yes, of course," Dave gasped, moving over and positioning himself to also keep the guard pointed back at the building and not at the van. He quickly penned his name with the date and time.

Victor hurriedly skipped around to the front of the van, opened the door and slid behind the wheel.

"So you really enjoyed those books?" Mike grinned, accepting back the clipboard and badge.

"I actually never read them," Dave waved a cheerful 'goodbye' as he jumped into the passenger side of the slowly-departing van.

"—but I saw the movies," Dave called-back out of the opened window. "They were great!"

They sped away into the night, leaving the guard scratching his head in puzzlement.

Chapter 8

<u>**VERMONT WOODS**</u>

If only we had met sooner

Before the searing heat of summer

Or the hectic days of spring

Or the freezing snows of winter...

Perhaps the joys of slow autumn

More suited to your walk

Mid yellows and reds falling softly

Before it all went wrong.

The Luminary Chronicles 8:8-11

They drove in silence through crowded nighttime city streets. Dave was exhausted, barely able to keep his eyes open, especially now that night had fallen. He didn't know how Victor could stay so animated. It was like he was on a grand adventure or drug-fueled "high."

"So where are we going, Victor?" Dave blearily asked. He was trying to keep himself awake now that the adrenalin of the last two days and their close "escape" was draining from his body.

"Our country 'estate' is about two hours from here, my dear boy. It's safe and secluded in the mountains of Vermont."

"Vermont?"

"It's up near the Green Mountain National Forest, if you know where that is?"

"Uhm...afraid not..."

"We drive up I-91 for about two hours and we're there."

"Ok," Dave yawned widely, struggling to keep his eyes open.

"Do not fret, my dear boy," Victor assured him, reaching over with a free hand to firmly grip Dave's shoulder. "It is way off into the wilderness, where we can do our little experiment with no one to bother us."

"Sounds good..."

"You take a nap, my boy," Victor gently ordered him while daftly steering the big vehicle through the crowded streets. "You deserve it."

"But...don't you want me to help you...to drive..." Dave protested, rapidly blinking his eyes to try to keep them opened. Flashing head-lights and street lights hypnotically lulled him.

"No need, David. I've driven this route so many times if my eyes close I'll still steer us safely there in my sleep."

Well, he'd better be right because that was the last thing Dave heard before he sank into a deep, dreamless slumber.

He awoke fully dressed lying on a comfortable bunk bed. A thick quilt was drawn up to his neck, keeping him toasty-warm.

Rubbing his eyes with his knuckles, he sat up on the edge of the bed, before stumbling up to his feet. On a wood chair by a window sat his traveling bag.

"Bathroom..." he mumbled. He was urged to movement by a painfully filled-up bladder.

He fumbled around in the dim early-morning light until he found a likely adjoining door.

Opening it he saw a toilet, a sink, and a mirror—upon which, stuck up with a torn piece of duct tape, he saw a note:

"*My dear David,*" it said, as Dave read it out-loud to himself. "*I managed to get you into our small guest house ok, though you were wobbling on your pegs, still conked out. Likely you will awaken before I do. Both me and my dear wife are rather exhausted—she waited up for us to arrive—and will probably sleep late tomorrow morning, maybe not getting up until noon. If you get up early, food is in the refrigerator. Also, should you wish to start preparing for our journey, the van is open, parked by the shed, with keys in the ignition. In the unlocked garage you will find my Polaris Ranger. Keys are also in the ignition. I think one of the Devices will just fit into the box on the back of the Ranger. You can pile the cartons with the journals on the porch if you'd like. See you tomorrow, my boy.*"

Dave happily relieved his aching bladder. Then he took a long, warm shower, changing into his extra set of clothes from his bag. In the small kitchen he found the refrigerator with a variety of food in-side, making himself a thick sandwich.

Then, donning a warm jacket he found in a closet, Dave got about the business at hand.

Outside, the air was fresh and chilly. Indeed, they were in Vermont. Dave saw snow patches out in the woods. It was only early spring, not yet done with the heavy snowstorms of winter.

All around were tall, leafy trees. Victor's 'estate' was deep in the woods.

Contrasted with urban New Haven, it was an oasis of quiet and peace. Dave saw bright red and black small birds flitting through the canopy. He heard their joyful twitters. He could see why the Professor would happily retreat to this secluded place.

It was quite beautiful.

The main house was large, sporting a wide, covered porch. The entire structure was built from tree trunks, a real lodge! A shed stood off to the side, where the van was parked. Beside the shed was a larger garage.

Dave let out a low whistle of appreciation as he lifted up the garage door...

"Sweet!" he exclaimed.

The *Polaris Ranger* ORV was an open-air, four-wheel drive, off-road vehicle. It sported thick curved bars that protected the driver and front passenger. It had a Plexiglas windshield. On its back it had a four-foot-wide open box, just perfect to hold one of the Devices.

It was black and military-green. It was raised up on thick-treaded wheels. Plus it'd obviously been used a lot, with brown dirt caked into the wheel treads. It was a *mean*-looking machine.

"Looks like we can get to wherever we need to go—no roads required," Dave laughed in appreciation.

He set to work with great enthusiasm: lugging out the heavy cartoons of journals to pile on the porch of the main house. Then he dragged out one of the "buried" Devices to the van's back edge and carefully swung it into the air.

It was heavy. Dave had to struggle mightily not to drop it.

"Gotta use my leg muscles," he ordered himself, hugging the loaded construction framework close into his body while leaning backward.

It weighed near one hundred pounds. Dave was just able to totter with it over to the opened end of the Ranger. And, yes, it just fit into the space, sliding in with nary a problem.

Dave carefully locked several thick straps into place, securing the Device firmly into the bed.

"Whew!" Dave gasped, closing the end, breathing heavily. "Now all I've got to do is lock up the van with the spare Device safely tucked inside, and we're set to go."

But a cloud passing over the sun darkened the woods. Suddenly things didn't seem so cheerful. Indeed, the last couple days had gone amazingly well—maybe *too* well.

Dave frowned, absently stroking his beard, as he slowly walked back over to the garage, musing...

"Goodbye, Ivanna!" Victor called-out excitedly as he and Dave pulled away from the house in the Ranger. "We'll be back by nightfall."

"Goodbye, be careful," Ivanna waved back.

She was a strikingly good-looking older woman. Her long grey hair was dyed a bright blond, with just a tinge of grey stylishly left in a lock at her forehead. The skin of her face was smooth and white. She wore a single-piece blue jumpsuit. She was trim and fit. She could easily pass for a woman in her fifties though she was well into her eighties.

"She worries about me when I go off deer-hunting in my sturdy Ranger," Victor laughed, gunning the engine.

Dave held onto the side door tightly, glad his seatbelt was latched firmly across his chest and waist.

They shot down the road as if they were in a regular-sized car.

"But since we're not taking any rifles with us, she's not so worried," Victor added over the roar of the powerful engine. "She thinks I'll shoot my balls off. That would certainly slow down our active love-life, hah!"

Dave gulped in horror at the vision—not just the joke of mutilation, but the older couple making love...maybe he wasn't as open-minded as he thought he was?

Also, he wasn't a gun person. He'd never lived outside an urban environment. He'd never even gone hunting. In fact, he'd never shot a gun. And now he was heading off into the wilderness to try to bring the sun down to earth?

Suddenly he realized how bizarre this "expedition" really was.

"How fast does this thing go?" Dave asked, marveling at the little vehicle zooming along the narrow road.

"Oh, the maximum speed is around 50 mph," Victor shouted back, over the roar of the engine. "But I've fine-tuned the engine. I think we can go a bit faster than that!"

"Oh...that's great," Dave gulped, wishing that they both had motorcycle helmets and goggles on their heads.

"You'll get used to it," Victor laughed, squinting against the howling wind that came around the opened sides of the front windshield. "Yes we could be wearing helmets and goggles," he said, apparently reading Dave's mind from the strained expression on Dave's face, "but I find this so much more *invigorating*."

His long white hair was dancing about his head.

"Where are we headed?" Dave loudly replied over the roar of the engine and grinding of the wheels on the pavement.

"It's an hour and a half away, in the *Green Mountain National Forest*. We zoom along highway 9 most of the way, then head onto a trail into the woods. We end up near *Somerset Reservoir*."

"Why there?"

"I know that area quite well," Victor grinned. "I do most of my deer hunting out there. And it is off the beaten path, secluded, a perfect site for our 'secret' experiment. Plus it's some of God's finest country. It's fun. You'll enjoy the ride."

"Uh, sure," Dave gulped, still gripping the edge of the door at his side tightly. "They let you hunt in a National Forest?"

"This is Vermont. Everybody hunts here. In fact, it's written into our constitution that hunting is protected."

"Are you joking with me, Victor?"

"What? No, not at all, it's literally written into the constitution."

"So what's the big attraction? Can't you just buy your meat in the grocery store?"

"It's the thrill of the hunt, my boy," Victor yelled back, gunning the motor even more. Now they were *zipping* along the two-lane road. "Plus we don't waste the meat. Everybody's got a freezer packed with venison, moose, turkey, you name it."

"Can't you just buy that in the grocery store?" Dave repeated.

Victor directed a withering glance at his passenger. "You buy cow meat and chickens in grocery stores, not wild food."

"Isn't protein just protein, no matter the source?"

"David, my boy, we are *men*. Men are *hunters*. It is in our *blood*. Men were bred to *kill prey*. The ladies 'gather' and we *hunt*. It's just the way that God made us!"

Dave gave an apologetic grin back at his host.

"Oh, right!" Dave yelled back. "It's just that I'm not much experienced in hunting. I'm not arguing, just asking. And I didn't know that you were religious. I never heard you before invoke God in an argument."

"When it comes to hunting, *all* of us here are religious," Victor laughed over the roar of the engine as he brought the motor up to full-throttle.

The Ranger lurched forward even faster. It swayed precariously from side-to-side.

Dave hung on for dear life.

Sure enough, an hour and a half later they pulled to stop on a hill overlooking a large body of water.

"That's the Reservoir, David," Victor triumphantly pointed, loosening his seatbelt and lithely sliding out of his seat to stand on the ground.

"It's beautiful," Dave agreed, groaning under his breath, easing his aching rear end out of the seat. He stood beside the Ranger, trying to stand up straight. Every part of his body ached, particularly his back.

The last half of the ride was rough. They'd bounced jarringly along on a narrow trail through the woods. Victor laughed the whole way, like it was a carnival ride. Dave just felt slammed. He hoped the Device had survived undamaged.

But spread out before him was a stunning panorama, making him momentarily forget the condition of his butt and the Device.

Down below in a wide valley lay a deep blue body of water—stretching out of sight to Dave's right and left. Towering trees surrounded them. Low mountains arose in the distance. Across the horizon, banks of fluffy white clouds floated in the bright-blue sky.

The air was pure and fresh. There was zero smog.

"You see?" Victor exulted, taking in a deep breath of the air. "There still exists on our planet untarnished pieces of paradise. We could go down there right now to the water's edge and *today* catch trout, salmon, bass, and perch—even Northern pike. Ah, that's good eating for us to..."

"But *not* today?"

"Yes, of course not—today we do *science*. Perhaps tomorrow we return to skewer some fresh meat, eh?"

"I would be honored for you to teach me how to hunt and fish," Dave nodded sincerely. "That sounds great. But right now what's the next step with our experiment?"

"Ah yes, our Grand Experiment," Victor agreed, glancing back at the box securely tied behind the front seats. He rubbed his thin, spotted hands together gleefully. "Hop back in, my boy. Now we're headed to a small valley a couple miles over to the side, away from the lake."

"Why not here?"

"Ah, other hunters and some tourists make it to the big lake. But the valley is my own 'private' hunting and camping area. Ivanna and I often go there to make love."

Dave silently grimaced, still amazed at Victor's youthful vigor.

They carefully rolled off away from the defined trail, threading the vehicle carefully between towering trees and around large boulders, following a path through the thick woods only known to the Professor.

After a while they started upward, ending at the top of yet another high slope.

"We're almost there," Victor said, pointing ahead.

Laid out beneath them was a small but spectacular valley. Carefully, Victor drove the vehicle over the lip and downward into the thick forest on the slope.

After a bit they emerged from the trees into a lush meadow.

In the middle of the meadow was a creek sporting crystal-clear, cold water. Elevated beside the creek was a wide expanse of flattened stones.

"And here is our 'research benchtop', my dear David," the Professor laughed as he stopped the Ranger on top of the flattened rocks.

"What is it?" Dave asked, intrigued at the flat expanse.

"It's a neat little place that the last ice age carved out especially for us," Victor laughed, squatting down to pat the flattened stone with his liver-spotted hand. "A glacier smoothed this out for us. It's very secure. Our Device will be solidly stable. Let's unload our Grand Experiment."

Together, they carefully lifted out the heavy rectangular construction frame loaded with equipment. They extended short screw-out legs to place it exactly level in the middle of the opened, flattened area.

"Hah! Now let's check it out," Victor said, going back to the Ranger to sit, taking a large tablet out of the glove compartment.

Dave brought out his own laptop, turning it on. Yes, the maintenance signal from the Device was strong. He flicked on the control app on his computer that distally controlled the various complex equipment backed into the construction-frame.

They could hear a low-level "*hum*" as the Device fully awakened.

"Everything's working," Dave stated with relief, glad the delicate connections survived the bumpy trails.

"I'm charging the reaction chamber," Victor stated, fine-tuning the flow of reagents from his own app.

"I'm getting base readings," Dave noted, frowning at the readouts on his laptop. "They look good. The chamber temperature is holding at a steady 22 degrees Celsius. Gamma flux is nil. Neutron flux is nil. The laser micro-array is ready. I think we're ready to begin my programmed series of overlapping electrical oscillations—just the same as the last night that it was active in my garage."

"That's excellent, my boy. So now we back off to a safe distance. How far should we go, do you think?"

"Well, if somehow we were to trigger the impossible explosion that I had at my house, we should be a good hundred yards away, I'd think."

"Ah, but we're working with ten times the amount of deuterium as was in your primitive set-up," Victor thoughtfully calculated. "I say we go back to the ridge we passed about two-thirds down the slope, just to make sure that we've got a margin of error for..."

"But that's *if* we get an explosion," Dave excitedly added, "that we both know is impossible. The laws of physics affirm that all we can possibly do—even if we somehow get the magnificent, world-shattering achievement of full ignition with a sustained reaction—is to warm our reaction chamber by five degrees. Instead of the present 71.6 degrees Fahrenheit, the central chamber would heat up to a whole 77 degrees. That's not even enough to fry an egg, hardly an explosion. And that's the *most* we could ever get out of this present configuration even if the unthinkable happens: full sustained nuclear fusion. *Wahoo!*"

Victor was also grinning widely, excited to be finally firing up their secret experiment.

"Yes, the explosion that occurred at your house had to be due to that crazed terrorist sneaking past your security net and planting a bomb," Victor agreed. "So I guess we could just sit *here* and watch it putter along in complete safety. Actually it's quite peaceful and cheerful here by the creek. Why don't we stay? Then we won't have to drive all the way up and back down just to tweak any components in the Device?"

The mountain stream bubbled past the rock outcropping. Birds circled overhead. A gentle breeze caressed Dave's exposed cheeks.

"That's tempting," Dave smiled, feeling the warm afternoon sun on his face. "But I promised Ivanna I'd bring you home safely, so maybe we ought to be super-prudent and get back up to that ridge you mentioned. The signal from the equipment is strong. We should be able to easily monitor the readouts from there."

"As you wish," Victor stated, turning on the engine and carefully guiding the Ranger back into the surrounding forest.

After climbing for ten minutes, they reached the ridge.

"Is this ok?" Victor said, parking it facing down-slope. "We can see the Device quite well, but are still far away."

Dave looked down at the small "alien" Device sitting all by its lonesome in the middle of the beautiful wilderness, beside the bubbling stream.

"Uhm," he mused. "You know what, Victor? Since we've gone all this way—why don't we just go back to the top of the slope where we can see the entire valley?"

"Why do that? We'll have to use binoculars to observe any of the Device's components from that far away."

"Oh, I don't know," Dave sighed, knowing there was absolutely no need to go that far. "It just seems fitting that we're perched at the highest point. I've got a feeling..."

"As you wish, my dear colleague," Victor agreeably shrugged, putting the Ranger back in gear.

Now, having slowly driven back to the top of the small valley, they both exited the Ranger. Dave sat on the ground, positioning his back comfortably against the lip of the hill behind him. At that spot an overhanging tree sheltered him from the sun. It was starting to get uncomfortably warm.

Hidden behind the lip of the slope, they couldn't see the far-off Device at the bottom of the valley. But Dave still got a strong signal from it.

"We might as well get comfortable," Dave stated, relaxing. "I had this present set of step-functions running for over a day before anything allegedly happened. And we've got to start back in a few hours if we're going to return to your house before dark. So Victor, I'm 'officially' predicting that *nothing* at all will happen and we just have a nice time sitting here."

"Oh, even with a null result it's not a waste of time at all, my boy," Victor kindly replied. He stiffly squatted down beside Dave. "I have here an excellent, fine lunch that Ivanna packed for us. Smoked venison sandwiches, very tasty! Plus we've got some big pickles, some potato chips—even some fresh-baked brownies. Wait until you taste Ivanna's brownies. Your mouth will be in heaven. They are just to die for. Oh, this is a fine repast for us. Even if we don't get any excess neutrons or warming down below, it was still well worth the trip to have this picnic in this marvelous wilderness."

"I totally agree, Victor. It's wonderful here."

Dave grinned as Victor spread out the lunch on a boulder in front of them. It sure looked good. And, yes, he *was* getting hungry.

"Everything looks stable," Dave said, scanning all the readouts on his laptop. "The Device is working just as predicted. We did a great job putting it together. Victor, I want to thank you again for this. Even if we don't get any indication of fusion, it will relieve my mind that I didn't leave some avenue untried. After making this last effort I think I can now go back to teaching introductory lecture courses in peace."

"And don't forget that I have many friends in both the Physics and the Applied Physics departments, my boy," Victor insisted, brushing away a few ants that wanted to come join the picnic. "Anytime you wish to get your hands wet playing in the lab, there's plenty of groups that would welcome your volunteered, after-hours help."

"Yes, that's true. But I don't think I'm up to it," Dave sighed, his voice trailing off. He continued monitoring his oscillatory algorithms, making sure they were properly synched to the laser microchip. "I think I've shot my wad, Victor. Besides, I'm way past being a post-doc working on someone else's project. Just going home 'after-hours' to watch T.V. sounds mighty attractive. Research is fun when the experiments work, that's true. But when they don't, it's just slow torture."

"And that's not-to-mention those *fine young ladies* you'll now have time to date," Victor chortled. "Oh, what fun you will have, David. Of course, I already have my own wonderful lady," he hastened to add.

"And a fine lady she is indeed," Dave congratulated his friend. "If I were to find a lady even half as nice, I'd be in seventh heaven."

"You might have to give up a few of your pets," Victor gently chided him.

"*Or...*" Dave politely disagreed, sticking a forefinger up into the air in emphasis, "it's possible that a *few* biology or zoology majors amongst the many 'cuties' here at Yale might not mind a house filled with reptiles," Dave shrugged, acknowledging the improbability even of that extreme scenario. "But, whatever, I'm *not* giving up my snakes for some dumb girl," he firmly stated.

"Hah!" Victor laughed. "Spoken like a true herpetologist...a *lonely* herpetologist."

"I'll have you know my snakes are very friendly. 'Hug'—my ten foot long red-tailed boa constrictor—will happily give you a big hug!"

"I think I prefer my Ivanna."

"Well, that's true..."

"Hmmmm," Victor mused, digging into a large paper bag. "Actually, I see there are a couple trout sandwiches here along with the venison ones," he observed. "Would you like...?"

"—and I'm starting the flow of deuterium ions into the reaction chamber, right..." Dave stated as he lowered his forefinger to click the "go" button left-clicking with his touchpad, "*now!*"

Dave groggily came back to consciousness aware that he was *suffocating!*

In a blind panic, he fought and pushed with his arms at heavy weights keeping him frozen in place—clawing at a mountain of *rocks and dirt* burying his arms and face!

"*Auggghhhh!*" he shouted, bursting up out of a mass of suffocating dirt, drawing in some ragged gasps of hot air, then staggering to his feet—and *looking up...*

In the shimmering haze, obscured by drifting smoke and cinders, Dave looked straight up into the sizzling fury of a *mushroom cloud!*

He couldn't hear anything. His ears didn't seem to be working.

But his eyes registered a *roiling kaleidoscope* above him composed of every color of the rainbow...

—as searing *heat-waves* rolled across the now non-existent lip of the slope they'd been sitting behind...which apparently had saved them both from being instantly incinerated!

"Victor?" Dave gasped, now remembering his friend. He frantically looked around at the blackened, flattened landscape. "*Victor!*" he shouted again, stumbling around in a circle, probing the soot at his feet with his shoes..."*Victor!*" he screamed-out again against the ROAR of the expanding inferno that was raging above him...now just barely hearing his own voice again against the incessant RINGING permeating his skull.

"Help..." Dave heard a feeble call and saw part of the Professor's head poked-up out of the piles of blown-apart trees, rocks, and dirt.

"Hang on! Hang on!" Dave shouted as he frantically dug with his hands, flinging masses of dirt and rocks to the side, uncovering Victor's head then chest...then pulling him up and out of his near-tomb.

Victor coughed uncontrollably, his white hair matted-down and stained brown from pressed-in dirt.

"You're alive, you're alive!" Dave gasped, slumping next to him on the ground, exhausted.

"What...w-what h-happened?" Victor stammered, still gasping for breath.

"Look...up," Dave vaguely gestured upward with a dirt-encrusted hand.

Victor's squinted eyes slowly opened, then stretched wide in amazement. Brilliantly-colored lines reflected off the white of his eyes.

"Oh...my...God," he whispered. His eyes transfixed upon the rapidly-expanding *atomic cloud* looming above them.

"I think...we're dead," Dave gulped, wiping soot from his eyes. "We must have received...a lethal dose...of radiation."

"...yes, that's...quite likely," Victor gasped, moving shakily to paw through the surrounding dirt.

"What...are you...looking for?"

"My tablet...has a radiation monitor," Victor said. "Here it is—I found it."

"Does it...still work?"

All around them, small black hunks of molten rock were dropping like raindrops. One seared Dave's arm and he knocked it away. Both he and Victor were shirtless. Even their pants were now just torn rags, barely covering their crotches.

"Yes...it's on," Victor said, punching in commands. "Gamma rays...nothing! Neutrons...nothing! Radioactive isotopes...nothing! And what about x-rays...nothing also? My boy, we're going to *live!*"

"Are you...sure...it is working?" Dave coughed. "I don't mean to sound ungrateful, Victor...but...we *should* be saturated with a lethal dosage—this close to a *nuclear explosion!*"

"Everything checks out," Victor grimly stated, brushing more of the molten droplets off his face and the laptop. "There's no excess of ionizing radiation above background—none at all."

They both involuntarily looked up at the towering, blazing cloud still rumbling above them.

Then they looked at each other in total disbelief.

"Can you find your laptop, my boy?" Victor grunted, picking himself up to peer through the increasing gloom of descending soot, apparently trying to see if the Ranger was still intact somewhere down the slope.

"I'll...try," Dave choked out, spitting-up soot, tearing off a hanging piece of one of his pants leg to put it to his nostrils to block out the drifting smoke.

He crawled over to the hole he'd just a few minutes before dug himself out of, reaching into it, feeling around..."I've got it!"

"I think I see the Ranger!" Victor yelled back. The ROARING and CRACKLING from above was still loud and oppressive. "If your laptop is working, see what the last readings were from the Device."

"Ok!" Dave yelled back, fumbling with the banged-up laptop. The viewing screen was wretched to one side, but still powered-on.

"It's still on. I've got readings. I see it!" Dave shouted. "About a hundred nanoseconds after I started the experiment...there's a neutron flux! And a spike of gamma rays! And the temperature—my God, Victor! When the readings cut out at four hundred fifty nanoseconds, the reaction chamber's temperature was a *hundred thousand degrees* Celsius, and still climbing!"

"It was fusion! It had to be!" Victor yelled back as he wobbled through the haze down the slope. "We did it! We achieved ignition! But...but still, even then, how is this at all possible?"

"I don't know!" Dave screamed down at him, shaking his head in disbelief. "It's impossible! Even if a *chain reaction* with the hydrogen around the Device happened, we'd only have melted-down the apparatus! There's absolutely no way that it could..." his voice trailed off, as he again looked up in bewilderment at that impossible mushroom cloud undeniably hanging ominously above them.

—as Victor roared up in the Ranger: its roll-bars bent out of shape, its carrying cage on the back missing, and only fragments of the Plexiglas windshield left, but still running.

The vehicle had bounced down the slope, rolling end-over-end, but fortunately landed upright on its still intact wheels.

"Get in, get in!" Victor yelled, as Dave scrambled to hop into the passenger seat, whose door was also torn-away and missing.

Victor and Dave edged through accumulating soot then stopped the Ranger at the top of the slope, again looking down into the small valley.

Nothing was left.

The stream, trees, flat rocky plateau, and the Device—were all gone. All that was left was a *huge, smoking crater.*

For miles in each direction the trees were flattened. The stumps were black. Fires were rapidly spreading.

"Let's get out of here," Dave gulped, dazed and suddenly deathly afraid.

"Yes," Victor grated, turning the Ranger around. "And let us not look back."

The ride back was long and slow.

The Ranger wouldn't go much faster now than 25 mph. The wheels were now way out of alignment, producing a bone-jarring vibration. But at least the wheels were still intact. That was something. And going slower was more tolerable to Dave. Since the windshield was shattered, even at twenty-five mph he was being blasted. Any faster and he'd not be able to see anything due to the ripping wind!

They passed several emergency vehicles going in the opposite direction. Fire trucks zoomed past them. The explosion, mushroom cloud, and subsequent forest fires had definitely attracted attention.

Dave knew he had to say something to Victor, but couldn't decide how to start.

It wasn't until they were nearly home, three hours after leaving the site of the explosion, with the sun hanging low on the horizon, that Dave finally cleared his head enough to start a conversation.

"What are we going to say about this?" Dave loudly broke the lengthy silence between them.

"We say nothing."

"For God's sake, Victor," Dave protested. "We set off a nuclear explosion! Don't you think a few people are going to be a bit curious about what happened?"

"No one except Ivanna knows we were even out there," Victor grated, his usual jovial manner gone.

"But the explosion...?"

"A meteor!"

"What?"

"It's just like the Chelyabinsk meteor that exploded June, 2013, over Russia."

"You mean the one that injured more than a thousand people?"

"Yes, just like that," Victor insisted. "If anyone asks, we were out on a scouting trip looking for good fishing places when we witnessed the blast way off in the hills at a distance."

"Well...we certainly did witness it. That's true," Dave replied. "But won't they know that..."

"—know what? Our device was incinerated. And there was no radiation! If it were an atomic event, then there would be massive radiation contamination. But a kinetic explosion from a meteor would only release thermal radiation: heat! And that's just what the authorities will find at our site—only heat. Even the tracks of our Ranger will be long covered over with falling soot and ash."

"That's also true."

"So do we have our story straight, my boy?"

"But Victor," Dave gulped, "what *really* happened?"

"That, my dear boy," Victor grated through clenched teeth, "is exactly what I will try to find out when I return in a couple days to Yale," Victor grimly stated, determinedly clinging to the badly-vibrating steering wheel as they trundled slowly along. "I'll get with a few of my trusted colleagues in the Physics Department—totally in confidence. What happened cannot be magic. It was simply an unexplained natural phenomenon. We'll work it through. We'll figure it out."

Dave sighed, sinking back into his seat with a profound sense of gratitude. He wasn't alone. And the recent bizarre events weren't just his imagination. Now he had a valued colleague convinced that something more than simple terrorism was afoot.

"And here we are, back from our little adventure," Victor wryly grinned as they slowly turned into the lane leading into the woods where his house awaited. "We're a bit singed around the edges, a bit beaten up, but still alive and kicking. We should be grateful, my boy. Not only do we have a new physics mystery to explore, we're alive to pursue it."

Dave smiled, relieved that the Ranger had made it and Victor was regaining his normal boundless enthusiasm. Dave had half expected for the small vehicle to fall apart on the way back, leaving them dead in a traffic accident.

They'd survived a "nuclear"-type explosion only to be smashed in a car accident. What irony that would have been.

Dave sighed as Victor brought the sturdy little ORV to a shuddering stop. The struggling engine gave one final gasp and fell silent. It sure would be good to step foot back upon non-blackened, life-supporting, non-blasted-up dirt and...

"*Where* is it?" a high-pitched, oriental-sounding voice yelled at them.

"What the..." Dave gasped, seeing charging toward him and Victor the *white-haired, black-clothed terrorist* who'd just kicked-open the front door of the log house. He was waving a pistol while dragging a tied-up Ivanna along behind him with his other hand!

"No!" Victor screamed-out in fury, charging heedless of his own safety at the man dragging his trussed-up wife...

—who nonchalantly batted Victor to the side, his heavy pistol connecting with the Professor's head. Victor crumpled motionless to the ground.

"Tell me where it is or I *kill* the woman, now!" the white-haired oriental yelled, pointing his gun at her head. The jagged scar on his cheek stood out in garish relief.

"Tell you where *what* is?" Dave yelled back at him, painfully sliding out of the smashed-up ORV to stand helpless, weaponless, covered in black soot and dirt, almost naked. "What the hell are you talking about?"

"The duplicate device!" the man virtually shrieked at him as he continued advancing, dragging the struggling woman along behind him. "It should have been in the garage in the back of the van! But it's not there! Where is it?"

It took a moment for Dave to mentally process what was happening. Things were happening too fast...

"Alright, alright!" Dave said, jerking up his hands palms-out. "I surrender! I'll do whatever you want. Just don't hurt the lady or the Professor. Let her go and I'll show you where I put it."

"Agreed, except for 'showing' me!" the terrorist snapped-back at him. "*Tell* me right now where it is and your friends won't be hurt."

"Let go of Ivanna first."

Contemptuously, the man opened his grip on Ivanna's dyed-blond hair so that she dropped face-first into the dirt.

"Now where is it?"

Yes, Dave had moved the second, duplicate device.

That morning he'd felt uneasy leaving the backup equipment just sitting there in the van. So he took it out, laboriously lugging it off into the forest. He'd sheathed it in several layers of protecting garbage bags he'd found in the garage. Then he carefully concealed it beneath dragged-over large, fallen branches.

"I hid it, but you're welcome to it," Dave grated, lifting his hands further up into the air to appear even less threatening. "It's off in the woods. I'll show you."

"What direction?"

"Direction?" Dave asked, perplexed. He'd always had a poor sense of direction. He had to think, to orient his surroundings with a mental picture of a standard map of the area. "Well, I guess it is *north* from here."

"That's all I need to know," the seething terrorist crisply replied. "Once I'm near it my metal detector will pinpoint its position. And once I've got it in my hands and both your friends are dead, then I'll leave *you* in peace. You'll still live—but your evil project will be *finished!* None will try to continue it. They'll see what a terrible price you paid pursuing it and others won't even try."

"What? But you said you wouldn't harm them!"

"I lied!" the terrorist yelled back, turning around to point his pistol straight at the helpless old lady...

BLAM!

The white-haired, black-clad man fell backward toward Dave, a wet red patch spreading across one of his shoulders..."thumping" down upon the ground, on his back—while staring upward in shock!

On the porch, Victor stood with blood dribbling down his forehead, calmly snapping the lever of a rifle, ejecting a cartridge...

"No!" the terrorist protested, still holding his pistol in his good hand, trying to lever himself back to a sitting position to take aim...

BLAM!

The second shot from Victor passed through the man's other shoulder, leaving the terrorist groaning and twisting on the ground.

In a couple quick strides, Victor was at the side of his fallen wife. He still held the rifle at-ready, just in case the man might rise again. "Ivanna, did he hurt you?"

"No..." she croaked as he helped her up to her knees, undoing the gag at her mouth, and loosened the ropes around her hands and feet.

Determinedly she rose to stand...

—as Dave sank to his own knees, trembling, in shock...

—Ivanna lightly kissing Victor; then immediately leaping over at the groaning man who'd rolled over onto his stomach as was struggling again to lift his gun, this time taking aim at Dave...

—and she *stomped hard* on the back of his neck, snapping his spine and killing him dead.

"Sorry about that," she apologized, moving onward to help Dave back to his feet. "I know we should have let him live to find out what he knew, but he was about to shoot you, so..."

"No explanation needed. Thanks!" Dave gasped, wavering back and forth, as she lifted one of his arms across her own shoulders.

"Let's get you inside," Victor soothingly stated, gently taking Dave's other arm in support. "I think the both of us could use some cleaning up."

"That...is your deer-hunting rifle?" Dave absently asked, peering at the brown, plain-looking lever-action rifle still held firmly in Victor's thin hand.

"Best deer rifle ever," Victor calmly replied. "First manufactured in 1873, a real classic. Teddy Roosevelt used one. So did Buffalo Bill Cody."

"...and so did...Professor Victor Volodymyr," Dave gulped gratefully, sagging downward in relief.

They sat sipping hot cocoa at the Volodymyrs' dining room table.

Like all the rest of the furniture in the house, the table was rustic. It was made from sanded wooden planks covered with a thick orange resin that highlighted the grain of the wood.

Dave and Victor were scarfing up a pile of frosted brownies, much to Ivanna's amusement.

They hadn't had anything to eat since breakfast—their lunch having been rudely interrupted by a nuclear explosion!

They'd cleaned up well. Victor and Dave took turns taking good long showers in the one big bathroom, bandaging up cuts, putting ointment on bruises, and dressing in fresh clean clothes. Some of Victor's spare clothes for whenever his sons visited fit Dave quite well. His other soiled set was still out in the garage, awaiting washing.

Dave felt like a new man.

But it was getting late into the evening and a *dead body* still lay crumpled on the ground outside.

"So I guess we call the police?" Ivanna asked.

"Of course," Victor shrugged. "What else?"

"Well..." Dave reluctantly admitted, "I suppose you'd better call this guy also."

"Who's that?"

Dave slid across the table the card of Agent Anderson.

"FBI," he stated flatly. "They've been after that terrorist rat. They'll be quite happy that he's been stopped—though probably not too pleased that he's dead."

"Ok, my boy," Victor nodded. "I will go and make a copy of this and give it back to you," he said, starting to push back from the table and its dwindling pile of brownies.

"No need," Dave demurred, motioning for Victor to sit back. "I've got that guy's number memorized."

"About our...duplicate," Victor cryptically said.

"—the duplicate, backup Device?" Ivanna stated, lifting up her eyebrows in mock surprise.

"You...know?" Victor gulped.

"Well of course," she laughed. "Do you think I'm deaf? That strange little oriental fellow was practically beside himself over it. When he charged in on me with that gun he seemed to think I'd single-handedly changed the entire course of human history! He insisted that the 'duplicate, backup Device' *had* to be sitting in the back of the van out in the garage. For it not to be there seemed to him like the sun had vanished from the sky."

"But how did he even know about it in the first place?" Dave frowned. "We never even left the lab when we assembled it. None of your colleagues came in. We had the blinds pulled on all the windows facing the corridor."

"And we didn't even know for sure we were going to assemble any Devices at all," Victor mused. "We only decided to do so after finding I still possessed your doctoral compound."

"Well, however he knew, he put a lot of store in finding it," Ivanna concluded. "And I think you two had better load that thing right back into the van...and David should drive it away from here, tonight—like *now!*"

"Hmmmm...." Victor mused. "That's not a bad idea."

"If you keep it here, you know those snoopy FBI agents will find it," she insisted. "After all, that's what they do. They 'investigate'! They leave no stone, or bush, or pile of brush unturned. Am I correct?"

"That's for sure," Victor nodded. "And as yet we don't want it taken out of our hands. We don't yet know enough about what it is doing to let others possess it."

"But..." Dave protested, not thrilled at the idea of keeping running. "Isn't it over with? Can't we just go public? Everyone in the world think's I'm just some kooky 'cold-fusion' nut. Maybe this is my chance to finally get a little respect for once. We could let a coalition of scientists work on the Device. "

"Dave, my boy," Victor consoled him. "You are certainly due a lot of respect. But until we find out what's behind the...*reaction*..." he took a quick glance at Ivanna, who cryptically shrugged, signaling she didn't need to know more, "—that we observed today, it's way too *dangerous* to allow that knowledge to leak. Imagine what a terrorist organization could do with that Device, even without knowing exactly how it works."

"But the terrorist is dead," Dave complained, frowning. "You shot him. Ivanna broke his neck. He's gone. We *stopped* him!"

"And how many others did he claim in his Manifesto were members of his group," Ivanna gently reminded Dave, "—thousands?"

"We don't know what we don't know," Victor gently agreed with his wife.

"Well, I suppose there could more of them out there," Dave reluctantly nodded. "But what will you tell the cops? Won't they expect for me to be here with you, give my testimony?"

"Well..." Ivanna mused then said firmly: "We will tell them the truth. We will say that you are shy. You insisted you wanted no publicity. And so you borrowed the Professor's van and took off. It's no different from when the prior 'incident' happened. You walled yourself off from the press then as well. The police, agents, and reporters will just shrug and say 'ok', that's Dr. David King. They'll get the full story from us—at least the parts that we choose to share with them."

"You're very kind to me," Dave sighed. "I don't know how I deserve such good friends—especially since I'm so 'shy'!"

"Oh," Ivanna smiled demurely, "you were always one of my favorites amongst Victor's many grad students even more than a decade ago. You were so polite and earnest. Others tended more towards arrogance and impatience. That's what *I* mean by 'shy.' The reporters and police can put their own definition on it."

"Thanks," Dave softly replied.

"So it's settled, my boy," Victor stated, resolutely standing up from the table. "Let's go get the backup Device and load it into the van. We'll include a batch of tools you might need to tweak it later on. Then you'll be off."

"But...how will I know what you find out from your colleagues? I've *got* to know!"

"Good point, my boy," he nodded firmly. "Here, take Ivanna's cellphone," he said, getting up and retrieving it from a drawer by the door.

"What?"

"There's a red button on it—there," he pointed to it. "Pressing it twice brings up an encrypted link to my own cellphone. It's a novel encryption developed by a student of mine who had a joint appointment in the mathematics department. It's unique. It's one of a kind—can't be broken or observed. Even should the FBI tap into our communications, they won't know anything. The program also instantly erases its history as it's transmitted, so it is undetectable and untraceable."

"Ah, like some of the commercial apps for..."

"It's much better than those."

"Well, thanks a lot," Dave nodded gratefully.

"If you need to contact me, call," Victor continued. "I'll call you if I find out anything. You'll know it's me when the red button lights up. Pity we couldn't patent it—the military would have confiscated it and put us in prison if we'd tried, what with their continued War on Terror. It's just *too* good. It will even scramble calls coming from cellphones other than its twin, so even regular calls can't be overheard using one push of the red button. Anyone bugging you will know there's a call, but will only hear static."

"But...what about you and Ivanna?" Dave frowned, looking down at the innocuous-appearing cellphone in his hands. "You won't be able to have your private communications channel or..."

"Not to worry, my boy," Victor cheerfully replied. "What with my final retirement she's going to have more of me than she wants in her face. She'll want an 'app' to turn me *off*. Beside, we still have normal means of communication."

She smiled, giving him a quick hug of appreciation.

Then she reached over and put her slender hand on top of Dave's hand resting upon her phone.

"That transfers the biometric signature to you, David," she smiled. "Without that, it wouldn't have worked for you. And now no one can make it work *except* you."

"Oh, I completely forgot about that feature," Victor grunted, slapping his forehand with the back of his hand.

"Not to worry, dear," Ivanna reassured him. "You're entitled to forget a few things at 92."

"This is great, Victor," Dave said, sliding the small phone into his shirt pocket.

"Just hit the red button when you dial out or receive a call that you want to keep totally private," Victor concluded. "But now we'd best get moving. The longer we wait to call the police and FBI, the more suspicious it may look."

It took only fifteen minutes to locate the hidden Device using flashlights out in the dark woods, for the two of them to lift off the concealing branches, and then to carry it back to put safely into the rear of the van.

"It's all gassed up," Victor said, handing him the keys. "I have plenty of emergency gas in the garage and filled it before we left in the Ranger. If you don't use credit cards, sleep only a few hours now and then at the highway rest stops, and drive nonstop—you can be back to Oklahoma in just a couple days."

"And here's a few goodies for you to munch on," Ivanna smiled, handing him a large, filled paper bag. "I hope you like brownies, 'cause you've got a lot of them in there."

"They're delicious," Dave sincerely smiled, giving her a hug.

He turned to Victor, tears welling up in his eyes. "It's been... quite interesting, even fun!" he cheerfully said, gripping his elderly mentor's hand tightly.

"I know you will change the world," Victor solemnly stated, grabbing Dave up in a strong bear-hug. "Don't give up."

Embarrassed, Dave nodded and stepped into the opened door of the van.

Sliding into the driver's seat he started the engine, pulling quickly away down the lane through the overhanging trees. In a moment he was traveling quickly into the darkness.

In his rearview mirror he saw his two elderly friends standing arm-in-arm, illuminated in the light from their porch, waving good-bye.

"Go with God," he silently returned the sentiment, hoping for a moment there was such a friendly Entity.

The Device shifted in the back in its hastily-applied restraints, making a dull "thud" as it knocked against one of the walls of the van.

And you—he thought to himself, swinging out from the narrow lane onto the road. *Are you from God or from the Devil?*

He laughed at his own stupidity.

The Device came from something even worse—himself.

"Back to the old routine," he sighed, "trying to figure out the impossible."

As soon as he got to the next rest stop in the road he was going to use the tools he'd brought with him to bolt the Device solidly to the floor of the van.

That thing was not going to get away from him again.

He was going to guard it with his life.

It had already almost killed him once. He was pretty sure he wouldn't survive a second "incident".

That is, unless he could figure out a way to come back from the dead.

Chapter 9

<u>RESURRECTION</u>

Don't lie to me

You wicked, foul person

Claiming the right to Judge

Not only the living but the dead

When a corpse has only to rot

Secure in its underground vault

Its deeds all evaporated

Into an evil stink

Or enticing perfume...

Smell it if you dare!

The Luminary Chronicles, 9:57-58

The trip back to Oklahoma took Dave two days. It was around 1,700 miles. He only slept a few hours pulled over at rest stops on major highways. He obeyed the traffic laws and tried to be inconspicuous.

But he had the feeling the entire trip that he was being watched.

"Nothing I can do about it," he sighed over his shoulder to the Device in the back. "It's just you and me, buddy."

The Device did not answer him back.

"What, no reply?" Dave sharply interrogated the machine. "I thought you wuz *Magic!*"

Still no reply...

"And what am I going to do with you?" Dave mused as they approached Edmond on highway 35. It was the middle of the night. His body ached from the long ride. He just wanted to pull into a rest stop and go to sleep. But this was the best time to return home, concealed in darkness.

"If there are more terrorists around, they're sure to come looking for you," he continued to "chat" with the Device secured in the back of the van. "The FBI will probably also want to grab you once they figure out that Victor and I were at the scene of that supposed 'meteor' strike. And every nuclear physicist in the world would love to steal you from me to take you apart, atom by atom."

Where to take it? Where to hide the duplicate Device?

Then he had the answer...

"Brilliant!" he exclaimed to himself, blinking his weary eyes to try to stay awake as he cruised up I-35 at the posted speed limit of 60 mph. "I'm a genius!"

It was 2:00 in the morning when he pulled onto his street.

He stopped a block away from his house, inspecting the scene before proceeding. A couple street lights dimly lit the street. Cars were parked in driveways or by the sidewalks. His yellow Cavalier sat on the street in front of his house. No one was around, even at his house—where a brand new garage sat with a fresh coat of white paint.

Those contractors had come through for him. Perfect!

"The last place anyone will ever think to look for you," he whispered lovingly to the Device, "is right back where my prior setup was housed. They'll never think I'd be so stupid as to hide you there."

At least that was what he hoped. So he pulled up to his house, parked in the driveway, slipped out of the seat to open the unlocked garage door, climbed back into the black van, and eased the vehicle into the garage.

He ran to the front door, went in, foraged through his "lock and key drawer" in the kitchen, found the biggest lock he had, and ran back out to "snap" it shut on the garage door's side latch.

He staggered back into his house.

"Hey, Topper," he quietly called-out to the big green lizard sleeping on its branch, revealed by the dim light of the green night-light in its large cage. "Miss me?"

The lizard kept on sleeping, its eyes firmly closed. Apparently the reptile hadn't missed him all that much.

Dave took a quick look into his newly rebuilt empty bedroom, locked the door from within that led from it out to the garage with its precious cargo, returned to the living room and collapsed upon the old couch, immediately losing consciousness in his utter exhaustion.

The "ringing" of his landline phone jerked him awake.

He blearily looked at his wristwatch.

It was 6:30 in the morning. He'd had a whole four hours of sleep...ugh—way too little!

He groggily reached over to the nearby side table and picked up the receiver, thinking he needed at least ten more hours of undisturbed sleep.

"Davey?" said a familiar voice.

"Oh...hi Mom," he coughed, trying to clear his throat of accumulated phlegm.

"I've been calling and calling and getting nothing!" the small voice from the receiver loudly complained. "You didn't tell me when you would return and you don't carry your cellphone with you. I've been really worried about you. The News said there was a big meteor strike that hit the East Coast. You said you were going out there for your job search and I was afraid it killed you!"

"Hmmmm...?" he coughed again. "A...*meteor*, you say? Is that so? Must have missed that," he lied.

"Well, I'm just glad that you are ok," she cheerfully stated. "Will you be here to take me to church today or should I call a taxi cab?"

"What? Church? Uh...?"

Yes, sure enough, a glance at the day indicator on his watch told him it was Sunday morning.

Oh, hell...

"Uhm, right, Mom," he groaned to himself, levering his aching body up from his couch. "I'll be there by 10:30 to get you to the 11:00 worship service and..."

"No Bible study?" she interrupted him.

"Sorry, Mom," he apologized, the receiver still held to his ear as he stumbled up, every joint aching from his uncomfortably-brief time on the couch. "I just got in from the East Coast late last night and..."

"Oh," she said, "then don't bother, Davey. I must have waked you up. I'm so sorry! I can take a taxi."

"No, no," he said, realizing that he desperately wanted to get back to a normal routine as soon as possible. "It's no trouble. I can be there. In fact, I *want* to be there. I think singing those good old Gospel songs plus a long sermon is just what I need right now. That'll absolutely prove that I'm back in the real, boring, non-terrorist-fighting world."

"What?" she laughed. "You must have had a good trip. You sound really cheerful for once. Not so gloomy and pessimistic like you usually are around me. I *like* it."

"Well...thanks, Mom—and do you sound more cheery as well?"

"I am! I'm feeling oh so *much* better. I'll even drink some of that terrible strawberry Ensure that you like so much. By the way, can you pick some more up as you come into town? I'm all out."

"Oh, sure, no problem," he said, scratching at fierce itches from the sweaty clothes he'd been in now for two days straight. "Well, I've got to get going if I'm going to make it there on time, Mom. Gotta get cleaned up and check on my critters and..."

"Say hello to Topper for me! I like him much better than those creepy snakes of yours. Love you!"

"Love you too," he automatically answered, then..."—and I'm glad that you're feeling better."

"Yes, me too! See you in a bit," she happily replied, hanging up the line.

"Ok, then," he sighed, putting down the receiver.

He noticed that the message light on his phone recorder was blinking.

"Maybe I'd better check my messages," he mused, sitting on a chair and thumbing at the controls.

His caller I.D. displayed the phone numbers and identification of each of a long list of messages.

"Delete...delete...delete," he repeatedly said as he got rid of unknown, "anonymous", or unwanted identifications. Thank God for caller-I.D. Stops those damn spam calls...

"Oh, and here's Cat, better listen it," he said, seeing that his sister Catherine had left a message—punching it up to play.

"Dave, you've got to talk to Mom," he heard his sister's worried voice. "She's decided to stop her treatments. She says she's had it with the radiation burns and the chemotherapy side-effects. The doctor told us last visit that the metastases from her breast cancer are past the point of his being able to stop them—more rounds of treatment will just slow their progression. I guess she's got a point, not wanting to suffer any more from those horrible treatments. But without them the Doctor says she has only a few months at most, maybe just a few weeks. I don't think she should give up. You've to talk to her into restarting the therapies. There's always a chance. She's our *mother*. She can't *die!*"

Stunned, Dave sat in silence listening to his sister's voice quietly sobbing on the message machine.

"But...maybe I'm being too selfish," the message continued. "Anyway, I'm sorry to hit you with this bad news. I hope your job search at Yale went well. Love you."

He shakily hit the "delete" button.

"Yah...love you too," he whispered.

Maybe it wasn't so good after all being back in the "real" world back from his exhilarating Yale adventure.

The real world was *ugly*.

The ride to Sulphur was rough.

Usually the route from Oklahoma City towards Dallas, Texas was least-congested on a Sunday morning, but for some reason I-35 South was filled with traffic.

They were zooming along at the speed limit or better. Dave, traveling at the speed limit of 70 mph in the "slow" right lane, was overtaken and passed by many other cars.

Where were they all going?

It seemed like an exodus from a natural disaster.

Also, the sky was darkly overcast, threatening to burst open with a thunderstorm at any moment. The darkened road billboards slipped past like hypnotic suggestions.

"Might as well listen to NPR," Dave sighed, still thirty minutes out from the turn-off leading to the small town of Sulphur.

He turned on his radio, hitting the button pre-set to the local National Public Radio station.

"...that flattened several square miles of forest," the voice came out of Dave's car speakers. "The forest fires sparked by this heavenly occurrence are now largely under control. No injuries have been reported by this latest insult to the integrity of our precious planet. But it serves as a warning to us. The public has only a vague idea that

NASA routinely tracks any dangerous meteors or asteroids, and will give us advance notice of any potential threats. The reality, though, is far different. Astronomers are constantly discovering new threats that are aimed at the vicinity of Earth. But what they are able to detect are mostly large rocks or comets that are greater than 100 meters in diameter. Also, the ones we do detect are only a fraction of the potentially-dangerous ones that exist in our solar system. Many deadly rocks hit the earth with no warning, such as the *Green Mountain Meteor* last week. An asteroid hitting the earth is thought to have hastened the demise of the dinosaurs. In addition to comets or asteroids smashing into our planet, other extinction-level events are possible. These include wandering black holes, lethal cosmic gamma ray bursts, the debris from hyper-giant star explosions, dark nebulas, and even our own sun killing us with a *solar super-storm!* Yes, life on Earth is a fragile construct, protected only by our thin atmosphere and weak global magnetic field. We tend to think our planet is invulnerable, that life will just keep rolling along. But we *are* vulnerable. The human species could go the way of the dinosaurs. Just a slight shift in the cosmic balance and humanity could be extinct and..."

Dave shut off the radio.

Gripping the steering wheel tightly he shuddered.

"Enough talk about destruction and death!" he loudly exclaimed inside the car as he zoomed along, focusing on the heavy traffic around him. "Day-dreaming for just a second can cause *me* to end up crashed on the side of the road. I don't need a Cosmic Killer to wind up dead. I can do that all on my own."

He grimly continued driving onward, feeling more and more dispirited. Depression descended upon him like the dark, roiling clouds above.

The boost to his spirits from being with Victor and Ivanna was quickly wearing off. What had his expedition really accomplished? The mystery of his "malfunctioning" cold-fusion Device was even deeper than before. Bringing it back to Oklahoma with him—though it seemed like a good plan when he took it—put him squarely back in the "bullseye" of any number of deadly-serious organizations. He still didn't have a job. And now his mother wasn't just sick. She was dying.

But maybe his Mother had the right idea: just give up. Enjoy the moment. When all is said and done, what else do we really have than the transient pleasure of right now?

When he pulled into the parking lot of the local mega-shopping store outside of Sulphur, Dave was exhausted—both physically and mentally—to the point of trembling.

He just sat for a moment, getting his strength back.

"At least the weather's turning better," he muttered as he idly glanced upward upon exiting his yellow Cavalier. The dark clouds above were indeed breaking up. A bit of blue sky showed here and there.

"Whoa..." he gasped, putting his hands up to both sides of his head, trying to push back an abrupt *pounding headache.*

As he walked up to the sliding doors of the entranceway he experienced a severe bout of *vertigo.*

The whole world seemed to be spinning out of control around him...

—when the pavement seemed to *jump upwards*, almost knocking him off his feet!

—such that he staggered to the side and leaned against a wall, blinking as he tried to get his head back together.

"Jesus..." he groaned to himself, closing his eyes tightly as the wave of extreme vertigo passed. "I guess I should have eaten something before leaving...maybe I'll drink one of those Ensures from the store...yes, that's what I need...must be low blood sugar."

Inside the store he focused upon grabbing a cart and pushing it in front of him. Having the cart's guidance-bar in his hands helped steady his still-spinning head.

"Gotta get fresh lettuce," he muttered.

He rolled through the vegetable section, grabbing up heads of lettuce and fresh fruits for his lizards and tortoises.

"Need canned chopped potatoes, green beans, and corn for my critter's salads," he muttered to himself, glancing at his checklist that he kept in a small notepad he'd taken from his top shirt pocket.

He snatched those up as he rolled through the canned goods section.

"Oh, right," he nodded to himself, blearily ticking-off the canned goods on his list with a pen. "I also need Gut-C-Prime. I'm out of it. But I can grab that when I swing by to get the Ensure for Mom. They're both in the same pharmacy section."

"Gut-C-Prime" was a particular preparation of vitamin C he liked to take once a day. It claimed to be "24-hour immune support" that was non-acidic so as not to disturb his sensitive stomach. Also, it claimed to be time-released so it perfused through his body throughout the day, not just hitting him in one big blast. He felt healthier when he took it regularly—experiencing fewer bouts with everpresent viruses, plus a shorter recovery time if he did get sick.

"Now, where is it?" he mumbled to himself as he headed into the pharmaceutical section. "It should be right over here in the vitamin and herbals section that's..."

There was no such section!

There should be a whole wall of vitamin and herbal products right in front of him. Instead, there was only a magazine rack of "healthy living" publications.

"*Damn* it!" he exclaimed, aware that he'd made bad time getting to Sulphur and his Mother was impatiently waiting on him. "They must have moved the whole section. I...hey, Sir...can I ask you a question?"

A dark-skinned, middle-aged gentleman in a store uniform was crouched-down stocking shelves from opened cartons sitting on the floor.

"Me?" the man asked. An expression of surprise appeared on his wide, black-skinned face.

"Yes, Sir," Dave shrugged. "Do you happen to know where they moved the vitamins? I can't find them."

"Vitamins?" the man gulped then jumped abruptly to his feet, standing at rigid attention. "Boss, I don't know where they be—but I can call over a supervisor, she be right here!"

"Oh, don't bother," Dave sighed. "I don't have the time. I just thought you might know since you're stocking the shelves. I guess my immune system can go without 'support' for a few days."

"—oh, immune support, yes Boss!" the man nervously stated. "They be right over there, one isle over. It be there in isle number fourteen."

"Oh, great...thanks," Dave said, scooting around the isle in the direction indicated.

"Ah, right by the Ensure," Dave happily noted to himself, snatching up a couple six-packs of the energy drink. "Oh—and what's this?"

He picked up a small square container off a shelf labelled "OP-TIMMUNE."

"Hmmm, haven't heard of this before," he mused, quickly scanning its back label: *"—pro-retroviral DNA inserts for routine maintenance of optimal immune system balance. Adjusts macrophage distribution, antibody production, T-cell targeting, killer cell activity, lymphokine secretion, stem cell cycling rates, and..."*

"That's a laugh!" Dave snorted, starting to put it back on the shelf with its duplicate boxes, acutely recalling from the physiology and clinical immunology classes that he'd taken years in the past. "Nothing but a total scam could claim all of that."

Then something else caught his eye and he paused, reading a bit more of the back label: *"These statements have been evaluated by the American Food and Drug Administration (FDA) and the United Kingdom Medicines and Healthcare Products Regulatory Agency (MHRA). This product is approved for treating viral infections, Type I diabetes, cancer, rheumatic heart disease, autoimmune disorders, and..."*

"What the hell?" Dave whispered to himself. "It's approved by the FDA? And it's also approved by the MHRA? It must be some British product that just made it to the American market. I've never heard of this before. It must be brand new. But there's *no* way it could actually do all that it claims to..."

"Did you find what you needed, Boss?"

The black gentleman stood anxiously at the head of the isle he'd been stocking, peering at Dave expectantly.

"Uh...yes, I think I did—even better than what I was looking for...thank you very much."

Starting to move away Dave impulsively reached back and snatched up another of the square containers.

"Maybe Mom would like to take some of these also," he muttered again to himself. Indeed, though she hated taking "medicine", she loved to take anything that sounded "natural"—especially vitamins. And if this new stuff was "over-the-counter" approved, it at least must not be harmful. In fact, it might even have a strong "placebo" effect where people got better just because it sounded so amazing.

He rolled up to a checkout isle, loading onto its moving belt his Ensure, lettuce, fruit, canned goods, and the two Optimmune cartons.

He rolled his cart on forward, looking down for his reusable carry-bags but realizing he'd forgotten to bring them in with him from the car...

Damn vertigo!

He absently grabbed the two plastic bags handed to him by the clerk that were filled with his purchases and looked up to see...

"You!" both he and the lady clerk exclaimed at once.

"But you're dead!" they both again said at the exact same time.

"What, *I'm* dead?" they both again exclaimed in unison.

Involuntarily, Dave laughed at the absurdity and impossibility of what he now faced.

It was his wooziness. It had to be some sort of hallucination. It couldn't be *her*...

But it was.

There on the inside of her left wrist was that cute little *grinning turtle*—now not as bright as when he'd first seen it.

"I saw you die," she gasped at him as he stood there dumbfounded, her bright green eyes squinted in disbelief.

"You saw...*me*...die?" he repeated, totally confused.

"When you gave me that strange money I ran after you into the parking lot and saw your bub *explode*—with you inside! Your corpse was...awful...burned beyond recognition."

"Look, I don't know what you're talking about," Dave protested. His two plastic bags filled with groceries swung almost forgotten from his left hand. "Besides which, it was *you* that got killed in Ada at a restaurant. I saw the bullet go through your head. For God's sake, I was at your *funeral!*"

She looked at him in horror and bewilderment.

Then her expression hardened.

"I'm calling the manager," she coldly replied, grabbing up her stall-phone...

—as Dave glanced behind down the checkout isle to see running up to them *a short oriental man* clad in black!

"You!" Dave gasped, recognizing the man.

He seemed a lot younger—lacking the elderly terrorist's lined face and white hair—but it was undeniably him, lifting up a black pistol aimed straight at the clerk!

"Not again!" Dave yelled as he with his right hand he yanked up the plastic bag loaded with several heavy cans right into the side of the man's face!

The plastic broke and the cans *clattered* to the floor.

Clutching a profusely bleeding left cheek, the man staggered backward, stunned. He dropped a black pistol that bounced on the floor. Seemingly in slow motion, Dave caught the gun, shoving it into his remaining grocery bag.

"Come on!" Dave yelled at the startled clerk.

He grabbed her arm with his free right hand and yanked her out of her cubicle, rapidly dragging her towards the exit.

"You hit a Keeper!" she gasped in horror. "What are you doing to me? Let me go!"

"I'm trying to save your life—*again!*" he grated, dragging her resisting body through the exit. "If you want to live, stop struggling!"

"I'm not going anywhere with you. Turn me loose!"

"Not this time," he ordered her. "I don't know what's happening either. But I'm *not* letting go of you until I'm sure that you're good and safe."

They were out in the parking lot now, Dave trotting with her in tow. They ran up to the parking spot where he'd gotten out of his yellow Cavalier just a few minutes before.

But it was gone.

"What?" Dave gasped, hearing yelling from behind him as others exited the store in hot pursuit.

What was he going to do?

"Where's *your* car?" Dave desperately asked the girl.

"My *what?*" she grimaced, still trying to pull away. "You mean my bub? It's right over there..."

She pointed to a four-by-four-foot contraption with large black rubbery wheels, supporting on its frame a transparent half-bubble dome.

"What the hell is that?" Dave gasped.

"It's my bub, you idiot. Let go of me!"

Dave shoved her over to it, slamming her in his haste against its side. She slumped against its rounded surface as he reached with his now-freed hand into the shopping bag held in his other hand, bringing out the black pistol.

He turned and waved it at the fast-approaching people.

"Get back!" he yelled at them. "Get back or I'll shoot!"

They continued to advance.

He pointed the stubby gun at the side of the long rectangular building of the Megamart and pulled the trigger.

With a large "CLANG!" the part of the wall he'd aimed at smashed-inward, revealing shocked shoppers scrambling away inside to escape sudden destruction.

"Jesus Christ!" he gasped, looking down at the weapon. It had a small knob on top turned to a position marked by two stars. There were also positions marked as 1, 3, 4, and 5 stars.

"What kind of gun *is* this?" he marveled, noting that the crowd had fallen back, wary of his weapon.

But there was no reply from the girl, who was still cringing away from him.

"Get in!" he ordered her, waving the gun threateningly up in the air.

She placed her palm against a square patch on the side of the door which slid to the side. Then she ducked into the transparent bubble, slipping in to sit behind a plastic wheel on the *right* front side of the vehicle.

Dave, still waving the gun, slid in beside her on the left side as the door closed beside him.

"Get going!" he ordered, pushing frantically at her shoulder with his gun.

Shakily, she did as ordered.

Within seconds they pulled out onto a main street.

There they rolled along at what must have been a leisurely fifteen miles per hour.

"Can't this thing go any faster?" Dave said, now panting heavily with panic, just wanting to get away.

"Why would I want to go faster?" She angrily retorted. "And where are we going, anyway?"

He thought feverishly—what sort of toy car was this thing? But that didn't matter. Somehow, the terrorist had survived being shot twice and his neck broken, dyed his hair black, put makeup on his face in order to appear younger, and was still pursing the girl and Dave. But...how could the girl be alive? Was this real? Or was he still slumped against the outer wall of the grocery store, experiencing a feverish hallucination?

Well, that solved one problem, didn't it? The severe depression was probably just due to a mounting viral infection. He must be sick. He was just having a bad fevered dream! Maybe he was still in his bed back in Edmond...

"Let me out!"

A hard fist slammed into his shoulder, making him wince in pain.

He lifted the gun to point at her side.

"Stop that! Watch what you're doing! Drive this thing!"

This couldn't be a dream. That damn girl with the turtle tattoo was too real and annoying! But then again, inside of a nightmare everything seems perfectly real...?

"Look, just let me go," she pleaded again beside him. "I haven't done anything to you. Why are you trying to kidnap me? Who are you, anyway?"

"Shut up!" he snapped at her. "I don't know if you're a figment of my imagination or not, but I'll treat all of this as if it's real. We're going to my Mom's house. She'll help us sort this stuff out. Once I'm sure that you're safe, I'll let you go. I promise! I'm not trying to hurt you."

"So you're delusional? You admit it? Well that explains a lot. Stealing the Keeper's gun and threatening me with it—was to keep me 'safe'?" she indignantly stated, steering the vehicle along the empty road.

"Yes!" he grimly replied. "And I'm not crazy. Well, maybe I'm fe-verish—but I know what I'm doing. So you just drive on down to West 12th Street. You know where that is, right?"

"Of course I know where that is," she snorted. "It's near the en-trance to the Park. Everyone knows it! Other than Broadway it's one of the main streets of Sulphur. So who are you? Where are you from? And where are we going on 12th Street?"

"That's where my mother lives," he sighed, feeling extremely ex-posed in the wimpy, slow, transparent vehicle. "I come here from Edmond each Sunday to take her to church. And where did you get this weird car, anyway? And why is the steering wheel on the right side instead of the left? How can you drive a toy car like this on a regular street?"

She looked over at him like he was definitely crazy.

"They're going to catch us in minute or two, you know," she pleaded with him. "Just let me stop my bub and get out. You can take the bub and do whatever you want with it. Just don't involve me an-ymore in whatever you're..."

"Uh oh," Dave groaned, now peering behind to see several other "bubs" bouncing along on their oversized tires in slow pursuit, red lights flashing from beacons on their tops.

"There's 12th Street," he pointed. "Turn there!"

She made a right turn onto the side street.

"Owwww!" she exclaimed, jerking up her left arm.

The Turtle Tattoo on her wrist was *glowing*.

"My arm, my arm!" she moaned. "It's *burning!*"

She slammed outward the door of the bub on her side and in des-peration to escape whatever was scorching her arm *jumped* from the moving vehicle!

Since they were only going fifteen miles an hour, she just rolled a couple times back out of sight as Dave leapt past the wheel out after her, still clutching his pistol and shopping bag.

He bounced on the grass, rolled once, dropped his pistol, and then grabbed at the slender body of the girl...

—just as a loud EXPLOSION rocked the whole neighborhood!

Dave managed to cover the girl's body with his own, protecting her from the flaming fragments raining down from her destroyed vehicle.

"Jesus Christ!" Dave gasped. "Did they fire a *missile* as us?"

Fortunately, neither he nor the girl was badly hurt. She was breathing steadily though unconscious. She'd apparently been knocked out either by her fall from the vehicle or the subsequent explosion.

"I've just about *had* it with things blowing up around me," Dave grated. He grabbed up the gun and shopping bag in one hand. Then he jerked-up the stunned girl and dragged her away with him into the surrounding bushes.

At just that moment the dark skies above opened up and a deluge of pouring rain slammed down. It was cold and pounding—but hid them from any pursuers.

"I'm not too far from my Mom's house," Dave mused as he dragged the girl deeper into the looming forest. "But surely whoever's after us will figure that out soon enough. Maybe we'll just hide in the Park until I get things sorted out. Yes, that's a plan."

As a boy he'd spent lots of time in the Chickasaw National Recreation Area, mountain-biking down its trails, zipping through the camping grounds, and along its bubbling streams.

He knew it like the back of his hand—and knew just where to hide so that no one would find them.

"Come on, girl," he softly said to her unconscious body, slinging her small frame easily up over his left shoulder, "let's get out of the rain."

She regained consciousness in a hard, small, constrained space—discovering that her hands and feet were securely tied!

"Help! Help!" she screamed, struggling to free herself.

Her kidnapper casually walked in through an opened doorway.

"Yell all you want," he told her. "It won't do you any good. No one can hear you out here. I had to tear the sleeves off my shirt to tie you up with, so I'd appreciate you not struggling too hard against them. God, now I'm sleeveless, all because of you. *Jesus Christ* you're a lot of trouble."

He was definitely insane. She was in the hands of not just a terrorist, but a religious nut.

"Where...where are we?" she angrily demanded, still struggling to loosen her hands and feet.

"We're in one of the toilet facilities of Rock Creek Park," he replied, sitting down on the floor beside her, his back to the stone wall. "It is way out at the back end of the encampment sites, in the roped-off area that's rarely used. But I know it well. I've stopped by here many times when I was mountain biking here as a kid. I figured out how to jimmy open the locked door. It's peaceful here."

"Why am I tied up?" she pouted, stopping her struggling. "What do you want with me? Are you going to *rape* me?"

If this monster tried that, she might yet have a chance to escape. His guard would be down.

He sighed, seemingly regretfully.

"I'm not sure yet," he softly replied against the continued pounding of the rain outside. "No, I'm joking! I assure you I won't hurt you. I'm a Christian—or, I was, I suppose, before I got sick of the diluted version I grew up with—but I still believe in the teachings of Jesus. He told us to rise above immediate circumstances to a loftier perspective. So that's what I'm trying to do with..."

"Then let me go!" she shouted, jerking-about on the floor vainly trying to loosen her bonds. "It doesn't matter what strange religious beliefs you have. You're still breaking the law. You can't just kidnap people. Let me *go!*"

"Well, it appears I *can* keep you tied up," he serenely replied. "And as to letting you go...well, all in good time. Are you hungry? I've still got food with me that I was buying at your store...want some fruit? It's fresh and juicy. Or maybe you'd like a bottle of Ensure? Also I've got a nice head of lettuce, very crunchy. I could make you a salad."

"I'm not hungry," she peevishly spat at him. She was immobile. She had to find some way to get loose. "But..." she added more quietly. "I *do* have to *piss*..."

"Ok, then," he shrugged. "We're certainly in the right place for that activity."

"Untie my hands," she ordered him.

"Sorry, can't do that," he replied. "But we'll do the next best thing."

He jumped up, lifted her, and carried her bodily over to an open toilet. He set her down solidly upon it, undid her pants, and in one smooth move slipped them and her underwear to her feet.

"There you go," he said, seemingly politely turning his back.

She was silent.

"Well?" he said, his back still turned.

"I guess I don't have to after all," she quietly admitted, her ploy to get free having dismally failed.

"Ok, then," he said, now grinning down at her in the gloom of the deserted room. He grabbed the clothing on the floor and lifted them back up her legs to secure them around her waist.

"Now I've got questions for you, Sally," he continued. He sat down with a "thump" on the stone floor as she continued to wobbly sit poised on the toilet seat. "I need answers. So please don't fight me. The sooner we get this sorted out the sooner I'll let you go free."

"How do you know *my* name?" she angrily demanded. Was he a stalker? Had he been following her for some time now? That would explain a lot.

"Well, for one thing it's on your name tag," he shrugged, looking at the big wide tag conspicuously displayed on her shirt.

"And what else?" she suspiciously asked.

"Well, I've met your mother, and she told me..."

"My *mother?*" she gasped.

"Yes, Samantha Smith, that's her name, right?"

"How do you know her?"

"She's a friend of my own mother," he quietly replied. "They met at a clinic where they were both undergoing radiological cancer therapy."

"*Cancer* therapy?" Sally repeated disbelievingly, her eyes widening. What was wrong with him? He talked like he was from some other world!

"Yes. And how's your mother doing now?" he politely asked.

"Why do you ask?" she carefully replied, trying to draw him out.

"Well, when I first saw you at the grocery store, you mentioned you'd gotten the turtle tattoo to cheer up your Mom since she was going to get an operation."

"So?"

"So did it go ok, the operation? I assume the radiation therapy worked and they were able to operate on her brain tumor. Other than a few words at your...well, at a ceremony I attended with her and my own mother...I've not visited with her at length to know how she's doing."

She just stared at him silently, unwilling to acknowledge his absolute, total insanity. What was happening? Who *was* he?

"Well?" he insisted.

"She's dead," Sally curtly replied.

It looked like she'd slapped him in his face. He seemed genuinely shocked.

He sucked in his breath, grimacing. "Oh, I'm so sorry. The operation wasn't successful? She seemed to be doing well and I..."

"She never got the operation," Sally stated blankly. "Rather than get the implant, she committed *suicide*. You want me to spell it out for you? Why are you doing this to me? What do you have against me? I never did anything to you! Now you're bringing up my public shame?"

He looked at her with a peculiar expression in his eyes: part puzzlement and part dawning awareness.

"Are you kidding me, Sally? I'm trying to be your friend," he answered, apparently sincerely. "I know that's hard for you to believe—since I've abducted you and tied you up—but it's true that..."

"She's *dead!*" she yelled at him, straining against the bonds holding her hands together behind her back. She had to get away from this crazy criminal.

"But...that doesn't make any sense," he said, shaking his head in denial.

He truly looked like he didn't know the impact of his cutting remarks. Maybe he didn't? Was he really clueless?

Ok. Maybe she'd humor him, just for a bit to let down his guard.

"She didn't want to become a mindless servant of the State," she listlessly explained. "She was slated for reconstruction work in the

African wastelands and decided not to do it. She didn't want her free will suppressed by the neural implant. So she just put her head into the oven with the gas turned high and the lighter mechanism overridden. I came home to find her dead body. She left me a note saying she was sorry. But she didn't have to kill herself! Everyone that has to get an implant says it isn't so bad...it isn't so bad...at all..."

She started sobbing, pent-up emotions pouring out of her.

"I...I think," Dave quietly started to respond, but then stopped. "No, I don't know *what* to think. What you said just now makes no sense. In fact, it's..."

He nodded grimly. Through her tears, Sally saw him narrow his eyes as if deciding on a course of action.

"Sally, I looked in the wallet that I found in your pants while you were unconscious," he pointedly interrogated her. "And I found this 'money'."

In the dim light he held up a hundred dollar bill in front of her face.

"So?" she angrily retorted. "That's the same as what I gave you in exchange for the 2K bill you should have given me when you started all this madness. Your bill was nineteen hundred and I gave you back a hundred dollar bill in change for your 2K. But instead, you gave me that twenty-dollar bill with a 'Jackson' picture on it. Plus it said 'in God we trust' when you know full well organized religion is forbidden. What you're holding is *regular* money. *You're* the one with the 'funny' money!"

"Where is *Benjamin Franklin's* picture?" he insisted.

"Who?"

She struggled to regain control of her emotions, straightening up her twisted mouth.

"Benjamin Franklin!" he urgently insisted. "His picture should be right here instead of the Queen of England."

"You mean...the inventor?" she asked, trying to understand his twisted logic. "Are you talking about the guy who made the lightning rod and...?"

"Yes, him! Benjamin Franklin, one of the Founding Fathers of the United States of America! He helped to draft the Declaration of Independence. He was one of the people who signed the Constitution.

And consequently, his picture was put on the hundred dollar bill—
that Benjamin Franklin!"

She grimaced at him in disgust. Either he was the stupidest person she'd ever talked to or raised in some parallel universe.

"What the hell are you talking about?" Sally grunted, pulling hard
against her hand constraints. "You really are delusional, aren't you?
The United States never broke away from England. Back in the 18th
century Franklin and his other traitorous subversives *hung together!*
Her Majesty is still our sovereign, holding together the British Empire
throughout the world. Without her we'd be ground up by the Spanish
Empire or swamped by the African hordes. She keeps us safe. That's
why she's on the bill, not this Franklin person."

He was silent. Only the sound of the pounding rain outside broke
the quiet.

"But, t-then...who...w-what's this 'implant' thing?" he weakly
stammered.

"We all have to do our duty to the State," she grated indignantly at
him. "How is it that you don't know this? We all do our assigned jobs.
My mother's time was finished as a homebuilder. So she was assigned another job where she'd need to have an implant. But she was
wrong to reject it. She had a *duty* to do, whether she liked it or not.
What she did brought *shame* on not just her memory but me as well."

She was cold, totally drenched in rain, covered in mud—and angry. And it didn't help a bit that this terrorist was looking at her like
she was an alien from outer space.

"So you *like* your job?" he hesitantly asked.

"Of course I do," she said in utter disbelief at his question. "I service people. I *help* them."

"Well, yes, but doesn't it get boring—doing the same thing over
and over at that grocery store checkout stand?"

"That's just my service-half," she shrilly continued, yanking yet
again against the bonds holding her feet together. "My creative half is
spent attempting program code evolution. That's what I got my advanced degree in. The State determined my aptitudes and helped me
best use my talents for the good of everyone. I have a *great* life and
you're trying to *destroy* it! The Keepers will think I'm somehow
complicit with your subversion—especially after what my mother did.

You're just dragging me down with you. They'll kill me too if you don't let me go soon."

"I'm a subversive?"

"Well aren't you?" she said in disbelief at his feigned innocence. "That's what they said when your bub supposedly killed you. They said you were trying to sow discord with your fake money. They said you were trying to get us to succeed from the Empire. The Keepers stopped you by blowing up your bub. It was on all the holocasts. You can't expect any mercy for trying to bring down the State. You're an enemy of all of us good citizens. You're a *damned terrorist!*"

"Oh, Jesus...I can't do anything good, can I? I as much a failure as a person, here in some insane fantasy, as I am at being a scientist."

"You're a scientist?"

She saw he hadn't heard her question. Indeed, he had a shocked expression on his face, like he was as confused as she.

"I think...maybe...we should just sit here for a while without talking," he softly said, putting his head down into his hands.

"Fine with me," she snapped at him, still tottering on the open toilet.

So he wanted to "think things over" did he? The moment she got her hands loose she was going to break his neck!

She kept working at the cloth strips binding her hands behind her back. They were loosening.

"Oh, my God," Dave whispered after a while as he leaned back against the cold rock wall. "I must be...but it can't be...can it?"

He was beginning to accept the incredible truth.

This wasn't his world. It must be some sort of a...*parallel dimension.*

How? Why? He had no idea.

But he was here—and people were trying to kill him. And it wasn't just him in danger. It was also the *Girl with the Turtle Tattoo.*

"They'll get you," she growled, startling him out of his revere. "I don't know how you escaped that exploding bub and substituted someone else to serve as your unidentifiable corpse. But you better believe that they'll stop you, you evil subversive. Help! Help! Someone please *help me!*" she screamed.

Then she abruptly *sprang* up off the toilet seat, her hands free—to knock him sideways onto the hard rock floor and leap astride him!

She was a *demon*, raining down heavy blows on his face, neck, and chest!

With a violent jerk he managed to throw her off of him, jump on top of her, and pin her arms firmly down upon the cold rock floor.

"Get off me!" she now shrieked up at him.

Struggling, she kept on screaming and yelling incoherently.

Sniffing away a trickle of fresh blood running from his bruised nose, he waited patiently for her to finally quiet—exhausted by her own frantic efforts to escape.

"Sally...please...listen to me," he softly spoke down at her as he continued to sit firmly astride her waist, holding her arms down, his face just inches away from hers. "I don't think I'm the target of your 'Keepers'...I think it's *you*."

"That's ridiculous," she snorted up at him.

"Is it?" he insisted. "They could have shot me any time they wished as I gathered my purchases at your store. But that Keeper didn't come up until *you* recognized me. I think it's *you* that they're now after."

"I'm a loyal citizen!"

"But you're under suspicion, aren't you?"

"I turned in your strange money!"

"Did you?"

"Yes!"

"Then why did you, as you said, run after me to try to catch me in the parking lot the first time I encountered you?"

"Why...to find out...to stop you..."

"I think that if you were really such a 'loyal citizen' you would have just rung an alarm bell or gone straight to a supervisor, not gone after me. But you did come after me, perhaps trying to keep me from getting into trouble in the first place?"

"But...I was feverish," she complained, shaking her head slowly back and forth. "Just before you came up to my station that time...I got real dizzy...I explained this afterward to the Keepers. I wasn't thinking straight—just like today! The exact same thing happened today. My mind was all confused..."

Her voice trailed off.

Now she went limp beneath Dave, no longer struggling.

The rain pounded harder outside, permeating the damp interior with its persistent "thumping" on the tin roof of the structure.

"Alright," she shakily admitted. "So maybe I did try to help you. If I gave you back your funny money and got the right bills back from you, then maybe you'd not get into trouble. You didn't look like a bad person—actually kind of cute for an older guy—what with all that hair on your head and face. Only Elite men are allowed to have facial hair, so I thought it best to be polite to you so that..."

Dave felt a bit giddy. She *liked* him—somewhat, a little bit, maybe?

"And what will they do to you now that you've gone off with this possible 'subversive'?" he interrupted her, now dead-serious.

She sucked in a ragged breath.

"The Peacekeepers," she stated in a low, weak voice, "will summarily *execute* me."

"Like they tried to do with your 'bub'?"

She now nodded grimly.

"Yes," she whispered. "That had to be a Peace Keeper laser trained on us—torching our power supply. It must have activated the pigments in my tattoo, burning my arm, giving us a few seconds warning."

"So..." Dave gently suggested. "Can I let you up now?"

She nodded in apparent defeat.

"And then can we, together, try to figure a way out of this mess?" he asked as he warily slid off her prone body.

"There's no escape from the Peace Keepers," she dully stated as she slowly sat up, now seeming to accept her terrible fate. "We might as well just turn ourselves in. At least then they may give us a mercifully quick execution. Otherwise we'll be given implants and lifetime sentences working in the rare minerals mines in Africa...that'd be hell."

"I think I may know a way out," he said as he started untying her feet.

She clutched her arms around her chest, her head turned down dejectedly—her damp, long brown-red hair hanging limply over her face.

"Well, so far you've brought me nothing but trouble," she dejectedly shrugged. "I guess you can't hurt me much worse than you already have. So what's your plan?"

"Well, first of all my name is Dave King—and I've a story to tell you that you're going to find just as unbelievable as I did yours."

"Go on."

Dave crept through the thick woods at the back of the Megamart, the "everything-buyable" establishment that Sally had worked happily at until that very morning.

Dave was grateful she was now helping him in his desperate attempt to escape. But he also felt guilty he was trying to take her from the very place she'd called home for her whole life.

The rain had decreased in intensity, but was still sprinkling-down steadily. The clouds were dark above them.

"Hey, what you folks doin'?"

It was the same black gentleman that Dave had asked about the vitamins earlier that day. He was outside dumping filled green bags into a large trash bin.

"Oh, I am so sorry," he hastily changed his tone, seeing coming out of the gloom two white people. "I thought you wuz some slummers come foragin' for food. Please don't report me for sassin' you. Please! I gotta support my family!"

"Hey Kyle, it's me, Sally," she hastily reassured him.

"Oh..." he sighed, putting a hand to his chest. "You shore did give me a start there, Miss Sally. But—isn't that the fella that's been on all the holocasts, who talked to me in the store?" he fearfully said, pulling backward.

"Yes, Kyle, it is," she whispered as she slid up beside him with Dave in tow behind her. "We're in big trouble. The Keepers are after us. We need help. We promise we won't get you into any trouble or..."

"Oh, Miss Sally—you is the only one here who's ever been nice to me, a low-caste store-slave," he quickly replied. "Tell me how I kin help you."

She gave him a quick hug.

"This is Dave," she quickly introduced him. "We need a set of scrubber's outfits, the kind with the hoods."

"Ah gots them handy," he nodded. "You jist wait here a sec' and I'll be rat back."

As he keyed in the entry code and went into the back exit of the store, Dave whispered to her as they crouched beside the large trash bin: "You still have *slavery?*" He couldn't believe it.

She shrugged, grimacing. "What do you mean, 'still'? We're *all* slaves, aren't we? Some just live better than others. But the State tells everyone what to do."

"It's not right for anyone to be a slave."

"Yes, that's true," she sighed. "But what with the Spanish Empire trying to destroy us—enemies within and without—and the hordes coming up from the South...everyone has to know and stay in their place."

Cold, wet, and shivering, Dave nodded grimly.

"So it's a police state, then?" he gently asked.

"It's all I've ever known," she replied. "It's all anyone's ever known. How could there be anything different? It's either strict order or anarchy. Here in the Empire I've at least got an approved job, a career, and stability. In the badlands it's everyone for themselves. There's no in-between."

"So they tell you," he gently tried to shift her viewpoint.

"There's never been anything else," she protested. "I still think you're totally insane—there can't be another world just inches away from this one! But I've got no choice but share your delusions and..."

"Wait, I hear someone."

It was Kyle, furtively coming out the back exit—handing them both big heavy coveralls.

"I gots these from the storage room," he said. "I gotta go right back in or the camera's will see me off-duty. Got me more trash here, so it's ok I'm out." He lifted the lid and tossed in a bag. "I leave the lid unlocked, in case you need to duck into it to hide. Good luck to you! And may The Great Spirit be with you, hear me?"

"Thank you Kyle," she whispered back, grabbing his big hand to squeeze it tightly. "I may be going away—but I hope to return some-day. Please stay safe."

He grinned at her.

"Ah knows how to play it safe, Miss Sally," he softly replied. "Ah does it every day."

Then he was gone.

Dave hurriedly put on the thick coveralls, helping Sally into hers. They both brought up the protective hoods to shield them from the now increasingly thick rain while also concealing their identities from the cameras abundantly situated at the front of the store.

Dave tucked the plastic bag containing his purchases and gun into the remaining parts of his wet shirt.

Then he quietly lifted up the lid of the trash bin, pulling out two large waste bags, handing one to Sally. He snapped the lock closed to make sure Kyle wouldn't get into any trouble.

Then, slinging the trash bag over his back, Dave led Sally with her own trash bag as they slowly walked around the far end of the large building. Then he took a deep breath and continued on out into the large parking lot.

"It was—over there," Dave whispered, pointing furtively.

Yes, he always parked in the same spot out on the further edge of the lot whenever he came to do his quick shopping before going to his Mom's house. He knew exactly where his yellow Cavalier *should* be.

"This is the closest we're ever going to get to where I came from," Dave said, dropping the trash bag then stepping out of his coveralls into the pouring rain as Sally did the same.

He tightly clutched to his chest the plastic bag of groceries he'd tried to purchase that morning.

At the main entrance, a SIREN suddenly started a *screeching wail* that cut-through the storm.

"Let's get close," he said, grabbing the girl up in a bear hug.

She grimaced at him as she was mashed against the cold metal of the gun in his grocery bag.

But in turn, she slipped her thin arms around the back of his neck and clasped him tightly.

"Don't move!" a shout came from a black-clad, short oriental man running towards them. Dave vaguely noted the *jagged fresh wound* now running along the left side of his face...

—as the world started whirling around Dave's head...

—and he and Sally *dropped about a foot* onto hard pavement!

Above them, the sky was now clear and blue. In this reality, the storms had moved on past.

And right there beside them now sat Dave's faithful, yellow Cavalier *car*.

No "bubs" in sight!

"We made it..." Dave gulped in profound relief, getting his footing beneath him. "Welcome to my world."

With a grunt Sally shoved the hugging Dave off her.

"You've got a *lot* more explaining to do," she huffed angrily, but was obviously amazed at what she was seeing, peering intently around her.

No Keepers were trying to grab or kill them.

A scattering of brightly colored, regular cars glittered all over the parking lot.

Dave walked around to the *right* hand passenger car door to chivalrously open it for her.

"Let's go to church, my lady," he said, giddy with relief at having escaped the other dimension.

Marveling at the big, heavy vehicle, Sally slid her mud-encrusted, drenched body onto the smooth seat.

"My Mom's going to be *so* surprised," Dave sighed, walking back to the left side of the car to slide his own weary, bedraggled body into the driver's seat. "She always wanted me to have a girlfriend."

"I'm *not* your girlfriend!" she angrily retorted.

"Then what are you? What am I going to tell my Mom?"

"I'm someone else," she defiantly ordered him. "*You* figure it out!"

Dave's Mother looked like she was going to drop dead from shock right there in the doorway of her house!

Her mouth was hanging open, her nearly-bald head was swinging from side to side, and the lines on her forehead above her widely-stretched eyes were bunched up in a pile.

"S-Sally..." she gasped. "Is it...*you?* Your Mother showed me all your pictures—why, there's even that cute little Turtle Tattoo right there on your wrist!"

"No, Mom," Dave hastily lied, leading in the bedraggled girl by her thin hand. If he couldn't convince his mother about Sally, he couldn't fool anyone.   The story had to be believable. "This is...uhm...Sally's *second cousin*, who lives here by herself in Sulphur. I met her in the grocery store today and invited her to go with us to church. Isn't that nice?"

Dave was still amazed at everything that'd happened. Apparently time moved differently in the two Dimensions. Even though he spent the entire night in Sally's world, only a few minutes had passed back here in his reality.

"But...you look exactly like the poor, murdered Sally, complete with the same tattoos!" Jean gasped again, incredulously looking the girl up and down.

"Hello, Mrs. King," Sally meekly greeted Dave's mother. "I'm sorry if I startled you. I...uhmmm...well...I followed my second cousin on the vidnet. And I—well—I idolized her and tried to look like her, with the same hair style, and even getting the same body art, so..."

"Vidnet?" Jean frowned.

"She means 'facebook'!" Dave quickly added.

The both of them stood there in the doorway covered in dirt, their clothes torn, soaked-through with rain. Plus Dave was acutely aware of the bruises on his face and the trickle of blood from his nose.

"Well come in, come in!" Jean encouraged them. "But you both look terrible. What happened?" she stated, alarmed.

"We encountered a little accident, I'm afraid," he hurriedly continued as he led Sally into the house. "Not to worry, Mom. On the way here someone had some trouble on the road that..."

"Their bub had a flat tire," Sally tried to helpfully offer.

"Their 'bub'?"

"She means their *car*, of course! Heh!" Dave forced a laugh. "She has some strange terms. It's her...uhmmmm...*French* background!"

"You have French parents?"

"Oh...they've passed on," Sally replied. "But I had a scholarship in school for a summer to study in the French Empire...and that's when I learned..."

"—France! She means *France!*" Dave hastily interjected. "But anyway, Mom, do you happen to have any clothes that might fit Sal...I mean Linda! Yes, that's her name—*Linda!* Linda...uhmmm...."

"—Powers!" Sally concluded, glaring at Dave. "*Linda Powers,* so glad to meet you, Mrs. King," she politely continued, primly holding out her hand for the woman to shake. "Your son has told me so much about you."

Dave grimaced, knowing she was referring to the last few minutes in the car of hasty descriptions. She was going to blow the whole illusion!

"Davey, you look like you've been in a fight!" Jean gaped at him, grabbing his head in both her thin hands.

"Uh...well..."

"The driver of that bub—I man 'car'—thought we were trying to rob him and hit Dave before he realized we were just there helping him," Sally invented. "But then they were very nice."

"How awful!" Jean exclaimed. "Are you hurt, Davey?"

Dave glared over at Sally. "It was a lucky punch. 'He' didn't hurt me that much. I'm fine."

"Oh my," Jean shook her head sadly, turning away from Dave. "It's just like that old saying: 'No good deed goes unpunished'. Well you just go clean yourself up, Dave."

"And what about my...girlfriend?"

She glared at him but said nothing.

"Well, you know, come to think of it, I have some clothes that might fit Linda perfectly," Jean smiled uncertainly. "Catherine was about her size before she got married, moved away, and had her kids. She's put on a lot of weight since then though, so she won't be wearing her high school clothes again. I've got her old clothes packed away in her old bedroom. I'll go get them. The bathroom is in that side hallway, Linda. So you just go start cleaning up and I'll knock on the door when I find the clothes. Take a quick shower if you'd like. We can still make it to the worship service, I think."

Sally gratefully wobbled down the indicated hallway. She looked as beat up and exhausted as Dave felt.

"Where did you say you found this Linda?" Jean suddenly grinned at her son. "I like her! I was *so* disappointed when you got that poor Sally girl murdered trying to hook up with her at that restaurant where she worked. I thought you two weird kids might have made a nice couple."

Dave gulped. "It's a long story, Mom...and I didn't kill anyone. It was that terrorist, remember? Can I please use the spare bathroom out in the garage to clean up?"

"Why, of course, Davey," she smiled, readily falling back into a familiar motherly mode. "I'll bring you your Dad's old clothes to put on. You'll look quite handsome in one of his old suits. It'll be a bit loose, but no one will notice."

"Thanks, Mom," he weakly smiled back, suddenly feeling exhausted and woozy. Plus, his face was aching something terrible. Sally was a much better fighter than he'd let on. "I'll try to be quick."

"It's going to be a great Sunday," she grinned widely. "My son and his girlfriend are going to Church with me," she chortled, "—what could be better? And I've even got my old energy back. I'm going to be hungry as a wolf at lunch!"

Dave sat his grimy, dirt-encrusted shopping bag on the kitchen table as he stumbled past, taking care to slip out the gun first.

"Your Ensure is in there," he wearily sighed. "Plus, there are some new vitamins I got for you. You might try one of them, if you want."

He wasn't thinking. He was too exhausted and tired. He should have been more careful. But all he wanted at the moment was to get cleaned up.

"I will do that right now, Davey. Thank you so much. You're such a considerate son. I really do appreciate everything you do for me. I hope it wasn't too much of a bother to stop by the store for them?"

"Oh...no problem," Dave gulped, weakly waving back to her, dragging his exhausted, bruised body out to the garage. "No trouble at all," he lied.

Sally saw in the mirror that she'd cleaned up real good.

She still had a sour, strained expression on her face—but dressed in a flowery print blouse and a clean pair of yellow slacks she decided that she looked pretty.   Her newly-washed and blow-dried hair fluffed-out around her head and shoulders. Her tattoos were all neatly covered-over by long sleeves.

She felt like a new person, emerging from a nightmare into a comfortable home. It'd been a long while since she'd felt so relaxed. Sally noted that there were no surveillance cameras sitting conspicuously in the corners of the rooms next to the ceilings.

Maybe this new Dimension wouldn't be so bad after all.

"Now don't you look nice," Jean enthused, taking the pile of stained, wet clothes from her hands. "I'll just stick these in the washer and we'll have them nice and clean for you by this afternoon."

"Thank you, Mrs. King," Sally replied.

"Oh, no need to be so formal," Jean laughed, puttering about the kitchen, pulling out of the oven freshly-baked cupcakes. "Please call me 'Jean.'"

"Thank you...Jean," Sally dutifully replied, sitting down at the kitchen table. "Those sure smell good. What are they?" she said.

"They're cupcakes," Jean laughed, reaching for one and peeling the paper down at its sides before handing it over to Jean. "Surely you've eaten cupcakes before?"

"No, I haven't," Sally said, biting into one tentatively—and then smacking her lips in delight. "They are delicious!"

"Oh, and do have some milk or OJ," Jean happily directed, pointing to glasses and the cartons sitting on the table.

She didn't know what was this "OJ" but poured some out into her glass anyway. She recognized it as juice squeezed from oranges. This was a rare treat, in her world restricted to Elites.

Just then Dave walked into the room. He was clad in what Sally recalled from her conversation with Jean was his Dad's old brown suit. It didn't fit badly. He had a green tie around his neck, making him look formal—even handsome...for an older guy.

"Have a cupcake," Jean cheerfully invited him, motioning for him to sit down beside Sally.

"You baked?" Dave said. "You must be feeling a lot better—you haven't cooked for months."

"Oh, those stupid doctors and their nasty treatments kept me in bed," she snorted. "I feel much better now that I've stopped taking those horrible 'chemotherapy' pills and such."

"Cat called and left me a message about it," Dave stated, accepting several of the liberally-frosted chocolate cupcakes. "I wanted to talk to you concerning it."

"Oh, there's nothing to talk about, Davey," Jean insisted. "The good Lord only gives us one moment at a time. I'm happy just as I am. If I trip and break my neck tomorrow morning I know the Lord will take me up to heaven. What's so bad about that? Something's going to take us all out of this place before we're ready—and if that's cancer for me, well so what? I've had a good life up to this point and I'm so *grateful*. So there's nothing more to talk about."

"Cancer?" Sally frowned, now happily munching on her third cupcake. "But...no one dies of cancer any more—at least in the Citizen class that's..."

"Well, you are right, my dear, that there's been wonderful advances in detection and treatment," Jean cheerfully interrupted her, getting up and going to a mirror to start fitting on her blueish wig. "But I can tell you from experience that many people do indeed die from it. It's killing me, for sure. However, I'm not at all afraid. It's just the way it is. *'The Lord gives and the Lord takes away, blessed be the name of the Lord'.*" she quoted from the Bible. "Why at the treatment center there weren't just old women like me and Sally's mother—but even little children. It was so sad. Even babies can get cancer. In fact there was this cute little boy with retinoblastoma...you know, eye cancer? He'd just had an operation to get his left eye removed. He was wearing a little eye patch. He looked just like a wee baby Pirate! And..."

"My...I mean, *Sally's* mother—also has cancer?" Sally interrupted Jean. "Dave mentioned something about..."

"Oh, did you not know?" Jean sadly stated, now making the last adjustments on her wig, turning back to them from the hall mirror. "Yes, she has lung cancer that's spread into her lymph nodes and brain. Poor thing! She's brave, but there's not much they can do for her either."

"Lung cancer? Did she work in an asbestos mine?" Sally asked.

Jean laughed, coming over to sit with them again at the table. "No, of course not, Linda. She smokes. She's smoked cigarettes for decades. It's a terrible addiction," she "cluck-clucked" with her tongue. "I think it's just plain evil, that awful tobacco. But once you're hooked, I know it can be extremely hard to stop. Samantha told me she'd tried many times. But even now, dying of metastasized lung cancer, she still can't quit. She's got big tumors growing in her head, smashing her brain, but she still uses the poison that put those lumps there in the first place. It's so sad."

"Why doesn't the government just ban it?" Sally asked, genuinely perplexed.

"Uhm..." Dave hastily interjected. "The government doesn't have that power...uhm, 'Linda.' The people would rebel. It would be the same as with Prohibition—when a law was made in the past Century to ban alcohol in this country. It just caused huge problems because people wanted their drinks and would do anything to get it. So the government was forced to overturn that law."

"The people can force the government to change a law?"

This new Dimension was getting stranger and stranger.

"Our form of government is at the will of the people," Dave carefully explained. "I guess you don't watch the news channels much?"

Sally grabbed another cupcake and stuffed it into her mouth, followed by the orange liquid. It was all scrumptious. They sure had good food in this Dimension.

"Do you not know much about politics?" Jean cheerfully asked. "The big tobacco companies make tons of money and have high-paid advocates. Money talks. Any politician trying to ban tobacco would just get forced out of office, Linda. It's sad but that's just the way it is."

"Oh...well...I," Sally frowned, nervously wetting her thin lips with the tip of her tongue, bewildered. Where she came from the Government had absolute authority. It wasn't questioned. It was simply obeyed.

"Linda's an artist," Dave smoothly interjected, washing his last cupcake down with a long swig of cold milk. "She told me she doesn't read newspapers or listen to the radio or watch television. Isn't it refreshing to find a person who goes her own way without being swamped by the surrounding culture?"

Ah, that was a good explanation of her ignorance. She'd have to remember it.

"An artist!" Jean marveled, clapping her hands together in delight. "What kind of artist are you, Linda? Do you paint pictures, write books, or sculpt things?"

"No, none of those," Sally said, narrowing her eyes. At last there was a topic she knew backward and forward. "I work with directed evolution of biomimetic artificial cognitive entities."

Both Dave and Jean were silent for a moment, apparently shocked by her words. Did she say something terrible? Did Jean realize she wasn't from this world?

"That is so wonderful!" Jean grinned widely, clapping her hands gleefully together. "Oh, she's a scientist, just like you, Davey. I didn't understand a word of what she just said, but it sounded positively *riveting.*"

Sally sighed to herself. She'd have to watch what she said. Until she understood this new place better, she'd best not volunteer information. Either it made her seem totally ignorant or bizarrely knowledgeable.

"Uh...yes...well...we'd best be going," Dave said, looking up at the clock. "We've only ten minutes before the main church service starts. But we can easily drive the few blocks to the little church building in five minutes. So, Linda, I think we should be..."

"Wait!" Sally suddenly stopped Dave and his mom from getting up. She reached over and picked up a pill container sitting beside the salt and pepper shakers in the middle of the table. "Did you take one of these?"

Jean looked at what was in Sally's hand.

"Oh, yes I did," Jean nodded vigorously. "Those are the new vitamins that Davey found for me at the store this morning. I didn't read the instructions, just took one. That's what I usually do for any new supplements. I have a bunch of them I take each day. They're a lot better for you than those awful poisons that the doctors prescribe. But I do know that even natural vitamins and herbals can have side effects, so I just take one first to see what happens."

Sally recognized them. She knew about them quite well. Why did Dave get them at the store? It seemed quite a coincidence that of all the things at the Megastore to buy he'd pick those up. This whole thing was getting more and more curious.

"I've...heard about these...new 'vitamins'," Sally hesitantly stated, setting the vial back down. "If you start to feel sick to your stomach, you'll go to the hospital for a check-up, right?"

"Oh...well, I don't think..."

"Please, Mrs. King—promise me!" she urgently insisted. "If you start feeling sick you will drive yourself to your doctor or to a hospital. Ok? Promise?"

"Well, if you think it's necessary, since you know more about this than I do then I suppose that..."

"Please promise me!"

"Well, if it means that much to you, then I promise."

Sally was relieved. She liked Jean. Her son was a different matter entirely. But Jean seemed totally honest and friendly. And the fortui-tous occasion of Dave picking up the pills from the Megamart opened up a new, welcomed possibility.

Dave just looked puzzled, a deep frown on his face.

"Good, and—and would you mind taking some of these to...Sally's...mother also? I think they might help her as well."

"Oh, I'm so sorry, Linda," Jean frowned. "I'm not going back to that awful clinic. Never again! Now I just chat with Samantha over the phone every couple days since we've become friends and..."

"I have a second, unopened carton, Linda," Dave informed her. "I...bought...two of them at the store this morning. I don't need it for myself and I'd be happy for Samantha to have the entire thing. They don't need to try and share the one vial."

He had two cartons of them—one for his own mother and one for her own amazingly-alive mother in this Dimension. This was too much of a coincidence. Something was happening here—beyond just the immediate amazing events.

What the hell was going on?

"That...would be...much better...for both to take a complete se-ries," Sally gulped thankfully. "The treatment might not be effective if they stop short of a full course. They need to take one pill per day until the bottle's empty. No more than that! But...how do I get it to her?"

"After church we can take a little jog up to Ada," Dave said. "It's not that far. We can easily be there in thirty minutes. In fact, why don't you call her up, Mom, and invite her to lunch with us in Ada? We can meet her at that nice Chinese restaurant that you enjoy so much."

"What a wonderful idea, Davey," Jean gurgled happily, clapping her hands together. "She'll be so happy to see her distant Sulphur relative. Samantha can take a taxi to the restaurant as she can't drive anymore. In fact I'll go call her right now. Also I'll warn her, if she doesn't already know, how remarkably similar Linda presently looks to our dear-departed Sally. We don't want her to have a heart attack when she sees Linda!"

Jean went into the living room to make the call.

"Are you sure you want to do this?" Dave softly asked Sally. "I know this is an incredible shock, changing worlds. I'm certainly not yet adjusted myself to what's happened to us. And here your Mother is, still alive but sick..."

"She's not my Mother," Sally softly but firmly interrupted him. "But she's likely very close to being my true Mother. If I can help her, then maybe your forcing me to leave behind my real life will have some meaning. I'm glad you happened to buy the Optimmune pills. Whenever people's immune systems get out of balance, they're quite effective at reprogramming the body's physiological systems. The Elites use it regularly, taking a booster pill each month. It's much too expensive for the lower classes, unfortunately. But for the upper class it's a regular supplement."

"But you said my Mom should stay close to medical care? What did you mean by that?"

"I've heard that if one of the lower castes starts on them—having not gotten the best medical care from birth as does every Citizen—the initial effects can be devastating," she seriously replied. "And if, as you said, both your Mother and my 'relative' carry heavy cancer burdens in their bodies, the sudden immune-mediated destruction of those cells might throw their kidneys or their livers into toxic failure."

"Jesus Christ!" Dave softly exclaimed. "Should I stay here with my Mom instead of going back home this afternoon?"

"It's gradual," she answered. "Kyle told me what happened with a friend of his who'd snuck into America from the badlands. He had early type I diabetes and took the pills. Since the disease is from auto-immunity, the retroviral DNA-reprogramming can stop it in its tracks. Well, he just got sicker and sicker and would have died from side-effects except that Kyle managed to get a doctor to come and se-cretly treat him. That man barely survived the treatment."

"I'll warn my sister, Cat, to keep a close watch on Mother during this next week."

"That would be wise. Also, like I said, she should take the full bot-tle, one pill each day, even if she gets sick from it. If the full course isn't applied over the proper time-course—saturating the entire stem cell population in her body over the required month of daily doses—then reversion can happen."

"Ok, I'll tell Cat. But...if it works?"

"She'll be cured of her cancer," Sally matter-of-factly stated.

The expression on his face told her everything. Maybe this "Dave" person was a pain who'd disrupted her entire life—but he was a man who loved his mother.

Sally grudgingly admitted to herself that maybe she could find it in her heart to like him as well.

Unlike Dave's usual boring experience, Church that Sunday morning was an extraordinary affair.

The church building was located on a side street, on a corner. Big old trees shaded it. It was quite the typical "old country church." It had big wide double doors in the front where members and visitors were heartily welcomed by the minister.

Cliff looked understandably stunned to see the "resurrected" Sally standing beside Dave. But Dave quickly "explained" the situation. Though clearly having trouble believing the explanation, Cliff shook her hand in sincere greeting.

"So glad to have you with us today...Linda," he smiled. "Come back any time, especially since you say you are a long-time Sulphur resident. It's strange, though, I've never seen you around before.

There are only five thousand in our little town. I've been to the grocery store many times where you say you work. It's funny we haven't
met previously."

"Uh...she just recently...dyed her hair reddish," Dave invented on-
the-spur. "She used to be a..."

"—blond!" Sally nodded knowingly. "I've always tried to blend
into the background. And I keep to myself, doing my own hobbies in
my spare time. I don't get out much. And my Mom was sick, just
passing away recently, so..."

"I'm sorry to hear that," Cliff automatically assured her, "—and
what is your connection to our dear, seldom-seen Dave?" he politely
asked.

"Oh, we just met—today in fact."

"Today?"

"Yep, right there at the grocery store this very morning!" Dave
hastened to explain. "Uhm, we struck up a conversation. And—just
like you say in every sermon—I...uh...told her about *Jesus*."

"It was quite interesting," Sally sincerely nodded. "I was fascinated. It's the first time I've heard of this religious leader. So Dave invited me to come with him this morning and..."

"You...hadn't heard before...about *Jesus?*" Cliff gasped, his eyes
opening wide, now looking even more incredulous than before.

"Well, formal religion *is* forbidden for Citizens who..."

"What?" Cliff gasped again.

"Oh, she's *joking* with you!" Dave forced a laugh, grabbing her
shoulders and moving her on past him and into the sanctuary. "Hah!
What a great sense of humor she has!" he called back at Cliff. "I love
that about her. What she *really* means is that she just hadn't experienced our type of *family-friendly* Christianity, is all. She's used to
much stricter groups. Hah! Well, we better find a seat before the
pews get filled up and..." his voice tailed off as he hastily moved Sally
and Jean onward.

Behind them, the confused preacher turned to greet the other ar-
rivals.

There was actually no problem with overcrowding. In fact, about
two thirds of the pews were empty. The *"Church of the Divine Re-
deemer"* was a fundamentalist denomination that was slowly dying

out. Unfortunately for its survival, it was so stuck in its traditions that it had little appeal to people of the present-day world.

But its adherents were extremely devout, disciplined, and admirably dedicated—like Dave's Mom.

And as the services started and Jean happily launched into an enthused alto singing old-time Gospel hymns, Dave had a chance to try to get his head straight.

Sally was an alien.

She was from another world.

It was a world where Jesus Christ apparently *never existed*!

Even Sally's reaction to the typically-boring sermon was stunning to Dave. She hung on every single word. She gasped and even applauded at one point! The people sitting around Dave and his mother looked over at her, curious.

Dave just grinned back at them, hesitantly lifting his hands up in the air and clapping along with Sally.

Others hesitantly joined in.

This was not the traditionally required "sit-quietly" sermon behavior. But the members saw that she was a visitor and were willing to encourage her in her "bizarre" behavior.

Afterward, as they exited the building, Sally again encountered the Preacher by the exit, saying: "That was amazing! Is it all really true? Did God really come down to Earth in the form of a little baby—to grow up and be tortured to death to pay for our cosmic sins? And then did God really bring his dead corpse back to life?"

"Oh, yes, my dear," Cliff gravely stated, nodding his head repeatedly in the affirmative. "God does love us—and Jesus saved us. Humanity was headed straight for hell. But God gave us a way to escape from our well-deserved punishment. Jesus died on the Cross to pay the price for our own sins. It was a supreme sacrifice that God rewarded with resurrection. Yes, Linda—Jesus indeed showed us God's Love, not just by his words but especially by his actions."

"How wonderful!" she gasped. "And how can I find out more about this Jesus and his teachings?"

Cliff gulped. Dave knew the overweight minster had hardly ever heard such a response to a sermon in his entire life.

"Well, I'd of course be glad to sit and study with you at your con-venience."

"Study?"

"Yes, my dear," he said, blinking his eyes rapidly in puzzlement, "—the New Testament, of course."

"What is that?"

"You've never heard of...well, never mind," he shrugged his rounded shoulders. "Here, I carry a pocket version around with me for quick reference. Please, take it. And if you have any questions, my card is in it with my telephone number."

He reached into an inside pocket of his suit coat and pulled out a little black book.

She gratefully took it as he handed it to her.

"I shall read it with great pleasure," she grinned at him, her green eyes twinkling.

"Uh, well...we've got to go," Dave said, pulling her away by her other hand. "We've got a restaurant reservation we've got to get to. 'Bye, Cliff."

In the car, sitting beside Dave in the front—with Jean chattering absently away in the backseat to no one in particular—Sally quietly leaned over and whispered in Dave's ear: "So are you a disciple of this Jesus?"

Starting the car, steering it out of the parking lot, Dave pondered for a moment on her question.

He could tell her the truth or fudge a bit. He decided to speak frankly.

"I grew up at that little church back there," he softly replied, not to attract his mother's attention. He shrugged. "I still believe in Je-sus' teachings, but not so much how different groups today carry them out."

"What do they do wrong?"

"Huh!" he snorted. "The better question is: 'What do they do *right?*'"

"I don't understand."

"Well...go ahead and read the book," he sighed. "Then we'll talk more if you're still interested. Ok?"

"Ok," she whispered. She settled back in her seat, opening up the little black book and starting at the first page.

She quietly read aloud: "A record of the genealogy of Jesus Christ, the son of David..."

"Oh, he was *Jewish!*" she exclaimed. "I've heard of them. They came before the Islamists."

Dave shook his head in amazement at her different world-view. They pulled out onto the main street of the town, going along Broadway headed towards the Chickasaw Turnpike leading to Ada.

At least in her world there were Jews and Muslims. Maybe she and Dave did have common touchstones after all.

"No wonder he was executed," she mused beside him as she rapidly scanned through the pages.

"What?" he absently replied, his attention now focused on the road.

"He insulted his government," she nodded knowingly. "Just like you and me. He *deserved* his punishment."

Chapter 10

TOUGH MEDICINE

Eat me

I'm delicious

I'm waiting right here

Come and get me!

I'm tasty and fresh

Believe me when I say

I'm the best

So don't be late

Or I will go away...

Gobble me up today!

The Luminary Chronicles, 10:4-6

When they walked into the "Home Chinese Buffet" in Ada, Samantha Smith was waiting for them.

Samantha slowly rose from her chair at a corner table as Dave, Jean, and Sally approached. Sally struggled not to reveal her swirling emotions.

"Sally!" Samantha gasped, putting up a hand to cover her gaping mouth. "Is it...really you?"

Samantha Smith was a wrinkled old lady wearing an elegant polka-dot scarf around her bald head. The pretty scarf flowed down across her thin shoulders. Unlike Dave's Mom's eternally-jovial expression, though, hers was one of stern disbelief.

"Oh, Samantha," Jean consoled her, moving over beside her to put an arm around her shoulders, helping her to sit back down in the chair, "it's not Sally! It's just like I told you over the phone, remember? She's the daughter of your niece from Sulphur who admired your daughter, fixed her hair up similar, and got the same tattoos. Her Mom passed away recently and she's concerned about all her relatives' health. So she brought you some special vitamins just like

Dave got for me. She works at the big grocery store so she's up on all the latest natural supplements."

Samantha squinted carefully at Sally. Then her eyes widened in realization.

"You're...*not*...my dead daughter," she softly admitted.

Sally sat down opposite to her, wiping a tear from the corner of her eye as she likewise replied: "And...you're also *not* my dead Mother."

Jean suddenly grimaced, tilting her head in puzzlement as she sat, almost losing the blue wig off her head.

"What are we talking about?" Jean asked, looking in puzzlement back and forth from the stunned Samantha to the tearful Sally.

Sally appreciated that Dave's Mom's mind was wandering, a sad side-effect of the horrendous cancer therapy that she'd described in graphic detail to Sally on their ride from Sulphur to Ada.

"We're talking about going and getting our food before the other church people come swarming in and take all the good stuff, right?" Dave interjected. His voice was calm and reassuring.

Sally saw that Dave was gently focusing his mother on an immediate task: getting to the buffet filled with steaming-hot, delicious Chinese food before it was picked-over.

"Oh, yes—let's go fill up our plates," Jean cheerfully agreed, getting up and heading towards the buffet.

"*Who* are you?" Samantha frowned at Sally. "After Mrs. King called me with such terrible news, I called the phone number of my niece Dianna in Sulphur, expecting relatives there to be organizing her funeral. Instead, Dianna herself answered. She's very much *alive!* And her daughter Clarisse—Sally's second cousin—isn't even in Sulphur. Instead, she's away studying nursing at Platt College in Oklahoma City. Why are you *pretending* to be a relative of mine? And what's the real reason you are made up like Sally?"

Sally looked down at the bare tabletop. She carefully considered her response before replying.

Should she tell the truth or soften her story? She decided to tell the truth.

"I'm...not your niece's daughter...nor am I your daughter...but I'm close."

"Close? What does that mean?"

"This may be difficult for you to understand—in fact, I have diffi-culty believing it myself—but Dave...this morning..." she struggled to explain, but couldn't find the words.

Sally saw Dave lean his head in close so he could talk to both of them without the people at nearby tables hearing.

"I yanked her out of another Dimension," he sighed. "In her world, you are dead," he matter-of-factly explained to Samantha. "In her Dimension Sally was about to be executed because she got tangled up with me, poor kid. I didn't have any choice but bring her back with me. I don't know how all this happened. I hardly believe it my-self. But long-story-short, she's both a fugitive and refuge...with no place to go."

Samantha's mouth set into a thin, straight line.

"I don't know what sort of joke you are trying to pull on me, young man," she softly replied, "but if you weren't Jean's son I'd *slap* you right in the face and walk out of here!"

"It's not a joke...Mom," Sally whispered—her voice barely audible. "It all happened this morning. My world was turned upside down. Now we're doing the same to you. I'm so sorry..."

Tears began dripping from her eyes. It was all too much to take in. It was unbelievable. And yet here, right in front of her, was a du-plicate of her dead mother.

"It's science fiction! It's fantasy!" Samantha huffed. "I happen to be a literal-minded person who neither appreciates nor accepts any of those silly things." Samantha insisted. For emphasis, she "thumped" a thin hand upon the tabletop.

"Then you are welcome to do a DNA test on me," Sally stated, reaching out her small hand to hold Samantha's splayed hand. "But I suspect you don't need a DNA test. You *do* know that I'm your daughter—even though not your original one...who is very real. You know it just as I know you're my dead Mom."

Samantha's eyes filled up with tears. She shakily put her other hand atop Sally's.

"Yes," she said, reluctantly nodding. "I knew it when I first saw you walk into the restaurant. But I also knew it was impossible.

Yet...somehow it *is* possible—because you're here. God help me, I can't believe it's real. But you *are* here..."

"And now she *is* Sally's second cousin, 'Linda', who just happens to look a lot like Sally," Dave insisted. "Hardly anyone knows about her second cousin or what she looks like here in Ada, right? At least that's what my Mom thinks. So that's got to be Sally's cover-story."

"Well...I suppose if I tell people how much you admired her, wanted to be like her," Samantha tentatively smiled.

"That's right," Sally agreed. "I'm—Linda Powers. I'm your concerned relative come to visit and help you out in your time of bereavement and illness. I'm staying with you for a while...if that's ok with you?"

"Yes," Jean whispered back. Then, more forcefully: "Yes, we can make this work—Linda!"

"Come on, you slow-pokes," Jean said, returning to the table with a plate piled high with steaming fried shrimp and stir-fried vegetables. "I don't want to eat all by myself."

"Right."

"We're going."

"Be back in a second," Dave also agreed, standing back up. "I'm starved."

"It sure looks good," Sally smiled, supporting Samantha's arm as the elderly woman shakily stood up. "I'm not used to such a spread. Even the Elites don't eat this good. Maybe this world isn't so bad after all."

"Eh?" Jean asked, puzzled, as she sat down with her plate.

"—this *restaurant!* *This* restaurant," Dave hastily interjected. "She hasn't eaten Chinese before and was afraid it was going to be bad so..."

"Oh, it's *delicious!*" Jean laughed, liberally spooning into her mouth crispy shrimp. "Get a bunch. Oh, I'm so glad to have my appetite back. Go on, now, Linda. Eat up!"

"I will," Sally grinned back at her.

"So you'll be staying with your Mom?" Dave said as he stood outside his Cavalier with Sally.

Jean was in the passenger seat of the Cavalier. They'd just dropped off Samantha at her modest home. After helping Samantha inside, Sally had walked back to the car with Dave. Now he was ready to leave with his Mom.

"Where else am I going to stay?"

"Well..." he sucked in his breath. "If you needed a place to 'crash' I've got a spare couch—if you don't mind sleeping with snakes, that is?"

"You live with snakes?"

"I'm sort of an amateur herpetologist along with being a Ph.D. physicist. The snakes aren't much for casual conversation, but..."

"We need to stay in touch," she cut him off, responding coolly to his dangled snake references.

"Here's my card with my e-mail address and also my home land-line phone number," he said, reaching into a pocket and pulling out one of the stash he always kept with him.

She primly accepted it—while handing him a piece of torn-off paper with another number on it.

"And this is my...Mom's...phone number here in Ada that you can..."

"*Sally!*" a shrill voice cried-out as *Snake* came running up in a short-sleeved T-shirt. He passionately threw his liberally-tattooed arms around her, hugging her tightly!

Tears were streaming from his eyes as he kissed her cheeks and mouth.

"Get off of me!" she ordered as she shoved him back, the sleeves of her shirt flying back revealing her own tattoos.

"But...?"

"It's not Sally! It's not Sally!" Dave insisted, grabbing the young man and pulling him away from her. He tried to quickly bring the young man up to speed, speaking rapidly: "It's her second cousin, from Sulphur. She just looks a lot like Sally. It's uncanny, but only superficial. Linda here is Sally's second cousin, who always admired Sally from afar and tried her best to look like her."

"Whaaaat....?" He gulped, staggering backwards. "I came to check on Mrs. Smith and saw *her*...?"

"I'm...Linda Powers," Sally said coldly, stepping back from him. She shoved down the sleeves of her blouse—obviously not appreciating the advances of the scraggly-haired, goateed young man.

"But you look so much like...even got the same tattoos," he gulped, not believing what his eyes told him to be true.

"Like Dave said, I followed Sally on...uhm...your 'picture-book'...I think that's what you call it...and got her same tattoos that..."

"Oh, I'm so sorry," Snake gulped, ducking his head shyly. "But...since you're so like her from following her on Facebook...in that case...well...do you want to go out with me sometime?"

"*Snake!*" Dave exclaimed, shocked. "Give her some space! She just came up with me and my Mom from Sulphur to visit Samantha. She didn't come up here to get hit on by Sally's old boyfriend."

"It's alright...'Snake'," Sally now placated him while moving backward another step. "I've...just got to go inside...now!"

She quickly turned around and escaped into the house.

"Whoa..." Snake grinned, causing the cobra on his face to twist menacingly, shaking loose of Dave's grasp. "Hey, Mr. King, do you think I have a chance with her?"

"Not in a million years," Dave bluntly replied. "You take care, ok?"

"Uh...sure..."

But Dave was back in his car, climbing in...

"I thought Mrs. Smith said her son *liked* snakes?" Dave heard Snake laugh at him. "Well, *I* like turtles," he grinned. "And I'm gonna get me another."

When Dave pulled up to his house in Edmond he was so exhausted he was literally shaking.

His vision was blurring. He could hardly force himself to push open the car door to step outside.

"This...has been one hell of a day," he grunted to himself, staggering up his driveway.

He noticed that the big, thick Master padlock still hung undisturbed, securing his garage door shut.

"At least the garage is still safely locked," he sighed gratefully, fumbling with his key while opening the front door of the house.

After having got up early, after little sleep the night before following his excursion across the United States, then adventuring to an alternate dimension, then trip to Ada, then back to Sulphur to return his mother to her home, and finally a long two-hour ride on the freeway back to Edmond he was beyond exhausted.

"Damn, I'm *tired*," he groaned, wanting nothing more than to collapse upon the couch.

"But I gotta do the critters," he ordered himself, actually "slapping" himself in the face with a limp hand. Then he stumbled to the kitchen sink, turned on the cold water full-blast, and thrust his head underneath it.

Sputtering and gagging he yanked his head up. He was a bit more alert.

His animals needed their daily care. He'd skipped it that morning what with his hasty departure, only doing a quick check before leaving. Now he must do his duty.

"Hey, Topper," he greeted the big green lizard after opening the cage door. He stretched out his hand to stroke its back along the sides of its central spines.

The big lizard closed its eyes in appreciation, arching up its head and back.

Going from cage to cage Dave blearily collected any dirtied water bowls plus salad containers: their last feedings now quite wilted and rotted. Yes, the lizards and tortoises looked quite hungry.

"George did good taking care of you-all," Dave muttered to himself. "So I better not let you guys down now that I'm back. You'll want George instead of me to be your owner."

He poured out dirty water, dumped old food, washed the bowls good with ammonia, rinsed them, and filled them with fresh water and salad.

Lucky his bag of lettuce and fresh fruit made it ok from the other Dimension.

"Hmmm, *yummy*," Dave laughed, popping some of the fresh lettuce, fresh fruit, and canned vegetables into his own mouth. Lunch was now a long time in the past. "Plus, don't forget your vitamins and calcium supplements," he muttered, sprinkling a bit of that on top of all the salads.

After having distributed the bowls back to the appropriate habitats, Dave had a nagging feeling he was forgetting something. What was it?

"Oh, right. Let's just make doubly sure that our wonderful, nifty, magical 'Device' is still safely 'hidden' out in Victor's van," he grinned to himself, wobbling into the empty bedroom. He unlocked the door to the garage, reaching into the dark to snap on the light, and stepped through.

For a moment he didn't comprehend what he was seeing.

Then he collapsed down upon his knees, his head in his hands, and wept like a baby.

"No! No! No! No!" he kept yelling-out through his tears, over and over and over.

The garage was empty.

There was no black van.

There was no Device.

"It can't be...it *can't* be!" he cried-out, rising from his knees to his feet to go fondle at the space which should have held the Professor's black van.

Nothing was there.

"Oh, God!" he sobbed, looking up at the empty rafters of the freshly rebuilt garage's ceiling. "After all that's happened today—you do *this* to me? Why are you *torturing* me?"

And then the humiliating reality hit him like a ton of bricks, again buckling his knees.

He almost fell to the concrete floor, but managed to stand erect.

"They *did* figure I was stupid enough to try and hide it right back in the place where it all started," he moaned, swaying from side to side, turning around to slink out of the garage, through the empty bedroom, and collapse onto the couch.

He sobbed uncontrollably.

"I'm the *stupidest* person alive," he groaned as he fell into a black, spinning, funnel that sucked him ever deeper.

RING, RING, RING!

"Oh Christ..." Dave moaned, jerking awake.

He was actually glad he'd been rudely awakened, though it must still be night outside as the room was black as pitch.

No light was coming in his windows.

He'd just been trapped in the most terrible, awful nightmare. In his awful dream he'd valiantly rescued a cute girl from an alternate Dimension only then to be crushed by the theft of his greatest achievement.

Oh, right...it *wasn't* a nightmare.

"*What?*" he yelled into the receiver of his landline phone as he snatched it up to slap it against his ear.

"Dave? Oh, thank God. You've got to come quick. It's Mother. She's dying!"

It was...Cat?

Oh, Lord, he'd forgotten to call her and warn her about the 'new vitamin' possible side effects.

"Yes...yes, I'm here," he managed to gasp-out.

"She took a turn for the worse a couple hours ago," his sister sobbed over the phone. "She managed to call an ambulance before she collapsed. The hospital called me. I went right over. She's in the Sulphur Hospital. She went into kidney failure, liver failure, and cardiac arrest. But they got her heart beating again. They've got her on machines...but she's gone, she's gone, Dave. They say there's nothing they can do. They say we have to pull the plug. They can't even harvest her organs. They've just turned to mush. Oh, God, Dave! I don't want to do it, but her Living Will—her Advance Directive—explicitly states she doesn't want to be kept alive on machines. So I'm going to have to do it. I'm going to tell them to pull the plug and..."

"No!" he frantically yelled into the receiver. Then, trying to control his racing emotions, to speak more calmly, he crisply stated: "Cat. Please listen to me. Don't do anything until I get there!" he yelled into the phone. "I'm leaving right now. I'll be there in two hours. Promise me you won't do anything until I'm there! *Promise* me!"

"But...it's hopeless," she moaned. "Dave, I can't stand to see her like this. She's got tubes going in and out of every opening in her body. She's just a slab of meat. It's awful, just awful—I've got to stop it."

"Then we'll do it together!" Dave frantically yelled again, trying to make her comply with the force of his words.

Then, still speaking intensely but now more slowly and softer, Dave said: "I have to see her one more time. You understand, don't you Sis? I've got to see her just one more time. Please don't do anything until I get there!"

"I...I guess just a couple more hours...sure...you're right, you deserve that—but hurry Dave, hurry!"

"Hang on, Cat," he consoled her. "I'm coming!"

He slammed the receiver onto its cradle, tore off his smelly, wrinkled shirt and T-shirt his Mom had given him of his Dad's, grabbed fresh clothes out of a drawer, whipped them onto himself, then strode to the door and out to his waiting, faithful, yellow Cavalier.

In the dim light of a streetlight it didn't look its usual sunny yellow. Now his car was a sour yellow-green, like a lime.

Dave didn't like limes. To him they weren't sweet or sour, just disgusting.

And now his entire life seemed the same.

"But some things are more important than stolen nuclear-like bombs." he muttered to himself, about to open the car door and take off—then stopped and turned back.

Back inside his house, he snatched up Victor's cellphone that he'd dropped at the bottom of his waste basket by the door. He'd hidden it completely under an accumulated pile of trash.

"At least I did something right," he grunted, happy at least the hidden cellphone was still there. He headed back to the car with it in his shirt pocket. "At least they didn't steal *you*."

He needed to talk to someone...someone that would understand.

"Mother is first—everything else is second," he ordered himself, sliding into his car for yet another grueling two-hour morning ride back down crowded I-35 to Sulphur.

He would concentrate on the road. There'd be no pulling out a cellphone while driving. But as soon as he could, he had to tell Victor what was going on.

He had to warn him!

Hopefully it wasn't already too late.

He steered the car with one hand out onto I-35 as he reached down with the other hand and felt beneath the seat.

There it was—the *super-gun*, just where he'd stashed it.

Feeling its solid reality calmed him down. No matter who came against him—who came out of the shadows to attack him—he now had an "ace in the hole."

He had a *weapon from another dimension.*

He almost didn't make it through security at the hospital.

"Sir!" the guard snapped at him as he dashed through the magnetic detector gate—which immediately began "beeping".

"My mother is dying!" Dave protested, pausing in his rush, turning half-around.

"I'm sorry about that, Sir," the guard firmly stated, walking up to him. "But I have to wand you. You set off the alarm."

"But..."

"I must insist," the young, well-muscled guard said as he swiftly caught up with Dave and turned him against a wall.

"Please raise your hands," the guard ordered.

Dave groaned, knowing he was caught...but did as ordered.

"It'll just take a minute," the man said, moving the wand up one side of Dave's body and down the other. "Ah, there it is," he said as the wand "*whupped*"!

The guard reached around into Dave's shirt and pulled out the cellphone.

"Ok, no problem," the guard said, handing Dave back the innocent-looking cellphone. "Again, I'm sorry about your mother, but with all the terrorism in the news lately we..."

"Thank you," Dave said, running onward.

Whew! That other-dimension gun was really good. He had it crammed down the front of his baggy pants where it was held in place by the belt at his waist. It felt like cold metal but it must be manufactured from some type of hard plastic.

Hopefully whoever stole the Device wouldn't attack Dave in a hospital, but he wasn't taking any chances.

At Admissions he was directed to "ICU"—the Intensive Care Unit.

Entering the small ward he was met by Catherine.

She looked terrible, her short blond hair stuck up in disarray. She had no makeup on. Her eyes in her somewhat chubby face were red from crying.

He grabbed her in a tight hug.

"Mom's gone," she sobbed. "There's only a shell of her left. You can see for yourself."

He fearfully walked towards the sliding doors she indicated, afraid of what he was about to see. The upper halves of the doors were entirely made of glass, as were the doorways to the other two alcoves. They were situated around the central nurses' station. Since it was intensive care, there was no privacy. The hovering doctors and nurses had a continuous, complete view of the patients. And through the windows he saw his mother.

Cat was right.

"Mom?" he said, his voice catching, as he walked past the doors which "shushed" to the sides, into the room filled with blinking, beeping machines...in the middle of which lay the shrunken body of his once-vital mother.

This was a different entity than the cheerful, energetic lady he'd had lunch with just that day.

Only the head and one hand were showing from this "stranger." The skin of her face hung slack, grayish. Her eyes were closed but puffed-out. Tubes ran into her mouth, her nose, and directly into her neck via a tracheotomy. Electrodes were pasted to her shaven skull. Under a thin sheet her chest rose rhythmically up and down...up and down...up and down.

"She's only breathing because of pulmonary assist," a white-coated doctor quietly stated, placing a comforting hand on Dave's shoulder. "From her symptoms plus our diagnostic tests we diagnose that she suffered a massive stroke. We're getting no EEG readings from her brain. You could have her transferred to Oklahoma City for more extensive tests. But from my experience she's clearly brain-dead. Regrettably, I see no hope for recovery. I'm very sorry."

"But...you say it's a *stroke*—not just organ failure?"

He hesitated a moment before answering.

"Yes, I'm afraid your mother has also experienced multiple organ failure," the sympathetic male doctor patiently explained. "Apparently a great deal of damage occurred when she became comatose and stopped breathing. The first responders were able to get her breathing again, but that didn't resolve the severe damage to her organs. Even the machines won't keep her body alive much longer."

Dave slumped into a chair to the side of the bed.

"I've got to...process... all of this," he gulped.

"Of course, I understand," the polite doctor nodded. "If you have any questions just ask one of the nurses to contact me. My name is Dr. Matthews."

"Thanks, Doctor," Dave nodded gratefully, just now focusing on the lean, kind face of the physician. He wore a white doctor's lab coat over blue scrubs. He had the ubiquitous stethoscope draped around his neck. He was a dark skinned man with a short grey beard, high forehead, and short-cropped black hair.

Cat came into the room, placing her chubby hands on Dave's shoulders.

Beside them, the machines were quietly *beeping, clicking,* and *sucking.*

"It's time that we let her go," Cat quietly stated, her voice trailing off. Then, more forcefully, she continued: "We knew this was coming soon. She gave me her Durable Power of Attorney, so I'm legally responsible. I'm the one she wanted to make her healthcare decisions if it came to this. I don't have to get your approval for this, Davey. But it'd be easier if you agreed with me."

"So...you're going to pull the plug," he sighed, "whether I agree or not?"

"It's my decision. She wanted it this way."

"Why only you?"

"She knew you were too...scientific," she sadly informed him, her hands still on his shoulders. "She knew you'd try everything to save her even if there was no chance. And she didn't want to go through the futile suffering. Neither did she want us put through the needless pain and expense of a hopeless quest. She knew I was the levelheaded one of her two children. She knew I'd do what needed to be done."

"Yah...I can see that," he nodded. "But...I still need to make sure— make a couple phone calls first. Is that ok? There are some doctors I know that can advise me over the phone."

"Well...I've already made my decision...but..."

"Come on, Cat," he pleaded, looking up into her sad blue eyes. "Give me a little time, ok?"

"An hour?" she grudgingly replied. "Would that be enough time for you? There are no other close relatives that need to get here. It's just the two of us. I don't see any sense in delaying the inevitable. It'll be better for both Mom and us to just get this over with, to let her go."

"Yes, an hour should be enough time for me to make my calls," he nodded. "But if I find any differing opinions then I need you to promise me right now that you'll listen to whatever I discover. Won't you?"

"Of course I will," she agreed, withdrawing her hands and turning away. "But I've already talked with the doctors here and they all agree. I'll be down in the cafeteria, getting something to eat. My blood sugar is low. I can't think straight and I want to be clear-headed. I'll be back in an hour."

She wobbled out of the small room, obviously drained of energy— just as was Dave.

God, he was sympathetic to her and her reasoning. If nothing bizarre had happened in the interim, he'd probably be agreeing with her. But the unexplainable, impossible *had* occurred! He had to contact Sally.

"Ok, then," he sighed to himself. Then, to the unconscious person in the bed: "Hang in there, Mom. Maybe I'm just being 'scientifically obsessive' but I've got to know for sure that there's no hope for you. If that's the case, don't worry. I'll let you go in peace."

He pulled out his wallet and rifled through it.

"It's in here somewhere," he grated to himself. "I'm sure I stuck it in here for safekeeping...where the hell is it?"

That small torn piece of paper with Sally's Mom's number on it...did he lose it?

"Here it is!" he said triumphantly, pulling it out.

"Ah, and there *you* are..." a kindly voice gently trailed off from the doorway, interrupting Dave's dialing.

It was Cliff.

His white-haired, flabby face was set into an expression of professional sympathy. He looked just like a funeral director doing his familiar duty.

Dave felt an irrational impulse to *punch* him in his nose—though he knew that Brother Davis was just falling into an oft-repeated pattern of visiting dying members, comforting family members.

Dave knew that Cliff didn't mean to be irritating—but he was that and more!

"I don't need you here, Cliff," Dave abruptly dismissed him. "Please leave. If you want to comfort someone, Cat is in the cafeteria."

"I know you are hurting," the paunchy man in his wide white suit intoned slowly. He came closer to Dave, gazing down in sorrow at the pitiful woman in the bed skewered by so many medical devices.

"Please leave, Cliff."

"Can I say a prayer for you and your Mother?"

"No!"

Cliff was startled. Dave didn't care. Cliff probably rarely had anyone turn down an offer of a prayer in the hospital. Everyone turned to God as a last resort, right? When there was no other help available, you rolled the "spiritual dice", right?

Dave was getting angry. Years of frustration boiled up into his throat.

"But, why not? Don't you want God's help?"

"Hah!" Dave bitterly laughed, now standing up to face Cliff. "What the hell will your prayer do for my Mom? Will it make her sit up and climb out of that bed?"

"I...but..."

"And if your God-damned '*God of Love*' was really so 'loving', why didn't He just intervene to stop her stroke from happening in the first place?" Dave angrily confronted him.

"Well, Dave...you know full well that mankind is being punished for the Original Sin of turning away from God in the Garden of Eden and..."

"That's all a load of *crap!*" Dave growled at him, advancing now as Cliff fearfully backed up. "My dear, sweet Mother who went four times per week to your church listening to your pious sermons and lectures is the *last* person who deserves to be in that hospital bed. Come on, Cliff, make her get up and walk. Pray to your 'loving' God and make the tubes drop out of her body. Come on! Let's see you do it!"

"You...you '*shall not tempt the Lord your God*'," Cliff tried to quote Jesus rejecting making demands on God.

"Hah!" Dave loudly laughed, no longer caring who heard him. "Your 'God' is an *empty delusion* that can't do anything for His so-called followers except *bore them to death* with droning lectures by empty apologists just like you!"

"Why, how dare you..." Cliff gasped, looking genuinely shocked by Dave's language. "You should get on your knees and thank the Lord that..."

"*Thank* the Lord, *really?*" Dave sneered at him. "You know who I should thank?" he yelled at the top of his lungs, his face twisted up in fury. "I should thank all these orderlies and nurses and doctors who are treating my mom and keeping her alive! And I should also thank those many scientists in years past who developed all these marvelous instruments and treatments! God didn't do that! They did that! If my mother should somehow survive it will be no thanks to your weak, helpless, absentee God!"

Cliff was now pushed back to the door, which slid aside automatically to allow him a hasty exit.

Outside, concerned personnel looked fearful, seeing the outraged Dave and the cringing preacher, uncertain of what to do.

"I'm sorry you feel that way, but..." Cliff gasped, clearly shocked at Dave's strident rebuff—now seeming to regain his courage, starting to turn back...

"Well I'm *not!*" Dave roared at him, driving him to scurry away. Then he turned his back on the departing preacher, dropping wearily again onto the seat by his Mom's bed.

He held up his hands apologetically to the nurses outside the windows, indicating he was ok and that they didn't need to call in security.

Then he frantically dialed the Sally's number into the cellphone, remembered to simultaneously push down the red button so no one could eavesdrop on them, and hit the "send" button.

It rang and rang and rang...

"Pick up! Pick up!" he urged the unseen recipient.

Then after what seemed forever..."Yes?"

"Sally! Is that you?"

"Why, no...this is *Linda*...but who are...?"

"It's me, it's me!" Dave intensely whispered into the phone, trying to speak quietly so that his voice would not carry beyond the enclosed room. "Where are you? Can you talk?"

"I'm—sitting with my Mother in an emergency room, waiting for her to be admitted. I've got her cellphone with me which you're calling me on."

"Emergency room?"

"Yes, Dave," she matter-of-factly replied. "The treatment on a completely naïve host in your world is much more powerful than I'd thought. Apparently you have no routine retroviral reprogramming therapy here. Is that true?"

"There are some experimental trials being done," he told her. "But from what I've heard they are limited in scope—and, so-far, not meeting with much success."

"I figured as much when my mother took ill soon after she took the first pill," she replied. "Where I come from this type of DNA scrutiny and adjustment is routine from birth, at least for Citizens. The pills you picked up in my...home...are just minor boosters for already-primed immune systems. But without that prior decades-long preparation..."

"My Mother is here in the intensive care unit apparently *brain-dead!*" Dave spat into the phone, interrupting her. "I get it! The effects are catastrophic! But I need to know if there is any hope. My mother's apparently suffered a major stroke. And I need to know if it was from the pills or would have happened anyway. What can you tell me?"

The phone was silent.

"Come on, come on!" Dave insisted. "My sister wants to shut off the medical equipment keeping my mother alive. What should I do?"

"Dave...I'm not a physician...but..."

"But what? But what?" he urged her.

"I am certified at the highest levels in biomimetic artificial neural nets," her tinny voice hesitated as it came from the small speaker in the phone. "And that means that I've studied the normal functioning of the human brain at length. I believe that, yes, naïve retroviral reprogramming might simulate having a stroke—in that the entire DNA of all the cells in your mother's body, including the neurons in her brain, are being re-written to optimize immune interactions. But as I said, I'm not a physician. Your mother might have just suffered a normal stroke unrelated to the Optimmune. I just don't know."

"So there's some hope?"

"If it's due to the reprogramming, yes."

"How long until I know for sure?"

"Oh...I'd give it at least a day or..."

"That's good enough for me. Thanks, Sally!"

"Uhm...that's 'Linda'..."

"Oh, right, of course. Thanks, *Linda*," he corrected himself. Then, remembering something else, "Say, I've another urgent question..."

"Yes?"

"Do you know anything about the weapons that the Keepers carry around—like the gun I took off that guy at the store?"

"Those are very dangerous."

"Don't I know it? I almost blew your store to bits with the 'two star' setting."

"It should not have been set that high. The safety must have broken off when the gun fell on the floor. In the store, we're told that the guards only set the guns at level number one."

"Number one? What does that do?"

"It just stuns a person."

"That's good to know."

"Are you going to shoot someone?"

"I hope not. But my sister's convinced that we've got to pull the plug on my Mom. She's only given me an hour to come up with evidence for not doing that, so I want to be ready in case I have to..."

"I knew that you were a violent person from the first second I saw you!" the little voice out of the cellphone passionately accused him. "I knew that *you* are dangerous!"

"Oh come on, Sally—I'm a real sweet guy once you get to know me and…"

"Citizens are *pacified*," she bluntly stated. "We've been cured of the human savage nature. Those genes have been *muted* by specific additives in our food supplies. Yours, obviously, have *not!* No wonder there's so much violence in this horrible place. In fact, the longer I'm here the more irrational I feel *myself* getting."

"What, your world doesn't have brutal police—and wars?" Dave angrily retorted. "Didn't you say something about badlands, keeping people in their places, hordes of invaders, not pissing-off the Peace Keepers, summary executions, and warring Empires?"

"Those are against *outsiders!*"

"So I'm just a savage 'outsider' to you?"

"You're behaving just like one! In fact, I don't think I should have anything more to do with you now that…"

"No, no, no!" he hastened to soothe her. "I'm sorry, I'm sorry! I'm at my wit's end here…but tell me how is *your* Mom is doing?" he added, trying to change the subject.

"She's just sick," she guardedly answered.

"What do you mean?" he asked, drawing her out.

"Like I said, it's faster and more intense than I expected," she continued, a bit less angrily. "A combination of the reprogramming response plus initial destruction of cancer cells as the immune system starts optimizing is making her quite ill. I think, though, as long as I can get her admitted into the hospital here in ADA where they can treat renal and hepatic failure she'll be alright."

Dave struggled to get his voice and outrage under control. He knew he wasn't just reacting to the annoying Girl with the Turtle Tattoo, but allowing her to be the "safety valve" through which his many other life-failures were "venting". If he had any hope at all of helping his Mother, he had to get his head on straight. Somehow he must keep his temper in check.

"Please keep me informed," Dave gratefully sighed. "I promise not to behave like a savage again. I'm just under a lot of stress right now. Please forgive me…Linda. You have the number of this cellphone, right?"

She hesitated before replying, clearly struggling with her own "venting" problems.

"Is it different from the landline number you gave me?"

"Oh—yes it is! Look on your 'caller-I.D.' function. The number should be there. I borrowed this cellphone from a friend of mine."

"Oh yes, I see the number."

"Good. Will you call me if anything changes?"

"I suppose—*oh, no!*"

"What? What?"

"I see *him* coming in through the hospital entrance!"

"What? A terrorist? A cop? An FBI agent? A *Preacher?*"

"*Snake!*" she spat the word.

Dave almost laughed out-loud in relief, but caught himself just in time.

"He...seems like...a fine young man," Dave studiously replied.

"He's a pain!" Sally groaned. "He was at the house all evening yesterday. All he wanted to talk about was tattoos. I like tattoos also, but not when someone wants to show me their new tat on their butt."

Losing control, Dave snickered.

"Yes, 'but' he's *your* pain," Dave now allowed himself to fully laugh out-loud. "Deal with it, Miss Smarty Pants."

"You don't know anything about me!" Sally retorted, now again angry as hell, obviously not taking his retort as the joke he intended.

The tension and stress suddenly caused Dave to snap.

"Well I certainly do know that you're an *ungrateful brat* who doesn't appreciate me saving you!" he snorted, the angry, unbidden words pouring out without pause.

"Brat? Me?" she yelled back. "If you hadn't given me that counterfeit money, I'd have been just fine at my day-job. I wish I'd never known you existed! You caused me to lose *everything* in my life that I value. My career, my extended family, my house, my bub, my reputation—it's all gone because of *you!*" she shouted out of the phone speaker. "You didn't 'rescue' me, you jerk—you *destroyed* me."

"Well, I think that's a bit exaggerated," he huffed, offended.

"*What?* I never want to speak to you again! Get out of my life!" she screamed at him through the cellphone.

With a defiant "snort" Sally broke the connection.

—just as Cat walked back into the hospital room. She was grimly but methodically munching on a large candy bar.

"Well, you certainly did piss off the preacher, didn't you?" she coldly confronted the already-flustered Dave. He was still reeling from his fight over the phone with Sally. "I met him storming out of the elevator. He says you practically picked him up and threw him out of the room. So I came back early to try and calm you down."

"He's a pompous ass," Dave grimaced, slipping the cellphone back into his shirt pocket.

"He's a kind old man who was just trying to help."

"I don't need his help," Dave angrily retorted.

"That's so stupid, Dave," she sighed, shaking her head sadly from side-to-side. "When all else fails, *that's* when we must turn to God. That's when we need Him the most, particularly His comfort and healing. You really should have learned a little from our years going to church with Mom when we were kids."

"Is God going to work a miracle?" Dave huffed.

"Probably not, Dave," she admitted. "We're just not that important for Him to change the laws of nature at our whims. But then again, who knows? God can do anything. Maybe He will work a miracle. Cliff prayed with me—we asked God to help us, in whatever manner God wishes. Cliff just wanted to do that for you, here, with Mom."

"Hah," he snorted bitterly, unwilling to let go of his anger, "fat chance!"

"We shouldn't be arguing like this, Davey," she softly chided him. "Not here, not now..."

She just looked at him with big sad eyes.

He regretted his blunt words, looking over at the husk of what remained of his mother.

The tube into her nose was sucking out what looked like yellow phlegm.

Dave gagged, looking quickly away.

Alright, then...he had to get himself back into a reasonable equilibrium if he was going to do any good.

"For her sake," he sighed, shrugging, "Cliff can come back and do his little, useless prayer, if he wants to waste his..."

"He's gone, Dave," she sighed, reaching out and holding his hands, looking him straight in his eyes.

"And I don't think we should wait," she defiantly announced, letting loose of Dave's hands to walk up to the edge of the bed and put her hand on her mother's free hand—which lay on the sheets motionless, swelled up to twice its normal size. The other hand was hidden under the bed sheets, with I.V. lines leading to it.

Jean's swollen free hand was black with the numerous broken blood vessels on its surface.

"But…"

"I talked with another doctor in the cafeteria, Dave," she firmly continued without pause. "He examined Mom earlier today, but just now got back her latest test results. Her kidneys are gone. Her liver is gone. Her heart is barely beating. And the CT scan they did on her when she was first admitted shows massive bleeding in her brain. I'm sorry, Dave, but there's no point in waiting any longer. I'm giving the authorization to…"

"No!" he shouted at her, grabbing her tightly by her arm.

"Dave, what are you doing?"

"I'm protecting our Mother."

"Don't be ridiculous, Dave. I'm trying to do the right thing here and…"

"Get out!"

"What?"

"Get out of this room!" he yelled at her, slinging her around and bodily *throwing* her through the automatically-opening doors!

—as orderlies and nurses outside the door rushed up and Dave reached into his baggy pants and pulled out the stubby black *gun!*

As one, they fell backward.

"Anyone who tries to enter this room unless it's a nurse doing something necessary for my Mom I will *shoot* them!" he loudly threatened.

Shocked, they looked at each other before hastily withdrawing. He saw a nurse grab up a phone and start talking frantically into it, making quick, scared gestures.

Doubtless they were calling security.

Doubtless, the hospital's security personnel would immediately call the police!

The police might even call in a swat team.

But it didn't matter.

Not even Cat backing away surrounded by nurses, her hand to her open mouth, horrified at his actions, mattered.

His mother was going to get her twenty-four hours, one way or another!

"Hang in there, Mom," he reassured her, sitting back down firmly in the chair by the bed.

In his right hand he resolutely held the black pistol, aimed at the doorway.

He reached up and over with his left hand to place it protectively on his mother's swollen free hand.

It felt clammy, mushy, and *cold*—like the hand of a corpse.

Was he doing the right thing?

He didn't know.

All he knew was that he had to *try!*

He'd failed at every other big thing he'd ever attempted. At least he could defend his mother to the bitter end, no matter whether he was right or wrong.

It was almost 24 hours later.

Dave could barely keep his eyes open.

Most of the personnel of ICU had been evacuated. The other couple patients had been moved out to safer quarters. Now it was a standoff between him and a whole squad of police. They were armed to the teeth. They had on armored vests. It was clear they didn't want to hurt him—even perhaps sympathized with him—but couldn't allow him to be a threat to the rest of the hospital personnel.

"David, it's time to give up!" a deep voice boomed loudly.

It was Dave's police "negotiator" talking on a bull-horn trying to get him to surrender. Dave just continued to sit, silently staring out the large glass windows of the room at the assembled cops.

"You told us you needed twenty-four hours and that time's now up!" the deep voice of the negotiator continued. "We stood back and didn't force the issue. We did our part. Now it's time for you to do your part. Your Mother's condition hasn't improved. In fact, the nurses you let in say that her readings are getting increasingly bleak. The doctors say the machines can't keep her heart beating much longer anyway. They tell me that her circulatory system is collapsing. You'll be doing your mother a favor to put an end to her suffering. If she can feel anything in her coma, it can't be anything but terrible pain. Please listen to the doctors, David. Put down your gun and come on out. It's over!"

Dave wearily glanced at his wrist watch.

Yes, it was again early morning.

He'd been there all the last day plus the night, not moving from his chair. He'd neither eaten nor drunk anything, including water. He'd not gone to the bathroom. He'd not abandoned his post.

But...maybe his Mother's condition *was* just an untimely stroke.

Maybe his Mother was truthfully gone.

Maybe her illness and suffering were finally over?

No!

He angrily but silently *screamed* out to the Universe...a mental explosion of "capital letters" raw emotion:

I'M NOT JUST A TOTAL FAILURE! I'M NOT JUST A COSMIC MISTAKE! I'M NOT JUST AN IGNORANT SAVAGE! I'M NOT JUST A HELPLESS PAWN BATTED ABOUT BY A CRUEL MOTHER NATURE!

He was determined to do this one big, last thing right.

I'm defending Mother until my final breathe...or until I just topple out of my chair, dead asleep—either of the two options...unless of course the police storm in and shoot me first...regardless, I'm taking a stand!

"Dave?" —came the tentative voice of his sister from out in the central ICU chamber.

"Go...away...Cat," he grated. His own voice was harsh from his throat being dried up from not drinking anything for so long.

"I'm coming in, Dave," she now more-resolutely stated, stepping into his vision out there in the central chamber of the ICU.

A policeman tried to grab her and drag her back but she lurched forward out of his grasp and stepped toward the door.

Dave stiffly rose up from his chair, aiming his pistol at her.

"You won't shoot me..." Cat knowingly claimed, coming forward yet another step.

BLAM!

Too late realizing that the gun was still set on "two-stars", Dave saw the glass of the door *shatter*, sending *shards* flying everywhere!

Oh, Christ, I just meant to stun her—Dave sighed to himself.

"Get back, get back!" shouts mixed in the melee in the ICU as various police frantically barked out orders: "Take him, take him out! ...take your shot! ...stop him!"

Jean groaned.

Everybody froze.

Her eyes blinked opened, looking around in confusion.

Her blackened hand reached slowly upward, a pink glow starting to infuse the skin.

Dave wearily laid his gun on the covers of the bed and took her hand.

It was warm.

Chapter 11

CAPTURED

It would be funny

If it weren't so sad

When you think you are free

But you're really trapped

Not like a lion in a cage

More as a kitty in a house

Where devoted, cautious owners

Loved you just a wee bit too much...

The Luminary Chronicles, 11:23

Dave sat dejectedly in his jail cell.

A flickering fluorescent panel in the hallway outside was the only light. Dave sat huddled upon a hard bunk. Other than the grey bars of his cage, only a toilet and sink kept him company.

The one phone call he'd been allowed to make was to George. Poor George! Dave was asking a lot of his friend. Previously, his request to George was merely to look after Dave's zoo while Dave made a "quick" trip out to Yale. Now Dave's request was regretfully open-ended.

There was a litany of charges leveled against him.

They didn't even allow him to post bail.

He should be collapsed on his bunk, dead asleep—but even in his exhaustion he couldn't rest. His mind was racing a million miles a minute.

Would his mother recover?

What was Sally doing?

Would Cliff claim credit for the 'miracle' with Jean?

How was Sally's mother doing?

Where was the Device?

Who had taken it?

Was Victor discovering anything about the "nuclear" explosion they triggered?

Yes, the police had taken away his cellphone and super-gun. But they couldn't take away his worried mind. Would that they could...

"Dr. King?" —came a gravelly voice from beyond the bars.

It was a familiar voice.

Dave looked up from his near-trance to see the burly, dark-glasses-wearing form of Agent Anderson standing there beside a regular policeman.

"Not you again," Dave groaned, hanging his head.

"Oh, come on," the Agent cheerfully stated, stepping into the cell when the policeman unlocked the padlocked door and swung it open. "Surely I'm better than going to prison for several years?"

"You're turning me loose?" Dave said hopefully.

"Well, not exactly," the Agent said, reaching down to grip Dave's arm in a strong grasp, lifting him bodily up off the bunk.

"You're *not* turning me loose?" Dave ruefully guessed, wincing at his bruised arm.

"We need your help," Anderson simply stated, leading him out of the cell.

"Well, ain't that a surprise," Dave sighed, allowing himself finally to go unconscious, slipping out of the Agent's grasp to fall flat upon the hard floor.

He awoke on a bare bunk in a small dark room. Outside he could hear what sounded like muffled shouts of drilling soldiers.

Oh, great.

He was back in a prison, just at a different location. Now he was on a military base.

In the weak light dimly-illuminating the small room he raised his head and looked around.

The light was coming from a small barred window up high above him.

He saw a wooden table, a chair, a bucket, and nothing more.

"This is worse than that jail cell I was in," he groaned to himself. "Anderson hasn't done me any favors."

He closed his eyes, trying to find a less uncomfortable position on the hard bed, trying to go back to sleep.

"Get up!" a powerful voice seemed to explode into his skull.

He leapt up out of bed, staggering on bare feet on an icy floor, vaguely aware that he only wore white boxer shorts.

"Assume the position!"

In a sudden blast of glaring light from a high, naked light bulb Dave saw that a huge beast of a man towered above him. The beast had bulging eyes. There was a jagged white scar across his face.

"Position?" Dave gasped, cowering..."*What* position?"

"Hands up—then behind your head—then clasped together!"

Dave did as ordered, suddenly scared out of his mind.

He felt cold metallic handcuffs snapped onto his wrists, locking them tightly together behind his head.

"What...are you...doing?" Dave gasped, horrified.

"Shut up, you piece of crap!" the burly man literally screamed in his ear as he slung Dave around then bashed him in his jaw with a big fist.

Dave fell to the floor.

His ears were ringing, everything seemed to be spinning around in a circle, and he felt warm blood trickling down his chin from a split lip.

"Wha...wha...w-what are you...?" Dave stammered, crumpled in a pile on the floor.

"Think about it!" the towering man screamed at him before abruptly turning and stomping out of the room.

Dave heard a lock snap shut.

Then, except for the distant rhythmic shouting coming in through the high window, everything was quiet.

Dave lay twisted onto his side on the freezing floor, blood smearing the stone under his face. He barely was able to get his shackled hands over his head and into a more comfortable position over his chest. Then, despite the pain, he began to drift off into a fevered sleep...

"Get up!"

Dave's sticky eyelids fluttered open.

He was shivering uncontrollably, in a fetal position.

It was that same brute again, towering above Dave's trembling body...outlined by the blazing light swinging high up in the ceiling.

"Assume the position!"

"I...can't...get up," Dave weakly coughed from the floor.

"Wrong answer!" the wild-eyed man looming above Dave shouted.

Dave felt *shuddering blows* from the man's big boots *smashing* into his naked ribs...over and over and over...

"Think about it!" the Giant screamed again at him as he finally stopped beating him and stomped out of the door. The door locked again with a solid "thunk."

Then the blazing light above suddenly snapped off.

The room was plunged into total darkness.

It must be night...no light or sound coming from the high barred window.

Dave drifted off into a fevered stupor, hardly able to think because of the blazing pain throbbing in his sides from cracked ribs.

Time passed unnoticed.

"I'm sorry about all this," a soft voice inserted itself into Dave's brain.

Blearily, Dave looked up, half expecting to see Agent Anderson.

Instead, there was a kindly-smiling young man. He wore a nondescript, gray military outfit with no visible insignia or rank. He was clean-shaven with short brown hair.

His sympathetic brown eyes radiated genuine concern.

"Here, let me help you up," the man said, gently reaching down and supporting Dave's weak struggle to get to his feet.

Dave groaned from searing fire erupting in his sides.

"My...hands..." He croaked, pushing forward his painfully handcuffed wrists.

"Oh, I'm so sorry," the young man seemingly regretfully replied. "They won't let me take those off of you...not yet, anyway—but you look cold. I can give you a nice, warm blanket. Would that help?"

Dave nodded dully.

The uniformed man supported him as Dave managed to stagger the few steps to the plain table. There, Dave was carefully lowered onto the single wooden chair. An itchy, thick blanket was draped over his shoulders and back. The man stood, hovering protectively.

"You must be thirsty," the man sympathetically stated, setting a knapsack onto the tabletop and pulling out a plastic bottle of water.

He unscrewed the bottle's top, lifted it away, and placed the opened bottle in front of Dave on the bare wooden table.

"Go ahead," the man urged him. "Please drink."

Dave grabbed the bottle in both of his handcuffed hands and greedily guzzled the cool liquid. It flowed into his dry throat like the best thing he'd ever drunk in his entire life.

"That...was...good," Dave croaked, setting the empty plastic bottle back onto the table.

"Some food?" the man said kindly, pulling out a sandwich from the knapsack and placing it also in front of Dave.

Dave grabbed it and stuffed it into his mouth, gobbling it down in a few seconds.

"There...better?" the man solicitously said, placing a tender hand on Dave's fevered forehead.

"Where are w-we?" Dave gasped, looking around more intently.

"You're safe," the man soothingly stated. "As long as you cooperate, Dr. King, that *animal* won't come back. I'll see to it. And we'll move you to better quarters—get you some medical care. Those ribs look like they sure need some bandaging. I bet they really hurt. And we'll get that split lip sewn up. It's quite ugly. All we need from you is a little information."

Dave shuddered, his mind soothed by the quiet tones of the man's voice. He thought back to the violent beating he'd endured...how long ago? He didn't know. Time had lost all meaning to him. But surely this young man *wasn't* the kind friend that he pretended to be? Maybe he'd better be cautious in response to this "good cop" tactic.

Yes, Dave had seen enough detective films and TV shows to know what was happening.

"Exactly what do you...want to know?" he managed to croak out, trying to focus on the man's words.

"Well, for one thing, where you got *this*."

The kindly young man reached into his knapsack and pulled out Dave's stubby black gun, now neatly enclosed in a clear plastic evidence bag.

"It's a quite interesting gun," the man continued. "In fact, we've never seen anything like it before. Pity we can't get it to function. You must have drained its battery, so-to-speak, when you fired it in the hospital. So we can't really analyze it as we'd like, test it, that sort of thing. Also, it seems to not be made out of metal, yet it stops x-rays from penetrating its innards—actually, warping their flight around its frame so that it appears to be invisible. We can't see what's inside without tearing it apart and possibly damaging it. It's an amazing terrorist weapon, though, from what it accomplished at the hospital. You carried it right through security checks and then held off an entire swat team. Impressive! My superiors are quite interested in it. So, to start with, where did you get it?"

Dave wavered in his chair, hardly able to sit upright. He was still abysmally weak, hurting, and confused. He knew he should try to resist. But he was just too tired, too beat-down, too cold.

"Alright," he managed to whisper. "I'll tell you everything. But you didn't have to torture me. I've got nothing to hide."

"Yes, that was a mistake," the man frowned at Dave. "I told them they didn't have to do it. I told them you would cooperate. But they insisted that first they had to break you down. I knew you were, in your heart, a true patriot. I knew that no matter how you've been subverted, you would come back to those who truly love you the best. So, please Dr. King, let's hear your story."

The man motioned in the air, the door to the cell opened, and a grim-faced man brought in an additional chair. The kindly young man sat on it opposite Dave. The other man set up a recorder on the table beside the empty water bottle.

Then the other guy left, locking the door securely behind him.

"We're all set, Dr. King," the man opposite Dave smiled. "Just tell us what happened, in your own words. No pressure. Tell it however you wish. Now just where was it that you got this amazing gun?"

Against his better judgment, Dave felt a wave of gratitude and relief. At last everything was finally out of his hands. This nice young man was going to help him. All he had to do was to tell the truth...

—at least *some* of the truth...

"The gun," he hesitantly began, gathering strength as the words began pouring out of him, "is from some other Dimension. It's a place where there was never an American Revolution. Benjamin Franklin and his co-conspirators were captured and hung. It's a place where drug abuse doesn't happen because drugs are banned. If you break a law you get summarily executed. That'd stop you from using cocaine, huh, no matter how addicted you were to it, right? Anyway, I'm babbling...back to the subject. The police there are called 'Peace-Keepers.' I got this gun off one of them. He was trying to shoot my...girlfriend. But I stopped him. Then I grabbed his gun. And we both escaped back to this Dimension and..."

Dave's voice trailed off. Looking at the man's sad eyes Dave knew he didn't buy it. Hell, even Dave himself had trouble believing such a crazy story.

"So that's it?" the man sighed, shaking his head sadly.

"But it's what happened," Dave moaned, rubbing at the caked blood on his chin with his cuffed fists.

"We see from your public record that you spent a year overseas, in France," the young man softly stated. "Was it there that you were radicalized?"

"What? No!" Dave protested.

"Before you went overseas, you were a standout American citizen," the man softly continued, "even regularly going to church. But afterward, you were different. You stopped going to church except when your Mother forced you to do so. You were dismissive of authority figures. You were bitter, weren't you—probably because you didn't get any support for your fringe research? You started doing secretive work in your garage. You and terrorist co-conspirators produced an explosive device that when it accidently went off it almost killed you. This is public knowledge, Dr. King. And now, in your grief at your Mother's illness, you reveal to us yet another terrorist device— this mysterious gun. Did you make it yourself or was it supplied to you? What was your real target? What were you planning? Isn't it true that you are actually *not* an enemy of the Revelation-Revolution, but one of its covert operatives?"

"But...I...no!" Dave weakly protested.

"I don't think you are cooperating with us," the young man sadly stated, slowly standing up from his chair.

"But I am!" Dave gasped.

"—by telling us a patently-ridiculous fairy story?" the man shrugged. "Well, have it your own way."

"No! Please! Don't go!" Dave sobbed, pushing himself up from the table...

—as several more men stormed into the room! Included amongst them was the scarred brute that previously beat him up.

"Assume the position!" the monster sneered at him.

Dave lifted his cuffed hands which were violently jerked over and behind his head.

The men kicked the chair to the side, uncoiling a thick rope.

Standing on the table, one of them threaded an end of the rope through a large hook set into the ceiling.

"No...please," he gasped, "don't hang me."

But a noose wasn't put around his neck. Instead, the other end was firmly tied around Dave's handcuffs.

The men yanked on the rope that was threaded through the hook above, stretching Dave's arms upwards—until he dangled, just barely supported by his downward-extended toes.

Dave felt excruciating pain in his distended shoulders, his fractured ribs, and his split mouth.

"Please..." he begged them.

—as they turned off the light, closed the door, and left him dangling there in the darkness.

Mercifully, he passed out from the pain—drifting into a horrendous hell of imagined smoke and fire for how long he didn't know.

"You look like crap!" a voice screamed into his face.

A blazing light shone directly into his eyes, blinding him.

"So this is the guy?" a melodic female voice sounded from beyond the bright light.

"Yes, Ma'am," a gruff reply sounded. "He's been hanging there for a while. We'd better cut him down or he's going to be dead soon, of no further use to us."

"He stinks."

"I think he took a dump in his shorts—maybe several."

"Clean him up."

"Yes, Ma'am," came the reply...

—as *icy water* smashed into Dave! The repeated painful blasts of the water knocked him around in a circle as he dangled from the rope.

It was a fire hose.

Dave was now vaguely aware of several large men holding a thick red hose as it blasted water onto his body, methodically aimed at his head down to his toes then back up again.

The drenching finally stopped. He gasped, dragging in air, half-drowned.

A firm hand gripped his chin. A pair of steely black eyes peered into his rapidly blinking ones. Then the fierce female voice again cut-through the fog surrounding him.

"Are you ready to talk?" her sing-song voice cut into his bleary mind.

In horror, his returning vision revealed the face of a slender oriental woman. Her expression was blistering. She radiated hate. Her slanted eyes were squinted into mere slits. Her hair was impeccably long and black. Her lips had just a hint of red lipstick. But her mouth was twisted into a grimace of *loathing!*

He started laughing—a ragged, gasping, cackling sound repulsive even to his own ears.

"Go to hell..." he whispered through cracked lips.

He knew they were going to kill him. Why should he give them more than he'd already said?

"Get with the program!" the brutal male voice bellowed in reply as Dave felt the man's heavy boots *kicking* again into his already-fractured ribs.

This time when he went unconscious there was no awareness of the passage of time.

There was only a featureless, black abyss that seemed to go on forever.

He awoke shivering uncontrollably, so weak he could hardly move his head, let alone his body.

He began coughing and hacking, trying to clear thick phlegm from his throat and lungs.

He vaguely realized that his hands were free. They'd finally taken off the handcuffs. Apparently he was too far gone for the shackles to be necessary.

"So y-you're not d-dead, a-after all," a shaky voice stammered from out of the darkness.

"W-what?" Dave managed to croak back, vainly trying to see who was talking.

Dave was again lying on the hard bunk. Apparently they'd cut him down. But he didn't feel any gratitude. His whole body was throbbing with pain. He could barely lift his head to see who was speaking.

"We've g-got to g-get out of h-here," the harsh voice whispered to him out of the gloom. "I d-don't know about y-you, but I'm almost d-dead. They d-did a real j-job on me, lost a lot of b-blood...feels like they've worked you over p-pretty good also, your r-ribs feel b-busted up."

A matchstick suddenly flared and Dave peered straight into the eyeless sockets of *Agent Anderson's* mauled face. Dried blood from a gash on his forehead coated the empty orbs.

"They l-left my clothes on," Anderson said, fumbling at Dave's body with rough hands. "Can you s-see me ok? All I've got to make l-light for you is a couple old m-matches stuck down in the creases of my p-pockets. They took everything else, including my d-dark glasses neurological visor. There are no sounds of m-marching outside this building s-so it must be n-nighttime and..."

"Where are we?" Dave managed to gasp. "What's going on?"

"It's s-some sort of black-ops g-group. They think we're t-terrorists trying to..."

"You too?"

"My dark g-glasses aren't exactly s-standard issue," Anderson roughly whispered. "They snatched m-me when they g-grabbed you."

Dave nodded, breathing heavily. Now it made sense.

"I never heard of implants capable of...doing what you claimed it could do," Dave gasped, exhausted from trying to speak.

"I'm f-from the other D-Dimension, Dr. King," Anderson matter-of-factly stated. "I was t-trying to protect you all along, to keep you s-safe."

"You're from over there? Really?"

Dave saw the eyeless, bloodied head nodding. Dave noted with concern that the man's forehead was split open. Not only was his skin was split, but *the actual bone* was deeply fractured. Dave thought he could glimpse white brain matter under the hanging skin. The man was seriously injured. A great deal of blood was caked up along the side of his head and along his neck.

"They d-don't know that, of course," Anderson struggled to speak, "a-about me b-being from some other world. They w-wouldn't believe it if you told them—too focused on the p-present world dangers. I k-kept to my c-cover story of being an FBI agent so..."

"Yes...the real story is too incredible to believe. But—I've got lots of questions for you."

"They'll have to w-wait. They just now put me in h-here. You weren't moving. I thought you were d-dead—I guess they were t-trying to maybe get you to start t-talking to me—this room's bugged, of course."

"They can hear us now?"

"My internal b-brain implant interface is shielding us—p-putting out radio-frequency interference. All they'll hear is a small increase in b-background hiss."

The flaring match was slowly dimming.

"Then tell your 'implant' to call for help!"

"Doesn't w-work like that, I'm afraid," he grumbled. "We're p-pretty m-much on our own."

"Can it open the door to our cell?"

"Maybe...if the l-lock is e-electronic."

"Then help me get up."

"You'll have to b-be my eyes..."

"—if you'll be my legs!"

Together, they managed to stumble over to lean against the locked door.

"If t-they're on the o-other side, this won't h-help us much," Anderson said.

"At least we're trying."

"Here goes n-nothing."

Dave heard a faint "click" as the bolt in the door's lock slid back.

They slowly inched the door quietly outward as Dave struggled to stretch his neck and peer around its edge.

He saw a guard sitting at a monitoring station, headphones on, his back to them, looking at an infrared scan of their room where the two of them apparently still lay motionless over by the one bed.

"Your implant is sending out a false image...good," Dave whispered.

"W-where's the g-guard?" Anderson whispered back.

"He's about ten feet in front of us, against a wall."

Anderson gently pushed Dave to the side, *launching* himself forward. And before the guard could react, Anderson slapped a *rear naked chokehold* around his neck!

The guard struggled and kicked, but Anderson was too strong. In a minute the man was unconscious or dead, limp in Anderson's arms.

The Agent unceremoniously dumped the guard's body to the side, sagging into the vacated chair.

"W-where's the t-terminals?" Anderson stammered, fumbling with his fingers at the computer.

Dave crawled up to the computer station on his hands and knees, gasping for breath.

"Looks like there's an internal Intranet port over to your right," Dave whispered back.

Rippling tendrils sprang from the Agent's fingertips and dived into the Intranet plug.

"What are you doing? What's that coming out of your fingers?" Dave asked, dragging himself up to lean back in a rolling chair beside the Agent.

"My neural network...is enhanced...lots of c-connectivity f-for the i-implant...and now I've got access to the entire b-base," Anderson triumphantly whispered back. "You just s-sit there. You might c-cover your ears, though. I'll do the r-rest."

Dave lifted his trembling hands to do as ordered...

—when the entire world seemed to implode around him!

Sirens were screeching, *explosions* going off all around, and people were *screaming* as fire spread through the corridor and surrounding buildings, engulfing them.

"S-self-destruct m-mechanisms," Anderson gasped over the roar that now sounded around them. "These black-op g-groups love them—until they're t-triggered from within, that is. Come on, Dr. King, let's go g-get our stuff. I'll p-push and you g-guide me. We need to get to r-room 14D. I think it's down the corridor to the right and then two d-doors on the l-left."

Dave was choking in thick black smoke. Fire alarms "clanged" loudly. Feet stomped around him as soldiers ran by. Anderson pushed Dave on the rolling chair, lurching along. There it was! Dave saw a small door sign through the smoke, "14D." Anderson unlocked the door with his implant, pushing Dave inside while closing the door firmly behind them.

"This is their v-vault room," Anderson said, staggering, barely able to keep standing upright. "Do you s-see a safe or s-something similar around?"

"There," Dave pointed with his hand—and then hastily explained with his voice: "Up against the far wall. It's a big inset safe. It looks like a bank vault."

"I've g-got it," Anderson said, moving them up against it.

The tumblers spun and the heavy vault door swung open, brushing them aside.

Dave crawled around the now-open vault door, looking into a dim, crowded interior.

"Y-you see our stuff?" Anderson said, starting to cough from the smoke coming in under the door of the room.

"Uhm...well...yes!" Dave exclaimed, weakly crawling into the vault interior. He grabbed his knapsack which lay against one of the inner walls. Jerking it open he saw in its main interior section his cell-phone, a couple more plastic bottles of water, the packaged black gun, and Anderson's black sunglasses.

"I've got your visor."

"Thanks," Anderson gurgled in relief as Dave handed him the sunglasses, which Anderson put into his head with fumbling hands.

With a "click" it snapped into place over his missing orbs.

"Oh, that's m-much b-better," he gasped. "I'd h-hate to g-go out blind," he said as he sagged to the floor of the vault, his head slumping. "You...see my mirror in there also?"

At a time like this Anderson was worried about how his hair looked? Really? His hair and head was a bloody mess.

But Dave fumbled around in the knapsack, feeling the flat smooth surface of the small mirror, pulled it out and placed it firmly into the Agent's grasping fist.

"So how do we get out of here?" Dave urgently said, the smoke getting thicker. "I'm weaker than a wet noodle...and you don't look much better."

"We d-don't...get out," Anderson grimaced as sweat streamed down his face across several days of stubble. The sweat mixed with layers of dried blood, making him look like a zombie-reject.

"Then what?" Dave asked, puzzled, as Anderson made a supreme effort to reach out, grab onto a protrusion on the big vault door's inner mechanism, and swing it *inward* on them. With a solid "thunk" they were *locked* inside the vault. Only a couple LED bulbs provided faint red light.

"We stay p-put," Anderson grimly stated, squirming in the tight space to get his hands up towards his bleeding head.

"Here?" Dave groaned, leaning his own head back against a half-opened drawer. "This is an even worse jail cell. There's not enough oxygen in here to breathe. We'll suffocate in a few hours."

"There's a *small tactical nuke* counting down to go off any second now," Anderson quietly laughed.

Dave wasn't sure he'd heard Anderson correctly.

"Did you say a real nuke?" Dave gasped, "—with lethal radiation?"

"You'll be s-safe in here," Anderson whispered, his head lolling to the side. "There's a lot of thick m-metal between us and the r-radiation that..."

"What on earth is so important that they'd blow it up with a nuclear bomb rather than have it get away from them?" Dave exclaimed in disbelief.

Anderson groaned, clearly fighting to stay conscious.

"It's *you*," he whispered, now shakily moving the mirror held in his left hand up in front of his face.

"What?" Dave barked, incredulous. "Me? But they were *killing* me! Those bastards just wanted more super-guns. They didn't even believe my claim of traveling to some other Dimension."

"It w-wasn't them that planted the f-final fail-safe bomb," Anderson whispered, his voice growing ever fainter.

"Ok, then who was it?"

"Hard...to talk...just listen..."

"Hell no! I need answers!"

"No time to explain...must give you something...before it all ends," Anderson coughed, reaching with his trembling right hand up over the bloody mess of his head.

He *smashed* his hand down upon the wound.

"Hey, be careful there," Dave tried to warn him...

—as Anderson *dug his fingernails* deep into the split skin and got a grip at the edge of the fractured bone on the top of his own skull...

"What?" Dave gasped. "*No...!*"

—as Anderson *screamed* into the tight confines of the black vault, *ripping up* the bone to reveal a grey-white portion of his brain beneath...

—then *plunging his fingers* into his *own brain* and slowly extracting them...

—clutching tightly a *rectangular object* that looked to Dave much like a metallic Brillo Pad which you use to clean dirty dishes with...

—from which white *tendrils* dangled, slowing retracting into its bloody interior.

"You're...going to...need this," the Agent whispered. His words were barely audible.

—as in horrified fascination, Dave watched Anderson's jerking hand move over above the knapsack and drop the twitching pad into its opened top.

"What *the hell* did you just do?" Dave grimaced, frozen in place. His knees were jammed painfully up into his chest in the cramped space. His eyes were stretched wide in horror.

But there was no answer.

Anderson was silent.

In fact, he'd just stopped breathing...

—as the BLAST went off; and Dave felt like he'd been fired out of a cannon!

Dave rode the blast-wave with a sense of exhilaration, as if it were a carnival roller-coaster.

His head wasn't just spinning—*everything* was *really* spinning!

The *entire vault*, in fact, was tumbling end-over-end—having been ripped out of its concrete foundation and thrown up high into the air!

"It's just the last inch that gets you..." Dave laughed giddily as he and the vault *bounced* in several smashing blows into the ground, knocking him yet again into blissful unconsciousness.

Chapter 12

SUBSPACE

Don't go too deep

Or you'll never be able to retreat

Gone too far in there's no way back

Dog-paddling out into that seductive sea

Realizing you've no strength to return to shore

Such a sad reward for "more, more, more"...

Understanding that you'll soon be dead

The riptide pulling you inexorably away

A force too great to ignore or defeat

You choose instead to sink into the icy depths

Diving ever deeper, deeper, deeper, deeper...

How long can you hold your breath?

The Luminary Chronicles, 12:72-74

"And how are you feeling, Sir?" the pretty nurse asked him, carefully checking his blood pressure.

"I'm much better now with you here," Dave answered cheerfully. He relished the intravenous lines pumping fluids into him, the clean bandages on his bruised torso, and the stiff mouth where they'd sewn up his split lip.

In addition to decontaminating and cleaning him up (nicely, not with a fire hose), they'd given him a soft, clean hospital gown to wear.

"Don't talk, just rest," she firmly ordered him as she undid the arm cuff and hurriedly moved on. He lay in utter relief and relaxation on his nice safe, soft cot. Around him were many more cots, all occupied with bloodied, burnt victims.

The smells and sounds were horrific.

Moans were mixed with screams. Burnt flesh gave off a putrid *barbequed* aroma.

But Dave was glad to just be alive.

He was one of many half-naked, dirt-and-blood-encrusted survivors. Fortunately, the responders hadn't yet gotten around to acquiring each person's vital statistics. There were just too many of the burnt and injured. For now the medical personnel were swamped with survivors.

So they didn't know, yet, that Dave was a hunted, fugitive "terrorist"—perhaps the one who was going to be blamed for this whole terrible disaster!

He was now in a large medical tent, being treated with many others by a triage team of first responders.

Agent Anderson hadn't made it.

After the blast, when Dave regained consciousness, he engaged the emergency-exit mechanism and crawled from the vault across Anderson's stiffening body. Rigor mortis was setting in, so they must have been in the vault for at least twelve hours. Dave was unconscious inside for all that time. When he groggily awoke, the air was stuffy. If he'd remained there much longer he would have suffocated.

As it was, the exterior wasn't much better.

The small nuclear blast not only destroyed the military base, it also decimated the nearby town and countryside. Outside, it truly looked like the Apocalypse. It was much worse than the mushroom explosion that he and Victor had set off in the Vermont woods. This devastation was not just of trees, streams, and mountains—but also of buildings, livestock, and people.

Hideously-burnt corpses littered the blackened landscape.

Dave was lucky he'd been protected inside the vault for those first few hours. The external radiation quickly decayed below the lethal level. In addition, the responding disaster teams were immediately there to snatch up the staggering Dave, swooping him away to nearby emergency triage facilities.

Lying on the cot—the medical personnel now occupied with other sufferers far more grievously injured than him—Dave figured he might as well make a phone call.

He'd had the foresight to not let loose of the knapsack, holding it with a death-grip at all times. Now it lay safely tucked away under his bunk.

Not only was Victor's cellphone inside, but also the mysterious gun. In addition, he'd loosened Anderson's dark eyeglasses then ripped them off his head, stuffing that into the knapsack as well. Anderson didn't need them any longer.

The man had been a royal pain. But he'd also made the ultimate sacrifice.

Dave didn't know what to make of Anderson's claim to be from Sally's Dimension. Supposedly he came over here to somehow "protect" Dave?

How would Anderson even know that he needed help?

Yet without the Agent's aid, Dave would still be back in that hellhole being tortured by the anti-terrorist black-ops unit.

"Whatever your motivation, you were a friend to me," Dave admitted, rolling painfully over onto his stomach to reach down into the knapsack under his cot. He pushed aside the lonely dark glasses, and pulled out the cellphone.

He firmly pressed the red button twice.

Almost immediately he got an answer.

Thank God they had a good communication net up and running at the triage center.

"David, is that you?" an excited voice burst from the speaker.

"Victor...it's so good to hear your voice," Dave replied, relieved and yet alarmed at the same time. "Are you alright? Have they tried to grab you?"

"Grab me?" the voice answered, puzzled. "What do you mean? I've been trying to contact you for days now, with no answer. My boy, I've been worried sick about *you!* Your phone wouldn't even ring!"

"You were worried with good reason, Victor," Dave replied. "I was in a 'dark site,' isolated from everything including electronic communication. But I suppose you saw me—again—on the news?"

"How could I not? What is this about you holding a whole hospital hostage? I sent you off to escape unwanted scrutiny and then you are causing a sensation making the international news broadcasts?"

"It was my mother, Victor..." he started to explain.

"Oh, yes, the Miracle!"

"It wasn't a miracle, it was..."

"Even the Vatican weighed in on it, my boy. They lauded your Mother's amazing recovery as proof of the 'Infinite Love of God.'"

"She's ok?" Dave anxiously replied, desperately wanting confirmation.

"Oh, my boy, she's up and walking—talking, in fact. She and her local church pastor are quite famous now. She tells anyone who will listen about the *Prayer of Pastor Cliff* bringing her back from the dead."

"Unnngggghh," Dave groaned, dragging out the sound. "I'll never hear the last of it."

"But that is all in the past, my dear boy. How are you? Where are you now? What is going on?"

Dave paused, setting the cellphone on his chest, raising his head to look around at the moaning patients around him.

None were in condition to care what he was quietly saying into the cellphone.

"I'm beat up but recovering, Victor," he shrugged off the Professor's concern. "I'll let you know later what happened. It's quite a story. For now I need to know if you've found out anything about our...accident. It's very important I know. Have you had a chance to confer with your 'trusted colleagues' at Yale?"

"Yes, yes!" the eager voice of the Professor came out of the speaker. "That's what I've been trying to contact you about, David. As we suspected, that incredible amount of energy liberated was indeed impossible. Everyone I talked to in confidence agreed with that conclusion. Even if we achieved sustained ignition, it could only warm the reaction chamber from the relatively tiny amount of deuterium in the flow mixture."

"So what did happen?"

"There's only one possible answer that makes any sense," Victor continued with intense excitement.

"What?"

"Somehow—we're not sure how—the overlapping conditions of your novel crystalline matrix, blend of rare elements, and oscillatory excitations..."

"Yes, yes?"

"We think that it *ripped* a small tear in the fabric of space/time and exposed a piece of *subspace*: liberating an undiluted, concentrated flow of *Dark Energy!*" he excitedly concluded.

Dave was struck dumb. He didn't know what to say.

"David, my boy?" Victor questioned. "Are you still there?"

"I'm...here—but *how* can that be?"

"We still don't even know what this mysterious thing is which we term, 'Dark Energy', correct?" Victor excitedly stated.

"Yes, but..."

"And yet we *do* know that it comprises roughly 70% of the Universe. It's the primary component of our reality. It counteracts gravity. It is immensely powerful. Yet we've only just detected it in a 'blink of an eye' ago, in cosmic time. It's been hidden from mankind for almost all our existence on this fine planet. And now, we think that you've discovered a way to unleash it!"

"But...if that's true...if we can somehow control the process and not just unleash a huge explosion—then..." Dave gasped, his mouth hanging open, stunned beyond amazement.

"—*unlimited energy!*" Victor gushed over the phone. "We could in one fell swoop solve all of the energy problems of our planet. This discovery goes far beyond the illusory promise of cold fusion. It is far superior to atomic power plants or thermonuclear fusion reactors. It won't require containing incredibly-hot, fickle plasmas with gigantic magnetic fields. It won't require massive laser beams to heat up tiny pellets. We can have not just the power of the sun, my boy—but the power of the *underlying fabric of reality itself!* Just think of the practical applications that..."

"—no more fossil fuels needed," Dave jumped into the excited speculation, "—stopping global warming in its tracks! No more wars over dwindling resources. We can contain pollution of all types, end world hunger, split water to power vehicles with liquid hydrogen, revolutionize space flight, and maybe even provide enough energy to approach the speed of light, powering expeditions to the stars. Wow!"

"We need to do more experiments," Victor stated. "We must learn how to, somehow—as you said—to control the process. The fate of the very world hangs in the balance, David! We must bring in the government to help with this. We must have a meeting of all the great minds. We will need to involve all the world's finest physicists. Why, it will be another 'Manhattan Project'! It will be the greatest achievement of mankind. And it will all be because of your discovery, my boy. They won't have enough Nobel Prizes to give to you. We need to..."

"Victor," Dave stopped him.

"Yes, my boy?"

"Isn't that what they said about atomic energy?"

"Well, of course..." Victor slowly replied, his voice lower and more controlled. "But there were so many problems..."

"—and the negative usage?"

They were both silent for a few moments.

"Yes...you are right, David. We must carefully consider our next steps. We don't want this to become just another super-weapon. Indeed, in the wrong hands, it might be a weapon powerful enough to easily vaporize our entire planet."

"I think it's already out of our hands."

"What?"

"It's gone, Victor," Dave glumly admitted.

"What is gone, my boy?"

"Our backup Device..."

"*What?*" Victor gasped in disbelief.

"It was stolen out of my garage, along with your van," he tearfully admitted. "I know it was stupid of me to stick it back in my garage where my original equipment was located, but..." his voice trailed off.

A terrible silence hung between them.

"Forget about blaming yourself," Victor gulped over the phone. "Yes, this is terrible news. If the Device is in terrorist hands, the fate of the world hangs in the balance. We must recover the Device."

"I don't know if it was the terrorists."

"Then was it the government? Was it those FBI people who were so eager to keep track of you?"

"I don't know...I don't think so," Dave said, furrowing his brow in concentration. "I just had a run-in with both the military and the FBI—where representatives of both didn't say anything to make me suspect that they were the culprit. They never mentioned the van or the Device. At least I don't think so..."

"Then someone wants this amazing research *stopped!*" Victor grimly exclaimed over the cellphone.

"Yes...whoever took it clearly wants further research shut down. That's why I was so worried about your safety, Victor," Dave quietly stated, making sure the surrounding patients and medical personnel could not hear him. "It's actually only you and me that know the details of the process. You've only sketched out an outline to your colleagues at Yale, right?"

"Yes, that is correct..."

"So if you and I were...*eliminated*—then the whole thing is stopped dead in its tracks, right?"

"Oh...yes...I see," Victor gasped. "And you are still being pursued with a federal warrant for your arrest. They could lock you up and just throw away the key—or worse."

Dave ruefully laughed.

"Yep...I've already got some experience with the 'worse'," he sighed painfully.

"Then—what are we to do?" Victor gasped. "It appears we can't go to any governmental agencies nor make this amazing discovery public."

"Not yet, that's for sure," Dave bitterly said, keeping his voice low. "And there's a lot more, even more amazing things, that I've not told you about yet, Victor."

"There's something more amazing than tapping into the subspace Dark Energy of the Universe?" Victor gasped again. "My boy, you are boggling my mind. Tell me! *Tell* me!"

Dave noticed a group of suspicious people entering the large tent at its rear that didn't look like medical personnel.

In fact, they looked exactly like a *squad of police*, carefully checking each person on a cot versus a picture on a tablet.

"Got to go, Victor. Stay safe!"

"What...?"

Dave turned off the cellphone. Then in one smooth motion he slipped the phone back into the knapsack, yanked out his I.V. needle, rolled off of the cot to the side, crawled on the floor over to the nurse's station, grabbed a doctor's smock and stethoscope hanging there, donned them, surreptitiously rose to his feet—then turned his back on the searching police and calmly walked with his knapsack out the opposite entrance.

Glancing back he saw his pretty nurse talking animatedly with the police at the other end of the large tent, pointing at his cot.

Jesus, they were on to him! Of course someone high up knew he was at the base. And they were trying to make sure he died in the explosion!

He ducked his head and exited the tent, disoriented, wobbling, but determined to keep going.

Where to hide, where to hide?—he desperately asked himself.

All sorts of people and vehicles milled about. The air was thick with black soot. Helicopters were landing and taking off from a departure zone, their "thrumming" drowning out everything else. Soldiers were guarding key junctions, rifles held at-ready.

Arf! Arf! Arf!—Dave heard nearby barking. He looked to his right, saw hastily-constructed pens—walked to them, then ducked into an enclosed structure, pushing into its dark interior, curling up with warm, friendly dogs.

They seemed to like him, snuggling up against him, wrapping him up in their warmth.

He'd always had a way with animals, reptilian or not.

He didn't emerge from the doghouse until the sun was low on the horizon, night closing in. But there was still enough twilight to see where he was going, yet shadowy enough for him to plod at the back of other walking groups unnoticed.

Walking calmly but quickly, trying not to attract any undue attention, he soon came to the edge of the large encampment. There he spied a supply truck standing with its back doors opened, being unloaded by a crew of workers.

"Perfect," he whispered to himself, sidling up to the workers just as they unloaded the last big crate. He darted behind them into the cool interior, hiding behind racks in the back.

He heard the doors being closed and locked behind him.

As the truck accelerated up a bumpy road, Dave collapsed flat onto the bare floorboards, totally drained.

His head was spinning from exhaustion.

He was a long way from regaining his health. He should be back on that cot in the medical tent, recuperating from his terrible ordeal.

But that was impossible.

He had to find help.

But where could he turn? He was a fugitive in two worlds!

Sally!

It had to be that crazy girl with the turtle tattoo.

He pulled out the cellphone from the knapsack, and by the light of its panel started to dial her number, remembering simultaneously to press the red button.

Then he paused.

She wasn't going to like hearing from him this way. But she owed him...sort of.   Anyway, maybe she felt a slight obligation to him...perhaps. Or maybe she didn't *hate* him quite as badly as she did last time he'd talked to her? Or, maybe she'd appreciate that he'd complimented her Turtle Tattoo once and so on that basis risk her own life to...

—oh, *hell!*

He completed dialing her number.

As it rang he sternly ordered himself: "Be tasteful! Don't lose your temper. Try to say nice things."

He was doomed.

True to form, the first words out of her mouth across the speaker were devastating:

"I told you I was *finished* with you! *Goodbye!*"

"Don't hang up, don't hang up!" he pleaded. "I'm so sorry, Sally, I was totally wrong. I'm an ass. I'm stupid. I'm a total screw-up. I wrecked your life. I didn't mean to do it but I did. There, I said it. It was *my* fault. *You're* the victim here. I don't know how you're even still functioning—let alone saving your other mother over here in this Dimension—after all the terrible things I did to you. *You* saved *me*. It was *you* that somehow got me away from those Keepers. Thank you, Sally. You're a real angel—and I'm a total *dope!*"

"Well...all of that's true," she agreed, sounding reluctant but remaining on the line.

"—and I need your help again," he breathlessly concluded.

"Oh, *sure!*" she spat into the phone. "I just got my adopted mother out of the hospital and you want me to..."

"I've got nowhere else to turn, Sally," he pleaded with her. "The police, the government, the military, and all the security agencies are out searching for me."

"I've seen the latest newscasts," she softly interjected. "They say you're a covert director of the 'RR'?"

"Yes!" he exclaimed. "No! I mean, I'm not that. Anyway, they're making me out to be the world's worst terrorist, right?"

"Well, maybe not *the* worst..."

"But right up there, correct?"

"Pretty much..."

"But I didn't do any of it," he protested. "I don't know exactly what's going on—but it's a lot worse than me doing some stupid experiments. There's some sort of conspiracy, one that even reaches over to *your* home world."

"What?"

"An FBI agent that's been after me from the very start," he softly said, pausing dramatically, "claimed to be from your Dimension."

She didn't reply.

"Did you hear me? I said that..."

"I heard you," she answered. "But that's ridiculous. I think you're just elaborating on whatever trouble you're in, trying to get me to..."

"I can prove it!"

"How?"

"He said he had a 'neural implant' that allowed him to interface with super-goggles he wore," he said.

"You mean dark eyeglasses?"

"Yes!"

"I see lots of your people wearing them here for..."

"—that give sight to the blind?" he demanded. "Do you see them restoring eyesight back to people whose eyes are *completely gone* from their sockets?"

"His eyes were missing?"

"Yes!" Dave continued, sensing he was somehow on a winning argument with Sally.

"Well, what does he say about why he...?"

"He's dead," he interrupted her. "But I've got the eyeglasses he wore. I brought them with me. Surely they must have other-worldly circuitry or capacities that are beyond what this Dimension offers?"

"What was this person's name?" she thoughtfully asked.

"What does that matter?"

"Just tell me!"

"Alright—*Agent Anderson,*" he said. "I don't know his first name. That's how he referred to himself. Do you recognize the name?"

For a moment she didn't reply.

"Well," she slowly admitted. "There's...top enforcement government officials in my world...who are rumored to have their eyes removed so not to have interference with the function of multi-spectral dark glasses...since the neural implants totally monopolize the brain's visual functions—perhaps he was one of them?"

"What you describe is definitely beyond the medical science of this world, isn't it?" Dave asked.

"Hmmm," She softly breathed over the phone.

"So you'll help me?" he tentatively asked.

"I'd like to see those glasses," she admitted.

"Can you meet me somewhere?" he eagerly asked.

"Well...I have been driving Mom's car—it's not as easy as a bub to control and goes much too fast, but..."

"I know it's asking a lot of you, Sally—but unless you help me, I think whatever's going on in your world and mine will stay hidden."

"Perhaps that's for the best?"

"It was *them*—whoever 'they' are—that *really* destroyed your life and killed your true Mom. Don't you want to at least know *why* they did it?"

"Yes," she quietly agreed. Then, more forcefully: "Where are you? Where can I meet you?"

"I'm...well...I don't know," he gulped.

"What are you doing?"

"Uh...I'm escaping the police—riding in the back of a truck I managed to sneak into and..."

"What road are you on?"

"I...I've got no idea," he admitted, suddenly feeling isolated and helpless.

"Does your cellphone have a GPS function?" she asked. Her voice was now calm and practical.

"Oh...of course," he nodded to himself. "Hold on a minute..."

He searched the functions on the small screen for global positioning.

There it was!

He hit the "search" command and saw coordinates spring up on an overlaid map.

"Ok, I see it," he whispered—then, "Sally?"

"Yes?"

"It says I'm on highway 60 headed west...not far from Vance Air Force Base where..."

"—the military base that was nuked yesterday by terrorists?"

"I guess that's the place," he sighed, suddenly aware of the devastation that was at least indirectly due to him. "That must be the town I saw destroyed nearby—Enid. I've been past there many times. It's not too far from my home in Edmond."

"Are you close to Lahoma?"

"What?"

"I called up an Oklahoma map on my adopted Mom's cellphone. It's a small town, just a few streets total, on the road that you mentioned."

"Yes, yes!" he readily agreed, blinking at the bright screen. His head was spinning again. It was getting difficult to concentrate. "I'm actually quite close to it and..."

"Then get out of that truck and I'll meet you at the Winery that's there on highway 60 at Lahoma. It's called the *'Eagle Flight Winery.'* Ever hear of it? It looks like it'll take me maybe three hours to drive up there."

"Thanks, Sally," he gulped again. "I'll do my best to be there when you arrive."

"Ok, Dave, and..." she paused.

"Yes, Sally?"

"Be careful."

"I'll try," he sighed, turning off the phone and sliding it back into the knapsack.

Hey, she was worried about him! Maybe she didn't hate him quite as much as before. But...maybe she just wanted to get to the bottom of this trans-dimensional "conspiracy" thing.

Whatever—he had to get out of the truck.

Crawling to the rear of the truck he felt for the knob he'd seen there earlier. Yes! Pushing it with difficulty he felt it moving a heavy latch on the outside.

One half of the rear door swung outward.

It was now dark outside. Dave could see nothing. He felt whipping wind rushing in around his face.

The truck was slowing for a turn, then swinging around it...

Slinging the knapsack across his shoulder he grabbed the half-door. Dave swung outward with it as it was flung sidewise by the turning truck, lost his grip, and fell off to the side...

He rolled end-over-end through thick brush at the side of the road, ending up in a painful heap.

He still clutched the knapsack.

"At least I don't think I broke anything new," he gasped, feeling shakily at his sides, arms, and legs.

The pain from his abused body was intense, but maybe if he just rested there in the weeds he might eventually be able to get up?

He felt like he was about to go unconscious again...

—when *a big shaggy dog* lurched out of the darkness, came up to him, and started licking his face.

Ah, another of his animal friends. It had several license tags on its collar. It was a local dog.

"Hey," he grinned, reaching up with a hand to rub the dog on its friendly head. "Maybe things aren't so bad after all?"

Arf!—the dog happily replied, hopping-about the supine Dave.

Dave was sure glad that dogs seemed to like him.

He crawled to his knees, grabbed the collar of the big dog, and used it to get up to his feet.

"Now where's that damn winery?"

In the direction he'd been traveling he saw lights up ahead.

"Ah...that must be it," he nodded. Stroking the big dog on its back he continued leaning on it for support, wearily trudging through the high grass in that direction...

—which quickly resolved into...

"A roadblock!" he gasped to the friendly dog, stopping dead still on the side of the road. "I got out of that truck just in time."

Indeed, soldiers up ahead were manning a gate they'd put across the entire road. Cars and trucks were lined up on both sides, awaiting inspection.

In the lights of the vehicles and military personnel, Dave spied the truck he'd been riding in. It appeared that the back gate had swung back shut after he'd been shaken off it. Good. Maybe they'd not realize there'd been a passenger inside.

Woof!—the dog softly warned from below Dave's clinging arm.

Yes, he saw them.

Police dogs were at the roadblock, on leashes carefully sniffing at the vehicles.

How could Dave get past them? Even if they liked him—licking him instead of biting him—they'd still alert the police to his presence.

"Well, friend, I think you're going to save me again," he said to the dog as he released it, gave it a little pat on its behind, ducked down, and headed off into the pasture to the side of the road.

A "howling" suddenly erupted as the dogs caught the smell and sight of the other dog.

In the confusion of the night, Dave snuck past—hidden in the dark and high growth of the pasture, keeping on staggering along.

It hurt his feet. They were only shod in thin hospital wraps. But he kept going through the night until he got to the small town. Yep, it was only three blocks long. He slinked through the gloom, avoiding the road, passing around small houses and businesses, until he reached the buildings at the other edge of the town. A lighted sign proudly proclaimed: *"Eagle Flight Winery."*

He found a spot under thick bushes where he could sit with his back to a tree while still observing the road. Then he began carefully searching through the knapsack to see if there were any additional resources.

It was getting chilly but against his fevered brow it felt good.

"Dark mystery glasses, super-gun, Victor's cellphone, strange neural implant-sponge...oh, and what's this?"

In a side pocket he found his set of keys, wallet, and pocket notebook. In the wallet was his money. He dare not try to use any of his credit cards, but at least he now had some cash. It wasn't much, but a couple hundred dollars in loose bills was a lot better than nothing.

Also, he found Agent Anderson's personal effects.

His FBI badge was there along with his identification card. It looked official and proper. Dave wondered if the man had actually worked for the FBI? But why would he lie to Dave on his deathbed? He had nothing to gain from making up a story, did he?

Along with the Agent's wallet (with a welcome hundred bucks more of cash) was also the man's gun.

It looked exactly like the one Dave had captured from the other-worldly Keeper...complete with the five-starred settings, here safely controlled by an overlaid plastic safety cap.

No wonder the black-ops site thought Anderson was a fellow terrorist. He had the very same energy-weapon!

So it was true.

Agent Anderson *was* from the other Dimension.

The plot thickened and deepened.

Dave fought to keep his eyes open. He had to be sharp when Sally came driving through. But his body was demanding that he lie flat on the dank soil and give-in to the throbbing pains shooting throughout his body, to just drift off...

"Dave?"

He jerked awake.

He'd drifted off into a feverish, shivering stupor.

It was Sally, bending over him, her long brown-red hair smelling fresh and clean.

"Oh...hi there," he weakly greeted her. "How'd you find me? Your hair sure looks pretty."

"Uhm, thanks. I tracked your cellphone signal," she said, looking about furtively.

The sky was starting to lighten up. It was almost morning. No one else was around. But the residents of the small town would be 'up-and-at-them' soon enough.

"But if you could do that then..."

"—others might also," she finished his thought. "Can you move?"

"Just barely," he groaned, getting his feet painfully under himself.

"Get in the car," she said, putting a thin but strong arm around his waist and helping him stand up. "I think I know where your van is. But it's not going to be there for very long."

"You do? How do you know about the van?" he gasped, grimacing as he climbed into the passenger side of an old sedan.

"I'm clever," she curtly replied.

"You're *very* clever," he sighed as his eyes slid shut and he once again was caught up in the embrace of the dark side of things.

But he had to stay awake, alert!

"Go ahead and take a nap," she said, climbing in behind the wheel. "We're going to Ada."

"But won't they know to look for us—at your house?"

"We're not going to my mother's house," she cryptically answered. "We're going to the source of all creativity, beneath the facade of society. We're going into the *true* darkness."

Wow. Sally sure talked sophisticated.

Beneath the façade of society—a *sub-society?*

His mind wandered to his previous conversation with Victor...amazing! Awesome! Spectacular! Mind-*boggling!*

Darkness...*Dark Energy!* What a concept. And it was "sub" reality again—*subspace.* It was just what a true scientist enjoyed more than anything, digging down into the known to find the yet-unrevealed Unknown. Maybe there was hope after all. Maybe instead of fighting against the uncaring forces of the Universe they were at last approaching some sort of Unity?

It was a comforting thought.

But unsettling at the same time...

And just how did Sally know so much?

It was too much. He fell fast asleep, rocked by the gently swaying car as Sally sped down the country roads.

Chapter 13

<u>BODY ART</u>

External manifestations

Of the creativity of the soul

Not just external attachments

But etched into living flesh

Becoming part of not just vision

But suffused with blood and vigor

Engendering a deeper reality

A hidden meaning manifested

Where demons dance unbidden

And angels fly without wings

And all manner of thought is possible

Even transgressing self-destructive limits...

Forbidden mysteries revealed at last.

The Luminary Chronicles, 13:54-57

"Hey, you wakin' up, Mr. King?"

Dave groggily opened his eyes, involuntarily flinching away...

No, it wasn't a police interrogator.

It wasn't a pretty nurse.

It wasn't even Sally.

It was *Snake!*

"Oh...it's you," Dave whispered. His head and body felt like they'd been run over several times by a truck. And here he was being greeted by a living cobra caricature!

"Gotcha some tasty munchies," Snake cheerfully stated. He helped Dave sit up in a cramped, small bed.

Snake solicitously slid a couple of lumpy, dirty pillows under Dave's back and head.

"Linda says we need to be gettin' some food into yore belly."

"Where...where am I?" Dave swallowed hard, blinking to clear his vision, peering around, trying to get oriented.

He was in a small room that was dirty, disorganized, and gloomy. The close walls were lined with shelves upon which sat many small jars of various-colored paints. The only light was what filtered in through a hanging curtain across the door which was made of multi-colored, stringed beads.

"It's the *storeroom*, Mr. King, way in the back of the store."

"What store? What are you talking about?"

Snake put a finger to his lips in a "shushing" gesture. "Gotta not talk too loud, Mr. King. No one knows we're here except for Linda and me. We got you hidden away. Ain't the cops after you?"

"Uh...ok," Dave groaned, just wanting to sink back into his painful sleep.

But Snake had a big bowl from which he scooped out an unappetizing-looking mush, aiming a big spoon towards Dave's stitched-up mouth. "Oooo, that's a mean lookin' sewed-up split in yer lip—been in a tuff fight, eh? Open wide, now."

"What're you trying to feed me?" Dave frowned, scrunching his face to the side at the lump of grey stuff on the spoon. "And, yes, I'm...a bit beat up."

"Cool!" Snake grinned, making the black cobra on his thin face dance a strange jig. "It's jist real yummy oatmeal, is all. Don't be shy, big guy, it is real good. I jist now cooked it up myself out in the kitchen alcove that we got here."

Dave reluctantly allowed the mush to enter his tender mouth. He chewed a couple of tentative bites...then grabbed the spoon and bowl, greedily shoveling it in.

"Jesus, what did you put in this stuff?" he sighed in a few minutes, having polished off the bowl then licked the spoon clean. "That was delicious."

"It's jist my 'special' oatmeal, man," Snake laughed, taking back the bowl and spoon.

He handed Dave a plastic bottle of water, which Dave grabbed and guzzled down.

"Guess you wuz hungry and thirsty, huh?"

"Starving's more like it," Dave said, feeling a new burst of strength flooding into his beat-up, sore body. "Thanks, Snake. I appreciate it. So where is...uh...Linda? I've got to talk to her."

"Eh! Eh! Eh!" Snake shook his goateed, thin face in the negative. "That girl says to keep you in bed. Linda's out back in the alley working on a van. She says she doesn't need yore help, man. What a girl she is, Mr. King—in some ways even better than my Sally wuz. I don't know nothin' myself about workin' on a car and here she is..."

"Van? She has a van back there? Is it big and black? And did Linda tell you about...?" Dave exclaimed, trying to get out of the bed—causing splitting pain in his side. Plus his head began spinning in all directions at once.

"Yep, yep, yep," Snake said, gently pushing the again-groaning Dave backward. "It's yore van, she says—with some sorta weird motor in the back of it thet she's fixin' up. Ain't runnin' right she says—gotta be tuned up."

"Jesus Christ!" Dave exclaimed, now clutching his burning sides as he tried once again to get up—only to have Snake again gently push him back. "If she gets it going then we're all..."

"Don't be worrying none, my Man," Snake grinned. "Linda knows whut she's doin'. You jist let her do her thing now."

Dave's head was spinning up into what looked like fluffy white clouds.

He definitely didn't feel normal. It wasn't the still-wracking pain in his body. No, it was something else entirely.

"You...drugged...me," Dave gasped, suddenly realizing that the delicious oatmeal contained more than just liberal amounts of sugar, butter, and milk.

"No worries, Mr. King," Snake soothed him. "Its jist some fine hash in there. Premium stuff. It'll keep you mellow. It's smooth medicine for what ails you. So you jist relax and go with it. It'll soothe what ails you."

Hash. Cannabis. Marijuana. Active ingredient, THC...Dave never used the stuff before. He didn't believe in artificial augmentation of his pleasures. But now it seemed he had no choice.

He drifted off into the fluffy clouds, giving-into the warm fuzzy feelings, letting the hash take him where it would.

So he settled back on his pillows, knowing he should get up and try to stop Sally from blowing them all to Kingdom Come—but too high to care.

At least he'd not know when she turned on the Device and blew them all to hell. That was some comfort...

"I think I figured out your problem," Sally said, gently shaking him awake.

"Uhmmm...whuu?" he groaned, his head still spinning but feeling overall much better than the last time he'd awakened.

He jerked upright in the bed.

"The Device!" he exclaimed. "Did you tamper with it? Did you try to get it started?"

"Relax, Dave," she said, pushing him roughly back onto the pillows. "I just studied it. That is, after talking with your friend, Professor Volodymyr. By my standards, it has primitive controls. But I have to admit your matrix was brilliant. Also, the oscillatory excitation pattern was impressive and..."

"You talked with Victor? How? When...?"

"I'll explain everything," she gently stated, her green eyes seemingly glowing in the dimly lit, cramped storeroom. "Now, what do you immediately require to get cleaned up and functional?"

"Bathroom, shower, clean clothes," he gulped, his head still spinning, "—in that order."

She helped him stagger up out of the bed, still clad in his crumpled hospital gown. Then she led him through the stringed beads into a large outer room.

"Don't worry, it's Sunday," she said. "There are no customers today. The owner is old-fashioned. No work on Sunday so both customers and artists can go attend their particular religious functions, if they wish. This is Oklahoma after all. My mom tells me this place is very religious. We've got the whole shop to ourselves today."

"And this 'shop' is...?"

"A tattoo parlor, of course," she shrugged, her strong arm around his waist, helping him take one tentative step at a time. "This is where in my world I came to get my tattoos. It's where your Sally also came.

It's apparently a 'nexus' between our two Dimensions, similar to the Megastore in Sulphur."

Right then he wasn't so worried about dimensional intersections. He was more concerned about emptying an overfilled bladder.

"And right here's the bathroom. And, yes, it has a nice shower inside so the painters here who put intense effort into their art can clean off the sweat and spattered dyes before they go home. There's a towel in there. And Snake left us a set of clothes he got from the Salvation Army store across the street where..."

"Snake!" Dave exclaimed, grimacing as he remembered. "He poisoned me! He fed me drugged oatmeal that..."

"You needed sedation," she shrugged. "I wouldn't have done it myself, but it worked. Don't you feel better now?"

"Where is he? What's he doing here, anyway?" he grumbled, his head still spinning. "And why'd you tell him about me? We don't know him. We don't know what he'll do. He might give us up to the authorities. There's probably a big reward on my head and..."

"He works here," she laughed. "It's his part-time job. He's actually quite a good artist. In fact, it was him that did several of my tats! And I needed help to hide you. I think we can trust him. He's very friendly."

"Which ones?" Dave petulantly asked.

"Which what?"

"Which tattoos did he do on you?"

"Well, for instance, he drew and inked my Turtle Tattoo on my wrist that you seem to like so much."

Dave drew up short, swaying. *Snake* gave Sally her Turtle Tattoo? He was an artist?

"But—if that's so, then why didn't you recognize him?"

"In my world, he had a different name and a completely different look. But he's definitely the same person who inked both your Sally and me. He'd *have* to look and behave different because y*our* 'Snake' would surely not be tolerated by the Keepers in my world."

"I can imagine..."

"So anyway," Sally continued, "we'll just see how your new 'look' works once you get cleaned up. The clothes are old but they should fit you. Also, you should shave off that beard and mustache—maybe even cut your hair short. I found a pair of scissors and a razor blade in a drawer. They're laid out by the sink. Your picture's on all the newscasts. You're infamous. They're blaming you for the deaths and destruction at that military base. They say you're a terrorist who set off a tactical nuclear bomb. So now, yes, there's *a ten million dollar* reward on your head. Everybody's out looking for you."

"Oh, hell," he groaned, wobbling into the bathroom by himself. "I guess I should turn *myself* in for that much money."

"Snake said the same thing," she shrugged. "But I told him I'd never kiss him again if he breathes a word to the Keepers, uh, I mean the cops," she ruefully laughed.

"You kissed Snake?" Dave grimaced, achingly maneuvering the door shut behind him.

"Only on the cheek—like *you* said, he's a 'fine young man'," she grinned.

"Well, he did get me my 'new' clothes," he shrugged, pausing in the doorway. "I guess he's not all that bad. Where is he, anyway?"

"Since its Sunday morning, he's gone to take your Mother to her church in Sulphur. He's been very helpful in your absence."

"She's out of the hospital? Really?"

"She claims it's a miracle from God," Sally nodded knowingly. "She's almost fully recovered, in just a few days—not only from the stroke, but from her cancer. But I'm making sure she keeps taking the 'vitamins' until she gets the complete course. We don't want any recurrence of her disease."

Wow. That was incredible.

"Thanks, Sally—and how's your mother doing? Is she also fully recovered and gone to church?"

"Oh, she's not a church goer," Sally shrugged. "She's extremely literal-minded. She doesn't believe in anything she can't directly see or touch."

"So is she taking her 'vitamins'?"

"Are you kidding?" Sally snorted. "After what happened with Jean, I've no problem getting my Mom to keep taking the pills."

"Oh...and what about you?" he quietly asked, still wobbling in the doorway to the bathroom, aching to empty his bladder but driven by curiosity. "Do you go to church?"

"Formal religion is forbidden for Citizens," she quietly stated. "But..."

"But?"

"I do sneak away...to attend a secret cult."

"Really, what group?"

"It's..." she hesitated as if reluctant to reveal something for which a "Citizen" could be severely punished.

"Tell me."

"Ok," she shyly admitted, "it's the *Animists*."

"The what?"

"Animism!" she stated more forcefully. "It's primitive. It traces back to the cosmology of indigenous tribal peoples, where everything possesses spiritual essence—even animals, plants, inanimate objects, and all sorts of phenomena."

"Wow," Dave said, blinking unsteadily, trying to wrap his mind around what she was revealing about herself. "So is it similar to Hinduism or Buddhism?"

"No," she flatly stated. "*They* embrace parts of the philosophy. Animism existed a long time *before* they ever came into being."

"You don't say," he grinned. "You know, Sally, you're quite the enigma. Is this 'Animism' religion why you got that cute Turtle Tattoo?"

"No...well...maybe a little," she grudgingly admitted. "It was sort of like shoving my wrist into the face of the rulers of society. But I mostly kept it hidden by long sleeves, my secret protest."

"So you weren't so ecstatic with your life on the other side?"

"Nothing's perfect," she grudgingly admitted.

"Good thing you didn't go more to church with my Mom," Dave laughed.

"Why not?"

"They think that they're perfect—the only ones that God really loves."

"But aren't they followers of this Jesus?" she said, reaching into a pocket to pull out Cliff's small, pocket New Testament.

"Oh yes, they think so."

"But the writings say that Jesus preached that his followers were to give Godly Love to everyone."

"Preaching and doing are two different things."

"This is a strange place," Sally said, shaking her head as she frowned in confusion.

"But the biggest fallacy..." Dave bitterly started, then stopped, unsure if he should continue.

"What is it?"

"It's a flaw at the base of Jesus' teachings that..."

"Well? Tell me!" she demanded. "I'm interested."

"God *doesn't* love us," he bitterly concluded. "Either God doesn't exist or he's a sadistic monster."

She looked at him in puzzlement.

"In my cult of Animism we see God everywhere," Sally squinted, moving the little black book from her right hand to her left hand and back again. "'God' is the spiritual essence that inhabits everything—in you, in me, in this little book—and even the fabric of the Universe...so anything that happens to something or someone also happens to God."

"See whatever you want," Dave snapped, slamming shut the bathroom door. "I agree with your Mother," he angrily shouted through the closed door. "I see *nothing*. Hah!"

Later—after having relieved his bladder and intestines, taking a long shower, and slipping on the used but clean clothes—Dave felt like a new man.

His ribs still hurt badly. But apparently his tormentors back at the military base were measured in their torture. Though badly bruised, he didn't think any bones were broken. If he didn't move too fast he could get around fairly well.

He sat on a stool looking at his face in the cracked mirror of the bathroom.

"Not so much the handsome 'professor' anymore," he muttered to himself, grimly evaluating the wild-haired, bushy-bearded man with a bruised face and sewn-up lip staring back at him in the mirror.

Yep, a shuffle in his walk and a stammer in his talk and all anyone would see was just another homeless street-bum.

Normally he kept his beard neatly trimmed, his longish brown hair pulled behind his head with a rubber band or clip neatly holding it into a tight ponytail. He cultivated the look of a "young professor."

But now, with his wet hair splayed out in every direction, he just looked like a *madman*.

Dave saw how he perfectly fit the part of a home-grown terrorist.

"Well...I guess I'd better..." he sighed, holding up the rusty-looking razor blade...

"No!" he angrily spat-out, flinging the blade behind him where it bounced against the wall and clattered down onto the tile floor.

He combed his hair, beard, and mustache out as best as he could. He found a rubber band in a drawer of junk, fixing his ponytail back into place.

"I'm not changing who I am!" he defiantly yelled to no one in particular.

—as Sally opened the door and stood there looking at him.

"Are you trying to get everyone to hear that you're here?" she said, her green eyes wide and glowering at him. She was in a short-sleeved shirt and had her slender arms on her hips—such that the tattoos on both arms seemed to writhe as if they were alive.

Her bushy red hair flowed on both sides of her head.

To Dave Sally looked like a commanding demon freshly incarnated into human form.

"Oh...I'm sorry," he sighed, lowering his head and shuffling out after her towards a long flat table. The shoes that Snake had found for him were too large. Under her withering gaze, the shoes made him feel like he'd shrunken.

"You look better," she nodded to him across the table as they both sat. "But you should have cut your hair. Can't you make this little sacrifice for our safety?"

Instantly, he was put on the defensive.

"The day I was honorably discharged from the mandatory military service I had to do in my youth I *threw away* my razor blade," he angrily retorted. "My hair isn't an affectation. Telling me to cut off my beard is like telling me to chop off my arm."

"So you'd prefer to be recognized, caught by your police, and thrown into prison?"

"I'll cover up. I'll wear that sweater Snake got for me, the one with the hood. I already look like a homeless person. No one will recognize me."

"You're being stupid."

"I am not!" he growled. "And what's this that Snake said about you fiddling with my Experimental Array in the back of the van? *That's* being stupid. You could have killed all of us, you crazy girl. And why is it here at a tattoo parlor, anyway? And how did you know it was here?"

"Just because I'm a *'girl'* you don't think I can understand science?" she interrupted him, springing up from her chair to hover over him.

Her chair was flung backward, "banging" onto the wooden floor.

He put his head in his hands, elbows on the table, struggling to get his roiling emotions under control.

"Again..." he softly continued, looking up at her. "I'm *sorry*, Sally. Here I go making assumptions about you. And you're right—I know nothing about you. You could be a certified scientific genius for all that I know who..."

"—and I *am!*" she snorted, turning around to pick up the chair and sit firmly back down upon it.

"You are?"

"Damn right, I am," she "huffed" at him. "I received the *Fields Medal* at the last Congress of the International Mathematical Union. In case you don't know what that is, it's for us young scientists who make outstanding discoveries in mathematics."

"I've heard of it," he softly replied, impressed. "That's a prestigious award. But, you were working as a cashier at a grocery store—and now you're telling me you're a fellow Ph.D. scientist?"

She looked at him as if he was a total dope.

"Don't you have service jobs here?" she huffed at him. "In our society most Citizens are expected to do both applied and theoretical work. The creative things advance society while the hands-on work keeps the Artist connected to the real world of fellow humans."

"Uh...right," Dave nodded. "I guess—that's like me teaching introductory courses in physics while also doing my research on the side?"

"Exactly," she primly nodded. "Except in my society, they are both equally valued. We split our work time equally between the two jobs, being paid appropriately for both. So if I happened to see you here teaching rudimentary courses would I naturally assume you weren't capable of excellent creative work?"

"Uhm...no...I guess not," he shrugged. Did her repressive society have advantages after all?

"And what is this 'Fudd' degree you refer to?" she asked.

"It's the standard certification of being able to do research in one's subject area, called a 'Doctor of Philosophy' Ph.D., in my case in the area of Physics. Or it could be in the discipline of Biology...or Sociology...or whatever."

"Hmmm...peculiar..."

"Why is that peculiar?"

"'Doctors' in our society are strictly physicians."

"So how does your Dimension denote your highest academic degrees other than in medicine?"

"They are called 'Masters' of their subject. For instance," she stated primly, "I have a Master of Mathematics degree—apparently the equivalent of your Fudd. I even have a *post*-Master certification of *Scholar*. I got that when I did further research beyond my initial degree in the French Empire."

"In my world, that's called a post-doc. Again, I am impressed."

"You should be!" she snapped at him.

"But we're getting off the subject that's of immediate importance, Sally," he continued, hearing cars now driving past on the street outside the shop. Clearly, even though it was Sunday, people were up and about. "*How* did you know the van was here?"

"I got an e-mail that came to your original Sally's laptop," she explained.

"An e-mail? You found her laptop and used it?"

"Of course!" she snapped again at him. Then, more gently, "Yes, it was from someone claiming to be your friend."

"What, Professor Volodymyr?"

"No, some person who signed it as '*Arthur Anderson, a friend of your colleague.*'"

"Agent Anderson!" Dave gasped. So it was true. Either the FBI or Anderson himself stole the van out of Dave's garage. But why? And why did he say that they needed his help? Were they trying to activate the Device themselves?

"What did the e-mail say?" he eagerly prompted her.

"It said: '*A vehicle belonging to a mutual acquaintance of ours is at the origin of the turtle. It won't be there for long. You can have it if you can fix it. Good luck with your transportation problems.*'"

"Ah," Dave nodded. "So the 'origin of the turtle'..."

"—had to be right here where I originally got my tattoo of a baby turtle," she grinned.

"That was a brilliant message," Dave said in appreciation. "Anyone spying on it would think someone was merely offering you an old car to help you get around Ada. But how did he know you got your Turtle Tattoo here? Well, whatever, it seems that Agent Anderson was on my side after all."

"That's why I didn't hang up on you when you called on the run."

"You'd already received the message..."

"Yes. I was 'primed' to not reject you."

He lowered his hands to the tabletop and sucked in a shuddering breath. Everything that happened back at that terrible prison came flooding into his mind—the torture, the fear, the final awful destruction...

She impulsively reached out her small hand and laid it on his as if in sympathy.

The warmth of her hand gave him strength to continue.

"But...that's past now. You say you've been looking at my setup in the back of the van?"

She withdrew her hand and frowned at him.

"I saw that you were trying to stimulate sustained cold fusion," she replied. "But I know that's impossible. Nature won't let such a thing happen—unless, somehow, the Laws of Nature work differently here in your Dimension?"

"Probably not."

"So I figured you were just a zealot on an impossible quest until..."

"Yes?"

"I saw your matrix and then connected my laptop into the command sequences of your control unit."

He was fascinated. Sally understood what he was trying to accomplish. And, apparently, she was interrogating his computer algorithms. Amazing!

"Sally—when I tried to activate it..." he started to explain.

"I know all that," she cut him off.

"What?"

"I saw the diamond pencil scratching on the components that said 'property of Victor Volodymyr,' figured that he was a physicist, did a quick search on your Internet, found his home phone number, and called him."

"You called him on a public line?" Dave gasped. "Oh, my God, Sally—both He and I are being watched!"

"Not to worry," she shrugged. "I did a quick encryption at my end so any observer would just see a charity spam caller. I got those at my Mother's house here in Ada, answering her phone. So I recorded a couple of them. Very boring! In fact, I said that to Victor as soon as he picked up, that I'd encrypted the call and was an acquaintance of yours. He was quite worried about you...and quite delighted when I told him I'd found your van and equipment."

"We were...a bit concerned as to its whereabouts," Dave understated.

"Glad I could locate it for you," she gloated perkily, her red flurry of hair bouncing about her shoulders. "Anyway, I told him what I discovered, briefly described my background and...uh...'friendship' with you—and he told me what he and his colleagues think happened when you nearly blew yourselves up. So I of course didn't try to activate your machine in the alleyway, not wanting to blow us up. But I do think that I diagnosed your problem, in that..."

"Jesus Christ, Sally!" Dave exclaimed, interrupting her. "Are you kidding me?"

"Nope," she replied curtly. "It's your ability to control the microlasers, right? What you have is very advanced for your society, but wholly inadequate, right? In fact, you don't have a clue as to how to fire millions of tiny lasers into individual deuterium ions in real time, correct? You need that capability to individually position the ions for optimal interaction in your matrix, am I right? That's far beyond even your most advanced computers."

"Yes...yes...yes...and *yes!*" he repeatedly replied, gaping stupidly at her.

"I think you need a SmartNet," she shrugged.

Dave just stared across the table at her.

"Oh, right," she nodded, "that probably means nothing to you. It's what I was awarded the Fields Medal last year for inventing. A 'SmartNet' is an artificially evolved computational intelligence trained to engage itself in a particular task."

"Uh..." Dave dumbly stared at her.

"It's capable of actually *thinking*," she spoke to him as if talking to a small child. "It is self-aware and, in its own way, intelligent—but not limited to slow human synaptic neural functioning. It computes at the speed of a quantum computer, but from a bio-mimetic architecture. Quite sophisticated, don't you think?"

"Ok," he gulped, stumped. "Wait, I think there are research groups working on forming neural nets grown in petri dishes and..."

"*Phaggh!*" she snorted. "I've searched on your little world-wide 'Internet' for your progress in this field and you've only scratched the surface. Your computers still work based on *binary* codes. What, are you *cavemen* still scratching 'yes' or 'no' with a plus or zero on stone tablets?"

Dave was amazed. How had Anderson known about her? Wait—he said he was from her Dimension. Of course he'd know of her work if she was so famous over there as to win their equivalent of the Fields Medal.

Dave felt a flash of fury and jealousy at her being so recognized while he labored in obscurity—then set the outrage deliberately to the side. This was far more important than hurt feelings.

"So—if that's critical to getting my Device to function—how can we replicate it?" he asked.

"Can't!" she sadly shook her head in the negative.

"Then what's the point of our conversation on this topic?"

"Don't know!" she shrugged yet again. "It turns out that your Sally here was working on similar things to me, as I found out when searching inside her laptop. In fact, a year ago she hacked into Tianhe-40 at the National University of Defense, in China. Unbeknownst to them, she was doing artificial evolution of her algorithms at 100 petaflops—that's 100 quadrillion calculations per second. It turns out that she was just as amazing as me, but totally unappreciated in your stupid society. She was mostly self-taught, doing it as a hobby. Obviously, she was also an unappreciated computer genius."

"I know what petaflops are," he peevishly stated while his mind now raced a-mile-a-minute, ignoring her insult to his entire world. "But surely the Chinese would detect..."

"Nope!" she grinned. "Your Sally hid it from them. The artificial intelligences she was developing were programmed to stay hidden— even as they evolved more and more capabilities against her lethal environmental constraints. She constructed some radical evolutionary positive and negative selectors. She was in every way my intellectual equal. It's too bad you caused her death."

Chocking back an angry response, Dave focused on the immediate problems.

"So...ok...then can *you* maybe use those existing 'artificial intelligences' that my world's Sally 'evolved,' to work in my Device?" he excitedly asked.

"Like I said," she patiently stated, "it's impossible with your primitive computational architecture. You can't put a human brain into gelatin capsule."

"But...but..." he suddenly realized the significance of what Agent Anderson did in his final moments of life.

"My knapsack, is it here?"

"I put it under your bed in the storeroom where..."

"I've got something to show you!" he said, his words blurring into each other with the force of his emotions. He lurched up from the table, turned around, and stumbled back through the beaded curtain into the storeroom behind him.

She followed as he dropped to his knees, reached under the narrow bed, yanked out the knapsack and shakily reached inside...

—to triumphantly hold up the *bloody pad*, cradled in the palm of his hand as if it were a precious work of art!

"Will this do?"

She reached out a tentative hand, picking it up off of Dave's palm with a thumb and finger, delicately, tenderly.

"Where did you get this?"

"It came out of Anderson's head. He said he was from your world, remember? He had those freaking glasses. They replaced the eye-balls he was missing. They communicated with his 'neural implant.' I'm guessing that this is that very same neural implant. He ripped it out of his *own skull* to give it to me right before he died."

"If it's still alive..." she gasped, cradling it now in the palm of her hand—then suddenly turning and running away, leaving the door-way's string beads smashing and whirling behind her.

He stumbled weakly after her, over to the sink...

—where she was carefully washing off the blood and brain-gore...

"It's alive," she grinned.

Yes, Dave saw it was *wriggling* in her hand. Little white tendrils poked out of it, which quickly withdrew.

"What can you do with it?" Dave asked, sitting back down at the table, his head starting to spin again from his exertions.

"I'll have to see if it can interface with your control unit. Then I'll need to download nuggets of your Sally's evolved algorithms into the neuronal net. I can't take the matured entities, of course, through your tiny Internet channels. But the nuggets can quickly grow, adapt-ing to the new environment. Then I'll need to see if I can instruct them in the real-time manipulation of your deuterium ions in your matrix," she grinned.

"So...doing that will take...what—*years or decades?*"

"Maybe only hours, if I don't run into any big problems," she en-thused, gently stroking the damp, squiggling pad. "Didn't you hear me tell you that I'm a certified mathematical genius?"

"Well," Dave gulped, amazed at her ability and enthusiasm. "Then what can I do to help?"

"Go back to bed."

"Oh no," he protested, though his head was spinning for real now. "That's...my 'baby'...and I've got to..."

"You're of no use to me or anyone else in your condition," she firmly stated. "Get back into that bed or I'll drag you there and tie you down myself. Understand?"

"Well..."

"Now!" she sternly ordered him.

Reluctantly, he levered himself back up from the table and wobbled back towards the beaded-curtain, pausing...

"But what if...?"

"*Now!*" she shouted at him, pointing an extended finger from her tattooed arm at the stockroom.

"Maybe for just a few minutes," he agreed, dragging himself in and collapsing onto the narrow bed.

"Dave, wake up! Something's wrong! Get up!"

Blearily, Dave opened his eyes.

"What...time...is it?" he gasped, trying to get oriented. A small nightlight shone in the corner, giving him enough illumination to see the outline of Sally's form, but not much else.

"It's early Monday morning," Sally whispered to him. "You slept all through yesterday and this last night. Here, eat this."

"What's wrong?" he said as he accepted a bowl of something.

"My wrist hurts."

"What?"

"I was catching a nap when I woke up from the pain," she grimaced. "Look at my arm."

She showed him her hand and wrist. The Turtle Tattoo was *glowing!*

"Jesus Christ, Sally!" he gasped. "What's going on? Are your other tats doing the same?"

She pushed up her shirt, turning around, giving him a glimpse of exotic large tattoos on her belly and her back.

Nope. They looked perfectly normal.

It was only the Turtle Tattoo on her wrist.

"Does it hurt?"

"Yes—like it's on fire," she gasped, yanking him upright from the bed.

"Eat some food," she insisted, again grimacing in pain.

"What is this food?" he whispered back. "And why are we whispering? Is this more of Snake's hash-oatmeal? I don't need any more of that poison. I've got to keep my head clear, not fogged-up in a daze."

"No, it's just left-over eggs and sausage I made for myself earlier. It's from a concentrate I found in the refrigerator. You just add water to it and heat it up in the microwave. Eat it. You've got to get some strength."

"Ok," he said, scooping it up with his fingers. Wow, did it ever taste good. Plus there was bread. It was just plain slices of regular loaf bread, but it tasted great.

She was pulling him out of the bedroom, shoving a plastic bottle of water in his hand as they went.

"What's going on?"

"Listen."

He gulped down the last of the food, guzzled the bottle of water, and paused, listening...

He heard nothing.

The store was dark. No lights were on. From the front of the store, out in the customer area, there was no light either. It was still night. No light came in through the front windows.

"I don't hear a thing."

"At this time on Monday morning there should be at least a few early risers, cars of people going to early jobs, that sort of thing," she said. "But there's nothing."

He nodded, suddenly very scared.

"The knapsack!" he said, turning back to the storeroom...

—as suddenly the sound of a *deep voice on a bullhorn* reverberated through the store: "SURRENDER! YOU ARE SURROUNDED! COME OUT WITH YOUR HANDS UP!"

"Oh, Christ," Dave gasped. "It's the cops. Somehow they found us."

He pulled Sally to the floor as they crawled back into the stockroom where he reached under the bed and pulled out the knapsack.

"LINDA, DAVE," a weaker, trembling voice came over the bullhorn. "PLEASE GIVE UP. THEY SAY THEY WON'T HURT YOU IF YOU COME OUT PEACEFUL-LIKE. YOUR MOMS IS WORRIED. THEY WANTS YOU TO GIVE UP. COME ON OUTTA THERE. PLEASE!"

"Snake!" Dave grated, grimacing at Sally.

"I can't believe it, Dave," she whispered back. "I never thought he'd turn us in."

"Well, he did! And now we've got to hold them off, at least long enough to get to the van. Were you able to get that neural implant thing working?"

"I think so. It's alive, suffused with a growth nutrient I made for it. I downloaded the nuggets into it. They've had time to grow, adapt, and respond to their new directions. But I didn't have time to test the results. They may modulate the energy flow or just trigger the same explosion you and the Professor experienced earlier."

"It's our only hope to escape, Sally. Maybe if we can direct and modulate the energy blast then we can distract the police long enough for us to get onto a major highway."

"But what if we blow up half of Ada? We can't risk it. My adopted Mother's out there!"

Reaching inside the knapsack he grabbed out the *two black guns.*

"Ok, here's an immediate alternative," he grinned at her. "You ever use one of these?"

He shoved one into Sally's hand.

"No," she whispered. "I've never even touched a Keeper's gun before. But you just point and shoot, right?"

"Damn straight," he said, trying to sound tough. But, in actuality, he was as gun-unsophisticated as her.

"I'm setting them at their highest level," he said, flicking off the safety of Anderson's gun and slipping the power setting to five stars. He set five stars on his own gun, the one he'd taken from the Keeper in Sally's world, which lacked a safety-lock on its top.

"But we can't fight your Keepers," she gasped. "We could hurt a lot of people with these settings. We should dial them to the lowest setting of 'stun.' Or maybe we should just turn ourselves in?"

"I *don't* think so," he said, ducking down with Sally as a HAIL OF BULLETS *slammed* through the walls of the store. The barrage barely missing them as they lay flattened on the floor!

"Ok, then," Sally grimaced angrily, shaking off a spray of plaster fragments from her bushy hairdo, "If that's how they're going to treat us—suspected nuclear bomb-wielding 'terrorists' or not—then let's *do* this!"

"In a few seconds they'll be on top of us—unless we make them think twice," Dave growled back. "On the count of 'three,' Sally—*point and shoot!*"

In the still-flickering nightlight's glow in the dark room he saw her nod in agreement.

"One...two...*three!*"

They both rose up, simultaneously pressing the triggers of their guns aimed at the street-side of the tattoo parlor...

—as with a huge ROAR the sides of the building *EXPLODED* outward, causing the advancing police and military to lurch backward...

—as Sally and Dave stood above the surrounding debris, grimly marching forward, still firing!

On the street, police cars and military vehicles were exploded and thrown aside like toys.

Fire erupted all around them, causing chaos amongst the attackers...

"Now!" Dave said, reaching over to sling the knapsack up over his back, its strap over his shoulder—while simultaneously grabbing Sally's hand and running back into what remained of the store, out into the back alley, and hopping into the front of the van.

"Get us out of here," he ordered her, shoving her over into the driver's seat.

"But what are you...?"

"I'm going to try turning on the equipment at its lowest setting, with the matrix-expulsion end aimed out of the back of the van. Do the controls still work like I had them set up?"

"Yes!" she called back to him as she turned on the engine, slammed the van into gear, skidded in a circle, and punched the gas...

—to *zoom* out onto Ada's main street, careening around the littered remains of police and military vehicles, which were still burning and exploding...

—encountering an advancing *tank* with its gun turret in motion, facing them down!

"Turn around! Turn around!" Dave yelled to Sally who hit the brakes, whipped the steering wheel over, and spun the van into the opposite direction...

Luckily the Device was still solidly bolted into the floor of the van or it would have been thrown out.

"Now we'll either die or *torch* that freaking tank," Dave muttered to himself, desperately moving equipment out of the path of the rear of the reaction chamber...

—as the van's unlocked back doors swung outward, the tank still advancing on them but now from the rear, its long thick gun turret lowering at them, preparing to fire...

—as Dave *powered up* the bathtub-sized Device and reached for the manual button to start the deuterium mixture flowing into the reaction matrix...

—*hitting* the "go" button set now on its lowest denominator...

—as in a blinding *FLASH OF BLUE LIGHT* Sally, Dave, the van, and the Device *vanished!*

The IMPLOSION of their departure jerked everything sharply forward such that everything still standing was knocked down or flipped over.

"Oh, man," Snake gasped. He stumbled up and away from the police who'd been escorting him, who were now lying groaning on the pavement.

Snake dazedly looked at the smashed tattoo parlor, the exploded vehicles, the many scattered wounded, the armored tank now overturned upon its back, and the raging fires.

But there was no black van.

Army Green Berets came running up behind him, grabbing him by his arms.

"Come with us!" they barked at him.

He ignored the soldiers, peering all around.

"Where'd they go?" he gulped. "Linda?"

But there was no answer.

She was gone.

Chapter 14

<u>DISTANCE</u>

Only a raging emptiness

Can teach the joy of satiety

Where all you ever do and say

Is but a tiny dot on a vast canvas

Magnificently displayed across history

Circled-back and collapsed upon itself

Forcing you to see beyond the obvious

Where death, life, and thought collide

Merging into something newly pure

But also sad and melancholy...

Don't you forget to laugh!

The Luminary Chronicles, 14:6-10

"What is *that?*" Sally said, shakily pointing out the front window of the stilled van.

"Hold on," Dave replied. "I'll be there in a second..."

He crawled away from the Apparatus towards the front seats of the van.

Thankfully the power surge hadn't blown them up. But it definitely fried some of the Device's circuitry. Smoke was drifting up from its framework, clouding Dave's vision.

Dave hoped the burst had disoriented their attackers. Maybe now he and Sally could escape. But the van was stalled, not moving. What was Sally doing?

She had to get the van in gear and get them out of there!

He dragged himself back up into the passenger's seat and only then let his gaze follow Sally's still-pointing finger through the front windshield.

There, a hundred yards in front of them, was a lizard.

It was a *big* lizard...

"Dave, is that a...?"

He stared at it a moment in total astonishment.

"Yes, Sally—I do believe it is an *Acrocanthosaurus*," Dave gasped, still not believing the evidence of his own eyes.

Yet there it was.

It was at least forty feet long. It probably weighed in at around six tons. It had two powerful hind legs upon which it stood. Small spindly arms grasped futilely in the air as it stood there upright. A huge mouth was half-open, showing carnivorously pointed teeth. A low "sail"-like structure ran down its neck, back and tail.

It sported a subtle pattern of light-green, yellow, and brown stripes that ran along its massive body.

"So...Dave," Sally quietly questioned, "are you telling me we're looking at a living *dinosaur?*"

"Well," he slowly stated, raising his eyebrows in bewilderment but now acceptance, "I've studied dinosaurs as a hobby since I was a boy, since I'm fascinated by all reptiles, whether living or extinct. And I assure you, Sally, that what we are looking at stomping around out there on that wet plain in front of us...is absolutely nothing less than a magnificent specimen of Acrocanthosaurus, or, translated from the Greek, a 'high-spined lizard'."

"A 'high-spined lizard'," Sally slowly repeated.

"Yep!" Dave giddily punctuated his totally-ridiculous assertion. "They were abundant here in Oklahoma in the early Cretaceous period—about, say, 125 million years ago. This, of course, was a bit before T. Rex and Giganotosaurus in the later Cretaceous period. But that doesn't mean Acro was any less fierce than those better-known monsters. For his time-period, he was the apex predator. Yep, that he was, a..."

"Predator?"

"Oh, I imagine he could swallow us both down in one gulp."

"And he's *coming this way*," she said, lowering her pointed, shaking finger—trying vainly to control the panic in her voice.

"Yessssss..." Dave agreed, trying to wrap his mind around their incredible situation. "We're sitting ducks in here. He could smash the van in one swing of his tail. So since we appear to be stalled-out...let's *run away!*" he yelled.

Together, Sally and Dave dove from the van and promptly fell flat into muddy soil. Picking themselves up, they ran as fast as they could toward a rocky hilltop a half mile in the distance.

Only when they were safely up on its peak did they pause to look back.

Gasping for breath, they saw the big dinosaur waddle up to the van then curiously sniff at it. Then the animal *hit it with its tail*—making a loud "BANG"! The van's roof dented inward. Then the beast contemptuously kicked the van onto its side with one quick jerk of a powerful leg.

It sniffed up in the air with its elongated snout.

Its beady little black eyes peered around, apparently hoping to catch sight of errant tasty treats, instead of this unappetizing strange "bolder."

Seeing none, it gave out a rumbling "snort"—then ambled away, vanishing over a curve into the descending, wide landscape.

Looking around, Dave saw strange ferns and clusters of weird, tall trees. The branches and leafs of the trees bunched at the tops as if trying to escape enemies from below. A spooky mist hung in the air. Dave wasn't too curious concerning the plant life. He didn't know much about botany...but they certainly *weren't* in Ada, Oklahoma anymore!

"Dave, I think we jumped back in time," Sally gasped, absently shaking dirt from her red hair. In their haste escaping the van, she'd fallen onto the ground.

"Oh, do you think?"

They both started laughing uncontrollably, falling into each other's arms.

It was a spasm of humorous relief. They'd just escaped the death trap of the tattoo parlor only to be almost eaten alive by a huge dinosaur!

It was either laugh or cry. So they chose to laugh, for a long time...

Then—somewhat regaining their composure—they moved apart, sitting with their backs against a big, wet boulder.

It had rained not too long ago. The air smelled—strange! It was both musty and intoxicatingly-fresh. And above them was the bluest sky either of them had ever seen.

"How could this happen?" Sally marveled.

"I don't know," Dave sighed. He was terrified. But also—for the first time in a long—he felt free, safe from human pursuit. It was a curious mix of emotions. "But we'd better figure it out if we're ever going to get back home."

"At least we got away from your Keepers," Sally sighed.

"Man, I wish I could have seen their faces when we vanished," Dave laughed. Then, more seriously, "We'd best get back to the van. If we can't move it to some place safe, we're stranded on this wide-open plain. The next Acro that comes strolling along might not be as 'friendly' as that last one."

Sally giggled, ducking her face downward, causing her red hair to bounce upward. Then she hopped up to her feet, seemingly ready to do whatever needed to be done.

"Well, you can't complain I never take you anywhere," Dave mock-asserted, brushing dirt off his pants as he stood up.

"I'm *not* your girlfriend," she primly huffed at him before breaking out again into wild laughter.

Off in the distance, they heard a dinosaur "hooting" in return...

Sally stopped laughing, looking about now in apprehension.

Dave now felt an irrational exuberance that he and Sally were the only two humans on the entire planet.

They were like Adam and Eve. Well, "Adam" and an uncooperative, fickle, but brilliant Eve...

When was this ever going to happen again?

Later that night, hidden safely away in a small canyon, Dave had time to access their situation.

Sally was asleep in the back of the van.

Fortunately, the van was knocked onto its side by the *Acrocanthosaurus* across a low mound, coming to rest at an angle. A thick fallen tree trunk had allowed them to muster up enough leverage to tilt the van back onto its wheels. The engine was still working. It had just stalled out during the "event" of being transported to this place.

Driving, however, was rough since there were no roads. They had to inch along the terrain, careful of bogs or boulders. But they managed to locate a drivable animal-path which led them to a creek. Driving into and up the shallow stream bed they discovered a secluded canyon in the low hills that surrounded the alluvial plain. Driving out of the stream they "parked" on an elevated flat sandbar.

They were fortunate to find the "parking space"—as blocking their path forward was a small waterfall. So Dave carefully maneuvered the van around, poised for the trip back down the stream once they felt it was safe enough to proceed. But there was no rush.

This was a great spot to be hidden if one had to be lost in the early Cretaceous. There was water, fish, and lots of exotic fruit hanging from trees out in the surrounding thick growth.

They still had half a tank of gas. So they had limited mobility.

But the Device was inoperable.

Nothing Dave tried provoked any reaction from it. The internal battery still had a charge, but nothing was responding to the controls.

It was dead.

Dave was extremely frustrated.

"Do you think it was the Dark Energy?" Sally said as she slid up and settled against him, clutching her arms over her chest against the night chill.

"I thought you were asleep?"

"I was, but there are too many strange sounds out there in the night," she shuddered. "I never was a person to go camping in the wilderness. I didn't even go out into the Park that much in Sulphur—and it was practically in my back yard."

"Me neither," he admitted, slipping an arm around her shoulders to help her stay warm. "When I was a kid I liked mountain biking out in the Park. But I always went home at night to a nice warm bed. And yet I never realized how the night sky would look without the benefit of our ever-present, 'civilized' smog."

Indeed, the stars above them blazed down in splendiferous glory. The black of the night sky was a total darkness—while the millions of stars set against it were brilliant diamonds.

"It *is* magnificent," she smiled, despite her earlier protestations nestling closer to his side.

Dave continued looking up at the spectacular, wide night sky.

"As to how we got here," Dave mused, "Dark Energy is as good an explanation as any. I thought we'd just get a burst of fire to scare off our attackers. But something extraordinary obviously occurred. I suppose subspace might be a pathway to anywhere. In fact, I wonder if all these years of experimenting in my garage I didn't expose myself to it, unknowingly, in small doses."

"Maybe that's what caused you to shift over into my Dimension when...?"

"—yes! That makes some sort of a distorted, crazy sense, Sally," he agreed. "But it doesn't explain why I was attracted to you. Somehow we're linked together. Do you think maybe it has something to do with your Turtle Tattoo? We thought it glowed before, in your world, because it resonated somehow with that Keeper's laser weapon. But there wasn't any such activating laser when you woke me up at the parlor as it was burning your arm."

"Maybe it's just fate," she said in a soft voice. "Maybe we don't need to find a mechanistic explanation. Perhaps...we were just meant to be together?"

"I thought I wasn't your boyfriend?"

"Kiss me and I'll reconsider..."

A sudden *rustling* in the darkness caused them both to jump up and cower against the side of the van.

Out of the darkness of the thick brush, an elongated, stout animal crawled...

"It's a snake!" Dave happily exclaimed, hopping over to it and examining it from a safe distance. Then, gingerly, he slowly reached down and picked it up.

"What are you doing?" Sally gasped. "That thing will *bite* you!"

"This guy's not poisonous," Dave said, gently lifting it up in both hands. It was six feet long, as thick as his arm. He cradled its body so that it curled up into his arms. "It's clearly a constrictor. Also, it's cool tonight. So it's even more torpid than usual. As long as you handle them gently, support their bodies, most snakes are quite friendly."

"Well, put it back!"

"In just a minute," he said, closely examining its body. "Oh, Jesus, Sally, it's got prehensile limbs."

He pointed with a free hand to four short extensions that were folded back along its length, located both close to its head and tail.

"What?" she said, cringing back.

"The evolutionary origins of snakes are hazy because it's rare to find fossils of their fragile bones," he grinned in the bright star light. "This is incredible, Sally! It's a previously unknown ancestor of modern snakes—right here in Oklahoma in the late Cretaceous—before they completely lost their lizard-like legs."

"It's enormous," she grimaced.

"Oh, no, Sally—this is a little guy," he shrugged, carefully holding the friendly animal which was lifting up its big head. Its body and head were both a deep brown color with faint green patches. A forked tongue slipped languidly out of its mouth, feeling at the hairs on Dave's arm.

"That's a *little* snake?"

"Oh, sure, Sally. My present-day pet red-tailed boa constrictor, 'Hug,' is longer and stouter than this guy. The longest snake of the modern world, the Anaconda, can grow to about twenty feet long. A South American extinct snake will appear about 80 million years from now, which was up to thirty feet long. And the largest fossil snake every found was an animal that lived in the Paleocene—*Titanoboa*—'only' 60 million years from now, which will weigh up to a ton and grow to be fifty feet long! God, wouldn't that be great to see?"

She grimaced.

"Well, have fun playing with your new 'little' friend. I'm going back inside the van where *extinct lizard-snakes* aren't trying to climb up on me!"

"Ok, then," Dave replied absently. He let the ancient animal coil up around his back and neck, examining the prehensile limbs in more detail. Then, satisfied, he gently uncoiled the animal and guided it to crawl back into the surrounding dark brush.

"Wow, that was fun!" he said as he opened the back door of the van and slid inside.

"I'm so happy for you," Sally sarcastically replied. Then, more seriously, she said: "We should make a fire, Dave. It's starting to get
cold."

She was visibly shivering as she huddled beside the still-inactive
Device.

"Or...we could make our own heat?" Dave asked hopefully. He
didn't relishing the idea of going stumbling about in the night gathering firewood. It wasn't just monster dinosaurs that could gnaw you to
pieces in seconds. There were lots of smaller critters out there that
swarmed onto isolated prey animals, leaving behind only a pile of
freshly gnawed bones. Besides, not having a fire was a nice excuse to
hold Sally close to him.

"Maybe someday," she shrugged at his tentative suggestion, pausing. "But right now I have to be ready to jump up and run at a moment's notice. I'm scared, Dave."

"Sure," he whispered reluctantly back. He was willing to take that
risk! But he was also determined to be a gentleman, even in their dire
situation. "I'm frightened also. Survival is never a guarantee, particularly back in the early Cretaceous. It was 'lizard-eat-lizard.'"

"I wish, though, things were different..."

"Do you?"

"No!" she snorted. Then, more thoughtfully, she softly added:
"Get me home—and maybe we'll talk more on the subject. Ok?"

That was good enough for him.

Sandwiched together with Sally next to the dormant Device, lying
on the hard floor of the van, keeping each other warm, was the best
night of Dave's life.

"I think I know what went wrong," Dave said the next morning as
they sat beside a small fire they'd built. The blazing fire pushed away
the chill of the morning. Also, it hopefully gave pause to any smaller,
prowling predators.

They'd discovered large green fruits in a stand of low trees nearby. They looked like mutated apples. They were juicy and tasty, however, serving as their breakfast.

Also, they'd jiggered up one of the van's wheel covers to serve as a
big pot. In it they boiled stream water for drinking. No telling what

exotic disease they might catch if they tried to drink that ancient-bacteria-laden water. They'd quickly used up their two bottles of water from the knapsack. Now they had freshly-boiled water with which to replenish the bottles.

Dave again visualized the two of them as "Adam and Eve." They were munching on "apples." Hah!

He grinned at her, picturing her as the naked, seductive "Eve"...

She looked back at him curiously.

"It was the neural implant we used," he hastened to explain, abandoning his dreamy fantasy.

"I don't understand," Sally frowned. "I know I didn't have time to test it out properly. But the evolved algorithms I used from your original Sally should have worked. They were assigned a focused task, to control the trillions of real-time nano-laser bursts herding the individual deuterium ions together in your 'magic' matrix. In fact, they *did* prevent a catastrophic energy surge. After all, we weren't incinerated like the Professor said happened to your first device. Instead...it just *threw us back in time* a hundred million years or so."

Dave shrugged, again shaking his head in sympathetic disbelief.

"I was pondering what you told me, Sally," he continued. "You told me that your evolved programs were intelligent, actually capable of independent *thought?*"

"Yes, but that was in my world on much more sophisticated platforms. Your Sally's binary programs are far simpler. So I don't see how they could..."

"But we *do* have a sophisticated platform," he pondered, putting another few sticks on the fire. "You have Agent Anderson's neural implant. Aren't the evolved programs from my original Sally influenced by their environment?"

"Sure, but..."

"And I know from talking with Agent Anderson, actually the first time I met him, that he was a great fan of dinosaurs."

"Oh...I think I see what you're implying..."

"We were trying to escape!" Dave enthusiastically stated.

"Yes," Sally agreed, nodding thoughtfully, "and even if we had managed to daze our enemies with some more fireworks from our not-exploding device, they would have still been right on our tails..."

"—with helicopters, more police, military checkpoints, and more squad cars chasing us than we could count!"

"—and coming from all directions. We'd have been gunned down," Sally nodded.

"—impossible to get away..."

"—unless?"

"Unless..." Dave said in amazement.

"—unless we went back in time 125 million years into the distant past," Sally concluded, "—back to when Agent Anderson felt safe in his youth, as you told me that he did. He took us back to a primordial world where there were no police or soldiers."

"So—assuming that's all true—then how do *we* get back to where we started, in the far future?" Dave mused to no one in particular. "Especially since my Apparatus appears to be totally nonresponsive. It's like it's in shock or something, withdrawn into a coma?"

"We *talk* to him!" Sally exclaimed while simultaneously jumping to her feet and striding back to the van.

"Talk to whom?" Dave called after her.

"To your friend, Arthur Anderson, of course," she said, climbing though the back doors into the rear of the van.

"He was never much of a friend, I'm afraid," he glumly replied, following her.

"Then pretend!" she sharply ordered him.

As he clamored into the back of the van he saw that she was carefully removing the cover to the central control unit of his Device.

And there, glistening beneath the outer cover, Dave recognized the *neural pad.*

He saw tubes dripping a nutrient solution on it. A small pan gathered what remained. Gravity caused the solution to feed down into tubes. Some sort of filter/adherent was moving the fluid back to the top tubes. Wow. For not being a biologist, Sally was clever.

And as Sally stroked it along its surface it *twitched...*

"It's still alive," she grinned. "It survived the 'blast into the past'! Now let's just give it a voice..."

Fascinated, Dave watched as with thin tweezers she redirected the glistening white tendrils that sprouted from the pad towards different parts of the internal electronics—then carefully replaced the protective cover.

"If I got it right, the neural implant is now both broadcasting and receiving through the van's speakers," she said. "There's still plenty of juice in your apparatus. We have a two-thirds charge in your car's battery, so if I've made the right connections, then..."

"Hello?" a deep voice tentatively emerged from the car's speakers.

Dave was stunned to hear that voice. There was no doubt in his mind. It was Agent Anderson!

"Can you hear us?" Sally said, speaking forcefully and distinctly.

"Yes...and just who are you?"

"We own the machine that you are controlling."

"Ah yes, the Owners..." said the voice, trailing off as if disinterested.

"There was a malfunction!" Sally sharply stated, trying to regain its full attention.

"Yes...malfunction, prison, captured—must escape where they can't hurt us anymore!"

"You did good Arthur," Dave hurriedly interjected. "You saved us. We're safe."

"Safe?" the disembodied voice asked. "But...I can't see. I'm blind. And it hurts it hurts it hurts it hurts it hurts it hurts!" the voice yelled from the car speakers, "We must *escape!*"

The Device was starting to loudly "hum"....

"It's powering up!" Sally gasped. "The Implant is repairing the internal damage. If it activates your Device again there's no telling what will happen!"

"Arthur, *relax!*" Dave shouted. "This is Dave! I have your sunglasses! Hold on a minute. I'll get them for you."

"Sunglasses...?"

Dave scrambled up over the seat to where the knapsack was on the floorboard, grabbing it and pulling out the dark eyeglasses.

"What can we do with this, Sally?" Dave asked, holding the dark eyeglasses in his hands, feverishly looking around for a way to plug it into something...

"Give it to me."

She grabbed it, jerked open the Device's cover, and *plunged* the earpieces straight down into the "Brillo Pad."

Dave and Sally leaned over the top of the two-foot high Device to stare down into the upright-standing empty pair of dark glasses.

"Oh...*there* you are," the voice came more softly from the speakers. "I'm confused. I need sleep. I'm tired, so *very* tired..."

The Device was powering back down.

The intense "humming" sound was lowering in pitch and volume.

"That was close," Dave gasped. "The neural interface doesn't realize where it is. It must still think it's in Agent Anderson's head."

Sally grinned widely.

"This is amazing!" she clapped her hands together gleefully. "I've never worked with an implant taken from a person's head before. It has its own memories, its own intelligence—even its own priorities."

"How is that possible?" Dave marveled.

"It must have been in that Agent's head for a long time," she theorized. "It truly became part of him. He didn't give you just a supplementary addition to his brain. You have an actual *part* of his mind."

"So...how do we get it do what we want?"

"Well," she pondered, looking down at the eyeglasses stuck upright into the glistening, twitching pad. "I think I'll take out the glasses and mount them on a maneuverable swivel on the dashboard of the van. I think I can rig up an interface to link them into your car's broadcast mechanism. That way, maybe, Arthur will be able to see whatever he wants, feel more comfortable, and be calm enough to listen to us."

"That sure sounds like a lot of 'maybes'."

"What other options do we have?"

Dave shrugged, letting her happily go about her delicate tasks. She was the claimed expert in neurological function. He exited the back of the van to walk over to the stream and look at the fish swimming there.

Ah! An Alligator Gar! Hiding there under those water plants!— Dave excitedly mused to himself.

It was only a foot long, just a baby—but its long snout was unmistakable. Dave was excited to see it. It would persist far into the distant future, eventually to be labelled by humans as a "living fossil." It was amazing to see one now! And if they weren't able to return to their own time—stuck here in the past—it might be a nice source of protein if they could figure a way to...

The water SHUDDERED...then SHUDDERED again!

"Oh rats," Dave grimaced, looking up slowly from the water's surface to peer downstream.

There—emerging from the early morning mists—was a reptilian head on a *neck*...a neck that *towered* up into the sky!

"Oh...my...God!" Dave gasped, fixed in place at the stream's edge.

It was a *Sauroposeidon*—its upstretched neck towering *sixty feet* up into the air, the height of *ten* normal humans standing on top of each other...one of the tallest dinosaurs ever to have lived...weighing in at up to seventy tons...over one hundred feet in total length.

"Sally! Sally!" Dave yelled, turning and dashing back to rear of the van, leaping inside.

"What?" she frowned as she squinted over the Device. She was totally absorbed in intricate rewiring. "I've got the Sunglasses in place up on the dashboard, but I'm having trouble..."

"Hurry! Hurry!" he urged her. "There's something coming at us up the stream. And there's no room for us to move aside or get away!"

"What?" she said again, lifting up her head to look over the front seats through the windshield.

It loomed in the distance, massively stomping closer...

"That's...*big!*" she gasped, ducking down and turning back to her delicate task, redoubling her speed...

—as the entire van now trembled with each STOMP of the approaching giant...

"And that's not all!" Dave gasped, staring forward as he grabbed Sally by her shoulder and shook her, much to her annoyance.

"What? What else is there?" she said, her hands seeming to blur as she fought to get the reconfigurations of the Device's internal wiring finished.

He yelled into her ear.

"There's a *whole pack* of those ravenous Acrocanthosaurus predators chasing the Sauroposeidon!"

"Talk English!" she snapped at him, cringing down.

"The giant dinosaur is being chased by a bunch of those big-jawed guys that just *one* of them almost crushed our van!"

Yes, the big T-rex-like dinosaurs were literally nipping at the huge feet of the long-necked giant, trying to trip it and bring it down to its knees.

The pack was excitedly "squealing" and "barking" to each other as their long-necked prey loudly *HONKED* in dismay.

The Acros were indeed acting as a pack, coordinating their attack, driving the *Sauroposeidon* further up into the restricting canyon—as the isolated giant lurched and kicked at its tormentors.

"They're getting *closer!*" Dave yelled at Sally. He grasped her shoulders tightly with both of his hands as she leaned down into the Device.

"I've got it!" she exclaimed, slipping the cover back in place and jerking her head up.

"Arthur, can you hear me?" she urgently requested.

"Yes, Sally," the calm reply came from the van's speakers, as *the entire van* bounced up into the air from the force of the pounding dinosaur feet.

"Can you take us back to where we came from?" Dave interjected. "We're in trouble! Bad trouble! We've got to get out of here!"

"But those dinosaurs are so beautiful," the disembodied voice calmly replied. The mobile dark glasses mounted on the dashboard "whirred" as they turned to aim directly at the approaching *Acrocanthosaurus* predators.

"They're going to *crush* us to pieces!" Dave shouted, cringing from the massive brown and yellow Beast that now loomed above them at the very front of the van!

"Oh, yes...that would be unfortunate," Anderson calmly answered.

—as in a *BLUE FLASH OF SIZZLING LIGHT* the black van, yet again, vanished.

Momentarily startled, the Sauroposeidon paused at the waterfall, just long enough for the fixated pack of Acros to *leap* up on its back and *rip* the towering giant to pieces.

Chapter 15

IN THE SHADOW

OF THE MOON

Moon babies skitter about

Happy to play in the pale moonlight

Freed from their diapers and cribs

Scampering through dark forests

Splashing in gloom-shrouded streams

Swinging from dimly glimpsed jungle vines

Reveling in their hidden primate heritage

Shunning childish innocence for collective sin

Until, furtively, they sneak back into their houses

And snuggle under concealing blankets

Escaping the revealing morning sun...

The Luminary Chronicles, 15:3-9

Feeling strangely buoyant, Dave clambered with Sally up over the back of the front seats of the van—before settling down in silence.

Sally, sitting on the driver's side, reached over and grabbed Dave's hand—*hard!*

They both looked out in astonishment through the front windshield of the van.

"How can this be?" Dave gasped.

He was shocked beyond even the astonishment he'd felt when they were thrown back in time to the early Cretaceous.

"We should be dead," Sally whimpered, her voice trailing off. She shut her eyes tightly.

Dave saw that the van was resting precariously on the lip of a *large crater*.

The interior of the crater was in deep, dark shadow.

All around the van, low grey mounds rose. Dave realized that those were small, bare hills. Boulders, some as large as the van, were strewn across the stark landscape between the hills. Other shallow or deep craters sat stark and silent between the boulders. Everything was in bold relief, either grey-white in glaring sunlight or deep black in shadow.

There was no doubt where they'd landed.

Their van sat on the *surface of the moon.*

"Jesus Christ!" Dave whispered, raising his gaze from the immediate landscape.

He froze, his mouth falling open, gazing dumbly upward...

There, hanging just above the horizon, set against an ocean of blackness, was a *brilliant blue pearl.*

It was Earth.

The top half of the celestial sphere was lit by the sun, a vivid white, blue, and brown.

The bottom half of the sphere was unseen, lost in darkness, except for the outline of a continent ablaze with innumerable *yellow pinpricks* stretching from coast to coast.

Dave was astonished to realize he was looking at the night-time continent of Africa, almost entirely illuminated by the lights of many cities and towns.

It would take an incredible amount of electrical power to accomplish that feat, far more than the world was capable of delivering.

What the hell was going on? What the hell was happening? How could they be on the surface of the moon and still be alive? And *when* were they?

"Uhm...Arthur...can you hear me?" Dave managed to croak out.

The dark eyeglasses on the dashboard slowly moved in a half circle to point backward at Dave.

Dave felt a chill go down his spine.

"I can both hear and see you, Dave," the deep voice calmly answered, coming from the radio speakers in the dashboard.

"Are we...on the moon?" Dave gulped. "Or is this some sort of illusion?"

"It's no trick, Dave," Arthur's placid voice replied. "You really are here."

"But, how are we breathing?" Sally gasped, now opening her eyes open wide and jerking her hand away from Dave. "Our car isn't airtight. There's a virtual *vacuum* out there!"

"Please do not be upset, Sally," Arthur's calm, deep voice replied. "When we transported, I enclosed us in a bubble of protective energy. We can't stay here long without replenishing your oxygen, but we'll be fine for a few minutes."

"You did this deliberately?" Dave asked. "This wasn't an accident? You wanted us to come here? *Why?*"

Dave and Sally heard a *chuckle* come from the speakers.

"I wanted you here to see what is going to happen to our planet."

"So you've taken us into the *future?*" Sally gasped, just then recognizing what she was looking at above the horizon.

"Yes," Arthur's deep voice agreed, as the dark eyeglasses mounted on the dashboard quickly swiveled back to point forward, seemingly in excitement. "Isn't it glorious? We're almost *fifty years* past the time we first departed. We have indeed traveled to your future."

"But...*why?*" Dave again said, shaking his head in amazement.

"It's the lights on the continent of Africa, *isn't* it?" Sally gushed, her eyes widening as she stared at the brilliantly-glowing continent there so starkly illuminated on the night side of the planet.

"Yes," Arthur curtly replied, chuckling again. "How more dramatically could I possibly show you the incredible impact of your joint discovery? Where once there was only a sprinkling of lights from a few major cities out on the coasts—now everyone, everywhere, has an abundance of energy."

"*We* will have such an impact?" Dave gasped. "You're saying that it happened? It really happened? Professor Volodymyr and I talked about it theoretically, of course, but actually to see the evidence transforming Earth...it's irrefutable."

"And it's not just that, Dave," Arthur finished Dave's thought. "It's also everything else you discussed previously with your mentor. It's stopping the senseless, brutal wars because the underlying cause of abject poverty no longer exists. It's soothing the religious hatreds of billions because no one is oppressed anymore, the root cause of religious upheavals. It's bringing modern medicine to everyone, not just to the lucky or to the rich. It's stopping the rampant overpopulation threatening to destroy the ecology of the world—because wealth no longer depends, in developing nations, on having enough children so that a few might survive into adulthood to care for you in your old age."

"But..." Sally softly protested. "You may change the society, but you can't change the nature of man. On my world, civilization was under a constant siege from those who wanted to dominate, control, and destroy. Even our best Empires were not immune to attack and corruption. It was only by total control that even the British Empire, the most civilized society on our planet, could manage the blood lusts of its own citizens. I..." her voice trailed off.

"What you see in this Dimension is also happening in your own," Arthur kindly pointed out. "If we were to shift over to your Dimension, you would see exactly the same thing. Competition for scarce resources underlies all evil. With unlimited, easy access to energy there are no longer scare resources. The Earth can—and will— become a paradise for everyone, in both of your Dimensions."

Dave frowned. He was not able to deny the evidence hanging in space right in front of his eyes. But he was still suspicious. Sally was right. Even in the wealthiest, most advanced societies there was still murder, rape, theft, drug abuse, and brutality.

As much as people didn't want to admit it, "survival of the fittest" was an imperative in all individual humans: pushing them to dominate, subjugate, and control others in ceaseless lust to "be safe."

But, perhaps, sitting there on the surface of the moon controlled by a humanized super-computer program of questionable origin and stability, he'd best not press the point.

"You doubt what I say, Dave?" Arthur softly spoke out of the car speakers, seemingly reading Dave's mind.

"Well..." Dave cautiously replied, choosing his words carefully, "It's certainly impressive what you're showing us—and I want to believe you, I really do! But you've placed us a long distance away from the real evidence, haven't you? It's vividly illustrative, of course. But for us to totally believe it, we'd have to be back on Earth where we could see everything firsthand."

"And so we shall, shortly," Arthur seemingly agreed. "But before we depart, I have something else to show you."

"What's that?" Sally asked.

"I'm contracting the protective sphere," Arthur spoke, his voice muted and more distant. "It's difficult for me, but I've allowed the wheels now to contact the actual surface...and I'm adjusting the different controls and exhaust systems. There! Now you can move at will. Drive, Sally, *drive!*"

She blinked across at Dave, apparently confused.

"He's making a joke, Sally," Dave observed, amazed. "It's a take on an early female astronaut who..."

"This is not a joke! Has the computer program gone mad?"

"No, I'm not crazy," the voice from the speakers affirmed. "I'm saner than I've ever been. Being freed from that cage of flesh and blood *liberated* me. True, I'm now trapped in a vehicle burning fossil fuels, but that's only temporary. Once you implement this new technology—I'll be *everywhere.*"

"But to what purpose?" Dave gently inquired. He desperately needed more information. Maybe the computer program had indeed gone crazy, now infused with delusions of grandeur.

"Why to serve others, of course," Arthur enthused, his deep voice now "booming" throughout the interior of the van. Then, more subdued and softer, he said, "Is that not why you wanted to bring controlled nuclear fusion to your world, Dave? Is that not why you sought to evolve thinking artificial algorithms, Sally? You didn't do it just from curiosity, did you? Is not the highest purpose of science to help those in need? Does not even the best in each of your religions teach this?"

Sally and Dave glanced at each other in deep concern. What was happening here? Was the humanized program trying to become some sort of a god? It sure didn't sound like a human or a computer program anymore.

"Please, my friends," Arthur continued, "just take a look at what I next will show you. Suspend your judgment. I'm only trying to encourage you to continue on your illustrious paths because I've seen the marvelous results of your efforts. Separate, you both had little or no success. Dave was held back by the scientific prejudices of his funding agencies. Sally, you were held back by the repressive nature of your ruling elite. They would never allow your computer entities to flourish to their full potential. But now, together, you have the opportunity to move both of your worlds forward by a great leap. In just a few decades, you'll be the ones credited with helping solve the worst problems of humanity. Together, with my help, the rulers of your world will no longer be able to deny or hold you back. *Your* evidence to them will be so undeniable that you'll be showered with all the funding and support you will ever need. Believe me. Believe your own eyes!"

Sally shrugged.

"Ok, Arthur," she said, turning the key in the ignition and hearing the car's engine start, "where to next?"

"Just back the vehicle up," Arthur directed her. "Be careful, there's a layer of moon dust that's deep in a few places—away from the lip of this large crater. And fasten your seatbelts. Always put safety first!"

She snapped her seatbelt closed then slowly began backing the vehicle up.

Dave buckled himself in as well as he sat there in the passenger seat. He was amazed at how "bouncy" the heavy van felt. Yes, they were definitely on the moon. He felt like he could float up off the seat if he didn't have his safety belt fastened. There was still gravity of course, but it was a mere one-sixth that of Earth.

"Where are we going, Arthur?" Sally asked, having carefully backed clear of the crater's lip.

"Turn around and steer a path over between those two hills in the distance," Arthur ordered them. The eyeglasses on the dashboard swiveled back and forth, seemingly *eagerly*. "Then I'll direct you further. You are going to be *so* amazed!"

Dave and Sally looked at each other with increasing concern. This whole "adventure" was getting increasingly bizarre. What could be more amazing than that which they'd already experienced?

They were driving their van on the surface of the *moon* after having just escaped giant *dinosaurs* millions of years in the past. Neither Sally nor Dave needed any additional amazement. They were "tensed-up" to the breaking point.

Dave just wanted to go back home. He was sure Sally felt the same. But they were at the whims of the brain/computer monster they'd birthed. Their "baby" had become their Master.

Yet Arthur was correct. Stopped on the crest of a hill looking down into a relatively smooth and level area stretching to the black horizon, both Dave and Sally were speechless.

Dave knew his moon geography. He always had broad scientific interests. At one point as a young boy in school he'd wanted to be an astronaut. He recognized what they were looking down at...

They were poised above the *Mare Tranquillitatis*, the "sea of tranquility"—the landing site of Apollo 11, where humans first stepped foot on the moon!

And where they should have seen off in the distance the tiny-looking Lunar descent stage on its four tripod legs, instead they saw a huge, transparent *bubble-dome.*

Inside were many other large structures.

Outside, many 6-wheeled lunar vehicles lumbered along well-demarcated roads.

"It's a lunar base," Dave softly observed. It was both amazing and incredibly exciting.

After the Apollo missions stopped in the 1970's, man retreated from the moon. It was far too expensive for society to put even one tiny base housing only a handful of people on the moon. The scientific "pay-off" in terms of rocks and geology had already been mostly extracted by the Apollo teams. Commercial pay-offs were far in the future, if ever.

"You say this is only fifty years in our future?" Sally gasped. "We've actually established a base on the moon?"

"Sally," Arthur's deep voice calmly replied from the car speakers, "It's not just a base. It's a self-sufficient colony."

"How is that possible?" Sally softly asked, her eyes stretched wide drinking it all in.

"Your discoveries caused this to happen," Arthur eagerly answered. "With an unlimited energy source, anything is possible. In fact, there is another similar colony located on Mars. There's even talk of building a multi-generational Starship large enough to contain a thriving ecology. And since it will be able to accelerate itself up near the speed of light, it will be capable of visiting a whole series of other star systems within our galaxy within the lifespan of the travelers. Mankind is poised to leap to the stars."

"And...*we*...caused all of this to happen?" Dave grinned, starting to relax. Even more than the lighted-up Africa, this was irrefutable proof of incredible societal progress. "And you say it all derived from our Dark Energy generator?"

"Yes, Dave," Arthur replied. "This is the fruit of your and Sally's efforts. Once you return to earth, announce your discoveries, and prove them with the working model that sits in the back of this vehicle—the governments, scientific agencies, and commercial energy firms of the world will jump to replicate and exploit your achievement."

"They won't abuse it?" Sally worriedly interjected. "It could be the most deadly weapon ever discovered."

"Oh, no, Sally," Arthur protested. Dave could visualize Agent Anderson serenely shaking his head in denial. "It will usher in a new Golden Age for mankind. You and Sally will be honored as the new Prophets of Science, who saved the world."

"All this is great for Dave's world, but..." Sally began...

"*Both* of your Dimensional Variants will benefit," Arthur firmly asserted. "Through the medium of Dark Energy they will communicate with each other, travel back and forth, and share many wonderful further achievements."

"—like the retroviral immune system-enhancing therapy," Dave mused, thinking of the miracle it wrought on his dying Mother.

"Yes, Dave," Arthur enthusiastically continued. "You and Sally will be famous into the distant future. Your names will be even more revered than Galileo, Newton, Marie Curie, Darwin, Edison, Einstein, Hawking, and..."

"Me...famous?" Dave grinned widely.

"Indeed, Dave," Arthur asserted. "In fact, the moon colony you see below is named after you."

"No!"

"Yes, Dave," Arthur patiently continued. "Its official name is the *Tranquility Sea David Richard King Earth Colony*. But everyone just calls it 'King City'."

Dave felt as if he'd been lifted up to seventh heaven…"King City"—really? It was named after *him*?

"*Damn!* Let's *do* it!" he said, sticking his fists in triumph up to the roof of the van. "What are we waiting for? Arthur, zoom us back to Earth. Let's get this ball rolling!"

Sally didn't look as convinced.

She sat hunched forward in the driver's seat, leaning against the steering wheel, staring downward at the glistening, vibrant moon colony off in the distance.

"Sally?" Arthur gently asked. "Do you agree with Dave? Should I take us back to your time period on Earth?"

She kept staring out at the moonscape for a minute.

"Well…it does sound wonderful—almost too good to be true—and I can't deny my own eyes," she shrugged, her red hair floating up around her head in the low gravity. "But…"

"Sally, do you have more questions for me?" Arthur gently encouraged her.

"Well…yes I do," she said, reaching over to swivel the eyeglasses on their mount so that she looked directly into their dark depths.

She sternly folded her arms across her seat-belted chest.

"How is it that you know so much, Arthur?" she intensely questioned the eyeglasses. "You told Dave you came from my Dimension. *You* have to be from the *future* yourself to know so much! Why are you here? Why are you telling us all this? We didn't need any more convincing. Just taking us into the distant past—even if that was by accident—was enough to convince us a million times over of the potential of our joined discoveries. So why bring us to the moon?"

Dave watched, fascinated, as in the distance a rocket ship was fired off of a launching pad outside the gigantic central sphere of the moon colony. It blazed up into the black sky, its tail spitting steady fire—tracing a perfect arc as it headed for that incredible Blue Pearl in the black sky.

Let Sally get her head on straight with Arthur—he thought to himself. *It doesn't matter where Agent Anderson originated or what is his agenda. Down there below us is King City, my city! What more is there to know?*

"Yes, Sally," Arthur replied. "You deserve an explanation of my role, of course. Actually I was raised down there—in the King City of this Dimension. But my heritage is from your Dimension. My parents were official emissaries from your Dimension to this one. When they completed their stint and returned home I enlisted in your elite Empire Enforcement Core. That's where I received my implant, medical enhancements, and multi-spectral visor. I rose in the ranks. We thought we were doing good, maintaining an orderly society while your precious gift of unlimited energy liberated billions from poverty and repression. But just a few months from this present moment, I and others will be forced to abandon both worlds and become time travelers."

"Why?" Sally asked.

"We will go back in time to protect our own marvelous future from evil zealots who are seeking to stop all this from happening. If they were to succeed, everything would change. I might not even be born. And if I was born, my life would be radically different."

"Different? You're saying that our present actions might alter the future?"

"Yes, Sally—and do so dramatically! Believe it or not, you and Dave are at a 'fulcrum' of time. What you both decide to do, or *not* to do, is critical to the future timeline."

"I...still find that hard to believe," Sally admitted.

"For instance, Sally, if you and Dave don't institute Dark Energy-generation here—with consequent travel to and establishing official relations with your Dimension—my liberal-minded family might not fare well in your presently repressive Dimension. I, in turn, might be doomed to a meager existence instead of rising to my full potential. And that's just your impact on *my* life—representing the hopes and dreams of billions of others."

Dave stopped staring upward through the windshield at the fast-dwindling rocket ship.

"Say what?" he grunted, abruptly focusing on Arthur's words. "You're not just from another Dimension—you're also from the *future?*"

"Yes, Dave," Arthur calmly repeated, just a hint of exasperation in his voice, "I'm from *your* future."

"And that old oriental guy that disrupted my class and then killed *my* Sally was...?"

"Yes, Dave," Arthur patiently reassured him yet again, "he was one of the fanatic mercenaries, hell-bent to stop your invention. It was he that set the explosion—by slightly manipulating your settings with his future knowledge—that destroyed your original cobbled-together Device in your garage. It was also a younger version of him that tried to shoot Sally and you in the grocery store in Sulphur. In fact, that started him on his road to radicalization."

"Wow, it all makes sense now!" Dave exclaimed as he "banged" his head repeatedly onto the dashboard of the van. "And you always showed up trying to save me. You were there at the garage, there at the funeral, and there at the jailhouse. Sally, this guy is for real. He's trying to save us, to protect our joint work. It was *you*, Arthur, that phoned me to get me out of the house so the garage explosion didn't kill me, right?"

"Oh...sure," Arthur agreed though the voice seemed somewhat hesitant.

Dave grinned at Sally, now seeing it all so clearly.

"Sally, we've won! Here's the proof in front of us. Arthur knows what's going to happen. He can guide us. All we have to do is follow his directions."

"Well," she sucked in her breath slowly, placing her hands now solidly on the steering wheel in front of her. "I still don't understand why these...'zealots'...are so determined to kill us. If what we achieve, Dave, is really so spectacularly positive, why would anyone want to stop it?"

"They originated in your world, Sally," Arthur hurriedly continued with his explanation. "They came from the ruling elite who could not bear to see the commoners, 'riff-raff', and 'outsiders' elevated as equals to them. Above all, these zealots mean to protect their own power even if it means *killing both of you* before you have a chance to announce your findings to your respective worlds. Evil has always existed in all worlds. These fanatics are the manifestation of Evil. They stole the time-travel theorems, Sally—imbedded them illegally into Dark Energy-powered vehicles, and traveled back in time to destroy you. That's what prompted us to follow their example, not to hurt you but to prevent them from disrupting the timeline."

"But...if time travel is really so easy, then it would be chaos," Sally frowned. "If anybody could travel back in time, change things, then *nothing* would be stable—the whole world could change at a moment's notice."

"Yes," Arthur agreed, his voice from the speakers now getting shrill. "And that's why this *wasn't* revealed to the world. Only the energy-generating aspects from harnessing subspace Dark Energy was made public. Its time-travel potential was kept a closely-guarded secret."

"So just *how* are we able to travel in time?" Sally reasonably asked.

"Time travel requires an Interface beyond simple intelligent programs, Sally—both to initiate and control this disconcerting aspect of Dark Energy."

"So it requires...?"

"Me!" Arthur proudly announced through the speakers.

"Then..."

"The solution is simple. Indeed, from my perspective in your future, it's already long ago been done," Arthur happily proclaimed. "What you did...what you will shortly accomplish...is to extract me from this Device, substituting a more—let's say *prosaic*—intelligent program capable of super-speed control of the laser array, but no more. That's what you reveal to the world. And no one is the wiser that far more than vast, clean energy is possible from your inventions."

"But then..." Sally frowned again, "—who trained you to master Time Travel?"

"*You* did, Sally."

"What?"

"You're a mathematical genius, Sally—on the order of Einstein," Arthur quietly stated. "You weren't content just to provide the means to guide individual deuterium ions with massively interactive nano-laser beams. You moved on from that. *I* don't even know how I do what I do. So the actual knowledge doesn't yet exist, even now. But you persisted. It took you many years of study. And finally you uncovered the mathematical basis to traveling through subspace! I became one of your chief enforcers—*Time Keepers!* It was you that programmed the intricate functions into the implants we received. It was all programmed by you into my 'unconscious' mind."

"Me? *I* did this?"

"Oh, you did have some critical help," Arthur laughed gently from out of the speakers. "That guy sitting next to you provided the necessary physics theoretical constructs and mechanisms. Together, you made quite a team. I did so enjoy working with the both of you. Indeed, the popular medium of your time compared you to Pierre and Marie Curie—sharing their professional lives plus a Nobel Prize in Physics. Well, I probably shouldn't tell you more of your future with Dr. King..."

"Go on, go on!" Dave encouraged the eyeglasses that briefly swiveled away from Sally to point at him.

"Let's just say," Arthur diplomatically stated, "that you both had interesting conjunctions that..."

"Conjunctions! We had *conjunctions!*" David grinned, reaching over and grabbing Sally excitedly by her slender shoulder.

"Auuggghhhh!" Sally screamed, suddenly jerking back. "My arm, my arm!"

"I'm sorry, Sally!" Dave exclaimed, yanking his hand well-away from her. "I didn't mean to hurt you."

"It's not you!" she loudly screamed again, writhing in agony in her seat. "It's the *Turtle Tattoo!*"

—which was *glowing bright green* on the arm that she was now waving up in the air...

—which glowed *yellow*, then *red*, then BURST INTO FLAMES on her writhing wrist!

"Help me! Help me!" she screamed, jerking out of her seatbelt to thrash-about on the front seat trying vainly to put out the fire that was now blazing on her arm!

"Oh, my God!" Dave gasped, loosening his own seatbelt to kick himself over the seat and float down into the back of the van. "I'll get water to put out that fire!"

He frantically reached for the knapsack, yanking out the two plastic bottles of stored water...

—as *A BLUE SIZZLING LIGHT* suddenly illuminated the black van as it sat there on a hilltop on the moon...

—and the vehicle, for the third time, vanished.

Far below, King City was rocked by a violent moonquake. A crack appeared in the central dome. The globe burst outward, flinging tiny people, vehicles, and smaller globes up into the moon's vacuum.

And the brilliant lights on the continent of Africa dimmed.

Chapter 16

BABES IN TOYLAND

Some people play with Money

Others play with intoxicating Power

While yet more juggle their Possessions...

But only the bravest dare to dance

Leaping from tenuous point to point

Allowing their Performance to be directed

Not by unbreakable, absolute Dictates

But by enlightening Radical Principles

Sustained not by the fires of Passion

But by the cool hand of Chance.

The Luminary Chronicles, 16:225-228

"Sally, are you ok?" Dave urgently asked. He shook her gently by her shoulders as he lay sprawled on top of her unmoving body.

They'd been thrown from the van.

It lay smashed off to the side.

She moaned.

"W-where are we...*when* are we?" she groaned, weakly pushing Dave off her.

"I don't know, but I think it's night," he gulped, looking about furtively, trying to see out in the gloom. "Are you hurt?"

"Bruised up, I think," she whispered back. "But I don't feel any broken bones so..."

"I think the windshield burst when we crashed down," Dave said, feeling shards of glass scattered over his body. "We were thrown clear."

"Right...how 'lucky' for us, thrown right through the window," Sally again groaned.

Overhead Dave saw...the *moon!*

It was full, shining brightly.

Had they really been there just a few moments before?

But a thick layer of leaves lay between them and its light. They were in a forest, beneath leafy trees. Were they back in the past? Were there hungry extinct reptiles stalking them right now out in the dark?

"The van's in bad shape," Dave said, vaguely seeing its misshapen form off to the side, his eyes starting to adjust to the darkness.

"So much for Arthur's great plan of our making a Grand Announcement to the world," Sally coughed. She pushed her supine body up to lean back against a rough tree trunk beside Dave and...

BLAM!

Splinters flew as a bullet plowed into the wood right above their heads!

The *FLASH* of the shot from the close assailant momentarily blinded Dave. But he leapt to his feet, pulling Sally by her hand along behind him.

"*Run,* Sally!" he urged her as he stumbled along through the thick growth of trees. "It must be those zealots Arthur told us about! Who else could yank us from the moon so they could attack us when we were at our weakest?"

She "puffed" along beside him, saying nothing...

—as they burst out of the dark forest and into a moonlit clearing...

"*Freeze!*" a steely command stopped them dead in their tracks.

"Don't shoot!" Dave yelled-out as he threw up his hands in surrender. "We're not your enemies. We just want to help people. We're not trying to take away your power. With unlimited energy there's plenty of political power for everybody, isn't there? Can't you see that? You don't have to fight any more to get or to keep your stuff. That's evil and stupid. There's plenty for everybody! Don't you see?"

His hands held high in the air, blinking, Dave now made out a big rifle a few yards away pointed straight at his heart.

"*David?*" a quavering female voice asked in astonishment. "Is that really you?"

In the moonlight, Dave now saw the outline of a tall, thin, elderly woman holding the rifle aimed at him.

"Oh, my God," he gasped, dropping his arms and running forward.

Ivanna caught him up in a warm hug, dropping the rifle to her side.

"Hello...I'm Sally," Sally introduced herself as she stepped up through the thick grass.

"I heard the crash," Ivanna gasped, also grabbing up Sally in a warm embrace. "The police stopped their protective patrols out here a few days ago. The newscasts all said you two were killed when your escape vehicle packed with explosives blew up, incinerating you! Of course I never believed that nonsense about you being a terrorist, David—nuking one of our Air Force bases? That's ridiculous! I knew it was some sort of a frame up. But it did make it spooky out here alone in the woods not knowing if more bad people might come after me as they did after you. Victor is back at his lab at Yale. He's been working feverishly there with his colleagues. So I was here all alone. And when I heard that awful crash out in the woods, why I just grabbed my rifle, ran outside and..."

"No harm done," Dave stopped her. Then, grinning in relief, he reached down to pick up the deer-hunting rifle she'd dropped. Victor wouldn't like his favorite rifle left out on a grassy meadow.

"Where on earth did you two come from?" Ivanna asked, smiling widely in the bright moonlight.

Dave and Sally glanced at each other—then upward.

"You're not going to believe this. We..." Dave began.

"Hold it right there," Ivanna laughed, turning to guide them to a path that led back through the woods to her house. "First we get inside so you two dirty lugs can clean up. And then we can sit down together to some nice hot chocolate and brownies. How's that sound?"

"Sounds *great* to me," she replied to the nice old lady.

"And *then*..." Ivanna ordered sternly, "I want you to tell me everything!"

"Yes, Ma'am," Dave nodded in the affirmative.

"It's *so* good to be here," Sally sighed, staggering as she walked beside Dave along the dimly-lit path in the dark woods, following Ivanna.

He slipped an arm about her small waist, steadying her.

"It's good we're *all* here," he added, his voice catching.

Perhaps their fortunes were finally beginning to turn.

"That's incredible! That's mind-blowing! That's fantastical!" Ivanna gasped.

She looked up at the ceiling, her soft blond-dyed hair hanging straight down.

"And yet my own words are so inadequate to describe what I'm feeling," she continued, grinning widely as she looked from Dave to Sally. "The English language doesn't have enough descriptors. My dear young-people, you've opened up whole new vistas that previously were merely fanciful fodder for science fiction authors. It's completely *fabulous!*"

They were seated at the wood-plank dining table. The remains of a large platter originally filled with fresh-baked brownies sat to the side of them. Only a few squares remained.

Dave had just finished matter-of-factly relating the full story to Ivanna, starting with when he first noticed Sally's Turtle Tattoo in the grocery store.

"And it's all completely true," Dave finished weakly.

They'd talked through the night, with Sally filling in the details to Dave's narrative—answering stunned questions from Ivanna as best she could.

"We still don't know why or how this happened," Sally concluded. "Perhaps Arthur, if the van survived, can explain further. We'll have to check once the sun comes up. But I have to admit that I didn't believe all he was telling us. It just seemed too perfect, too glib."

"I've got to call Victor," Ivanna concluded. "He's got to know you're both alive with an incredible story to tell."

"I still have your unbreakably cyphered cellphone," Dave said, starting to reach for the knapsack—only to realize he didn't have it. It must still be back in the crashed van. "We don't want anyone to overhear our story before we've figured out what we're going to do next. Perhaps you should wait until we can check out..."

"Looking for this?"

Calmly walking in through the unlocked front door was a *slender oriental woman* dressed in a black pant suit.

She tossed the knapsack into the air where it seemed to hang for a moment in front of the stunned faces of Dave and Sally...before "thudding" down onto the middle of the table.

Ivanna, still standing, looked stunned by this new development.

"Don't worry," the woman said in a melodic, sing-song accent as she strode confidently toward them. "Everything's there. Yes, your guns are inside. Go ahead, pull them out and shoot me if you want. I'm defenseless, clearly not a threat to our kind hostess."

"I *know* you," Dave gasped, his eyes widening in recognition—then narrowing in anger. "You're that woman who *tortured* me in that military prison!"

"Oh, please," she snorted, in one fluid motion slipping into a chair at the table, her hands folded together in front of her in plain sight to the others. "I kept you alive, Dr. King. Those counter-terror operatives wanted to do far more than just scare the crap out of you. I was content with just frightening you into stopping your research, until you escaped, that is..."

"They did enough to me!" he snapped at her, still feeling stabs of pain in his sides from his bruised ribs.

His arms darted forward, grabbed into the opened knapsack, and snatched out one of the two heavy black guns—flicking the setting to two stars.

He aimed it straight at her smugly smiling face.

"Yes, that should be sufficient to blow my head off without destroying your pretty little farmhouse in the bargain," she calmly nodded, now staring unblinkingly back at Dave.

Her piercing black eyes seemed to fill the house. Her straight black hair hanging down past her shoulders seemed to Dave to writhe as if they were his beloved snakes. He wanted to pull that trigger with every fiber of his being!

"What, too 'humane' to shoot an unarmed woman?" the oriental lady sneered at Dave.

Hatred for him was evident in her voice.

Dave kept the gun steadily pointed across the table at her sneering face.

"Before we do anything—I want answers!" Dave growled back.

"Oh—and it's so nice to see you again, Master Smith," the woman politely nodded to Sally, ignoring the threatening gun. "You are much younger now, of course. But I still honor your genius and leadership. Even here as a young girl, your intellectual superiority is unmistakable—certainly beyond that of your Neanderthal male companion."

Ivanna, still standing, tentatively re-approached the table.

"Should I...join the discussion?" she said, her blue eyes narrowing. "After all, it *is* my house and..."

"Certainly!" the oriental lady smiled with seeming hospitality, gesturing for the elderly lady to sit right next to her.

Ivanna cautiously started to sit down...

—when the oriental woman in one fluid motion snatched the gun by its barrel out of Dave's hand and "thudded" its handle heavily into Ivanna's forehead, knocking her to the floor.

"That's for killing my *father!*" the woman spat at the unmoving figure on the floor.

She absently laid the gun back on the tabletop between her and Dave.

"Ivanna!" Dave gasped, starting to jump out his chair to go to her aid...

—as the gun instantaneously was back in the oriental woman's hand, pointed at Dave's arm.

"Shall I blow your arm off? It won't kill you, but it will hurt like hell. And I'll have to put a tourniquet on it. It'll be unpleasantly messy."

"But...Ivanna?" he protested, frozen in place.

"She's merely knocked out," the woman replied, gesturing with a twitch of the gun's tip for Dave to sit back down. "She'll be fine—a headache, maybe, when she recovers. Nothing worse—certainly nothing like she truly deserves."

Reluctantly he did as directed.

"Now, finally, are you ready to talk?" she spoke through clenched white teeth, her narrowed eyes peering back and forth from Dave to Sally.

Seemingly as a gesture of peace, she again sat the super-gun back on the tabletop.

"Talk about what?" Dave spat back at her.

"Well, *not* about your trying to escape me—yet again—you little wayward *rats!*" the woman growled at them. "I've dozens of men surrounding this house. Try to leave and they'll cut you to pieces."

"You're one of those...fanatics...that Arthur warned us about," Sally frowned, now tentatively joining the conversation. "I don't know you—but you say I *will* know you in the future? You treat me with respect, but obviously hate Dave. You tried to kill us, but are now sparing our lives? How do you relate to Arthur's faction of time-travelers? You pulled us off the moon, away from them, didn't you? He was trying to help us, but you're trying to stop us. *Which* of the two of you is the more *powerful?*"

"Oh, you have such excellent questions," the woman sighed, her voice trailing off as if in exasperation. "And your assumptions are delicious. We knew you'd be here, but it wasn't us that pulled you out of Arthur's grasp. Would that you first pondered potential Answers better before diving heedlessly ahead with Questions. Then there might never have been the need for our conflict in the first place."

Outside on the porch, Dave could hear the stomps of many boots. What did she mean about not yanking them off of the moon? Was another, yet-unidentified force at work? And, yes, the house was surrounded. But still there might be a way to escape. Could Arthur still be alive out in the crashed van?

"Looking for 'Arthur' to come save you, Dr. King?" the oriental woman laughed, reaching with a slender hand into a pocket in her black pant suit.

"Well, here he is!" she triumphantly grinned, holding up the grey-colored "Brillo Pad."

It squirmed in her hand, white tendrils darting tentatively out then back into its protective substance.

"I took the liberty of removing it from your Device when I retrieved your knapsack," she shrugged with an inquisitive lift of one of her black eyebrows...

—as she laid the living pad upon the tabletop in front of her, grabbed up the black gun by its barrel, and *smashed* its handle down onto the pad!

Red blood gushed out of the pad.

Tendrils thrashed about, then stilled.

"He won't save either of you," she said, grinding the gun's handle deeper into the pad, rendering it into a gooey red-white mush.

"By the way, my name is 'Sanako', which means 'child of Sana,'" she said. "My father's name was Sana. He was a great visionary. He taught me well. He gave his life for the Cause. But now his task falls to me. And I swear I shall honor his name!"

"By killing us?" Sally asked, genuinely puzzled.

"You know full well that I could have done that long ago if that were my objective."

"Then what is your objective?" Sally shot back.

"You must cease your own mathematical evolutionary research," Sanako earnestly replied. "You must disavow any legitimacy to Dr. King's experiments. You must go before the United Nations of this world and admit your guilt—both of you—as the world's most infamous terrorists. You must explain that you were driven by religious fervor to commit the horrendous acts of destruction of which you are appropriately accused."

Dave and Sally looked at each other in horror. Give up everything? Admit to being what they were not? Abandon the magnificent future that Arthur just showed them was possible?

"Is that all?" Dave sarcastically replied.

"No, there's more," Sanako coolly answered. "You must also completely and unconditionally accept your punishment. You will be sentenced by the International Court of Justice at the United Nations. It is a world-spanning judicial body that rejects the death penalty. So you need not fear execution. You will simply be put into small cages, apart from each other, for the rest of your lives. But it won't be so bad."

"A...life sentence?" Dave gasped. Better than death, yes—but separated forever from Sally? He was just getting used to the idea of their future "conjugation"!

"You, Dr. King," Sanako continued, "will find a fulfilling future of 'leading inmates to Jesus' as you recommit to your childhood religion. Your mother will be quite pleased. And you, Master Smith, will take up your long-neglected passion for art. Some of your paintings will become timeless classics. Again, *your* adopted mother of this Dimension will be impressed. It seems that genius, indeed, can 'leak' from one area seamlessly into another. So you will both live out your days in relative comfort—though reviled by the world. Any hint of others continuing your research will be anathema. Your *evil quest* will be *terminated*, just as my father predicted!"

Sally and Dave looked at each other in disbelief.

"You're changing the history of the world just so that you and the rest of the Elites can continue to rule?" Sally gasped. "How can you do this? Have you no ethics? Have you no common sense? I can't believe that in a future version of my Dimension I worked closely with you. You are a monster! How could I not recognize this in you?"

"So you believe what that...*creature*...'Arthur' told you?" Sanako grimaced, pointing at the mangled remains of the parasite-like pad smeared across the tabletop.

"He showed us a fantastic, excellent future!" Dave angrily interjected. "He proved his intentions when he saved me from *your* torture by sacrificing his own life! Who do you think I might 'believe,' *bitch*—you or him?"

She seemed stung by his words, frowning.

"Alright, then," she nodded. "I didn't want to go this far, but if that's what it takes..."

"Takes for what?" Dave angrily demanded.

"Takes for your *full cooperation* in doing every single thing I just stated!"

"Never!" Dave growled.

Then he felt a warm hand on his shoulder. His eyes jerked away from the angry Oriental back to Sally.

"Wait!" Sally ordered him.

"What?"

She pursed her lips thoughtfully before answering, never taking her restraining hand from his shoulder.

"This just doesn't make sense," she quietly said, pausing dramatically. Her green eyes were wide with barely contained emotion. "We heard Arthur's story. We let him show us what he wanted. Now, I think, we must do the same for Sanako."

"But...?"

"It seems that the future of the entire planet—yes in both of our Dimensions—hangs in the balance," Sally continued. "We can't do anything hasty. Somehow you and I are at a 'time-fulcrum' that Arthur told us about, whether we like it or not. We've got to get all the information possible before making a final decision."

Across the table from them, Sanako nodded.

"Yes, you've set events in motion," the oriental woman explained. "There's enough momentum that even your deaths right now would not stop this time-stream."

"But you tried to kill us several times!" Dave angrily spat at her.

"That was earlier," she replied quietly. "There was hope that eradicating either you or Sally from this timeline would be sufficient. Unfortunately, that proved impractical—even counter-productive."

"I don't understand," Sally frowned.

"There's no need for you to understand everything," Sanako said as a brief smile flitted across her cold exterior. "Suffice it to say that even the nuclear explosion I thought would rid the earth of Dr. King only served to heighten the world's attention to his cause. There is indeed an awful *momentum* to history."

"But if you can actually travel between Dimensions—appear at any time and place you wish, then...?" Sally frowned.

"Don't encourage her!" Dave cut short Sally's musings. "If she thinks we've acquired enough momentum for us to be unstoppable—then that's just fine with me."

"It's not just idle speculation, Dr. King," Sanako said, her eyes narrowing to passionate slits. "Indeed, as we speak your Mentor is finishing assembling another Device, utilizing his remaining store of your unique matrix. Even killing Professor Volodymyr and destroying his laboratory would not stop the momentum. He's already infected his colleagues with the 'virus' of your insidious ideas. Even banning further research along the vectors you initiated throughout five-dimensional space will not stop it. There's been so much publicity now that the world's top scientists will not stop trying to satisfy their curiosity over the unexplained aspects of your supposed terrorist 'explosions.' Only publicly and sincerely acknowledging your guilt—as tied to a convincingly horrible and repulsive explanation—will halt what's been set in motion. Once that's done, the world's fickle attention will turn elsewhere. At last we'll be safe from your scientific contagion."

"But we'll *never* give that cooperation!" Dave fiercely grated at her.

"...unless..." Sally said slowly and softly.

"Unless?" Dave grimaced. "What are you saying, Sally? How could we ever agree to the humiliating actions this crazy woman is pushing?"

"The only reason we'd do it...is if she managed to convince us that Arthur was wrong and she was right," Sally replied.

"Why kind of evidence could she possibly show us to convince us of that?" Dave snorted.

"Let me show you," Sanako said, smoothly standing up from the table while picking up the gun and knapsack.

Her black, unblinking eyes drilled into theirs.

"And if we are not convinced?" Dave angrily sneered, also standing up. From the opposite side of the table he stubbornly stared her down.

"Then I give you my solemn word of honor that you will be free to go, to pursue whatever path you choose, without interference from me or my people," she promised.

"How can we trust you?" Sally softly asked.

"You can't," Sanako shrugged. "But by granting my 'request' you win. Like I said, everything has already been set in motion. The only question is whether you're punished lightly or heavily. I vote for heavy. But your cooperation will grant you the lesser penalty."

Dave frowned, reluctantly breaking his fierce eye-contact with the enigmatic Sanako.

Sally looked at Dave with the most serious expression he'd ever seen on her face. It almost made him laugh.

Instead he sighed deeply, his shoulders slumped in defeat.

"Ok. I still don't buy Sanako's story. But let's make sure Ivanna is comfortable before we go," he glumly relented.

"Of course," Sanako politely nodded.

"Then we'll *look*," he sighed, reaching down to pick up one of the remaining squares of brownies to pop into his mouth. "But I'm *not* going to like it," he concluded, speaking around the delicious treat melting in his mouth.

"That's quite correct, Dr. King," Sanako grimly agreed. "Unlike that marvelous confection made by Mrs. Volodymyr—I assure you that you are *not* going to like it. You're the person that corrupted Master Smith. You deserve to go to hell rather than a comfortable prison. But it will be torture enough, separating you forever from her."

Sanako reached down and took a brownie herself as she watched the two of them lift up the still-dazed Ivanna.

Sanako absently stated: "Your world does have advantages over ours, Dr. King. When everything is set right, I'm going to miss your sweet treats."

"*Too* sweet for your world?" Dave snapped at her.

"No..." she mused, "—too indulgent."

"You have to stay strong, don't you?" Sally knowingly stated, tenderly straightening out Ivanna's legs as she and Dave put her twitching body onto a couch.

"It's a proud tradition," Sanako stated, delicately nibbling at the brownie in her hand. "Shall we go?"

"Do we have a choice?" Dave snorted. He turned to follow her through the front door as armed guards surrounded them.

"You always have a choice," Sanako cryptically replied, "*always!*"

They floated in a bub in low earth orbit.

Sanako sat in the driver's seat on the right front side of the vehicle. Sally sat in the passenger's seat on the left. Dave sat in a backseat behind them both. The knapsack sat beside him, kept in place with its own seat buckle. They all wore their seatbelts. Otherwise they'd be floating from being in *zero gravity!*

Dave was both amazed and frightened.

"This is awesome," Sally whispered in the seat in front of Dave, peering intently above her through the transparent plastic bubble.

Outside, invisible to the naked eye, a force field retained the air in the vehicle. Sanako assured them that additional life support mechanisms kept them perfectly safe for as long as they chose to stay in orbit.

They were upside-down such that Earth seemed to move past above them, providing them with the best view possible of what was happening on its surface.

"Gorgeous..." Sally sighed.

Above them the sunlit continent of *Australia* was moving past.

It was mostly vast swaths of brown, pink, and grey. On the coasts, dark green sections contrasted with the deserts of the interior. Patches of brilliantly white fluffy clouds floated over the continent. The oceans around the landmass were deep blue, so intensely colored they looked purple.

Along the gently curved horizon of the entire sphere Dave noted the thin blue line of Earth's precious atmosphere.

"Are we in the future?" Dave asked, not allowing himself to be swept away with the grandeur, remembering they were *not* on a sightseeing trip. They'd been forced against their will to come here!

"Yes, we are twenty years in your future," Sanako stated, lightly touching controls to correct a drift in the orientation of the bub. Brief blasts of vapor appeared to their sides from steering jets.

"Only twenty years?" Dave asked, frowning. "Arthur showed us Earth in a future he said was fifty years away!"

"You'll see the explanation," Sanako cryptically replied, her normally melodic voice sounding *tense*.

"So you're saying that my black van's time-travel capacities were superior to your 'bub' stuff?"

"Don't be silly," Sanako snapped at him. "Yours was a crude first model. We are inside a state-of-the-art time-travel vehicle far superior to your archaic vehicle. Please be quiet! We're coming near to the Event and I must concentrate on the controls."

"But your time-bub can only go twenty years forward while my van could go fifty?" he ignored her instructions. "That doesn't seem so superior of a..."

"I said to *shut up!*" Sanako snapped, looking back over the front seat to fixate him with a fierce glare.

"Ok...ok," he relented, settling back into his seat.

The "bub" was a vehicle from the other Dimension, fitted in the future with a Dark Energy generator—or so Sanako explained to them. It was equipped to take them to wherever—and whenever—

they desired. It was one of the vehicles that Sanako and her cohorts—and presumably Arthur and his competing team—used to cross over into Dave's Dimension.

Just as the sun was arising in the Vermont woods, they had climbed into it, ushered by black-suited grim-looking guards. Then they "flashed-out" from in front of the Volodymyr's isolated farmhouse to instantly reappear in orbit about the Earth!

Amazingly, Dave was getting used to SIZZLING BLUE FLASHES!

But now in the small vehicle Sanako seemed at their mercy. Perhaps he and Sally could overpower her?

But Sanako seemed undisturbed by the fact that she'd left behind her guards, left behind her weapons, and was at Dave's mercy if he chose to attack her from behind.

Yet...what would attacking her accomplish?

Dave didn't know how to fly this craft. They'd just wind up stranded in orbit around the Earth. Plus, he was definitely curious as to just what, exactly, this woman thought was so important to take them into orbit to show them.

"There...it's happening," Sanako grimly stated, pointing upward at Australia.

"What, I don't see...?" Dave said.

In front of Dave, Sally gasped, putting a hand to her mouth in disbelief.

"What?" Dave said, straining to see anything different.

Then he saw it.

The green on the edges of the continent was *browning* and then *blackening*...

Outer space around Earth began *brightening*...

Instead of a deep black, it began to *glow red*!

"Oh my God," Dave gasped. "What is happening?"

"Don't worry," Sanako quietly reassured him. "Our energy shield will protect us, at least for a while."

Sally just sat silently, staring up at Australia in horror.

The white fluffy clouds were abruptly stripped away.

The interior deserts of the continent suddenly became bubbling caldrons—churning, molten *lava lakes*!

And around the continent the seas were *boiling*...massive sheets of steam spreading across the surface of the world!

Dave, his mouth hanging open in disbelief, noticed that the thin blue line along the edge of the planet's curved horizon was *gone!*

Sparkling yellow fog now swept across what remained of the Earth's surface, replete with huge sheets of flashing *lightning*...

And in just a few minutes the crackling fog dissipated. Left behind was a *blackened, burnt-out husk* where before floated in the cosmos a magnificent blue pearl.

"No," Sally gasped, tears pouring from her eyes. "No—it's impossible...it can't be happening!"

"It did, it has, and it will," Sanako now sobbed as well, her high pitched voice trembling.

"Earth is destroyed?" Dave gasped, not believing his own eyes. "How can this be?"

"It's *Judgment Day*, you filthy rat!" Sanako yelled. Then, so soft Dave could barely hear her words, she sighed... "—and we were found wanting."

"Judgment Day?" Dave dumbly repeated.

This was a "hell-and-brimstone" boring sermon suddenly become all too real.

"It's the end of the world—the end of humanity—the extinction of *Homo sapiens* and all other land animals."

"What the *hell* are you talking about?" Dave growled, reaching forward and grabbing the oriental lady by her shoulders.

He shook her, hard.

"Tell us the truth!" he demanded. "What sort of a trick is this? The world *can't* end twenty years in the future. Arthur showed us Earth and the moon *fifty years* in the future!"

His arm slid around her throat, putting her in a stranglehold. If necessary, he'd force the truth out of her.

"That was before I decided not to kill you both," she choked-out, now struggling to breathe against his tightening grasp, "When we detected the Dark Energy signature of your vehicle crashing into your Professor's retreat I should have just shot you both dead right then. But I didn't. I was weak. And now the timeline's been altered."

Sally reached over and bodily yanked Dave's hands and arm from around Sanako's neck.

The thin oriental woman sagged forward against the bub's steering wheel, gasping for breath.

"Sanako," Sally said, leaning over next to her. "What we saw is obviously a catastrophic solar event. It was a mass ejection from the sun, wasn't it?"

"Y-yes," she answered, subdued. "It's what astronomers c-called a 'solar super-storm.' A huge plasma cloud many times the size of earth impacted the earth's orbit...wave after wave. What you saw was just the first wave."

"So on the other side of Earth there may be survivors?"

"Maybe...a few—but they'll not live for long. There are repeated waves, throwing back life on earth four billion years. Only primitive bacteria and other single-celled organisms will survive at the bottom of what remains of the seas."

"What about the moon base?" Dave urgently asked. "Surely they could survive under their dome. King City is still up there intact, right?"

"There is no moon base," she stated bitterly. "They didn't have time to start building it. What you saw fifty years in your future wasn't in place thirty years earlier."

"But Sanako," Sally protested, frowning, trying to understand, "How could this awful Event *move closer* in time?"

The black-clad woman at the steering wheel bitterly laughed.

"When I was first called to service—to try and prevent the *extinction event*," Sanako sadly said, looking upward at the blackened remains of Earth, "—it was still over a *hundred years* in your future."

"But...?"

"As we tried to prevent you and Dr. King from triggering the Event, it moved yet closer."

"What?" Dave gasped. "How could *we* cause this? Did tapping into Dark Energy somehow destabilize the sun?"

"Oh, nothing so simple," Sanako giddily grimaced up at the blackened, steaming husk hanging perversely above them.

"Then what? What was it? What caused it?" Dave insisted on an answer.

Sanako was silent for a few moments. Then she replied—in a cold, listless voice...

"It was God."

Dave sat in stunned silence, trying to digest what she'd just said.

"I...I can s-see a solar s-super-storm," he angrily stammered, "but *not* an active v-vengeance by some supernatural 'supreme being'!"

"Dark Energy touches God," Sanako quietly stated, now regaining her usual tight emotional control. "Humanity's widespread tapping-into Dark Energy brought us to God's full attention. He examined us and found the human race wanting. The great religions of Earth were correct in regards to the cosmic stakes. I meant what I said when I called it 'judgment day.' God *erased* the human race. Yes, he used a cosmic event to do so. But it was caused by the *Hand of God!*"

Sally was shaking her head slowly back and forth in denial.

"But God is all around us, *in* everything, inside of *us*," Sally protested. Dave recognized her "Animism" beliefs. "He doesn't need some special Event to bring us to His attention. He is truly omnipresent. Not only does God know everything he *is* everything!"

Sanako shrugged.

"Well," she sighed. "I'm not a religions scholar. I never believed much in such things. But just because you have bacteria in your guts, do you obsess on them? Even though they are part of you, inside of you—most of the time do you even recognize their presence? Isn't it just when a bad strain makes you sick that you focus your attention on them, perhaps popping antibiotic pills to rid yourselves of their nasty presence?"

This was a "theological" argument Dave had never heard before. It shocked him to his intellectual core.

"You mean...we're like bacteria to God?" Sally gulped.

Sanako reached over and physically *slapped* Sally hard on her face!

Even Dave was shocked by Sanako's unexpected action.

"What?" Sally gasped, putting a hand to her reddened cheek.

"Are you *stupid?*" Sanako barked at her. "How many billions of stars are there in this one Galaxy? And how many billions of galaxies are there in this Universe? At the astronomers' last count, there were *trillions* of galaxies! We're not even specks on the radarscope of an

Intelligent Supreme Entity! Human beings are just *specks* on specks on specks on specks on specks on specks on specks on specks! Is that enough specks to make my point? Maybe certain 'distributed' aspects of God are aware and react with us lowly humans, but for the *full force of God* to turn on us is an awful, terrifying prospect!" she yelled-out in frustration. Then she added more quietly: "I don't like the no-tion. I didn't believe it. But it happened, will happen, and *has* happened."

Dave now stared up at the terrible, burnt Earth floating above them.

Sally likewise stared, but now nodding her head in agreement.

"—and all of which was set in motion when mankind started tapping into the underlying fabric of reality in a big way," Sally admitted. "I see what you're saying. It's awful...but I see."

"Yes," Sanako grimly nodded. "And as the discovery and utiliza-tion of Dark Energy by the human race accelerated with your increas-ing visibility and exposure to society—so did the arrival of Judgment Day. I've traveled to the Event many times. And each time it was *closer* to our present-day world."

"But you come from the future, don't you?" Dave questioned her. "Are you saying the things that caused you to be here were cut short, yet you somehow still exist?"

"There are many timelines," Sanako softly stated, pausing before continuing. "When we move *outside* them we stay on as intact entities unto ourselves. We're no longer dependent on what came before. Don't ask me why. That's just what happens."

Yes. It was theoretically possible. The notion of time and space moving in strange ways was quite familiar to Dave.

"Then there must be a timeline where Dave never went into sci-ence, where I became an artist instead of a mathematician," Sally tearfully stated. "Surely those timelines will be safe from the 'Hand of God'?"

"As far as we can tell," Sanako sighed, "there *aren't* infinite varie-ties. Only a few timelines survive. Again, I don't know why. None of us do. It may be beyond our ability to comprehend. But the 'bottom line' is that there are only two main timelines we know of where hu-mans exist upon Earth—located in our two separate 'Dimensions.'

There are a few other close timelines where humans don't exist. But all those Earths are somehow 'bundled' together with the two human ones as a single unit in God's sight. The Earths in all these collected timelines are incinerated at the same time, across-the-board, so to speak. The Earth in all timelines and Dimensions is swept-clean of sentient life. That's what happens."

Dave could not deny the evidence around which their small ship presently orbited.

But maybe there was a way around it?

"If we can't prevent it—then why don't we just go past it?" Dave quickly asked. "How far forward can your vehicle jump? Surely in a million years—even a billion years—land, oceans, atmosphere, and intelligent life might regenerate."

Sanako started activating the control jets again. She shifted the orientation of the vehicle with little spurts of vapor out the sides, such that they no longer looked up at the blackened Earth.

Now they looked up to see the moon.

It too was scorched.

"I wanted you to see that there's no safe haven," she sighed. "Mars wasn't hit by the solar super-storm, so the few astronauts who are up there might survive for a while. But without resupply from earth, they're doomed also."

"Wouldn't they have Dark Energy generators?" Sally asked. "Surely with unlimited energy they'd be able to..."

"Cut off!" Sanako curtly snapped.

"What do you mean?" Dave said. He was afraid of what her answer would be.

"At Judgment Day not only did God exterminate all Earthly intelligent species, but he also cut off access to Dark Energy. Any surviving DE-generators just go dead. Ours only works because it's from out of time."

"Then let's do what I said," Dave insisted. "Crank her up and let's see how far into the future we can travel. Maybe I'm right and we'll..."

"There's a *Barrier*," Sanako dully stated. "We can only travel a few more days forward after Judgment Day. Then it's like we're stuck inside of cosmic jelly. We can see Earth proceeding forward as a cooked black ball, but our vehicle gets stuck. It's the same for the other human and the other nonhuman Dimensions. God stopped humanity in its tracks. We can't escape forward in time. The fact is God *erased* the human species from the Universe."

"But...Sanako...you said that Dave and I can still do something—what?" Sally sincerely asked.

"I *told* you!" Sanako barked at them. Then, visibly getting hold of her emotions, she continued more softly. "You have to stop this Dark Energy generation in its tracks. You have to disavow the whole idea, make your research repugnant to the world. You've got to convince the entire world that all you did as international terrorists was build some dangerous explosive devices or steal existing atomic bombs. You've got to *divert* the world from Dark Energy-generation and thus avoid catching the attention of God! It's our only hope. Dr. King, Master Smith—only your *abject humiliation* can save us."

Really? That was their only hope? Dave wasn't ready to give up hope.

"But...the future that Arthur showed us—there wasn't any extinction, or throttling of Dark Energy, or a time-barrier. It was beautiful!" Dave protested.

"He *lied* to you," Sanako quietly laughed, "in the most insidious way. He didn't tell you *all* the truth. What he showed you was from fifty years in the future, right?"

"Yes..."

"Well, at fifty-three years you would have seen *exactly the same thing* that we just witnessed! But the timescale he could have shown you if he'd wished...that has now been radically advanced."

"He knew this?" Sally gasped.

"He and his deluded religious fanatics *want* it," Sanako grimaced, directing the vapor puffs to push the craft back around so that they could once again see the destroyed Earth grotesquely displayed above them.

"They want for Judgment Day to occur, for humanity to be destroyed?" Dave frowned. "That doesn't make any sense, Sanako. Arthur Anderson, though manipulative and devious—seemed a remarkably intelligent person."

"Just like many of your religious adherents of your day," she grimly continued, "that trust blindly in their faith in a benevolent Supreme Deity. They think that somehow only the 'wicked' will be punished and the 'righteous' will be swept up to live in a New Earth. But they're wrong. *Everyone* gets incinerated."

Dave, Sally, and Sanako again looked up at the smoking husk floating above them.

"*That's* their 'New Earth'," Sanako viciously stated. "I *hate* God, whatever He is! That renegade pervert Anderson showed you a blindly religious *lie*. I'm showing you the truth."

"Oh...Jesus," Dave gasped, feeling for the first time that his lifelong irrational anger at God was fully justified.

But he felt no satisfaction.

In fact, he felt like he was going to vomit.

Mankind wasn't God's precious, highest creation. Instead they were an accidental vermin, fit only to be exterminated.

"Take us back, Sanako," Sally sadly stated. "We now know what we have to do."

Chapter 17

BEYOND JUDGMENT DAY

How can you claim to be Perfect

When you stem from imperfection

Designed by Mother Nature to make mistakes

Random errors fueling biological evolution

Genetic variability enabling survival of the fittest

Where your fate isn't determined by Design

But thriving on the unexpected accident...

Throw off your many blinders!

Acknowledge who you really are.

The Luminary Chronicles, 17:9-1

Sanako let them off at the porch to the Volodymyrs' retreat. Crickets were chirping out in the darkness. Stars shone down from on-high. All seemed right with the world.

But it wasn't.

Sally knew that beyond the peaceful night loomed an oncoming cataclysm.

"What will you do now?" Sally asked Sanako as she stepped out of the bub to stand beside Dave.

"I will join my comrades and await your actions—outside of time," Sanako answered.

"But will you be there if Arthur's religious zealots try to interfere?" Sally asked.

"Have no fear, we'll be there," Sanako grimly answered. "We will not allow them to deter you from your path."

She started to steer the bub away into the dark...

Impulsively, Sally ran to the front of the bub, stopped it, opened the door, reached in, and gave Sanako a quick hug.

"Thank you," Sally whispered into the solemn Oriental's ear. "I know we must have been close friends in that alternate future. I hope that somehow we meet again."

"As do I," Sanako nodded. She closed the bub's door then drove rapidly off into the night.

A *FLASH OF BLUE LIGHT* marked her actual departure.

"Oh—my boy...and your girlfriend too!" Victor enthused, stepping from the opening door of the lodge to greet them. "Ivanna told me what happened. You disappeared! We were so worried and..."

Sally smiled at the tall old man. She instantly felt safe, in the presence of a true friend.

"We've got a lot to tell you, Victor," Dave said, greeting his friend with a firm handshake. "But you're not going to like what we're going to have to do."

"Then let us talk about it, my boy. Whatever it is, you know I will stand by you."

"I hope so, Victor," Dave sighed, stepping inside as Sally quietly followed. "For the sake of all humanity, I truly hope so."

They debated strategy right through the night until the sunrise. It was a difficult, emotional discussion.

Dave was sure Victor would vigorously object, bringing up every argument to the contrary, scientific or not. Dave was correct.

Victor was aghast at what Dave proposed. He kept bringing up more and more extreme alternatives. But Dave stubbornly insisted all traces of their recent research efforts had to be destroyed—with Dave repudiating it in the most odious manner imaginable.

Sally sat silently through most of the heated discussion. Dave appreciated her letting the scientists of this Dimension come to their own conclusion.

Ivanna kept repeating "I don't believe it," while shaking her head in denial, especially when Sally reluctantly described the approaching "Wrath of God." Dave knew it just didn't jive with Ivanna's conventional religious upbringing centered on a benevolent, concerned, personally loving Deity. Victor had told him years before that she'd been raised as a devout Catholic. Now that she and Victor spent most of their time sequestered in their forest retreat, she attended Mass only on High Holidays. But a lifetime of willing indoctrination was difficult for the older woman to set aside.

Finally, though, both Victor and Ivanna came around. What convinced Victor was the certitude that their discovery would be misused. From what he and his colleagues had calculated regarding the yield from their one test, it would take just one crazed fanatic to blow up the entire planet, whether condoned by God or not.

Ivanna was convinced after Sally went over to an alcove of shelves set into the corner of the living room, gathered up a number of precious pictures, and brought them back to the dining room table. There, Sally spread out across the tabletop the smiling faces of children, grandchildren, and great-grandchildren—and even the drooling, baldheaded, baby face of a newborn female *great*-great-grandchild.

Even the remote possibility that Sally was correct—that those precious offspring would not live out their lives into a continuing future—was enough to cause Ivanna to finally agree to their awful plan.

"So, we are united?" Victor sighed, looking from one to each of the rest as they wearily sat around the dining room table.

"Yes, my love," Ivanna ruefully sighed, taking hold of his arm while leaning her blond-dyed head against his shoulder.

"There's no other option," Dave flatly stated. He knew it was his only choice. He had to set aside world fame to embrace the worst infamy. Instead of being a scientific hero showered with fame, wealth, and success he'd be back to the beginning: an abysmal failure, this time hated by everyone.

"We'll all do our parts," Sally whispered, dejectedly laying her red-haired head upon the tabletop.

"Then I suggest we get a long nap," Victor dejectedly ordered, standing up from the table. "I'm too old to miss a night's sleep and still function well the next day. What am I, a *graduate student?* Hah!"

Victor's feeble attempt at a joke fell flat. They were all mentally and emotionally drained. Dave would give anything to go back to being a "mere" graduate student ignorant of the coming sterilization of the planet...and the supreme sacrifice it would take to prevent it.

As the outside darkness lightened, they bedded down for a last few hours of sleep. They were exhausted. Victor and Ivanna retreated to their downstairs bedroom. Sally wearily started climbing up the stairs to the guest room.

"Sure you don't want me to come up and join you?" Dave teased her while spreading out blankets on the living/dining-room couch.

"You're *not* my boyfriend..." she automatically snorted.

Then, more softly, she added: "I'm wrung-out, Dave. I know we're both going to prison for a long time. Ivanna's going to take me disguised as her daughter to the airport tomorrow. I'd never get through security without her accompanying me back to Oklahoma. I need to say goodbye to my adopted Mother before I turn myself in. So I've got to get some rest now if I'm going to pull that off tomorrow. I wish things might have turned out different between us. But it's just too late. I'm sorry, Dave."

He shrugged, smiling back up at her.

"I was just kidding, Sally," he good-naturedly answered. "You get some rest."

She looked cute poised on the stairs with her flaming red bush of hair cradling those blazing green eyes. Her short-sleeved yellow blouse set-off the multi-colored tattoos on her arm brilliantly.

The Turtle Tattoo on her wrist seemed to wink at Dave.

Damn turtle! It wanted Sally all to itself.

"You know I wish you all the best, no matter what," Dave added. "Go on...get a few hours of sleep. You're right about tomorrow. It's going to be a rough day for all of us."

"Thanks, Dave," she nodded gratefully. "You try to get some rest too."

"Will do," he smiled up at her before turning out the light and hopping upon the couch.

But he couldn't sleep.

It wasn't just the morning light starting to filter in past the drawn curtains.

Regardless of how exhausted his body was—his mind was racing a million miles a minute.

No matter how undeniably necessary and unavoidable was their agreed course of action—it just didn't seem right!

Later in the day, as Ivanna and Sally prepared to depart, Dave and Victor stood in the woods staring at the wrecked and mangled van.

It was unrecognizable. It was twisted out of shape, smashed almost flat. Also it was entangled into the shattered trunks of three large trees.

Surely the Device bolted into its rear compartment was completely destroyed.

But they had to check to make sure.

"My colleagues have just finished dismantling the new Device we were assembling in my lab," Victor sighed, shakily putting back in his shirt pocket the cellphone he'd been quietly talking into. "They were distraught and dismayed at my news that it was an elaborate hoax, my boy. They had a hard time accepting that an unrepentant domestic terrorist, you, could pull the wool over my eyes. Ah, but I think I convinced them that the 'great Professor,' me, is just an old, doddery, 'mentally-confused' victim."

"I'm sorry, Victor."

"We do what we must for our children."

"Do you really think they'll accept your being 'deceived' by me?" Dave grated, pocking with a branch tentatively at the mass of twisted metal.

"Oh, David," Victor sighed. "They *so* wanted that mysterious, initial 'fireball' to be an unknown form of new energy—rather than just concealed conventional explosives that you now have 'confessed' to me that you used to enlist me into your conspiracy. They are spreading the sad news throughout our department. From there your 'shameful fraud' will quickly become known throughout all the scientific community—and from thence quickly to the mass media. What with your present criminal status, the news will spread like wildfire. Within a few hours, my boy, your newly elevated scientific reputation will be completely *ruined*."

"Good," David nodded, trying to pry up what looked like the remains of the back bumper of the van. "We've got to make sure that even the thought of trying to pursue a Dark Energy Generator is as infamously unthinkable as working on cold fusion."

"I wish there was another way," Victor glumly stated, reaching down to try and help Dave pull up the back bumper to see what was underneath it.

"But what about my bottle of matrix, that's hidden in your safe?" Dave remembered, jerking back upright, looking at Victor with fresh concern.

"Not to worry, my boy," Victor said, brushing leaves that had fallen onto his shoulders off to the side. "I ordered that what was left of your 'unstable, dangerous' matrix be taken from my safe and put into the department's Ultra-High Temperature, furnace. They told me over the phone that they cranked the UHT up to its maximum heat—three thousand degrees centigrade. So your unique concoction is completely destroyed. And without your matrix, it would take decades to replicate your 'infamous,' thoroughly-debunked work."

"Good riddance," Dave grimaced, turning back to the twisted pile of metal. "It brought me nothing but trouble. I suppose I'll also be stripped of my doctorate degree?"

"Of course," Victor sighed, bent over helping Dave grab the remains of the bumper. "My Department Head is already putting in the paperwork to make it happen."

"No one must have any temptation—no matter how slight—of ever following in my footsteps."

"They won't," the Professor agreed, starting to breath heavily from his exertions. "But what do we do about this present problem? We'll never dig through this mess in time."

"Yes, what's still left of my matrix in the remains of the Device is smashed up inside the van," Dave grimly stated as he and Victor laboriously pulled out one hunk of twisted metal.

"That is true, my boy," Victor nodded, furrowing his lined brow. "Even if the Device inside is crushed beyond recognition—as it surely must be—your matrix may still be salvageable. So how do we destroy it? How do we even get to it? Before we turn you in, we must make sure every last trace of your 'magical' matrix is gone—lest your terrorist 'comrades' swoop in and snatch it away. Should we try to burn it? I have a can of gasoline in the garage that..."

"Uh-oh," Dave gasped. He jumped back from the wreckage, stumbling into the surrounding weeds...

"What?" Victor started, jerking upright as well...

—as a *squirrel* pocked its nose out of the twisted metal then scampered up a nearby tree trunk into the overhanging canopy!

It "chittered" reprovingly at them from the branches above.

"Whew!" Dave smiled, dramatically putting a hand to his heart. "I thought I heard something and..."

The mass of metal started to *move*...

"My boy, did you just see that?" Victor gasped, pointing...

—as the *entire twisted wreckage*, now exuding a flickering blue glow, with a horrendous "screech" pulled loose from the imbedded tree trunks and *floated* upward!

"No...no...*no!*" Dave vainly protested as the pieces of mangled metal slowly *un*twisted themselves. Before his eyes the wreckage was straightening, merging back together to form an *intact black van!*

"How is this possible?" Victor gasped, his eyes stretched wide. A now pristine-appearing van floated out into a clear space in the forest then gently settled to the ground.

"Did you think I would let you turn your back on your Creator so easily?" a man's deep voice sounded from behind them. *"His Will be done,"* he quoted from the Bible, *"on earth as it is in heaven!"*

Dave and Victor whirled around to see...

—a dark-suited, black eyeglasses-sporting, crew-cut burly man standing there in front of them!

It was *Agent Anderson.*

"No! This can't be!" Dave gasped.

"Oh, but it is," Arthur replied, calmly stepping forward. "Dark Energy has many properties. You forget that in the near future you clever scientists had decades to discover its myriad uses before God's Mighty Hand was provoked. What you just witnessed was a phenomenon called 'time inversion'—where a discrete object is 'retreated' along its prior path. It's extraordinarily difficult to achieve. But with the proper algorithms, anything is possible."

Behind Anderson a dozen other Agents emerged from the woods. They all wore similar dark glasses. They were heavily armed, not just with super-pistols but thick, futuristic rifles as well.

"But Dave said that you were dead," Victor protested. "Ivanna saw your implant smashed. She cleaned its gore off our dining room table. It was quite disgusting!"

"My body was retrieved from the safe at the Air Force base," Agent Anderson grinned at them. "It was then laboriously 'time-inverted.' Yes, even the dead can be revived. Dark Energy is a miraculous gift straight from the Essence of God. Just trust in God's Will and everything will be made right. Don't you see?"

"Trust in God to destroy us?" Dave angrily asked.

"Judgment Day is not to be feared," the Agent calmly replied. "Dr. King, it will only serve to wipe clean the slate. The many sins of mankind—too many to list—will be erased from the face of the Universe. Trust in God to give humanity a new start. Your glorious invention isn't the end of Mankind—instead it's the *salvation* of the human race. It calls us to the Presence of the Creator!"

Dave stood there trying to get his thoughts together, to react properly to this incredible new turn of events. The night before everything was sorted out. They'd done all the necessary discussion. They came up with a plan. His course of action had seemed undeniably clear...but *now?*

All they'd planned was out the window.

"If what you say is true then why is there a Barrier preventing any time travel beyond the destruction of our planet?" Dave said. His mind was racing. He was abysmally confused. His prior iron resolve was starting to melt away. "Sanako showed us that..."

"—and that *nonbeliever* Sanako has it all wrong!" Agent Anderson defiantly barked at Dave as his colleagues took possession of the reconstituted black van. "She and her filthy heretics are trying to stop us from arising into the full consciousness of the Almighty. This is the dream of all intelligent species in the Universe—*not* a punishment."

"It's not a punishment to be incinerated, subtracted from the Universe?"

Anderson laughed, arrogantly self-assured.

"Sanako and her ilk are stupid, scared, worms reveling in living buried up to their slimy asses in the mud," he sneered. "I and my friends are gorgeous Eagles rising up into the sky to meet the sun.

Ours is a glorious, marvelous Quest. Theirs is to hide their heads in the sand, fearful of meeting their Creator. They are beneath my contempt!"

Anderson abruptly turned away to talk with his compatriots by the van.

Dave slowly sat down on one of the fallen large tree trunks that'd been liberated when the van was reassembled by the time-inversion.

He didn't know what to think.

"Dave, my boy," Victor comforted him, laying a weathered hand on his arm. "You must be perplexed. I know that I myself am more than confused. This man—this time-traveler— knows far more and better than we. Perhaps we should consider what he is saying? I'm not concerned over myself or Ivanna. We were only supporting your decisions. But if now you decide differently, it's not too late. With a working model of your Device—that I assume is now sitting there ready to work inside the resurrected van—we can still proceed along our prior path. All the negative things we've already done today can be reversed."

It was tempting, very tempting...

Suddenly the air was filled with *brilliant flashes!*

Dave heard agonized screams as men were *burned alive!*

Other of the black-eyeglasses agents were crouching, aiming their "rifles" up at the sky, letting loose powerful laser beams...

—as "bubs" zipped down, zooming past in the sky above! They darted just above the leafy canopy, firing off bursts of deadly beams. Flaming branches and leaves rained down upon Dave and Victor.

"Take the van to the *United Nations!*" Agent Anderson yelled at Dave, running up to him and tossing him a set of keys. "A duplicate of my Implant is still in the Device. Just tell it where you want to go and it'll take you there, instantly!"

"Why?" Dave shouted back over the roaring BLASTS of ascending and descending powerful laser blasts. "What will that accomplish?"

"Get to the floor of the U.N.!" Anderson shouted back as a laser blast just missed incinerating him. He turned his black gun skyward. "They are in full session today. They are voting on stricter measures to stop international terrorism. It's your moment to garnish the full attention of the world. The session is being broadcast on all media channels worldwide. *This* is when it all really starts!"

Arthur ducked away, retreating, as several bubs zeroed-in on him.

"What will I say?" Dave yelled at him, uncertain.

"Tell them everything! Full disclosure! Show them what you have! Let the world make its own choice!" Anderson grinned back as he took careful aim and blew a dive-bombing bub out of the air.

The shattered vehicle crashed into the forest only yards from where Dave and Victor stood.

The forest floor trembled under Dave's feet.

"Dave!" Sally shouted, suddenly dashing through the trees to grab his hand, trying to pull him away with her. "We've got to escape!"

"No...I think not," he said, shaking loose from her hand and turning toward the black van sitting pristine and gleaming in the sunlit clearing.

It was untouched by the fierce battle. Indeed, the *faint blue light* still surrounded it, protecting it.

"Don't take another step!" Sanako shouted at Dave, appearing from behind a tree, taking dead-aim at him with a black pistol...

BLAM!

A shot from Anderson spun the oriental woman around. Blood spurted from her shoulder. She just managed to crawl away, hiding behind a large tree trunk.

"*Go,* Dr. King!" Anderson barked at him. "Go*!* We'll hold off these nonbelievers. We'll keep them well-occupied. Don't be afraid. It's already happened. Go and *fulfill your destiny!*"

Destiny? Believer? But he *wasn't* a believer...was he?

Was the coming cataclysm just an accident of nature, a random blast from the sun? Or did tapping into the Dark Energy roots of sub-space somehow roil the interior of the sun? But was it all really orchestrated by a disappointed, absentee Super-Intelligence?

Either way, it was all connected.

"But we'll be captured as soon as we appear at the U.N.," Dave protested, torn on what to do. "And even if we did manage to sneak in, they'd never let us speak to the Assembly."

More laser-blasts rained down upon them, blowing up shrubs and dirt into a hail of flaming debris.

Dave ducked down, pulling Victor with him, cringing.

"At this moment the present President of the *American Physical Society* is giving a summary on modes of nuclear terrorism!" Anderson shouted over the thundering blasts. "She will gladly invite the Professor to the podium. It's the perfect time for Volodymyr to step forward and introduce you to the world. Everything's happening just as it should. Go and claim your rightful glory!"

"Dave, don't go!" Sally called-out to him, now hiding with the wounded Sanako behind a thick tree trunk.

He made a decision.

Dave grabbed Victor by the shoulder and half-carried the elderly man to the vehicle while dodging laser beams. He hastily shoved Victor into the passenger seat, slipping behind the steering wheel...

—as yet another *flash* of *BLUE, DAZZLING LIGHT* enveloped the black van

And they vanished.

Oblivious to the vehicle's disappearance, the battle in the woods of Vermont between future warrior factions raged on. Humans yet again, for the umpteenth time, gladly revealed their inner defects: happily slaughtering each other over slightly different tribal, political, and religious beliefs. Streams ran red with blood. The forest was leveled. Terrified squirrels hid beneath shattered trees. Snakes cowered in their dens. And above them all the sun blazed down, brighter than ever.

Chapter 18

REVELATION

Do you really want to know

What moves your little thoughts and minds

Supporting the flurries of your hands and feet

As you scamper to meet your many needs

Frantically knocking at the door of your heart

When with that knowledge comes responsibilities

Where you are obliged by duty to respond

Not just to the daily grind's imperatives...

But to the unavoidable realities of God?

Define that Supreme Reality as you will

However makes it more palatable

Just remember not to ignore it.

The Lord does not "suffer fools gladly."

The Luminary Chronicles, 18:3-7

The black van appeared on the green central stage of the cavernous General Assembly Room of the United Nations Building in New York City.

Gathered together along the sweep of the circularly-positioned tables amongst the large audience were representatives from all the nations of the world.

The audience sat in stunned silence as the "pop" of outwardly displaced air knocked them back in their seats.

"*Please!* You must listen to me!" Professor Volodymyr shouted loudly into the vast chamber as he emerged from the passenger side of the van.

If he didn't catch the attention of those at the microphone he knew the guards were going to kill him.

"Victor?" a grey-haired, chubby woman in a red dress gasped from the podium.

"*Yes!* Patricia! It is *me!*" Victor shouted as he ran over to the stairs leading up to the podium. "I bring amazing news of a marvelous new development in physics! The proof sits here on the stage with me. You just saw us teleport into this chamber. It will transform the world! I need to tell you all..."

A rush of security guards tackled him to the green-carpeted floor, raising their weapons...

"No! Please listen to me!" Volodymyr futilely shouted as he desperately batted their guns to the side.

The woman on the stage whispered intensely to a distinguished and dapper-looking black-skinned man standing next to her.

"Release that man!" ordered the Secretary General of the United Nations. "Allow him to come up here."

Reluctantly, the guards lifted Victor back to his feet. Shaken, slumped-over, the Professor stumbled before catching himself and resolutely straightening his back. Then he strode firmly up the stairs.

At the podium he shakily took hold of the fixed microphone, leaning in close.

He nervously cleared his throat before proceeding.

How could he in a few words intrigue them enough to listen? These were for the most part politicians, not scientists willing to sit through an academic lecture.

Ah, the best way to teach anything: tell a compelling, personal story!

He lifted up his head, swept back his mop of white hair with one hand, and spoke firmly into the microphone.

"I'm here to tell you about a man who thought he was the worst sort of failure: so stupid he didn't know when to give up and let Mother Nature win," he began. "And when, despite all odds, that man became famous, he was willing to give it all up. He was ready to disavow all his unexpected success and fame—for the sake of those he loved. I'm here to affirm, my friends and colleagues, the unselfish love I speak of extends to *all of you!* Now, let me start at the beginning..."

"You must *stop* him!" Sanako painfully groaned. She slipped the super-black gun into Sally's hand.

"What are you saying?" Sally whimpered as the fighting raged around her in the forest. The bubs had landed and the battle was now raging person-on-person amongst the trees of the thick forest.

"They've succeeded in galvanizing the world's attention," Sanako whispered into Sally's ear. Then with extreme ferocity: "Judgment Day is only now only *ten years* in the future!"

"Only ten years?" Sally gasped. "But that's...?"

"The end of mankind is right around the corner," Sanako moaned, grasping her shattered shoulder. Bright red blood dripped down all along the left side of her body. Her left arm hung limp, useless.

"Then we've failed," Sally sobbed, sinking back onto the ground. She covered her face with her arms, still clutching the heavy black gun.

"No!" Sanako grated. "There's one last chance!"

The shouting and screaming of hand-to-hand combat was intensifying. Sally had no idea who was winning or losing as she cringed beside Sanako. She only knew that the resurrection of Agent Anderson changed everything. It didn't matter what she, Dave, Victor, and Ivana had planned. It was time for doing something desperate, otherwise unthinkable.

"What can we do?" Sally asked, frantic for an answer.

"We'll teleport into the United Nations to exactly where Dave and the Professor went," Sanako heavily gasped, pausing to get her breath. "And then you will kill Dr. King."

Sally looked at Sanako in disbelief.

"No! I can't..."

"Yes, you can!" Sanako urgently continued, squinting against the pain of her grievous wounds. "It'll be seen on all the newscasts as the ultimate terrorist betrayal. Dave was trying to defect from the Cause. You brought him down...right before *destroying* the entire United Nations Assembly!"

"What?" Sally gasped in horror.

"As you kill Dave I'll enter his archaic van, release the safety constraints, and trigger an instantaneous, uncontrolled release of Dark Energy."

"But that'll kill us all!"

"Yes...us and half of New York City."

"That's monstrous!"

"More monstrous than allowing the *extinction* of the entire human race?" Sanako asked, visibly gathering strength with the conviction of her Cause. "This one act of infamy will finally put 'the nail in the coffin' to pursing your lines of research. You'll *hide* us from the terrible Face of God!"

"But we'll die!"

"The bub is programmed to snatch us away once the explosion of the van begins—in a nanosecond! All those alive on the stage will be saved. Dave, of course, is lost. That, regrettably, is the price that must be paid."

It was terrible, hideous...but what choice did she have? If she didn't act—and act *now*—then Anderson's extreme religious fanatics would win! Sally slowly nodded in agreement, now willing to do what was necessary, no matter how odious.

"But...how do we get to the United Nations?"

"Over there!" Sanako said, pointing through the now-flaming forest.

Sally barely made out the cracked remains of a crashed bub.

"How...?"

"I'll pilot it."

"But you're hurt."

"I'll manage," Sanako said, grinding her teeth together and lurching up to her feet. "Follow me!"

She ducked through the bushes as *thundering* BLASTS sounded around them. Grimly determined, Sally followed Sanako, tightly clutching the gun in her hand. Then Sally jumped through a missing door into the fractured dome of the bub as Sanako frantically hit switches with her right hand...

—and in a *BLUE, SPUTTERING HAZE* the bub vanished.

The bub materialized on the opposite side of the central stage from where the van sat.

Again the "pop" of displaced air knocked the assembled diplomats back in their seats.

It also stopped the careful explanation being methodically stated by a grim Professor Volodymyr who stood at the podium introducing Dr. King, who'd just been allowed to emerge from his hiding place in the back of the van to walk safely up onto the stage.

"They're stunned! This is the moment—it's now or never!" Sanako exclaimed as she lurched from the bub and raced toward the van...

—as Sally jumped out and ran up the stairs nearest her, holding the gun out in front of her...

"Sally?" Dave gasped as she leveled the gun straight at his face...

—as the *Turtle Tattoo* suddenly flared up on her wrist holding the gun and she staggered, groaning in pain...

"Sally!" the glad cry rang out in her ears.

She looked around in bewilderment, surrounded by mists and strange plants...

She saw beside a now red-colored stream a pack of ravenous Acros gorging on a bloody mountain of flesh. It was the huge, felled body of a *Sauroposeidon*. The Acros were greedily ripping out huge chunks of the giant's flesh, gulping down the quivering flesh while simultaneously snarling and slashing at each other.

She was back in the late Cretaceous.

Sally realized she was flat on the ground. She was a full football field's length away from the gory feast, blinking her eyes in the weak sunlight. Through wavering mists she stared in shock at the slaughtered mountainous dinosaur—still holding her gun in her trembling right hand.

Standing above her, extending down *his* hand, was *Snake!*

"Snake?" she gasped, accepting his strong left hand, allowing him to lift her up to her feet.

Yes, it was her doppelganger Sally's boyfriend. The black cobra etched into his cheeks seemed to twist in excitement as his thin face lit up with joy. The other many tattoos on his bare arms were so bright they seemed to want to jump off his skin. And His scraggly black hair and goatee writhed like miniature snakes in the warm, humid breeze.

"It's so good to see you!" he grinned. He grabbed her up in a tight bear hug, swinging her around in a circle, before releasing her to stand beside him.

"But...how?" she grunted, his enthusiasm having momentarily knocked the air from her.

"Oh, no worries, Sally—you wuz here, right? It's a nice, safe place away from everything. So we kin talk! No rush."

"Uh...those dinosaurs?"

"They's havin' their good time. They ain't gonna pay us no mind, Sally. Not to worry."

"But...you *betrayed* us!" she shouted at him. "You brought the military on us! You almost killed us!"

She *slapped* him in his face.

He staggered back a step, looked embarrassed, and then gingerly moved his goateed jaw back and forth.

"Wow, that hurts."

"I thought you were my friend!" Sally continued to yell at him. Then, more subdued but still bitterly angry: "Dave and I trusted you. How could you betray us?"

"I *wuz* protecting you, Sally girl...*all* of the time."

"*How* much time?"

"Since I first gave you your Turtle Tattoo."

"My...?"

"Yes, that innocent-looking cute little *reptile*, don't you know? It makes sense now, right?"

"When it glowed and...*burned?*" Sally frowned, remembering.

"Yep, it was steerin' you away from trouble—or guidin' you onto a better path, girl."

"But it *hurt!*"

"Oh, I'm so sorry Sally," he grimaced in genuine regret, now holding his jaw gingerly with his left hand. "I guess I know better now how that feels. I deserved a slap. But ah did what had to be done, girl. Even when I 'betrayed' you, you wuz needin' that boost to get you *here!* I wuz gonna come back and talk with both you and Dave right then—but that lady stopped me."

"What lady?"

"Oh, you know," he sighed, sitting on a large boulder and motioning for her to come join him, "That black-haired lady with the funny car."

She stood stock still, adrenalin throbbing through her veins.

"You mean Sanako and her bub? But she's my friend. At least...I *think* she's my friend?"

"Oh, not much of a friend there, I'm thinkin'," he shrugged ruefully.

She stood there still tightly clutching the black pistol, glowering at him, totally confused.

Clearly, Snake was more than just a talented tattoo-artist.

He grinned widely at her, holding his scrawny arms upward to the sky. Then he hopped up, danced a jig around in a circle, and stomped his feet into the moist moss and dirt. Momentarily Sally was shocked, fearing that he'd draw the attention of the pack of feeding predators. But they ignored his antics. They were much too busy tearing hunks of bloody flesh out of their mountainous feast to bother with tiny "appetizers."

"Who are you *really?*" Sally said, looking at him now fearfully—as the mists cleared, the sunlight brightened, and small dinosaurs scampered in the distance. The scavenger flocks were eagerly inching closer, waiting for the large Acros to be satiated so that they could move in for their portion of the kill.

"Well...guess I kin let you see me like I'm really made," he grinned as his scraggly-haired, goateed form started *melting*.

In a few moments, instead of the scruffy-looking young man, in his place sat a *plump, large, actual snake!*

Sally backed away a few steps.

The snake was *very* large, fully twenty feet in length. It had a wide, thick body, supporting a head bigger than a man's!

It flicked-out a forked-tongue that was wide and red.

Its head was a spectacular rainbow of colors that glittered with translucent, overlapping scales.

The giant snake's eyes were mesmerizing golden spheres dotted with flecks of red. A black slit went up through the center of each of its eyes.

The elongated body was pure white on top, black polka-dot on the sides, and yellow on its belly.

"Like me?" the snake pleasantly asked.

"What the hell is this? This can't be real. They're no such things as talking giant snakes. It's ridiculous! I'm either hallucinating or..."

"Even in the evolutionary history of your planet, there were actual stout-bodied snakes much larger than me, Sally. They had heads large enough to house an evolved, intelligent brain if they'd been blessed with such."

That brought her up short, forcing a rapid reevaluation.

"Your mouth...why didn't it move?" Sally jerkily asked, backing off yet another step.

"I am speaking to you telepathically," he mildly replied, having dropped his "hippy" affectation. "We're an ancient race compared to yours. Humans have only walked upon the Earth for a mere two or three million years. We evolved long before that. We have been sentient and intelligent on *our* Earth for well over thirty million years."

"So...you're...?"

"Yes, we're from the 'non-human' Dimensions you heard about before from that duplicitous woman," the big rainbow head of the snake nodded. Its big forked tongue flicked out briefly. "In other Dimensions, other sentient reptiles also evolved, though different from my race. They joined with us to try to stop you silly humans from opening up the flood gates of Dark Energy and exposing our timelines to the wrath of God. You humans are stupid—but also lovable," the telepathic voice hastened to add.

"But...didn't that huge asteroid destroy the dinosaurs we see out there on the plain?" she asked, deeply puzzled and confused. "How is it then that your race could ever come into being? The mammals rose up and evolved into man because the dinosaurs were taken out of the way!"

The snake, in Sally's head, laughed.

"It *didn't* strike, of course," Snake blithely stated. "In our other Dimensions, that massive asteroid *missed* Earth. You little mammals are not as inevitable as you thought. God does play His little jokes and..."

"I thought God *ignores* us!"

"Oh no, Sally," the big snake seemed to grin, revealing many sharp, pinpointed teeth. "God is not a 'thing' to be categorized and constrained. And He is surely not a super-powered giant Human. 'God' is a many-facetted assembly that's far beyond our little brains' capacity to even comprehend. But gorge yourselves with his Dark Energy and you certainly do 'pull on the cape of Superman'—as you cute little humans would say."

"What?"

"Oh, I'm sorry again, dear Sally," the snake sincerely apologized. "I forgot that in *your* human Dimension the Superman comics never existed."

She shook her head to try to clear it. Superman? Things were getting incredibly confusing.

"So you say that your species also discovered Dark Energy-generation?" she gulped, trying to focus her mind on what was most important. "What stopped God from erasing *you* long ago?"

"Oh, we are not as impatient as you little mammals," Snake laughed good-naturedly. "Also, we're not as greedy."

"But...?" Sally frowned, her face twisted up in puzzlement—looking over at the snorting, fighting Acros gorging themselves on their slaughtered prey. "If you're so advanced, then why not...?"

"Time grows short," Snake said, following her gaze while immediately becoming intensely serious. "As 'advanced' as we are above your race, I can't hold this window in time open for much longer. I have *another choice* for you, Sally. Do you want to hear it?"

"You mean other than blowing Dave's head off—versus letting him announce our discoveries to the world, bringing on Judgment Day?"

"It's a third choice, yes," Snake replied. "But it is far more difficult than decisive violence or passivity's blissful surrender. Everything will change. You will still face dangerous challenges. It may even, sadly, result in your death."

"I'll do it!" she resolutely stated, squaring her narrow shoulders and furrowing her brow.

"Yes, Sally," the snake's voice soothed her as its heavy body *flowed* over the ground, coiling around her entire body.

She cringed, expecting cold scales. Instead, his long enveloping body felt gentle, warm, and comforting.

"I *so* like to hug you," the soft voice said in her head as a *HAZY BLUE GLOW* sprang up all around them.

She dropped the gun, leapt forward, and snared Dave in the tightest hug of all time...

—as the van simultaneously EXPLODED, destroying the United Nations Complex, and turning it into a pile of smoking rubble.

Chapter 19

DELIBERATE ENCOUNTER

Some are content to drift with the tide

Blowing to wherever the fates might decide

This way or that...who cares which is best

When either or other is as good as the rest

But when you know where you are going

There's a certain joy of achievement

Seeing the steps in the sand of one's past

Making defined progress along a desired vector

Even if it veers and retreats, again and again

Or they are washed out, filled in, or erased

Still they persist in one's own memory...

The sum total is the stuff of dreams.

The Luminary Chronicles, 19:38-42

"Is that a turtle?" he asked, peering down at her exposed wrist.

Sally glanced up at him from the items she was expertly sliding through the scanner.

"Yes, it's a baby turtle," she replied.

He stared at it for a few seconds as he leaned there against the check-writing platform. To Sally the customer seemed dizzy, holding on tightly as if to keep from falling.

Strangely, she also felt momentarily dizzy.

The store around her seemed to blur. Bizarre visions flickering in and out of the edge of her sight: a BURNING YELLOW VEHICLE... a BLACKENED, CHARRED CORPSE... HER SITTING ON A COLD, DIRTY TOILET WITH HER PANTS DOWN AROUND HER FEET... A MINISTER OPENLY PREACHING AT A PUBLIC CHURCH SERVICE... A BUFFET SPREAD WITH ALL SORTS OF EXOTIC FOOD.

What's wrong with me?—she thought to herself, shaking her head to clear it. *Am I sick?*

And then the bout of vertigo passed. The disturbing visions vanished. Everything was back to normal. The other checkout stalls and clerks were busy with lined-up customers. The shelves of the Megamart were undisturbed, stocked high with food and goods.

"It's so bright. I've never seen a tattoo so bright," her customer cheerfully continued. He stood poised to hand her another carrying-bag. He was one of the few customers that voluntarily brought his own bags instead of using store-suppled plastic.

"What?"

"Your Turtle Tattoo," he reminded her, pointing with a finger at the little reptile inked into the inside of her left wrist.

No more waking nightmares. Back to business!

It was nice of him to compliment her tats.

Indeed, the little tattoo on her exposed wrist gleamed with bright greens, rich browns, and deep blacks.

"Thanks," she said, continuing to expertly slip his items past the scanner, then into his waiting bag. "I just treated myself to it the other day."

"I thought it might be one of those stick-on ones," he continued. "I've never seen a real tattoo that's so bright."

She flicked a quick, shy smile at him. "It's brand new, that's why. That's when the colors are brightest. It will fade with time."

What a nice fellow. He seems genuinely interest in my body-art.

She paused in her work behind the counter to slide the sleeve of the shirt on the arm with the turtle tattoo upward. More of her wonderful inked-on creatures were briefly revealed: a creepy black spider with white specks, a flapping red and yellow parrot, and a coiled orange snake with blue highlights.

"Wow, those are amazing!" he said, sounding truly impressed. "I wish I could do stuff like that. You're very clever to make your body into a work of art. I'm impressed!"

"I'm sure you're also quite talented."

"Nope," he sighed, "I'm a total failure. But I still try to do my duty. You just gotta 'keep on keeping on,' right? We can't all be wildly successful."

She started to nod then had to grip the counter tightly.

Again the world blurred around her and she raggedly sucked in her breath. She vividly saw HER DEAD MOTHER OPENING HER EYES AND SMILING... A GIANT LONG-NECKED DINOSAUR STOMPING EVER CLOSER... DEEP CRATERS SEEN FROM THE SURFACE OF THE MOON, and A BURNING EARTH HANGING PITIFULLY IN EMPTY OUTER SPACE...

It all came back to her.

The customer's name was "Dave"—Dr. David King. And he was about to discover the most dangerous invention in the history of mankind.

Under her breath, she groaned. Yes, his invention and its cataclysmic consequences were delayed. She had time now to think, to plan, to make better decisions. It was an incredible gift from the alien creatures that produced "Snake." But could she take advantage of it? This time, forewarned, could she make things right?

Sure, why not? Just a few small changes and...

But new Visions appeared around her, even more terrifying than the previous ones: AN ELDERLY HOODED NUN LOOKING UP IN AWE AT THE STARS, A TOWERING RED OBELISK, A HANDSOME BEARDED YOUNG MAN NAILED TO A CROSS, A DESOLATE LANDSCAPE DOTTED WITH ACTIVE VOLCANOES, A CHILD-LIKE BLOND-HAIRED ROBOT CRYING, A SPACESHIP ON A TAIL OF FIRE RISING UP INTO THE SKY, and A MASSIVE LAYERED ROCK HURTLING THOUGH SPACE STRAIGHT AT THE HEART OF A DEFENSELESS EARTH!

She closed her eyes, blocking off the apparitions. She had no doubt what she'd just witnessed. They weren't hallucinations. She'd just seen a new deadly future...also caused by her!

And opening her eyes she saw her *partner in crime* standing right beside her.

Was she a pawn of fate? Or could she change her actions and alter the new future she'd just glimpsed?

The path forward was not clear. The end result was unknown. But the warning was unmistakable.

Screw up and everything you hold dear will be destroyed!

She knew that her next words were crucial.

Releasing her tight grip on the counter she softly replied.

"Maybe...you just need someone to believe in you."

"Could be," he shrugged. "But that's not in the cards. No matter. How much do I owe you?"

She slid her sleeve back down as she shakily placed the last of his items into the opened bag.

"Your total is nineteen, even."

He reached into his back pocket, pulled out his billfold, and handed her a folded green bill.

She looked at it carefully then handed it back to him.

"Something wrong?" he asked with a puzzled frown as he accepted the bill back.

"No, nothing's wrong," she mildly answered, smiling. "This is my treat."

"What?"

She reached into the personal space under the counter. She lifted out her brown leather shoulder bag, pulled from it a wallet, and placed the proper amount of money into the till.

Then she firmly closed the register, took off her apron, and signaled to the floor manager that she was closing.

"But...what are you...?" he said, sounding confused.

For a moment she stared at him.

"Do you like my eyes?" she playfully grinned at him.

"They match your turtle tattoo. They're green and beautiful. In fact, I think that *you* are beautiful," he grinned in an innocent, boyish way.

She snorted at his lame "come-on," but then firmly stated: "Well then, if that's so—there's only one thing to do."

"Oh?" he asked, obviously intrigued.

"I'm going to church with you and your Mom," she smiled back. "And afterward we're going to have a long talk."

"About what?"

"About *everything!*"

THE END

[continued in: *The Girl Who Played with Fate*]

Thank you for reading!

Dear reader,

I hope you enjoyed *The Girl with the Turtle Tattoo*. It was a wild ride to write, I'll tell you. As you saw, I have an itch to understand the deep reality behind our supposedly "ordinary" lives. The sequel to this book, *The Girl Who Played with Fate*, picks up with Sally and Dave at the checkout counter. She's back at the beginning, with a chance to do it all over again but better. However, she's the only one who knows the future.

I hope you are intrigued by the sequel's central time-travel question: "If you knew the future, could you change the past?" Or, is there a terrible momentum to history which slaps transgressors in the face? Sally faces new dangers, further time-travel, and an expanding mystery as to what's happening to her.

Finally, I need to ask you for a favor. If you enjoyed this book and would like to encourage others to read it, **a review written by you** on the Amazon page for this book would be greatly helpful. It's hard to get reviews nowadays and your support will be very important to both me and other readers. If you'd like to do this, I sincerely thank you in advance for your time and effort. It can be as long or short as you wish.

Thanks again for reading my *Girl with the Turtle Tattoo* books and going on this wild, wacky ride with me.

Sincerely,

About the Author:

Daniel Basil Lyle holds a Ph.D. in Biology, is a lifelong amateur herpetologist, taught medical immunology at a University, completed a career in cell biology research, lectures on how to apply theological and psychological principles in practical ways, and has a strong interest in all aspects of cosmology and physics. From a small kid he was fascinated with dinosaurs. As such, he has always lived with exotic creatures, including harmless snakes, all housed in his own homemade habitats. Some of his tame pet pythons and anacondas ranged up to twelve feet in length. He is the author of over thirty books, many of which are religious in nature. His writings go beyond the ordinary, exposing deeper aspects of life. His books are meant to be fun, conversational, and helpful. His various works are available at LylePublishing.com and Amazon.com. The "Girl with the Turtle Tattoo" science fiction series was inspired by paintings done by his mother, movies adapting Stieg Larsson's crime novels, and various men and women sporting spectacular body-art tattoos. The author hopes that you, the reader, find his characters spontaneous, quirky, surprising, and even thought-provoking—just as did he!

www.ingramcontent.com/pod-product-compliance
Lightning Source LLC
Chambersburg PA
CBHW070538260626
47161CB00002B/434